Nov 2016

Dear Warren

This and all my
best creative works
were done here
in this building —
and in my 'creative
cave'
5B

with Gratitude
and best wishes

Nitra

BLOOD WORDS
A Warrior's Walk

by

Manoshi Chitra Neogy

Copyright © 2016 Manoshi Chitra Neogy.

First International Media Publications Group hardcover edition
October 2016
International Publications Media Group and IPMG and IPMG logos are trademarks of International-
al Publications Media Group, LLC.

For information about special discounts in bulk purchases, please contact International Media
Publications Group at 1-917-604-9602 or Sales@ipublicationsmedia.com.

The International Media Publications Group Speakers Bureau can bring authors to your live
event. For more information or to book an event contact Francois Wilson at 1-917-604-9602 or
visit our website at www.ipmgworld.com.

Manufactured in the United States of America

ISBN: 978-1-632-67018-2 (Hardcover)

ISBN: 978-1-632-67021-2 (E-Book)

Portrait of Manoshi Chitra Neogy:

Winged Heart Woman

Painted by Scott Endsley

Edited by Jessica Pierce

Cover Design by Shannon Crutchfield

Back Cover Design by Yeisa Bouie

Layout Design by Yeisa Bouie

Table of Contents

Title Page...1

Winged Heart Woman Painting...2-3

Copyright...5

The Dedication...8

The Foreword...9-11

The Departure...12

The Inward...13

Book One: Birth...14

Chapter 1: I Eat Roses..15

Chapter 2: Feline woman soft brown and strong...24

Chapter 3: Lotus-the avatar, and the eveing raga of Solitude..45

Chapter 4: Oyster woman and the four arms of goddess Kali...58

Chapter 5: The gilded cage and my bleeding almond eyes...74

Chapter 6: the musk of the male sounds touches my skin...89

Chapter 7: My limbs were turn away from me As Isee the universe in the mouth of the saint beggar...101

Book Two: Sacrifice...119

Chapter 8: Pregnant and slaughtered in a Palace of wealth

Chapter 9: My lovers are with me My feet are bloody and my bones are transparent...139

Chapter 10: My sandalwood husband and the birth of savitri...182

Chapter 11: Wooden peacocks squeezing their way through narrow spac es...206

Chapter 12: knives will bleed and a baby woman will be born...223

Chapter 13: My beauty has been stolen from me And I walk with a half-eaten language...237

Chapter 14:I know that all the magicians are going to lead the way for me...256

Chapter 15: My tongue crishes raw almonds as it feels the silence of love...270

Chapter 16: The blood is on the floor and the owl visits each morning, and the lions eat gold bangles...291

Chapter 17: I weep with rain and the drops flood my wounds made by broken souls with fallen wings...307

Chapter 18: The birds are listening to my call and I will become my talent and my aspiration...321

Book Three: Epiphany...338

Chapter 19: I will always make love with poet men...339

Chapter 20: The child's gaze has saved my soul I will awake alive within the womb of my own creativity...384

Chapter 21: I stop souls

Index...390-391

Thank You's...392-296

This expression is dedicated to

my beloved mother,
my divine father, who made me write this book,
Dana who gave me his message,

Lord Ganesha, who sat on my head and sliced it
open with his divine trunk
The child's gaze
AND TO ALL THE WOMEN WHO RUN WITH
THE WOLVES

8

Blood Words Foreword   Sheril D. Antonio

"Every being in the universe is an expression of the Tao. It springs into existence, unconscious, perfect, free, takes on a physical body, lets circumstances complete it."

Tao te Ching

It is with subtle clarity and a profound resistance to the relentlessness and monotony of a comfortable existence that Blood Words stitches together in flesh and bones, all the remnants of a single life. Stasis is the enemy in this story and the book's refrain – "time is the sensible measure in the continuity of mediocrity" – is there to remind us of our main character's need to keep moving forward. In this elegant dance of words we see that in order to keep her balance she maintains equal movements– forward, backward–forward, backward. Blood Words carves its smooth surfaces out of a very jagged rock and the sharp chipping noises we hear are the many sounds of emptiness and loss. Mourning regains its rightful status and is done with gratitude for the ones who die bring us to life.

In Scientific American, they describe what takes place before the birth of a butterfly. "First, the caterpillar digests itself, releasing enzymes to dissolve all of its tissues." Unfortunately, it reports that observing this process in rare and dangerous for the life forming within. "Getting a look at this metamorphosis as it happens is difficult; disturbing a caterpillar inside its cocoon or chrysalis risks botching the transformation." In the case of this book, we get to witness the entire process. Pablo Picasso says "it takes a long time to become young" and Blood Words explains how it takes a long time to become whole.

I would guess that we understand confession as something we conduct towards the outward world, or towards someone of great significance - a trusted one. This author confesses to herself, to all of her selves past and present and does this valiantly for the selves to come. Whether you are a young or old soul, you need to know how this woman talks to herself and learns to love herself. Blood Words is a walk without fear of all of the possible paths presented, so prepare yourself, because our guide takes the ones very few of us would dare to. As I read the tightly woven text, I encountered words and phrases that were like threads in a dense and complex weave, giving each thread the ability to complete the many areas in the tapestry, changing as it moves along.

9

Chitra and I work for the same educational institution as teachers and mentors – but we are also eternal students. We see each other regularly by the indoor garden near my office where the bright sunny rug invites friends and visitors to sit. As much as has been shared between us, much more is left unsaid as we pass each other respectfully with silent acknowledgements that do not disrupt our intense focus. It is because of this practice that I can so appreciate the hushed and harsh language of this journey she invited me on. I had never known of the savage beauty that was encountered in its pages. This is a haunting story of a woman who belongs to herself, physically and emotionally, sexually and spiritually, a woman who welcomes outsiders to find her insides. She experiences the world as a place where the ordinary is quite painful. Reading the precisely placed words allowed me to understand why she had to free herself from traditional entrapments,superficial living and the claustrophobia of what we might call safety – to regain her eternal independence.

The fearful in us may experience this a cautionary tale, extoling the dangers of listening to your own voice, some will even say "see – this is what can happen when you dare to sing your own song," but if you know of the Tao or any such manifestation of wholeness, you can access the deeper meaning all this has for our main character. I tell my students that Picasso says that – "Art is the lie that gets to the truth" but never thought to ask what happens when art is born of many truths – where does that get us? Blood Words asks and answers.

"If you want to become full, let yourself be empty" – says the Tao. "If you want to be given everything, give everything up" and yet Chitra assures us that "nothing has been wasted and nothing is regretted." So, the sharp chipping noises produce shards that turn into flying creatures that lead our eyes towards the sky.

And, as we read, we understand.

As we listen we see.

As we see, we hear.

But only when we know do we feel.

I am just not that brave but was happy to meet someone who is,

"Namaste"...

10

THE DEPARTURE

After all was shattered and strewn with pain and memory
After all was bent, broken warped and even death stood still
After all was taken torn and stretched apart
After the sacred space was scattered with graveyards barren of bones
After even the sun felt cold and the moon cried with empty smiles
After even the trees were hollow and could not be touched
After self walked in unwashed knotted hair and tattered clothes and bleeding skin
After bodies were like fish bones empty and discarded
*After every hope of **Savitri** and **Satyavan** was cracked by the winds of doubt and disbelief*
After art was a distant sound and poetry choked the very chore of her being
And after she who died and breathed blood for air
In her blood became air and water flowed through
And the sun felt warm and the moons wept and stayed full and sickle for her
And poetry and art made love to her once again
And her heart became a sacred mantra
And teardrops remained on her face canvas like glistening virgin pearls

Inward

The blue table reflected the sky on it. I watched the scratched surface of the once smooth visage and felt the lines under my trembling fingers. It was long and endless. My eyes moved up to catch the tall clear vase filled with water and twelve red roses waiting to open their beautiful bloodlines.

I looked at the brand new black leather wallet by surprise. Some hundred-dollar bills lay across the shiny face. There was a finality and sadness about it. I moved back to the roses and quietly reached out to one of the buds and gently tore a few petals. They approached, the red petals and I suddenly began to tremble all over. My hands shook as I plucked more of them and one by one placed them in my mouth. They tasted quiet and sweet as though my whole self was entering a garden of memories and wounds.

A deep howl began to build within me and shaking and screaming I cried. The red petals fell on the wooden sky floor. and all around me as if weeping with and for me. The howl turned into a scream. I could not stop. It was not aloneness that engulfed me. It was a wilderness of sorts, a forest without trees, sand dunes without the rippling sand, a riverbed with no water and a human face without the sparkling shine of a soul.

It was the wasteland and I was in it. And then I saw my bride self, the one I had left in India when I walked away to sculpt life and art and weave the breath of life into the creative core. And I heard the chant always in me engraved in my being: 'I want to express myself. I will express myself.'

Book One:
Birth

Chapter 1: *I Eat Roses*

Sitting in the arrival area of JFK international airport I felt a sense of anticipation, sadness and a strange anxiety. I looked at the containers of the 16mm films around me and felt the presence of India. I had spent almost five months in Kerala. It was soon after my father had passed and this was my dedication to him in picture, rituals, poetry and memory. I was raw, open, trembling and exhausted.

I felt a light tap and looking up saw my husband. He looked at me absentmindedly and walked away to find a cart to place all the boxes. Returning with it he began placing everything carefully in. We sort of hugged. It felt empty and cool. He looked unusually slick and well dressed, almost like he was clothing his bird soul so no one could see it. I did. A few years back there would have been passionate hugs and wet kisses. Can a muse be forgotten so fast? Can the inspirations, the mad and hungry searching of two artists on a journey of spiritual and physical discovery be abandoned with such ease?

Everything inside hurt. Tightness enveloped my heart. I felt my skin howling in pain. He led me towards the car outside. I followed slowly. I was happy to see a mutual friend get out of the car and run to embrace me. Pedrillos was from Argentina. He helped with the luggage and opened the back door for me. He said I looked sun burnt and glowing.

My husband impatiently told him to get started as it was getting late. Surprised I asked him what the rush was. He casually mentioned that he had to take a flight back to Europe for some coming exhibition. I was shocked. All that I felt waiting at the airport became real. He said that he had told me about this. I had no recollection of it. Silence enveloped the car. My husband was uncomfortable. I felt like an alien.

My husband was from Austria. We met about thirteen years ago in New York City. It was on East. Ninth Street in Manhattan. He stopped me and enquired if I was from South America.

"I am from India."

He laughed. I asked him what he was reading.

"*Red and Black* by Stendhal," he said.

We stopped at the entrance of 63 E. Ninth Street, which was my abode then. He showed me some post cards from the Metropolitan Museum of Art. They were of Tutankhamen. My husband almost looked like the Egyptian prince. We met the next day. I introduced him to sushi which he never had.

I watched his expressions as I placed the first of this delicacy in his mouth. He spoke about five words of English then but even though I hardly knew any German, we communicated "grok-like" with ease[1]. About five days later he opened his pocket German-English dictionary and asked me to marry him.

The sounds of traffic outside filtered into the car and I watched the fleeting images as if in a daze. He casually asked about the shoot and how the filming went. I answered mildly without any enthusiasm. Everything in me was flying out. I felt like a trapped bird who had returned home to its nest to find it was gone. I wanted to cry but my tears had dried up. Nothing came out. I turned sharply and looked straight into his eyes.

"How are you?" I asked. Without glancing at me he replied that he was very preoccupied because of the exhibition. My fingers slowly moved towards his hand on the seat. They touched slightly but he quickly removed his hand. A pain pierced through and my eyes wept without weeping. I felt abandoned, rejected and lost. I was his muse. He had painted only me.

I thought of Picasso. I had gone to MoMA to see the retrospective of his portraits some time back; the exhibit concentrated on the feminine influences in his life. The early portraits had a fascinating reality about them with subtle suggestions of abstraction laced underneath the brush strokes. His initial fascination was with the women he portrayed and when that waned the lines changed from inspired compositions to almost aberrations of the same. The muse alive and the muse slaughtered. I was stunned. I could feel my breathing change.

Can a muse who inspired a whole motion and progression in a creative growth be disfigured and discarded due to the fascination of another muse? Had he found another muse and had I become the outsider? In my mind's eye I saw the big trunk filled with the letters he wrote to me quoting Rilke and Neruda and the dancing minstrels in the haunting language of Rumi. It was a love that inspired people to say that there was hope in the wasteland.

Looking out I saw the familiar cobbled street with the tramlines still visible. Pedrillos slowed down and drove gently to avoid the bumps. He was playing 'Blowing in the Wind', by Bob Dylan. I told him how I adored his music and his radical lyrics. He smiled. "He began in the sixties and now a decade and a half later the music is just as powerful, "I s-

---

1   To grok is to share the same reality or line of thinking with another physical or conceptual entity. From his book, *Stranger in a Strange Land*, Robert A. Heinlein wrote, "grok means to understand so thoroughly that the observer becomes part of the observed--to merge, blend, intermarry, and lose identity in group experience. It means almost everything that we mean by religion, philosophy, and science-and it means as little to us (because of our earthly assumptions) as color means to a blind man." The Oxford dictionary defines grok as "to understand intuitively or by empathy."

aid. We stopped at the entrance and jumping out he helped with the luggage. He avoided looking at me. He was a gentle soul full of love and I could feel his sadness. Walking up the stairs I looked back and half smiled at him as I waved good-bye.

My husband and I entered the building. In the elevator the silence was suffocating. Leading the way, he opened the door and brought all of the luggage inside. I paused before stepping in. It was beautiful and just for one moment my heart sang. I inhaled the familiar fragrance of the incense that he must have burnt earlier. He remembered, I thought. We entered together. I walked around and went to the bedroom. I felt exhausted and limp. I lay down and slowly almost fearfully he lay beside me. For the first time since meeting me at the airport he actually looked at me and said, "You look beautiful."

My eyes were wet and looking at him I seeped into what was the mad passion and the fertile soil of who we were once. My feet ran into that forest of desire and I was that wild bride child again. There were no boundaries. I was alive again. He was touching me and caressing me. The buttons on my shirt were giving way to his supple hands as he rained on me his voluptuous lips and liquid eyes. My left breast shone in appreciation. I remembered how he had often compared my physique to the temple sculptures in India. My eye closed and no more was I without; I was within. And then he suddenly stopped and my pores choked as though without air. My skin was without its shine. My beauty was in hesitation. Doubts surrounded me like crushed fallen and withered leaves.

My tantric vein lines felt tainted and Kama sutra sang no more. He sat up and looking at his watch said that he was late. Walking to the door he turned around. The light was dwindling. Dusk fell on his partially lit face and enhanced the contours of his bones and eyes. He seemed lost and yet impatient to leave, as though if he lingered he would be seduced by the interior tapestry which had flamed his desire so many times. He smiled and left.

I heard the footsteps as they pattered across the loft and then the quiet closing of the door. Unknowingly my hand continued where his had left off, almost as though driven by another force. My fingers paused on my **yoni** and felt listless. All my insecurities invaded me like hunchbacked thieves. Looking up I saw the Krishna door on which was engraved a blue/black life size Krishna playing his flute. I started and looked again. He was a vibrant shining blue. He seemed to emerge from the door carving and now stood in front of me. I sat up slowly, my eyes lowered in disbelief, and wept as his blueness surrounded and engulfed me. Krishna is an **Avatar**, a messenger from the heavens and I knew he came to tell me something. His translucent blue color is the symbol of all-inclusiveness. It is his energy and it is vast beyond our perception.

17

It is like the blue ocean sky. It is pure blue magic. He stood in front of me adorned with peacock feathers which had eyes on both sides. They had a hypnotic power and my gaze could not leave them. I was being pulled into the thousand eyes of the peacock feather and arrowed into the divine realms of Krishna's third eye. The room was radiant. I felt protected and the thieves had no choice but to leave me. The feathers embraced me as I ran wounded and devastated into an emerald forest of many hues. The light and the dark were standing together and both spoke to me. I heard his voice. The words fell all around and in me.

"I will tear you apart and swallow you so the magic mythos spreads within you and with my night-light, peacock-feathered, divine mind I will take your deepest secrets and sorrows and absorb and capture them in my liquid gaze. You have left your culture and your roots to search for your art and your dream within the ancient tapestry of your own Buddha-body-self. You will unleash the mysterious and give birth to a fresh new language and the pain you feel now will rise through your feet, carve your inner child, flow through your veins, and break through your back like the wings of an eagle. You will travel back and forth between both cultures. You will wed many men. I will be your bridge and when walking in the desert dunes of the Wild West, you will be held and nurtured by your bride-self, whom you left behind. Because you had to leave her. But you are both one and the same feminine mystique and you will always see each other in the mirror of your souls and the tall golden burnt tree will enter you and hold you both in harmony and beauty. You will never forget the ancient magnificence of your roots and you will sing their songs wherever you walk. You will enhance your bride-self because she too will learn from you as you will from her."

And as his blue aura blinded me I thought I saw my husband standing in the doorway looking at me with saddened eyes of longing at what he was leaving behind. I looked away and saw Krishna walking back into the carved door and as he slipped through the crack in the middle he beckoned me to enter. I followed him and I was back in India.

I was the bride that would have been. It was all crystal clear. The preparations, the music, the chattering of nervous women attending to all the rituals and to the henna on the hands and feet; the wet sandalwood leaving flower formations on the forehead and cheeks; the jasmine garlands being strung carefully, flower by flower. All around could be heard nervous echoes of relatives and in-laws and family. The haunting sounds of the *shehnai* were like sinuous snakes uncoiling in the base of my spine. Was that the rising of the *kundalini*?

The heaving breath of philosophy and spirit always quivered within and without me. –"Are you spiritual?" people often asked me. Though I hail from this ancient land my gypsy soul never felt it belonged to one place. This question always bothered me and defensively the answer would be quick and sharp. "No, I just like the sense of the other. Don't entrap me with your concepts and ideas and boundaries. I will be free and roam the unmade paths and be untainted like the lotus flower."

Someone tapped me on my shoulder and I was back in the midst of all the heady fragrances and silly giggles in anticipation of I guess a union. Why so much goddamn fuss and silly superficialities? I never understood weddings.

Suddenly there was a hush as the priest entered followed by the groom. I peeked and saw a handsome face crowned and jeweled like a would-be prince. His eyes were cast downward. I was untraditionally forward and looked straight at him. I was born with another eye, with a twin self in both worlds. An inner world of huge dimensions and an outer world of vast horizons and endless vistas. I had already traveled. I was all cultures. I knew no boundaries and felt no restrictions. The apple had fallen and the seeds were strewn in all soils. The godhead was always alive and the seven or nine chakras of ether body were familiar to me both in substance and vision. I know them. They speak to me while walking within the garden of trees and touching their sacred barks lovingly. They respond by caressing my inner circles and joyously I wander with back wide open. No one enters except them, and the truly pure ones. Not pure white and good and proper, but a warrior power that is the blood of the divine and a howl of the creative cry. I am very young. I am very old. Judge me not. I came back because someone was reprimanding me for looking. Who cares, I thought. But to avoid disharmony I lowered my glance, pretending some kind of mild shyness.

The ceremony began and the priest uttered all the appropriate mantras and **shlokas**. We fed each other; we were tied to each other. And we walked united around the fire as rice grains were thrown in the air, symbolizing abundance and fertility.

What kind of fertility, I wondered? Could a single rice grain express a poem or song or a verse cry and more? Noticing my absence from the present, someone brought me back again with an admonishing whisper. Finally, when all was done we were escorted to the room.

We entered and the doors closed. Sitting together on the bed we looked at each other. We were strangers. We had never met before. It was all arranged by our parents and astrologers and such. I guess we fulfilled all of the and requirements. It was silly and safe and completely protected. Or at least that is what was thought. Security and safety and never opening the gold-studded doors of the magical unknown. Who am I? My beloved mother said I had always talked to myself when I was little. "What did I say?" I asked her.

"I don't know but I knew then that you were a dreamer and would be an artist."

He touched my hand and I came back. "Where are you?" he

19

asked.

"An ant inside a lotus flower. I was just entering the center when you disturbed me."

His eyes seemed to have a glimpse of some kind of recognition and joy as though meeting a kindred spirit. We moved closer. I was excited and my breasts bloomed and sung. His fingers shyly began sliding the draped red sari off my left shoulder. I helped him. He began undoing the necklace. I stopped him because I loved the quiet jingling of the golden bells on them. His trembling hands stood me up and the silk sari began falling on the ground slowly like a melody of waves, unveiling a tangible vibrating bride body. I felt like a stallion on a desert dune strewn with jasmine and wild orchids. Pulling me to him he began kissing first my hands, then my feet as he caressed my thighs beneath the petal soft skirt underneath the sari red.

I never had but I had. I was the courtesan of the ages. I was a virgin and not a virgin. I did not know but I did know. He was surprised. I ate my surprise and felt a sublime surreal ecstasy. *Is this the Kama sutra? Is this what they talk about? Is this a merging of body and soul and the maddening desire of Krishna and Radha?* And as he bounded in and around me my red hands clutched the sheets, tore his white dhoti till it bled with henna stains and the howl of the wolves and the tinkling of the ankle bracelets around his spine created a passion raga. He whispered love words in Bengali and all around me was drenched in sweat. And looking through his beautiful almond eyes I began my wedded journey not knowing but still knowing what lay ahead. I could see it.

Trapped in a jeweled cage, ensconced in luxury and comfort and safety and expectations and familiar sounds and empty rituals and repeated motions. Suddenly my eyes hazed and I felt a separation from him.

"What happened? Where are you?"

"I am afraid."

"Why?" he asked moving even closer.

"I see walls all around me covered with ornaments and gold and I hear a distant cry calling me."

He started up and anxiously wanted to know whose voice it was.

"My child voice," I said, "the voice in me, the voice that guides me and reveals hidden truths, the voice of art and hunger and forest fires and vision quests. I hear them always and they never leave me in peace. They want me to be their warrior, their human expression, their compassion and their slayer of all that dwells in the stagnant ponds of mediocrity and death. That voice."

"I will do all I can so that voice never dies," he said.

Sadly, looking at him I replied that it was not him, it was them.
"Your parents will never understand me. I am fallen in their eyes because

I travel the worlds and cloak the earth. I am not beautiful to them because my skin is burnt amber and not a pale sickly white. Because I dance life and embrace what is ancient and free, because I was born old and know the sacred words and because I worship art and the breath of an artist and because I am different and will give them a daughter and not a son.

"How do you know that?" he asked.

"I know it because I feel it in every fiber of myself."

Looking at him I saw pain in his eyes. "Have I already lost you?" With a deep sigh he took one strand of my flowing black hair and looked at it deeply.

"You are my strand of life, my sun burnt beauty. You are everything. I love you," he said, "I don't care what they think and want. I worship You. I saw a herd of stallions galloping over smooth white hills, their black coats reflecting the light of the moon. I was startled and look-ing around the room remembered I was in New York City. I glanced at Krishna. His lips moved and his fingers gracefully found the notes on the bamboo flute. The magical crack through which he and I had slipped seemed alive and heaving like a forked tree bark. I thought of **Ardhanari**, Shiva and Shakti, the two selves in one--the one who stays and the one who leaves. They are of the same body, the same soul, and the same throbbing, beating wild tiger heart. I had left my bride-self in the bedroom deflowered and wild and doe-eyed looking at the journey that lay ahead of her, as I began my own on untouched paths and tiger walks and sharpened swords. I am the giant sable antelope with its coal black coat and horns that touch the earth balancing both worlds and both selves within me.

Slowly rising from the bed I glanced at my hennaed feet and could feel the lips of my Indian groom. I watched my red hands clutch-ing the gold sheets, reliving the scene of the wedding night. I knew that was not what I longed for even though the sweetness caressed my now wounded soul. But wounds heal and transformation happens and evol-ution rebirths and the rest dissolve.

Gathering myself I left the bedroom and slowly walked out. Everything screamed in me. The wounds ached. They were raw and open. I felt abandoned, empty, and absolutely alone. Everything shook. I couldn't move. My legs were still like the roots of a tree and trembling I fell to the floor. Nothing seemed real. He had left me like a thief taking away my pounding heart. Here was one more betrayal, one more lie, and one mo-re slaughtered self. I tried to rise but was not able to. I cra-wled towards the chair next to the sky table. Sand rippled all around embracing me with all its nuances and shades and whispering mytholo-gies. The grains entered my skin, consoling me with apologies of the frail humankind and the aberrations of me and mine and singular attachments. My eyes turned to the altar where the incense sticks that I lit on entering the loft had burned down and only the ashes were left, the ashes of a funeral where death had vanquished all obvious physicality.

I looked at the rolls of film on the floor in tin cans. Forty-seven rolls dedicated to my father who had passed recently. And here it was, another death, this time of betrayal and desire, of fear and insecurity and the pathetic poverty of a non-hero wearing the garb of an artist-painter. I crawled to the film rolls standing in isolation near the door. I pushed my whole self next to the cans, holding each one in my trembling hands with tears falling down my cheeks and on them. I knew then that my work as an artist had begun. Film was my language and my tool and I would breathe art into every celluloid expression. It would bleed and weep and capture the inner whisperings of mankind.

I felt the sand pushing me with its dune weight and giving me the strength to slowly rise from the ground. The sky table moved to lift me as though the sky itself was meeting the earth to help me. A blue hand reached out to me. It was Krishna again. He came to remind me of who I was and must become and as I rose he showered me with a hundred peacock feathers and I clung to one and drank his eyes. The table moved towards me. The twelve red roses formed a circle of fire and glistened and shone in front of me, inviting me to touch and feel them.

I was told that the red rose had one hundred and fifty high vibrations, the highest in the flower kingdom. And without realizing it my hands reached out to touch one glistening bud with a thousand love songs quivering from each petal. Placing one dew dropped petal after another in my mouth, all in me resounded with the birth of the flower and a haunting sensation of loss and separation fell into my being. I began a low bemoaning scream and as it got louder and louder even the table responded with its scratched surface and uneven tree lines. The howl filled the room and flew through the window on to the river outside. The water rippled in sadness and carried the wailing sounds on its glimmering liquid body. Once again I heard the blue God's voice thundering and silent as his words fell from the sky: "I am the beginning, middle and end of creation. Among animals, I am the lion; among birds, **Garuda's** eagle beak.. I am the conscience in the heart of all creatures. I am **Prahlada**, born among the demons, and all that measures, I am time." I knew his words were meant to fill me with a marvelous eagle power and I knew I had to inhale them and become more. Rainer Maria Rilke's figure descended from above and dropped from a transcendental source as Lorca's figure burst up from below, from earth itself and the middle was a liquid space of the creative core. It was itself life. I thought of my beginnings and remembered one of those ominous and frightening days when I first entered into the **duende** of the western world, here in the land of the howling wolves and ancient eagle warriors where the demon and the

22

angel dance together to create an irrational splendor of the deep song of creativity. Here in New York City. These were not memories of sentimentality. This was and is the story of a woman warrior who walks, crosses all worlds and knows no boundaries and eats all mediocrity and ignorance. She is a woman of the elements; she encompasses everything in us. She represents our most basic selves. She is complex and simple and is ready to live love and learn at every moment. She is two selves in one. The arrows of the Universe sculpt her.

Here I was once again in JFK International Airport, entering this country for the first time, a long time ago. The echo of my past in London where I was sculpted and molded and the longing whisperings of my passionate first love who had left this earth after a long illness circled within and without me. My song lines took me back and my dreamtime began.

According to the Australian Aboriginal, a song is both a map and a way-finder. Providing you knew the song, you could always find the way; an Aboriginal did not believe a country existed until they could see and sing it. Just as in the Dreamtime, the country had not existed until the Ancestors sang it. Rilke had a similar intuition. He said song was existence. One woman caught within the boundaries of her culture and the other connected with all the elements. The epic journey of one soul married to her birthplace and the other to the universal soul. This is the symphony of the feminine mystique, mine.

Looking around at this huge space of people and activity and motion, I felt tiny and intimidated. I was standing in a corner of the international arrival area surrounded by cloth bags of many colors People scurried by glancing at me curiously. I was a stranger in a strange land, indeed. That was me. My eyes traveled everywhere searching for the familiar face of the woman I had met in India. Smila was an elegant American who had gone to India on a search for her inner reality, and her own identity--a common theme of many who fly to the ancient land to discover themselves. That is where I met her, in Pondicherry, South India, a little place on the Indian Ocean that housed the center of Sri Aurobindo and the Mother, and whose Integral yoga was about the transformation of man into the supramental manifestation. "All can be done when the God touch is there", wrote Sri Aurobindo. This is one of my song lines and is where I had spent some of my youth and adult years.

The noise and empty sounds of relentless hurry brought me back and looking at the cloth bags around me and my hennaed feet and hands I began feeling the aura of where I came from and the power of what was beneath and beyond me. I suddenly did not feel small. I felt big and wide and vast and earth-wed. The hundred dollar note in the palm of my right hand was crumpled and red. I tried to smooth it and in doing that I caused my bound hair to uncoil, and the now wilted jasmine garland that weaved my braids fell to the shiny floor. Picking it up I inhaled its fragrance and my eyes closed as I felt the hands of the little fragile woman in India who had weaved it in my hair before I left and whispered in Hindi: "Your face is transparent and your songs will be heard by all who can hear and all who can see and all who can feel. Walk your path like

24

like the rhinoceros, fearing nothing and trembling at nothing and like the lotus flower, tainted by nothing. You are strong." I had never met her before. I touched her feet and drinking in her blessings walked away from my ancestors and all the hidden dreams of my heartland. Rising slowly I saw Smila in the distance running towards me. She was beautifully dressed with flowing silk fabrics draped around her. She walked towards me with arms wide open. I embraced her, and my long fragrant hair flowed around her and me. I did not let go of the withered garland and holding on to it began gathering all my bags from the floor.

"Let me help," she said. But I didn't let her help and, clutching all, followed her out to the parking area. She walked to a shiny streamlined car. It had beautiful lines and I commented on it. "Oh yes. It is very expensive and, you know, prestigious. It is a Bentley."

"A what?" I naively asked.

"Sort of like a Rolls Royce," she replied.

She opened the doors and I slipped my cotton entourage onto the back seat. She cringed as though they would leave a stain on the leather. Noticing that I started to move them onto the floor of the car, but she asked me to leave them where they were.

Opening the front door for me she beckoned me to climb in as she shut the door and walked to the driver's seat. It was magnificent. The hand carved wooden dashboard and the elegant interior were breathtaking. She noticed my awe and mentioned that this was her dream car and that she had worked very hard to own it. Settling in we cruised through the airport towards the exit and onto the highway towards New York City.

Smila was describing all that we passed by: the huge burial grounds on both sides and a ground scape of tombstones. I looked for my cloth covered notebook and wrote: "There is a walk that walks inside, there is a walk that walks outside, I see a certain dream at night, it hallows hollows all man's cry."

My gaze settled on the emblem of the car speeding along the highway. It dissolved to a vast desert-like place with dusty mountains in the horizon. It was dusk lit and barren and in the distance I saw a beautiful black stallion galloping arrow-like with a figure on its back who was one with the horse. She was robed in something long and was riding bareback. Her hair and clothes were flying in the wind, the only sound was the hoofs of the galloping horse and the whistling of the wind. *This is a symbol of my spirit, I thought to myself, I feel it. She will guide me and protect me with her fire wind song. She is my song line and will show me the sand-drenched path rippled with the shades of carved formations and ancient realities and words from all the sacred books embedded within the golden flow of mirrors. She is the flaming torch bearer of all the hidden languages of the blue light.*

As we moved through this visual hugeness, Smila spoke about

India.

"How are your parents?" She asked. "And your beloved father, who was so kind to lend me the money when I needed it so badly?"

"They are good and both send their warm regards. They wanted me to thank you for picking me up," I replied. "Do you miss them? "I miss them madly. And I feel their sadness too. But I had to do this, and I know they will understand someday. My father surrounds me with trust and that foundation allows me to flow freely."

As the car approached the city, the light was gentle and beautiful. I felt a throbbing familiarity and told Smila that it reminded me of Calcutta. She was surprised and said that she would never have thought that. There was a magic here. I felt comfortable. I felt a presence. And then I noticed the thick snake like formations of steam and smoke rising from the streets. "Would you mind stopping the car?"I asked Smila. Jumping out barefoot, I ran to the smoke and stepped right into it. I screamed from the scathing heat of the manholes and ran back to the car holding my scalded feet. I felt that I was standing on sacred ground. I heard the howl of the hundreds who were killed for land and greed and the treacherous screaming of the children, women and men who were brutally slaughtered at Wounded Knee. I could hear them. I had always felt a strong affinity with the American Indian culture and as a child I remembered wearing a feather in my hair and marking my face with lines of charcoal.

Smila laughed and said she would have stopped me, as she knew how hot the manholes could get.

"No," I said. "I had to experience this. I feel like I have been initiated by this land and this place and this is the beginning of my journey."

As we drove on I had an uncanny feeling of belonging. The Gods are alive, I thought. There was a rich silence in the car as we drove through the city, vibrating with smoke, people and noise.
And then leaving its limits we began winding through country roads. I watched the transforming scenes and marveled at the beauty of green trees and different foliage. Taking my cloth book I began my inner sojourn and wrote:

> The shadow of pine leaves
> Taking motion in art squares
> And the youth of sight walking
> through mud wet clay
> Watching a leaf held in earth
> The story of land existing to create
> And the red mountain whistling in blue
> And the green geranium resting in orange

The car slowly came to a standstill as Smila was describing exactly where we were and how exclusive it was.

"South Hampton," she said.

It was close to the ocean. I could smell the hungry sounds of the sea air and stepping out of the car stretched and inhaled deeply the mythic conch-sounding vibrations of the sea. Her home was palatial. Slightly limping from burnt feet, I entered the home. It was filled with geranium plants, and photographs of her teacher, Swami Satchitananda. I recognized him and remembered a time when in the midst of a huge crowd somewhere in India he approached me with his beatific smile and handed me the white flower which was in his hand. I still had it somewhere.

I bowed in front of the altar. Smila built a fire and lit the candles and soon the house was captured in soft hues of shaded light motions. She asked me if I wanted a bath. I said that I would love one. While the bath was being filled, she asked me if I would like a glass of wine and what kind.

"I would love a glass of red earth," I replied.

Candles were all over the bathroom and as I immersed myself in the warm, welcoming, fragranced water I closed my eyes and sipped the wine. The red blood howl sang deep truth songs and sensuously spread its sun-ripened self within me. I thought of Miguel, the man who had educated me about this ancient elixir of the gods, and who had given me so much when I began this journey in London. He was my lover of all time, as he took my hand and walked me into the mystery of this dance. He was always with me. He had invited me on a trip once. And when I arrived exhausted he had drawn a languorous bath for me and left me to unwind from the hours in the air. When I got out of the water I saw a trail of paper arrows. Following them I approached a table where an opened bottle was standing with the cork beside it. And next to the bottle was a piece of paper describing the wine and what region in France it was from. It also described all the blossoms that grew around the grapevines. The note ended by asking me to meet him in the dining area of the hotel. When I approached the table where he was sitting, he stood up and waited for me to sit down. He then poured a glass of red and lifting it up to me, he said that wine was water held together by sun and air. He spoke endlessly about the beauty and philosophy of the grape. Since then it has always been poetry and inner songs to me. It was my art companion of sorts and my infinite gratitude to this prismed sun-drenched soma of the gods. Slowly opening my eyes and pushing myself up a little I looked around for a piece of paper and pen:

> Walking in sandals on shaded sand
> Caught the serpent through my eye

Tiger flower clothed my ether
Textured stone give me my birth sight
Only only death deceives
Only only life conceives Feline
woman soft and strong you
are magic deep and brown.

Sinking back into the water and sipping from the etched crystal glass I
was on the beautiful Island of Formentera in Spain with my gypsy man,
Miguel, surrounded by crystal blue waters of the Mediterranean and the
sounds of flamenco and the passionate cries of the hota sung by the gypsies in Spain. To go to Formentera, we had to take a small boat from the
island of Ibiza. Often when on that boat Miguel would hum a haunting
tune. He was fascinated by it and looking at me he would just smile and
keep echoing it. He was a mixture of Irish and English and I had met him
in England where I was studying theater and film. He was my partner,
my lover, and we went often to this Island together. His rough gypsy face
and deep male magnificence showed me many vistas of the art of performance and voice. He was a master, a very well-known Shakespearean
actor, and with his exquisite skills he guided and chiseled my then un-
formed clay. We walked on the white sands watching the sun set, playing the guitar, writing poetry and making love under the sky. Our silken
skins melted into one another as we entwined the vibration of art and the
sensuous cat sounds of the *sutra* of passion. "Boot"--he always called
me that--"You light my fire. You have given me India. You are a sacred
stallion. I will sing songs for you. I will write stories for you."

I was back in India, in a beautifully shaded and luxurious colo-
nial home a little outside Calcutta. My husband was out working. I was
surrounded by help and had to oversee all the various chores being done
by each person. After completing my duties, I went to my study and
began reading Rabindranath Tagore's Chitranjali, a compilation of his
poetry. In the distance I overheard my mother-in-law speaking in Bengali with some visiting women friends. It seemed as though her voice was
particularly loud so that I would hear what she was saying through the
closed door.

"She is always leaving her duties and running to her room and
closing the door. Once I looked in and she was reading. She also has
some paint brushes and an easel. I have always to remind her to take
care of things. Not only does she have a dark completion, I am sure she
will give me a girl."

Looking away from my book I glanced out of the window and
raced into a sea of blue and green waves where I danced upon the heaving ocean. I felt I was not alone and as I wiped the tears from my eyes

the kohl smeared on my hands.

With those same shadowed eyes of a wounded deer from an ancient statue on the beam of light, I looked into Miguel's eyes as I caressed him wildly with the pores of my hair and the skin of my heart. I had taken him to India to meet my parents once. They loved him. We went to Pondicherry to have **darshan** with the Divine Mother in the Sri Aurobindo ashram. They got two fresh flower garlands for us and when we were led to her room my parents handed them to the Mother and asked her to wed us by exchanging the garlands between us. She had a smile and a knowing look in her all-seeing eyes. I understood what that look was many years later after I had left London and my Miguel had passed from an illness. My whole self wept. When we came down from the Mother's room Miguel and I sat side by side in the area underneath. He was very quiet. We still had the garlands around us. And then looking at me he softly said that when he was with the Mother he heard the same tune that came to him on the boat to Formentera. He was in an altered state. He radiated light and his whole face shone and was transparent. His eyes closed. I embraced him and felt some non-approving, judgmental eyes looking at us. I was oblivious to all except him and the resonance of the Mother. We were lost in her gaze and stayed there as long as we could.

There was a knock on the door. Remembering where I was, I told Smila that I would be right out. I walked out of the bathroom draped in a soft cotton robe with warm sun colors. Sitting on large fluffy pillows I flew into the tongue flames of the fire and watched a sliver of light floating from the sky. We were quiet with only some soft chants, and the crackling of the flames filled the atmosphere. I was still in the sand grains of Formentera as they lingered on my skin, leaving whispers of the embraces of passion, the dancing wind and a laughing heart. Smila slowly began to speak about India and meditation. I sort of listened. And as she went on and on about the blue light that she saw when she meditated, I drifted off and closing my eyes saw a bird flying in the blue sky, an iced river frozen. And many carp fish swimming against the current and the blue color of rainbow trout glistening in the light.

I thanked her for her hospitality and said that I would like to lie down. Walking to the bedroom, she turned down the covers and I lay down on a bed that felt as sumptuous as it looked. I slid in and dozed off almost immediately. It was a large bed and I felt Smila beside me. She began gently rubbing my back and neck. It felt good and comforting. But after a while the energy shifted and I felt uncomfortable and strange like a howling wolf. The strokes sat heavy on my skin. They exuded a murky odor as though the fingers were drenched in hesitation and greed. Smila's hands stopped as I moved away, shrugging off some creased, tainted skin and creating a distance from her. I was awake now and my eyes res-

29

ted on the glass filled with water next to the bed. Suddenly the water in the glass started to get smoky and hazy. My eyes slowly closed and I slipped into my ether world.

The dream world is my axis. Dreams inspire me and guide me and make me whole. They are my Art. They are my reality. I honor them. Two knives stand erect in a wide earth expanse, desert like. I am looking down into a deep cavern. I feel like falling but cannot, and then see a space filled with serpents. They become gold. And as I watch they transform into **shehnais**, the wind instrument played at weddings in India and in my dream state I see my bride self on my wedding night enraptured by my groom with the haunting notes of the instruments all around us. My twin-self is always with me. She who I left behind as we conversed with the blue stallion in a half-eaten language and our souls balanced each other and fed each other and held each other as our wounds became our ink. Now she holds and nurtures the culture garden and gently removes any invasive weeds, which may threaten to obscure my warrior sight. I watch the gold serpents and hear voices asking me not to enter. But I do. And get bitten. Something uncoils within me. I feel my body stretching and elongating. I feel happy and awake with a smile. As I slowly open my eyes to the cawing of a crow, dawn has seeped into the room with its soft sounds. Surprised and comforted by the crow calls, my eyes close again into that special light morning sleep where even death bows his head and weeps. Cloth figures are enacting a play on a vast expanse of rippling sand dunes. One of them approaches me and indicates that I should peel my finger. I do and underneath it is a crystal nail. They ask me to break it. I try, but cannot. The light catches it and it sparkles. I am walking and gropingly find a cave, which I enter. It is long and hollow and filled with light. Emerging from the cave blinded by the light they point at the earth and ask me to peel the earth skin. And as I am doing this an exquisite woman covered in silver approaches me. She has the most beautiful silver ornaments and I look at them quietly, wishing for them. Silver reflects my moon songs and its shining metal is fluid mind light embracing the compassion for the human walk. The woman then gives me a mirror and looking I see my own reflection as a bride and pride and dignity and strength are in the image.

I woke up and, remembering the dream in all its details, wondered at all the inflections and significances and noticed the still shaded water in the glass. I heard Smila busying herself in the kitchen. She popped her head into the room and greeted me with a warm smile. I nodded as she indicated the bathroom. My mouth felt parched and remembering the night's discomfort wondered at what all this would lead to. Entering the bathtub, I felt the warm water of the shower cleaning me deeply.

My mind remembered the beautiful silver woman in my dream

and I saw my other self in India near a window looking out as though searching for a part of her that had walked away. She is I. I am she. She weeps. I weep as my wet fingers wipe the tears away and my hand reaches out to dry her sweet tears. She is my beautiful child bride, my soul keeper. She is my sword sheath and sharpener enhancing me on my warrior walk with no hesitation.

Coming out wrapped in a large towel, I walked to the other room and lit incense, greeting Smila who seemed happy and undisturbed. She asked me to sit down. Slicing into a halved grapefruit urgently, I smiled. I was eating life. All boundaries and structures dissolved into my mouth with the pink, pearly juice of the ruby red fruit. Looking at Smila, I asked her how she had slept. She answered that she had slept well and asked me how I had rested. I replied that I had had some amazing dreams. To which Smila sort of mumbled that dreams were what was missing in her life. I spoke about dreams being one's personal myth, which was so amiss in today's industrial and linear existence. I read somewhere that the Greek word psyche means "butterfly" and also denotes the soul.

"Dreams give your soul wings and images from dreams are the exquisite patterns on those wings. Hold your dreams as you would hold a butterfly in your quiet palms. Pinning the dream down with interpretation will simply tear the wings off the butterfly and kill it. We can place the dead butterfly under glass, study it and admire its uniqueness but it will never fly again. I hold my dreams gently so they can always fly. I keep my dream catcher near me so I am assured that the negative dreams will be caught and the strong ones will fly away through the weavings of the catcher."

Picking up my cup and sipping the well-timed brew I noticed how silent she was. She glanced at me nervously and I looked back unabashed. She averted her eyes and changed the subject. Mediocrity has a million thorns that are not sharp enough to hurt the non-mediocre. They only try. She asked about my financial situation. Getting up I walked to where my bag was and taking out the now very vibrant red one hundred dollar bill I showed it to her. Some of the jasmine flowers fell onto the floor and I bent down to pick them up, making sure not a single petal was missed. As I did that I heard the voice of the bronzed woman who had given it to me, and all became clear. I raised my head with grace and walked into her gaze. She was shocked that this was all I had and quickly said, "Something will have to be done about this. I have contacts and I'll call around and see what I can set up."

"Thank you," I said quietly as I started to get ready for the trip back into the city.

"Maybe we should take all your stuff so you have everything there."

31

Placing everything near the door I sat in front of the altar for a few minutes. I caught her looking at me from the corner of my eye as I glanced around the house noticing all the furnishings and accessories.

"You have a beautiful home," I said. She thanked me.

The warmth had ebbed a little. There was just a hint of unease in the atmosphere. We got into the car and we rode back silently. I drifted back to Pondicherry where we had met, walking and sitting together near the Samadhi in the ashram. I had spent a year in Auroville, the city of dawn, a universal township in the making in South India, dedicated to human unity and based on the vision of Sri Aurobindo and The Mother. I lived in a hut I had built. This was at the very beginning, when the land was uncultivated and just a few people lived there. It was a simple A-frame structure, with a mobile ladder to climb up and down, and the only amenities were an outdoor pipe where I could shower in the open. I went there after my stay in London when Miguel and I had to separate for an unavoidable and sad reason. My heart was wounded and holed, and I had to renew and regain the rock garden of source. It was a time of solitude and growth, of being wed to the stars and the beginning of my journey into the adventure of consciousness. My feet were stained from the red earth, as I walked barefoot for a whole year. I biked to and from the Ashram in Pondicherry about forty kilometers away. And there I would wait in line to have **darshan** with The Divine Mother. She was gold and transparent. Of her Sri Aurobindo wrote: "The Divine puts on an appearance of humanity, assumes the outer human nature in order to tread the path and show it to human beings, but does not cease to be the Divine. It is a manifestation that takes place, a manifestation of a growing divine consciousness and not human turning into divine. The Mother comes in order to bring down the Supramental and it is the descent that makes her full manifestation here possible".

I met her when I was around seven or so. It was with my mother. She looked glorious and majestic. As my mother and I were being led towards her, I was overcome by her power and darted out of my mother's hands and ran away as fast as I could. I heard her say something in French to Champaklal-ji, a lion disciple always behind her, guarding and assisting. He followed me with silent pattering feet, grabbed me by my collar like a stray cat. He dragged me back and threw me at her feet. She placed her hands on my head and slowly and steadily began kneading my head as though it were a piece of dough or clay. All I remember to this day is a stream of light going right through my head and spreading all through my body. And even now in moments of anguish and life confusion I relive that experience and at once I am filled with her light arrows, and my inner eye awakens to that divine touch. I started to cry tears of joy, of wet fire that just poured out of my eyes. As I began to rise I remembered nothing, except her cotton-clothed feet in Japanese thong-

s. They shone. My head bowed. I started stepping back so I would only face her. And I heard my mother's joyful sobbing at what she had just witnessed. Taking my hand in hers she said, "You have been blessed."

"The hero who has come under the protection of the divine Mother cannot be harmed," I heard someone whisper in my ears.

A slight bump on the road brought me back and glancing sideways I noticed Smila looking at me.

"You were away," she said.

"Actually I was back in Auroville," I explained.

"That place gave me so much peace," she said. "I would love to go back."

As we begin to approach the city Smila suddenly lit up and told me that I was in for a surprise. We were driving through some very heavy traffic and like a child I was observing everything. The highway was parallel to the water and the blue expanse was soothing. In the distance I saw a tall shape, but I couldn't decipher it. As we got closer it got clearer and then, pointing at it, she exclaimed that what I was looking at was the world famous Statue of Liberty. Her left hand shot upwards holding a torch to guide all who came to this land, which belonged to the Native American Indians--the shaman warriors who were robbed of their land and held captive by the invaders and traders. The ones who believed that land could never be bought or sold because it belongs to no one. She was beautiful and as we got even closer her archaic weathered face dissolved into the Mother's face. I sat up startled. Smila looked at me wanting to make sure I was okay. I quietly said that she was magnificent and felt assured that she, the Mother, was right there with me. I was silent as I felt my burning skin piercing my body.

The car finally drove into Smila's building area and the doorman approached, opening the doors for us. He was pleasant and had a Spanish accent. It felt warm and sunny. She introduced me to him as he helped with all the baggage. We went up to the eleventh floor where the apartment was and she opened the door to a large sunny space with aesthetic furnishings, warm colors, Indian fabric, and Guru Photographs. She showed me my room and told me to make myself at home as she had all sorts of work to take care of. She also told me that she was going to begin making phone calls to people and maybe have a soirée and invite them to her place. I told her not to go to too much trouble on my behalf.

"I have to because you have no money and in this city," she looked at me harshly, "you really need it.

I felt sad and, lying down on the very comfortable bed, closed my eyes for a moment.

I was back in my bride-self in India in the luxurious home filled with affluence and comfort and security. It was a gilded gold cage. I was safe and trapped but the bird songs and the hum of nature were my hosts and friends.

Opening my eyes, I looked around at this room. It was simple and elegant but lacked a fullness and warmth. The cawing of the crow was absent and my jasmine fragrance and the haunting whiffs of the night queen were missing. I picked up the now wilted garland, and pressed it against my face till I felt blood flying out of my mind. Sitting up I began to unpack and placed my portable alter on the little side table next to the bed, and hung the sacred garland on my images. They were all there, all my warriors. Placing my cloth journal on the bed I opened it casually and smiled as the page opened to the following words, a Cree prophesy: "When all the trees have been cut down, when all the animals have been hunted, when all the waters are polluted, when all the air is unsafe to breathe, only then you will discover you cannot eat money".

Putting the bags near the wall closet, I began unfolding and hanging the clothes as thoughts visited me and inspired me. "Art is a sacred function and all art is autobiographical like the pearl is of the oyster," said Fellini, the great Italian filmmaker. "Unless you have been thoroughly drenched in perspiration, you cannot expect to see a palace of pearls on a blade of grass."

I remembered my days in London, when I was in my teens, when I studied and delved into the life of an actress. It was challenging and relentless. The same cattle calls from one audition to another and always hearing the same words over and over again. "She is very gifted and has a great sense of timing but unfortunately the look doesn't quite work." "What look?" I often wondered and even asked a panel once after what I felt was an excellent and appropriate rendition of the reading.

Well," one said, "you are just too exotic."

I asked him what he meant by that to which he replied, "Strange."

"Time is the sensible measure in the continuity of mediocrity", and after rejection after rejection, the stallion walk began faltering. I was even told that maybe I should go back to India and try there as I was talented. I cried out that I couldn't go back. The bark had peeled off the tree and it couldn't fit anymore. *I will walk, I will find, I will die, I will be reborn and I will evolve and never dissolve. I will show them and take them to wider horizons through the cell sounds that were given to me as gifts. And even if I falter I will express myself. They can outcast me and wound me and I will show them the strings of my heart and the shafts of my art. Finding the heart's voice that is what every artist is dedicated to. And that is my song line and my path finder.* Back then the money was not enough, and I did some modeling for photographers and magazines and some voice-overs. The hardest thing of all was being a clothes rack for boring styles and having to mingle with shallow people. But nothing could or would stop me. And through a maze of opportunities, some of some of which I refused because they would compromise me, I searched for a hand or a quest to hold me and lead me through. They came when I most needed them and steered me through. And now here I was in New York, and another journey was being launched.

I shivered a little thinking of all that I would have to go through again. Smila knocked and walked in the room.

"You didn't bring much," she observed.

"Anyway, I have set up some appointments for you to get you started in your career here, and when you're done I would like to go through the list with you."

Nodding I told her I would be with her soon. As she walked out of the room she noticed the altar and, smiling, sat down to take it in. She asked me if I always had it with me.

"Always," I replied.

After unpacking everything I went to her study and sat beside her. She walked me through all the people and numbers to call, explained each one to me, and what they could and could not do. It was a lot and I sat there looking at all the contacts, overwhelmed. Noticing my discomfort she assured me that it would be very productive and that she felt sure a lot would come of the effort.

"Just be confident and be yourself. You have nothing to worry about. Your beauty will see you through."

Shrinking at what she said and how she said it, I looked away. I remembered meeting a wonderful, warm woman once in London who said to me how easy and amazing it must be to be born with the gift of beauty. She went on to say that her whole life she spent being invisible because she was not good looking. I told her that beauty was a burden, to which she immediately replied that everything must come so easy for me and that she could not understand how that was possible.

The beauty that you see is often a lie to me because I don't believe it. My mother never validated me because she thought it would feed my ego, so I walked with a beggars bowl hungry to hear this from others and the scars that were caused are etched inside me. I can touch them.

"It comes with a price," I said. "It is like a huge test that is laid on you to see how you use it. It is a burden because if you walk on the shell of it, it cracks, and you never can ever enter the deep perceptions and realities of what lies within." She seemed confused but I continued. "Imagine an exquisite mask which you always look at and marvel at and make sure that it stays as it is in all its perfection. Your whole life your concentration is on the visage of this work of art and you try to make sure that nothing changes or distorts it. But it does change, and it does grow and enhance, but you cannot bear it and you are obsessed with trying everything so it does not chnage and in so doing you have never even tried to enter and go beneath that beautiful surface. You forget that underneath is the soil that feeds that pristine surface and needs all the consciousness and light it can get to maintain the exterior. But you have spent your entire life neglecting the within and when the without wilts you are devastated because your vanity is at stake. And at this point there is nowhere you can go and you spend your whole life trying to bring back what was and, moving into dark haunting shadows, you question all that is divine and true as the crust tries to get married to your soul. That is the danger and the burden. Carl Jung speaks of the individual soul of every decade and how monumentally important it is to nurture each one. Yet most of the time when one is at one point, one wants to either be beyond it or before it, one wants to be older or younger. And each soul is neglected and then when you finally are in the present space you are lost and empty and without because the present was never nurtured." Looking at her I saw that her face had lit up and she told me that she would never have thought of it in that way. She said she now truly understood and, thanking me, said that she would not demean herself ever again.

Thanking Smila I took the list and walked back to the room. She said that I should begin contacting people as soon as possible. There was urgency in her voice and I knew it was because she was very concerned about my finances or, rather, the lack thereof. My sleep that night was restless and even fearful. Glancing at the crystal tumbler of water and noting that it was clear, I closed my eyes with a deep sigh of relief. My hand reached out to the other side of the bed as though searching for someone.

I was in India lying next to my adoring husband. A flowing cascade of mosquito netting was tucked around us. My hand was on his. He was asleep as I looked at him quietly. He was at peace and it reflected back to me in waves of comfort and safety. Turning my eyes I saw the moon glistening through the little circles of the net as each one clung to the other in a joyous union. Smiling, I slowly crept out of the bed and, sipping from the steel glass of water, walked towards the window. The moon beckoned me to bathe in its silver rays. The tropical night sounds formed a symphony of heat waves and intoxicating fragrances. I stayed looking out, held by the moon and I thought I heard whispers. It was like someone was calling me. The moon's rays lit the foliage. All was familiar and embracing, and yet I felt a deep restlessness as though I was missing a part of me. I heard my husband softly asking if everything was all right. Turning I walked back and slipped into bed and pushed myself against him. He asked me what was wrong and I said that I felt as though someone or something was pulling me. Taking me into his arms he held me tight and stroking my hair asked if it was that voice again. "Maybe," I said.

The city sounds awoke me the next morning. I glanced to the other side of the bed and remembering where I was sat up. After showering I came out of the bathroom and noticed that there was a large mug of hot tea next to my bed. Sitting down I lit a stick of incense and, finding a secure place, put the burning fragrance near the altar. Taking a deep breath, I walked to the little table with a phone, and began dialing the numbers. Smila asked me to call the agents first and then follow with the others. She also said to mention her name, as most of them knew her. Appointments were made for the following days and weeks. Some were with agents, others with people who were casting for off Broadway plays, Independent films and commercials. I called and called relentlessly until I could feel my voice breaking. I stopped and walked out to see what she was doing.

How's it going?" she asked me.

"Good. Most of them were very accessible when I mention your name."

"Yes, - she said proudly. "I am very well known in those circles. They consult me about people, costumes and cultural nuances about themes they use."

I was impressed.

"You know without my name you would never be able to even speak to anyone except the secretary who would only screen your call and that would be that."

"I owe you a lot. How can I pay you back?"

"Oh you don't have to do that. Just be my friend."

I wondered what that really meant. There was so much within that sentence, and the night at South Hampton came back, and the murky water and the discomfort and unease that I had felt.

The next morning after a shower and light breakfast, I began my appointments. Smila looked at me approvingly and told me how to get to all the different places. "It is easy to get around here since the streets are numbered."

She suggested either walking or taking buses. "You look great," she said.

Walking toward the front door a man with a warm smile wished me a great day. There was something about him that made me feel very comfortable. I felt I could trust him. I showed him the address of my first appointment and he directed me exactly. The air was mild and fresh and I had a bounce in my step. I felt ripe and confident.

I walked into a very tall concrete building and went up to the top floor. The secretary nodded briefly when I told her my name and appointment time. "You are early," she said indifferently. "Take a seat." I did, and looking around brought out my journal. Opening the pages, I had just begun to write when the receptionist said that I could go in. She walked me to a very plush and ornate room. A well-dressed woman nodded, her head and asked me to take a seat. She mentioned Smila and asked me how I knew her. I told her that we met in India, and she nodded, saying that she would love to go there. She asked me what I wanted to pursue and about my background and training and so on. I mentioned that I loved theater and film and would be willing to do some modeling also. She asked me if I had a portfolio, which I handed to her. Glancing at the photos she remarked at the quality and asked me where and who had taken them.

"They were done in London by a very talented photographer."

"You do have a special look. Smila was right. Let's see what we can do. I'll make some calls and let you know. I'm assuming you are staying at her apartment?"

I nodded and said that was where she could reach me. Rising, she shook my hand and, walking me to the door, she wished me luck and reassured me that she would do what she could. Thanking her, I walked to the reception area and on towards the elevator. The receptionist quickly came after me with my journal in her hand. "You left this on the table." I gratefully took it and placed it carefully in my bag. Leaving the building I looked at the next address, and figuring it out walked towards another tall monument. Glancing up I noticed that many had very beautiful ornate designs on them. They were so huge and tall and felt like the sky.

This time I did not have to go too high and stepping out noticed another cold lobby area. I was on time, and the girl at the front desk showed me to a secluded office in the rear. She knocked and announced me. A suited, nice-looking man asked me to have a seat. "So you are Smila's exotic discovery." I shifted in the chair and rearranged myself self-consciously, not feeling comfortable in his presence.

"What part of India are you from?" He asked.

"Bengal," I said. I asked him if he was familiar with India and he mentioned that he had been there quite a few times on business. He went on to ask me why I was not pursuing a career there since India had such a vast film industry. I just casually said that I wanted to be here.

"Ah of course, everyone wants to be here," he replied, and I walked into my mind-ways and thought about flight and remembered the conversations with others who had stepped aside and not inside. Those who had forgotten the antelope prince as he shivered and trembled and ate his soul. And their empty meanderings of mind streams of whys and why nots and the naked questions of dissolved connections and judgments and accusations and I saw the dragon eye falling from a vast expanse into the red wet tongue of the Universal Mind. Taking a deep breath and looking back from the window, I noticed him watching me peculiarly. I was silent and he asked to see my portfolio. He began turning the pages and looked at the images and then at me and I felt my feet sinking into wet mud and earth and vision and abstractions and an opaque haze of a slaughtered gaze. He said he liked them a lot and asked me if I would be open to do anything.

"What do you mean?" I asked.

Hesitating he said, "You know there are numerous possibilities."

"Let me know what they are and I will consider them."

He said he would and, rising, walked me to the door. He hesitated before opening it, and said that he went to many parties and events and would like to introduce me around. "It could lead to interesting and productive opportunities," he added.

I nodded and stepping out of the heavy building felt I was walking on concrete skies. I heard the hesitant laughter from society's grey walls and the cry of the mediocre, and the stagnant repetitions of cobwebbed conversations, and the whale riders howling and calling for king. They came in remembrance of the sun of all suns, the symbol dawn, the walk into mire with lit wand, as the pebbles climb down and roll into my open palms.

I went to about four or five more of these appointments and finally exhausted from questions and furtive glances and uncomfortable silences I walked towards some trees in the distance. Getting a sense of where I was, I began sailing towards them. I entered Central Park. It was vast and beautiful with valleys and hills within its scope and the sky was lit like a mad raven dancing for his mate in the belly of the clouds. A tree with its sinuous trunk almost touching the ground beckoned me. Running towards it I sat down and, leaning on its trunk, I unpeeled my boots and pushed myself even further into its vibrating strong body, and felt the soft sweet texture of formed nature and the walk of the stone and the silent movement of the ethereal thought. I felt like the lion moving through unknown forests in search of food and light and art and grace. *I am not them. They are not me. But the walk continues within the hushed foliage of creativity and expression, and verse whispers, and the howl of the full moon wolf in search of the orchid bloom, and the heart in flight, and rippling crooked bamboos protecting the feng shuied entrance of the kingdom of the Lions.* Looking at the time I kissed the tree and, picking up my boots, headed towards the park exit. The sun was setting and the dusk painted streaks of light in the sky. Reaching the street I sat down at a bench and pulled my long boots up my legs. Unpinning my hair, I felt its soft waves caressing my cheeks. Moving my head like a stallion with its full mane running in the wind I called forth the gods of poetry, of passion, of word, of song and of mad love.

Walking alongside the park tiredness overcame me and, recalling the afternoon of appointments, I felt nervous and fearful. I thought of Smila and my footsteps faltered in hesitation. I was not looking forward to going back to her apartment. People walked by alone or with each other as I looked into their eyes and often they looked away or down. I felt alone and homeless.

And I am in India as flowers sail by me, and large images of the goddess Kali are hailed into the streets of Calcutta. People are invoking her through music and song, as she does her dance of destruction and creation. She is being taken to the river Ganges to be immersed back into the holy water. Stunned and excited I watch, until suddenly a slight honk of a car brings me back to the city.

I saw a yellow cab stop near me. I indicated to the driver that I didn't hail a cab. Rolling down his window, he revealed a warm grinning face, saying something in broken English. Not understanding him, I approached and bent down to listen again.

"Can I take you somewhere?" He asked. Hesitating a little I replied that I did not have far to go. "Please," he said again, "let me take you."

I felt I needed to get in and, thanking him, I did so. I could see him watching me through the mirror. I wanted to tell him where I was heading. But before I could open my mouth, he said that he knew. I smiled, and he then said that I had a gold chain on with a very sacred symbol that was blessed by an enlightened person. He continued, "You will also wear seven turquoise necklaces that will be given to you by an Indian elder." A warm breeze sang through me, as I quietly touched the symbol which was under my shirt. It was designed by my mother and blessed by the Mother, who put it on me before I left India. My eyes were moist with her light and I looked back at him. He smiled. His face was a weathered road map of beauty and trust and life, with lines etched into his dark visage. He was from Haiti. I looked out as the cab had stopped exactly in front of the building where Smila's apartment was. Opening the door I stepped out and was looking for my wallet when he stopped me.

"I don't want any money from you," he said.

Moved, I thanked him, and as I bent down to look at his shining, sage face, I removed the chain from under my shirt and showed it to him. Looking at it he touched his forehead as if bowing to the symbol and what stood behind it. He then said in broken sentences that I should always be who I was and never change. I clasped both my hands and bowed to him. A beggar saint, a wandering Guru of bold age and ancestors of pearled souls, I thought.

Diego, the doorman, was standing with the door open. I was happy to see him. I felt as though he knew me and understood me and before I could say anything, he said that Smila was upstairs. I thanked him and walked to the elevators still thrilled from what had just happened. I hesitated outside the door before sliding the key in the lock. Entering the apartment and seeing her I began telling her what had happened. She was shocked and angry that I had trusted a stranger.

40

"I didn't feel any danger at all," I protested.

"You are so naive and inexperienced and fresh out of India. Did you give him this address?" she screamed.

"No," I said quietly, not telling her that he had dropped me right outside the building.

She picked up the intercom and spoke to Diego, telling him to make sure that no stranger should be allowed in. She continued to reprimand me by saying that what I had done was very dangerous, especially in NYC, and that anything could have happened to me. I thought of the finality of smallness languishing in smallness, and the unripened spots of the non-being falling into blankets of fish and stale dreams. I felt alone and uncomfortable and frightened and walked towards my room. Removing my boots I lay down on the bed and began sobbing tears of blood and sand and the loss of humanity. My heart ached and I closed my eyes.

I was back in India as my twin self, my sweet silken doe-eyed bud bride. I was in the garden taking care of all the plants with the Zen gardener who knew all about each plant. He was explaining all their subtle themes. He talked about each one and the meticulous attention that they needed. We walked to the bed of roses filled with species from all over the world. I loved roses. Bending down to seep in the fragrance of these eternal storytellers, my eyes suddenly got moist, and straightening up I looked away and heard the call of a family of crows. Something stirred in me and I heard that voice again. I asked the gardener if I could have a few stalks. He smiled and cut five red roses. He watched me as I walked towards the temple.

My walk was faltering, and he had a concerned look on his face. At the temple - a small shrine belonging to our house - I caught the attention of the priest. He approached me and I handed the roses to him. He took the flowers and placed them near the image of the Goddess Kali. Her face, fierce and alive, walks the earth with a terrible compassion and a relentless intolerance of human ignorance. The priest did an offering to the image and then gave the blessed flowers back to me.

I passed by the gardener and gave him one of the roses. He accepted gratefully. On entering the house, going to the bedroom I placed them in a vase next to a little shrine on the mantel piece. The vibrant red roses reflected in the mirror and I glanced at this face embraced by the roses. There was a peace in my eyes as I took a deep breath.

Opening my eyes in New York I realized it was almost dark outside. I lit an incense stick and placed it on the altar. Removing my journal from my bag I started to write down the day's reflections. Smila knocked on the door and asked if she was disturbing me. She said she had peeped in before and saw me resting. She wanted to know how the appointments went. Two of them had called her and thanked her. They thought they could really do things for me. I thanked her and said I was going to have a bath.

"Can we have dinner together?" She asked. "I will order in. Chinese?"

As I was entering the bathroom she said she was very sorry for freaking out earlier. – "I guess I've lived in New York too long."

After dinner I got ready for the night. I could feel Smila's disappointment. Lying down I realized I had forgotten my glass of water and went back to the kitchen to get it. I quietly walked by her with the water when she stopped me with her hand. My body uncoiled like a sleeping serpent and I heard the hiss of the disturbed golden cobra. "I really need to speak with you," she said. "It's important."

"I have early calls," I responded. "Maybe we can do that tomorrow when I return." Back in my room, lighting a few candles, I began a journal entry. I thought of a quote from one of my favorite books by Odillon Redon, *To Myself:*

> "I have made an art according to myself.
> I have done it with eyes open to the marvels
> of the visible world and, whatever anyone
> might say, always careful to obey the laws
> of nature and life. Art is the supreme range,
> high, salutary and sacred; it blossoms. In
> the dilettante it produces only delight, but
> in the artist with anguish, it provides grains
> for new seeds."

Placing the journal under my pillow I watched the neon lines of light forming liquid waves on the ceiling and walls of the room. The flames in the candles were steady as they got smaller, leaving brush strokes of shadow images on the altar as though breathing visible life into their ancient forms. My eyes closed to the faint sounds of some sirens outside.

The next day was a series of appointments, of which one was a go-see for some kind of play. The assistant handed copies of lines to the several people waiting in line. There was no communication between anybody. Everyone was a threat to the others and each was absorbed in their own anxieties and fears. I glanced at the lines and at the other faces. My turn came and I read with confidence and professionalism. The panel was watching intently and yet why did I feel odd and uneasy? I had seen those looks so many times. They thanked me and told me they would call me. Right, I thought, and walked out. As I got ready to leave, I noticed one actor staring at me. He followed me out, and shaking my hand he said that he overheard my reading and was really impressed.

"Where did you study?" he asked.

42

"London," I replied.

"Wow, you're good.

"It won't matter," I said. "They will find me either too exotic or too strange."

"But that should be a huge asset," he said. "You have such a unique look and presence."

Thanking him, I started to walk out and I heard his voice in the distance saying he hoped we would meet again. I looked back, and waved as I quickened my pace.

Back in the apartment I felt anxious and was not really looking forward to what was about to unfold. Walking in I saw Smila working in her room and, hearing me come in, she enquired about my day.

"I did a lot and just left an audition for a play."

"Oh good," she said. "I'll let you unwind and then can we have our conversation?"

"Sure."

Taking off my boots I washed my hands and she walked in and sat at the table. I sat on the floor near the altar as she began to talk. "I'm just going to get right to the point," she said. "I'm very attracted to you, spiritually, emotionally, and physically." As she was speaking, I casually glanced at what I had quickly scribbled in the morning. Today I awoke, I tried to unleash the fear, I tried to crack the edge of the walk, and then as in process, I wondered what man could make me mad, what unfathomable weave of spirit could sprout my body and trace my space. Glancing up very gently I began to answer her. I felt like my words were coming as though from an undefined, surreal space. A familiar place where my muse resides and where I often hear and see her. She takes many forms when she shows me her physicality. A beautiful brilliantly feathered bird with a jewel embedded in her third eye. I have sat on that bird and she has flown me to lands and forests of ancient realities of myth and magic. Sometimes my beloved muse comes in the form of an ancient warrior dressed with all the tribal costumes and whispers chants and howls of a language that only he and I are familiar with. And sometimes a shape-shifting shaman enters my inner cave revealing many secrets and many visages, one of them being a white wolf whose piercing eyes unchain the human traps that bind, obscure, and demean me. I slowly told her that I understood what she felt and that I already knew everything, but that I did not feel the same. "If this causes any unease I will leave," I said gently. She immediately replied that it was unnecessary. "You can stay as long as you like."

There was a tangible silence in the room, as she shifted her legs and tried to make herself comfortable. "I adore the masculine energy. It balances me, caresses me, and completes me," I said. She glanced at me without any expression and said nothing.

My eyes drifted away to the window and the graceful sensuous see-through chiffon waves took me to a room in a beautiful hotel on the beach in Sri Lanka where I was in a contemporary German film production based on the love story of Radha and Krishna. I was to play Radha. I was reading the script when a knock at the door interrupted me. A waiter handed me a note on a silver tray. He had long white gloved hands. I picked it up and thanked him. I asked him who it was from. He said that it was found on the hotel desk with instructions to give it to me. Curious and excited, I opened and read its contents. It was a love letter. "I may never see you but will always adore you." I drank in the words softly and slowly, feeling every nuance and whisper. My hands traveled to my feet and legs and I could feel the breathing pores of my skin. Opening my eyes I realized that we would begin filming soon and as I started getting into the white dress for the next scene I looked at my reflection in the tall mirror and felt as though I was someone else. Walking to the window I looked out and felt his eyes like an invisible lover embraced by a forest of trees and crooked bamboos and jade dragons and silent powers. I started to leave the room and saw the letter lying open on the bed. It was alive.

Smila left the chair and was now sitting in front of me on the floor. She bent forward and touching my face said softly that she loved me. "I love Shiva," I said. "I love his mad dance and I love his mad passion. He is the motion of the world. He creates and he destroys and when he makes love with Parvati, his divine beloved, it is said that the heavens shake, the earth throbs and all is afire with the tantric howl of Shiva and Shakti, the yin and the yang, the two in one and the rebirth of the universal cry. The melding of God and Goddess."

Taking a deep breath I leaned back against the bed and stretched my legs out and closed my eyes. I looked at Smila but she had a cold expression on her face. Rising she said something about having to meet some people. Where was all that blue light and meditation and stuff that she always spoke of in India? I wondered. I felt myself shivering as though a cold wind just passed through the room. "Cynicism and coldness, they laugh at beauty," an American Elder once told me. I had tears in my eyes as I remembered how different she was in India. But that is India. It can strip one of all excesses and boundaries and gimmicks and false plays. It has a way of centering and stripping one bare.

Chapter 3: *Lotus - the avatar, and the evening raga of solitude*

Stretching out on the bed after she left, I watched the sun setting with its rich hues and textures in the bowing sky. Dusk, when Shiva does his dance of creation and brings all to life. I felt the rays of the sun touching my face with renewed energy and grace and saw the brilliant feathers of my muse-bird surrounding me with a halo of assurance and art, and of insight and the bold magnificence of the evening raga of solitude and solace. It was warm and glowing and then suddenly the phone rang. I hesitated. When I picked up the receiver and heard my own dusk-drenched voice saying hello, the person introduced himself. I remembered Smila mentioning him and saying that she wanted me to meet him. His name was Shane. I told him that Smila was out, but he replied he was calling to speak to me. He wanted me to dine with him. Startled, I told him to call back in an hour.

I like the sound of his voice, I thought as I walked to the shower. Enjoying the water I began to dry myself when the phone rang again. He said he would pick me up within the hour. "I will be ready," I said as I walked towards the closet to look for something appropriate.

The soft cotton touched me with warmth and sensuality. I ran my fingers through my wet hair. I felt radiant and excited to meet him. Picking up my cloth bag and strapping my sandals around my ankles and up my legs, I walked out of the apartment making sure the candle on the altar were blown out.

In the lobby I noticed a yellow cab entering the driveway of the apartment. Pausing, I watched to see who comes out. A tall, elegant man with tight jeans, cowboy boots, and hair tied back entered the door. Diego opened the door as I began walking towards him. "Stallion-like and sexy," I whispered to myself. "I like his look." When he saw me, he stopped as though surprised. We walked towards each other and I introduced myself. He really looked and I looked back. We both smiled as he led me towards the opened cab door. Looking back at Diego, I waved good-bye. I slid in the cab and bent down to relace my sandals. I felt his eyes on my hennaed feet, the feet washed with ancientness. Closing the door he told the driver where to go. I remembered the warm face of my mad mendicant driver who reminded me to always be.

"You smell of jasmine," he said, interrupting my thought flow. Smiling back I said how much I loved that fragrance.

"It has the sound of India," I replied, making him smile.

"You are beautiful," he said. "You are more than beautiful.

I looked directly into his eyes and for a moment we were locked into each other's gaze. I remembered the conversation with the woman in

London about the vanity of beauty and its burden. I felt big and unafraid. My spine felt erect and wide open. My heart felt strong and I was alive and awake. He excited me.

The cab stopped. We both climbed out as though emerging from a powerful experience and he silently led me to the restaurant entrance. The doorman opened the door and we walked in. The atmosphere was embracing and rich. I felt comfortable. It was beautifully lit and there was romance in the room. The candles on each table reflected live shadows on the walls, creating an intimacy that was tangible.

"Wine?" He asks me.

"Yes, red, dry, and full-bodied."

He smiled and chose a bottle. The sommelier obviously approved and, opening the bottle, gave him a first taste. He handed the glass to me. As it ran through me I thought of the sun and the air weaving stories and myth into this little luscious red grape. "Magnificent," I looked at him with world-eyes of dream caves and of texture and passion raining through the wind and whispering love songs as ancient as life itself. I placed my cloth-covered book on the table.

"What is that?" he asked.

"This is my book of thoughts, dreams and poems. I carry it wherever I go."

"How wonderful!" he said.

He ordered fish and asked me if that was what I wanted. I loved fish and I remembered the carp swimming upstream with a glistening blue light on its shiny body. He wanted to know why I came to New York.

"I just felt a strong urge, like something pulling me to this city. I like it. It feels like walking on a knife-edge. There is energy here and an atmosphere that makes me very comfortable. I am reminded of Calcutta, where I come from. There are many similarities."

"Have you a specific plan that you would like to follow?" he asked.

"Not really. Smila is introducing me to people and I am meeting and exploring and watching to see where all this will go."

"If I can help, I will," he said, "but you know it won't be easy. I feel that you have very strong ideas and would not compromise, and that will make it even harder."

"I know. I went through a lot of that when I lived in London. I did many things I did not like, but I did it as a learning process. I will do what I have to, but I'll make my own footsteps like the rhinoceros."

He looked at me quizzically and, very animatedly, I began to tell him about the rhino that never follows an already made path.

"That is how I feel about life."

He responded with a smile and as we started to eat he asked me why I had left India. And there I was once again. Sitting in my bride self in the luxurious house, my eyes followed the beautiful colored birds in the garden. All was lush and green, the first drops of the morning dew slightly bending the leaves with their glistening stories of night and dreams and hopes. In the distance I heard my mother-in-law instructing the servants and calling out for me. I achingly left the window of paradise and walked towards convention, duties, and social graces. She had a frown on her face as she told me to watch the cook because I needed to learn many things in order to be a good wife for her son. In the same breath she reprimanded me for never doing any household chores and duties, like a good wife should. After a long pause she told me that I spent my days wasting my time reading and dreaming and that I had no redeeming qualities, not even my complexion, which was dirty. Crushed, wounded, and bleeding I slipped into my hidden self. I said nothing and silently did all she asked me to do and looked for the peacock feather hidden somewhere inside my heart space.

Shane listened as I continued. "I had to leave the confining social structures that were suffocating me and not just follow what I was supposed to follow. I had to defy the boundaries, walk away from security and safety and follow a strange unknown hounding call. I was too young to even know what I was doing. I remember when I was a little girl people would ask me what I wanted to be when I grew up and I would reply 'I want to express myself.' that is all I used to say." I felt as if I couldn't stop telling him my story. "I broke the bark around me like a tree in order to grow. It was too tight. And all this was done against the approval of most of my family and elders. They were all set for an arranged marriage for me. It was not easy to walk away from all that security. No, it was not at all easy. Do you know what *"Numinosity"* means?" I asked him. "It means following your soul, your light, your own particular sound, your own ether. I did not know all this then, but something pushed me. And my father, my divine father supported me through all this. He saw it. He felt it. He understood it and he trusted me explicitly.

And with that trust and my wings unfolded I took flight and here I am."

"You remind me of a fairy tale or maybe a legend called Ondine. Have you heard of her?" he asked. "She was a water spirit and had to leave the water to find her soul. She followed a wild, mad life but she had to go that way and that's what you are doing."

Taking a sip of wine I leant back and closed my eyes. *The man-mate who will enter the aura will drink my soul and eat my heart and swallow my air. He will wash my life lines with wines of truth and trace landscapes on valleys of life. I will take him in my three hand structure; I will wet his flight to grace the entry. I will feel his eyes with the skin of my heart. I will hear his breath and write a line on my heart. I will take his mind lines and find stories of flight. I will rapture his limbs and flame the fire. I will watch his feet and wash them with ancientness. He will come*

47

through my dreams, through the visions of life. He will watch the waves, as my eyes will melt into ocean. He is my groom of many centuries and life times and youth. Him.

Opening my eyes I wrote these lines down. Shyly he asked if he could read them. Turning my journal towards him I let him see. He looked at me. I felt his hands wanting to touch my face but stopped.

"I did not come here to the west to imitate and lose my own special identity. I did not come here to fall into this huge global melting pot and dissolve into a vacant sameness and lose all textures of ancient-ness and presence. I did not come here to lose my identity and pride and dignity. No, my visions are elsewhere. The material stuff and all the so-called freedoms do not interest me. I am on another quest and in that quest there are no boundaries. They say the traveler is a true seeker. He is a traveler of the souls. He is of silence, of unveiled nostalgia, of new visions and new entries. I felt the invisible moving into the visible. What about you?" I asked him. " What are your dreams and passions?"

He laughed and talked about his life. He said it was nothing like mine.

"We are all different," I replied.

"I feel as though you are looking and searching."

"I am."

He said his interests were Zen and tantra. "I practice many disci-plines and with the right partner could reach many heights."

"I am my own tantra, my own yoga, and my own completion," I whispered to myself. Shifting my legs, the silver anklets tinkled in re-sponse.

"It sounds like India."

"Yes, that is why I wear them."

"Tantra," he said, "the exploring of all senses to go beyond the senses, the ecstasy of the senses into the ecstasy of the spirit, a divine madness and an absolute surrender."

A silence surrounded me.

"Some more wine?" he asked.

I almost couldn't hear him.

"Where are you?" he said.

"I am running in the emerald green forests of India, breathing in bird songs and butterfly thrills and tiger howls and ancient trees and the embraces of the wise trunks roughened by wind and rain. Their barked bodies speak to me. My skin is wounded and bleeding from the scratches of branches and thorns and the wounds of memory."

Laughing I bent down to touch my anklets and heard the ring of the bells again. Rising up I looked at him unflinchingly with the sky in my eyes. He started and said, "Your beauty has so many dimensions." As we finished the red grape wine I remembered my Miguel, and Spain, and our lips dripping in this soma as we swallowed our souls and cried into the night.

The New York City night was balmy and magical. He asked me if I would like to see his home, which was just around the corner. I saw the thorn marks on my thighs and arms. They left an empty and painful sound on my surface-self, but I am the wolf. I saw horse heads sitting on my lap as my henna palms fell on their wounds.

"I would love to," I answered.

We approached the house, which was in the sixties on the East Side. A beautiful little house tucked between bigger buildings. The inside felt warm and cozy. It was filled with Indian and Tibetan art. We walked up the stairs. He showed me the library, bedroom, study, and the meditation room on the top floor. It was my favorite room. We sat for a while.

"You can stay here whenever you want," he told me. "I am hardly ever here." He talked of his time in New Mexico and how the house remained empty a lot. "You would love it. The sky is like the ocean.. I would love you here even if it is only for me to enter a jasmine garden when I am back. And I do not want any money."

Closing my eyes I saw her again. She of many forms and many voices and many manifestations riding the black stallion. I had seen her when I first was entering this city and there she was again. She was crossing the vast expanse of sand dunes rippling with many colors and shades. I wished to see her face but it was hooded. As my eyes pierced through, the horse slowed down and the head turned slightly as if acknowledging my request. But it was not time.

We were silent. I felt a wild wind rainstorm weeping, howling, stumbling, frightening, enlightening process of what was to be. *I wait awake with eyes sometimes closed. I wait with eyes that cannot close. I call for help from the other kind. I feel my Invisible Structure of consciousness engulfing me. It is a silence filled with eyes. It is a silence of elegance.*

My eyes entered his as I very softly said that I would like to go back. He rose and helped me up and led me down the stairs to the door. I bent down to strap my sandals around my ankles and rising up picked up my little silk bag. Touching his shoulder I whispered how beautiful it was here.

"Yes, I love it here," he replied. "I would love to take you back if you don't mind."

He hailed a cab and began to give the driver the address on the West Side. I laughingly said that maybe the drive would already know where we were heading. He looked at me strangely and I told him about my experience with the cab driver. "Who are you?" he said, amazed.

The cab drove through Central Park. The trees were beautiful and sculpted the sky impressively. "Trees are my love. They are alive. Their souls howl through the skies as their roots enter deep within the earth. They connect sky and earth and link both together. They break all dualities. They are warriors of the silent kind. They stand in silence and observe and absorb. Have you ever touched a tree?" I asked him.

"Not consciously, I guess."

His eyes seeped into my skin and caressed me. Mine travelled to his face as though in response. He took my hand and passionately kissed it. Leaning back on the seat I felt his wet lips on my skin. I was a winged feline, walking into a new vast field of flowers trees and surreal sands, of hills and mountains and feathered minds, of cellos moving and of familiar humanity graced by time.

We finally reached the West Side and the driver pulled into the apartment building. I began to open the door but he placed his hand on my thigh and stopped me. He jumped out of the car and opened the door for me. Stepping out, I thanked the driver.

"That was beautiful. I truly enjoyed everything and thank you for all."

"I would love to do it again."

"Call me."

He walked me to the entrance where a different doorman opened the door. We walked in and as I said good night he clasped his hands to his chest and whispered, "Namaste." Walking to the elevators I looked back. He stood in the lobby hands clasped, transfixed.

Finding the key I quietly opened the door and walked in. Smila was not back. I felt relieved and walked towards my room. Closing the door my dress dropped down as I put on my long silk nightdress. Only the soft quivers of the moonlight streamed in. I remembered that beautiful French film, Les Enfant du Paradis, where Garance, the female lead, waits in her moon drenched room for her lover. I am waiting for him with a thousand rainbow vibrations echoing through every pore of his passionate being. Tell me tree man of flower and pain will I find him in this earth plain? Picking up my hairbrush I stroked my hair and sat down on the large cushions on the floor. Continuing to brush my hair with my eyes closed, I stretched my legs and felt like I was in a trance state. The whole room was beautifully lit and magic was everywhere.

And I was back in the little hut I had built in Auroville, looking at the symphony of the stars in the sky. The haunting night sounds of India and the enormous silence of this land merged within me. I came back to be part of and work for a New World, a new consciousness, to truly travel inwards, to get rid of unnecessary acquirements and to cleanse everything within. The Mother and Sri Aurobindo who were always close to me sought to find a new way of human development and they stressed that the aim was not to found a religion or school of philosophy or school of yoga but to create a ground of spiritual experience which would bring down a greater truth beyond the mind and accessible to the human soul. And The Mother by 1965 had begun to set in motion the process that would lead to the birth of Auroville.

My mind flowed within these thoughts. Not to shun life, not to shun the senses, not to shun the material self. Instead, to work through, to work with, and then to transcend and, after developing and perfecting, to bring down the light, to transform the basest and light up the roots. There is no escape in the yoga of Sri Aurobindo. The world is the place and this has to be inhaled and changed. And the start is always oneself.

I felt something in my hands. It was round and thick and pulsating with life. Looking down I saw an exquisite white lotus with a long full stem. I pulled the flower to my face and inhaled the essence.

I glanced at my hand and realized that the lotus was a dream and yet I had felt it. There it was again, my ether self-integrating and entering my being and always reminding me of the true reality. Smiling as if to myself my eyes go back to the moon and I thought of Shane. I felt warm and open as my fingers softly outlined my full lips.

Smila tiptoed into the room, and asked if I was awake. I nodded, and she sat down on the floor next to the bed. We both looked at the whole circle of the moon, bright, bold, and light.

"You are beautiful," she told me. "You are woman. You are different. You are India and you bring the essence of your culture here. ."

Rising up on my elbow, I looked at her surprised. I told her that this was how I had remembered her in India when we had met.

"I have not forgotten anything," she said, "when I am in your presence it all comes back. You bring it back, you remind me. You are like a mirror and that is what you will do in the world. That is your absolute mission: to remind people who they truly are and why they are here. I feel ashamed for asking you all those stupid questions about money. I see it so clearly now, so very clearly. And please excuse my attitude to you. I was angry and mean and selfish. Stay here as long as you need to, and don't worry about anything. In the morning I will call around and set up some appointments and interviews for you."

And she whispered, "My beautiful friend."

There was a vibrant silence in the room.

Smila rose, wished me good night and walked away. A presence filled the room and I told Smila that I had something to say to her. She returned and sat down near the bed eager to listen.

"I had to leave the deep-rooted banyan trees in my country. I could not formulate it then and maybe still cannot, but it was like a bursting forth of arrows of self-inquiry and lifetimes of other cultures and sounds and streaming waterfalls. Like a wondering minstrel in search of his own inner sound . It was so painful at times and then ecstatic at other times. I tore off the traditional skins like useless clothes. All I wanted was to walk with Self and Art. And in doing that I knew that I would be alone, walking on firestones and sinking sands. It was a monumental walk away from any structure or shelter and I never knew how hard it would be. But like night following day, I just walked and held a beat within me and heard it and felt it enter me more and more and at some time later even dared to call it my creative spark, my soul, the divine tune of life and art. I knew then deep inside me that very few would understand me and even fewer would accept me. But I threw care and concern to the winds and went the path of the wolves, of the wild woman and heard strange cries and whispers but always walked and danced with the waves of the Universe and with eyes all over my body. People criticized. People said strange things. I got hurt and defended myself and later wondered why I did even that. They were my own insecurities, because I did not always understand the value of the Walk. Now, I slowly begin to and know now that there is so much to learn. I am homeless in the traditional sense but not in the sense of the soul. That is why I had to leave the cave." Smila sighed and lay back. She took a deep breath and slowly touched my forehead and thanked me for sharing.

"Maybe I do not understand all, but I feel your quest. It is not ordinary; it is not small; it will require so much strength and so much support. I will try to be there for you whenever I can." And slowly rising she stopped at the entrance, looked at me, sent me a kiss and gently closed the door.

After Smila left I reached out for my cloth book and wrote:

> *The feather tongue of fire serpents, tears*
> *in raindrops from lifelong valleys, deep*
> *watching's with doe-like eyes, rivers*
> *flowing out of my mind wetting the*
> *banyan tree roots that grow and touch*
> *earth's many moods into the mystery of*
> *self and the hungry lion in the forest,*
> *paws wet, crushed crumpled and revealed*
> *to all.*

Lying back on the bed, book still in hand, I closed my eyes and slid into a moonlit sleep.

Dawn woke me with New York traffic sounds, and I slowly entered the approaching day. I left the dream world very carefully, making sure that nothing was missed. I always needed time to enter the world again. Tiptoeing to the kitchen, I put the kettle on making sure not to wake Smila. With a big pot of tea I knocked and entered her room with a tray. She welcomed the tea and sitting near her bed we began to plan the day. She said that all night she was thinking about all the different contacts she wanted me to make. "I will call them this morning and spread the appointments out so you have a few each day."

I left her to get ready. At the door she said how important the night before was for her. She thanked me for sharing and asked me again not to worry about the money situation. "I also owe you money that your father lent me in India."

Thanking her, I told her that she should use the money towards my stay at the apartment.

Back in the room I started to get ready for the day and touched a few clothes and choose something light and green. It was spring outside. I felt the young season gently giving birth to fresh saplings as they emerged from earth and tree trunks. I saw the white lotus in my hand and felt the firm stalk filling my palm. Brushing my hair I walked to the living room and waited for Smila to give me the addresses for the go-sees. "You look beautiful," she said as she sat down and went over the list of people and appointments. They were mostly theatrical auditions. Some photo shoots and some voiceovers. "They are all widely spaced so you have time in between and don't have to rush around."

A little nervous, I braced myself for the day.

Leaving the apartment, Diego greeted me with an energetic smile and wished me a beautiful morning. The first appointment was in midtown. It was on the fifth floor. I walked in, pushing the slightly ajar door, and noticed a long line of women and men sitting and waiting anxiously. There was no room to sit. The assistant handed me some lines to read and I walked towards the open window to study them. It was The Three Sisters, by Chekhov, and the part I was to read for was Nina. Luckily I was familiar with the role, as I had auditioned for it in a Chekhov retrospective while studying in London. Looking up from the lines I noticed all the bustle and frenzy of the streets.

****

I was in London walking somewhere on Kings Road with Miguel. He squeezed my hand gently. As we approached an old building he bent down to whisper something in my ear. He said he would wait for me. Walking up I looked back and saw his tall presence and rugged face smile with love and support as he drew out a Gitanne and lit it. I loved how he inhaled the full smoke as though it was life itself, and then traced his arch shaped lips that spoke of love and earth. I loved him. I still love him. My Miguel of madness and passion in a mirrored sky of night nipples and erect mountains. They glanced at me in approval and I walked out, head high as I heard the assistant director telling me that they would let me know. And there he was, standing waiting for me. Running down the unending stairs I danced into his open arms. I told him it went well. He

53

took my face in his arms and kissed my wildly. He came all in and touched the breath of smoke and tobacco and poetry lines and gypsy ballads. I
dissolved into him.

A voice brought me back and startled I remembered where I was.
A little dazed, I walked in and read my lines with a fresh energy and
thrust. I could feel them really looking at me, surprised and impressed.
As I walked out of the room I felt as though I had reached another height
and Miguel was there pushing me on. It felt amazing -- to be married
with the world of source and ancientness and the ethereal language of
the living beings who never leave me or left me. I am blessed, I thought.

Walking into the lit street I noticed it was Fifth Avenue and I
headed north. I felt the need to walk in grass and kiss the beautiful bodies of my trees. I looked for Miguel. I longed to fly into his arms. I felt his
rough face against mine. I heard him whisper, "I am here." He called me
Boot. I always wore high boots and he loved them. I had them on now.
I looked down and touched the soft leather. It was his skin. I began to
run through the street, heeding nothing and no one. I became the black
stallion on the desert expanse and felt the airy exuberance of the hooded being on me. I was carrying her. I was ecstatic and merged into the
winds and the howling waves of the ocean. I was in Paris rushing to a
fashion show where I was a runway model. This was the city of feminine
moods and love stories on every space and place. The city of vin rouge
and hungry poetry and heady glances and courtesan themes and the
wailing echoes of Piaf's cracked voice. It was my other city and I always
met her with warm skin tones and seductive smiles and sensual flutes
of romance. Yes, I loved Paris. I quickly changed and walked bravely and
powerfully on the runway with rhythm in my bones. I did not like this
world of fashion and modeling. It distracted me and robbed me of my
silence. It never was my world but it helped financially at that moment. It
was a vacant world with no sinuous layers of the themed cobra exuding a
language of flight.

Back on Fifth Avenue my pace slowed down as I noticed I was
close to the park. Peeling off my boots I ran barefoot the rest of the way
till I was on the grass and melted into the earth. And suddenly emptiness
overwhelmed me. I could touch it. It was dry. It was brittle. It cracked
like a dry leaf. And I saw her, my echoed self sitting at the window in
India. My eyes were tearing as the lush blossoms of fragrant languages
filled me. I felt my other self, always feeling and protecting me and reminding me in huge silences to continue and never stop or give up.

Back in the park, weaving through the trees, I remembered that
I had an appointment with a photographer who was a special friend of
Smila's. Looking for the address in my bag I headed towards the studio.
It was a long walk but it felt good to connect with the heartbeat of this
city, a jewel in a palace of thorns. It ignites, vibrates, invigorates, frus-
trates, annoys, fascinates, and sculpts you. It is a city of knives. It keeps

54

you awake. It makes you see through the mist of the evening fog. It rains one day. The sun pours through the next day. The light is like a Bergman film where the rays of the sun slice through a man praying in one single sliver of light. It weeps. It saddens you. It thrills you. There are the ones who have too much and the ones who don't. It is balanced and there are no boundaries. The poets feel. The writers share. The painters eat the light; the photographers capture the silence of a single homeless man bent behind the shadow of an autumn tree.

People were looking at me strangely and I realized that I was barefoot. Laughing I found a park bench and slipped my boots back on. I felt Miguel smiling. I heard his words in that cracked voice say, "walk away, but not too far." And touching my skin he reminded me never to slur my "r" or swallow my "t." He was a master of speech and language; he was my mad lover, my spirit homecoming.

Finding the address I rang the bell and spoke in the intercom. I pushed the door open and walked into a darkish hallway. It looked dreary and a little unclean. I walked up some stairs and saw a door slightly ajar. A voice greeted me and asked me to enter. It was a large studio with cameras, lights, and umbrellas strewn all over. It was hot. The photographer told me that I was on time as he had just finished a shoot. An attractive girl came out of a small room and smiled. She left and he started to explain what the shoot was about. Some test shots for an exotic commercial.

"That should work," I said with a hint of sarcasm

He looked up slightly and I told him that the word exotic was very familiar to me. "I can see why," he nodded. He placed me within a pool of light and began clicking. I have always been very brave and alive with the eye of the camera. Held by the right person it is the inner eye and everything peels and unfolds as I quiver and open. He was obviously inspired as I took various poses and forms. "Wow," he mumbled, "I don't even have to direct you."

As he frantically clicked and moved around me I began to feel just a little tense and uncomfortable. He stopped and asked me if I would mind trying on something in the dressing room. Walking in, I picked up a short, transparent dress. He noticed my hesitation and assured me that he just wanted to see how the light reflected on my face. Putting the dress on, I walked out into the studio. He looked admiringly at what he saw. Taking a deep breath I walked towards another light pool. He began speaking of Smila and asked me how we had met. "She always talks about you," he said. Not feeling like encouraging the conversation, I kept silent. I felt as though he wanted to probe deeper about the nature of our relationship. I felt distant.

After several hours he stopped and said he had enough shots. He was pleased and felt sure that clients would hire me. Walking back into the dress area, I began undressing and got into my clothes when I suddenly felt his presence. I looked at him surprised as he started getting closer. I pushed him away with all my strength. He commented that I should be aware of the business and how it worked. I replied firmly that I did know how it worked but was not going to be manipulated by it. He left the room unwillingly as I finished dressing. My India bride-self was there with me. I longed to be surrounded by the flowers and dancing shimmers of sunlight. But I was here and had to fight through this. As I tried to gather my things everything in the studio had shifted. He had turned the lights off and the darkness echoed the emotion in the studio. It was empty and angry and greedy. My steps quickened towards the door as though fearing his approach. He followed me and my steps got even faster. I saw my stallion goddess and spoke to her silently to be there with me. I heard the silent galloping of the horse hoofs on the sand as a whiff of wind brushed my face. She was here. I took a deep breath and turned around, looking at him with filled eyes. I thanked him and walked towards the stairs. The fear had changed into light and he sensed it as he watched me step down.

"I will contact you at Smila's," he said.

I thanked him, but I knew that my not responding to him and not giving in was going to change everything.

Taking a deep breath, I felt the street greeting me. I was angry. I was afraid. I was sad and I was alone. It was an aloneness that was familiar and necessary. It was a longing for my earth and the rust hues of that distant horizon. The light was falling and the temple bells surrounded me. I could inhale the incense. Seeing a phone booth I called Smila. I told her that the appointments went well except maybe the photo shoot. She asked me why and I told her that I was not responsive to his attention. She seemed angry and said she would speak to him. She asked me if I was heading back and I said I wanted to breathe in the evening air. I did not want to return yet.

Leaving the park I walked down Broadway and noticed a theatre that was playing The Seven Samurai, by Akira Kurosawa. I decided to go in. I loved his work and the timing felt just right. Finding a good seat I settled down, excited to be inspired. Mifune, the lead actor, was mesmerizing. His presence on screen was powerful and his performance had such a deep and captivating tremor. His Samurai sword was his soul, as he wiped it perfectly after completing the bloody destruction of ignorance, and then he carefully placed it back in its sheath he walked away with a symbolic shrug of his shoulders.

Outside the theater, I was exalted and felt like the famous De Chirico painting, 'Great Metaphysical Interior. There was a chill in the air and, bringing out my Moroccan wedding shawl, I wrapped it around me. It smelt of the desert and the gypsy sounds of pain and dream and love. I smiled and brought it even closer to me. I heard some Arabic music and noticed a small café. It looked inviting. Sitting at a table outside, I asked the waiter for a glass of red. The evening was magical and somehow reminded me of Paris, and the cafes, and the stories, the wild glances and excited conversations, with people everywhere.

I was sitting in a café called La Coupole in Paris with a slim glass of bubbling champagne in my right hand. In front of me there were six oysters inside their shells. I had never had one before. Their shells spoke of stories and ocean whispers and coral seascapes with seaweed colors. They looked fascinating. The waiter who was standing at a distance approached me and, sensing my hesitation, politely told me that they were very fresh and that I would enjoy them. I gently scooped one and placing it in my mouth felt the sensual burst of all its moods and flavors. I was eating the ocean and the waves weaved through my every cell. Something interrupted the smooth texture in my mouth and removing it I looked at it. I was stunned. It was a pearl, the story of the oyster wrapped and sealed in this exquisite round shape with which man enamored and courted woman. The waiter noticing it said that it brought great luck to find one. People were looking at me and across the way a woman raised her glass. I did the same. She looked familiar and later I found out that she was Jeanne Mourreau, that amazing, brilliant actress who I adored. Once I read that she used to sleep with a sword under her pillow and when asked about all her many loves, she replied that she would build a house where all her lovers would live. I dropped the pearl in the glass of champagne and drank it all till the pearl was in my mouth again. I wanted to feel its taste once more. And then, removing it from my tongue, I wiped it carefully and placed it inside a quiet pouch in my wallet. Paying the bill I walked out into the romantic night of Paris.

Out in the streets, still within the ocean cave where the little pearl had traveled to me, I felt embraced by dreams. The city welcomed my new discovery and glancing towards a softly-lit café entrance saw the name Rosebud. Citizen Kane, I thought. It was warm, cozy, and inviting. Walking in, I sat at a table that was rough and used and alive. It felt like a tree. I felt welcome. The maître-d' of the restaurant, who seemed like she could also be the owner, asked me in French what I would like.

"Your house red," I said. She was strong and well-built with a sensuous self-awareness within her. I liked her. She came with two glasses and a carafe and a plate with an assortment of cheeses. I told her that I had found a pearl in my first oyster. We looked at each other in recognition of an old friendship.

In the Arabic café in NYC I ordered some more of the humus and baba ganoush. Broadway was bustling with people and the evening was even warmer. Looking for my journal I made the following entry.

*To make an inner sound resound through any artistic expression is my life's passion. And whenever I see it I am inspired and assured. Film has always been my torch. When life is reduced to its barest essentials, art and poetry turn out to be among those essentials. In Inuit, the word "to make poetry" is the word "to breathe, both are derivatives of "**anerca**," the soul, that which is eternal, the breath of life. A poem is words infused with breath or spirit. "Let me breathe of it," says the poet-maker. "I have put my poem in order on the threshold of my tongue." These are lines from the book Eskimo realities written by Edmund Carpenter. And as I began to close the journal the following words flew out of me like the howling of a very white wolf.*

> *Of passion and color*
> *Of ecstasy and crimson flames*
> *The flight of petal in silent still waters*
> *In cloth of sky…the cracked earth sounds*
> *Of golden offerings' flight at dawn*
> *Of distances infinite in butterfly breath*
> *Playing the flute of the inner life*
> *Nestling in spirit…cracked between two worlds*
> *A resonance inner shaped in curve*
> ***Apsara** rapture on canvas and alive in art*
> *Playing with vision and sliding into self*
> *Seeing magic make its final shape*
> *Invisible structures…made tangible by ethereal thought*
> *Feeling the power of the source….*
> *Of passion and color….*
> *Crying the song of the soul….*

My mind wandered again back to the Rosebud Café and I was in Paris once again. Sipping from the heavy glass tumbler chiseled by time I sensed a presence and languidly looked up at a tall, wild-looking young man with piercing gray-green eyes set in a dark tanned face. The liquid soma of the red juice had entered me, leaving the sound of verse and flute ingrained in my eyes and skin.

"I hope I am not disturbing you" he said, "I am Tobias. May I?" And he sat down.

My femaleness glistened on my skin as I heard the echoes of the wedding red sari falling off my shoulders; my henna hands tearing his dhoti, my feet wrapped with silver anklets coiled around his tree spine, my Miguel pouring himself into me, and my somewhere-husband caressing my neck and the cave in between my two breasts. I was everywhere. We looked at each other. I placed the pearl in the center of my palm within the tree lines engraved into life and fate and love lines. He touched the pearl and gently closed the life hand. His ambiance vibrated with a feline maleness. He was wild. He was kind. I felt as though he was reading between my thoughts, as though he knew all. He was touching my mind.

"I love your eyes," he said smiling. "I have waited for your voice. I have heard it in my dreams. How many men have you destroyed?"

"Not enough."

He smiled. "You cannot be owned. No one can be. You are Sekhmet. She was a warrior goddess in Egyptian mythology. A solar deity sometimes called the daughter of the sun god Ra. You inspire because of who you are and what you carry. You never stop giving and being. And like the wind you caress the blossoms of every tree. You are free."

I looked at him. I was silent. I touched my arms and the nape of my neck. They are not my arms. They are the four arms of the goddess Kali. In one she holds a bloody sword after destroying the demons. The other holds a severed demon head signifying the destruction of ignorance and the dawning of knowledge. In another she holds the sword of knowledge, which cuts the binds and opens the doors to freedom. And in the other she holds the wheel of time and blesses all of humanity. These gestures are ethereal. They are reminders of who I am and where I come from. He watched me in rapt attention. The air was electric. It was the air before a huge thunderstorm. It was full.

Back in the Broadway café I looked at the empty plate and searched for the pearl in my hand. It was not there. The light was still golden. It was a summer sky and the day was late in leaving. I did not want to go indoors; I wanted to walk. Central Park was green and many people everywhere were enjoying the gentle evening. Looking for a bench near a tree and finding one that was empty, I sat down. Deciding to be even closer to the tree I walked right to it and sat down leaning against the old banyan looking one. I touched it. Tobias' eyes pierced through the smooth, rough bark and pulled me back in the Rosebud Café. He asked me if I was an actress.

"I am an artiste," I said.

"I am a revolutionary, - he replied, "and I am going to make a film in Algeria. I would love you to come."

"Tell me about your film?"

"A few years ago, in '62. Algeria and France reached a truce, and months later there was a mas exodus from Algeria to France. Nearly the entire Jewish community of Algeria left, and many Europeans as well. Days after the Democratic and Popular Republic of Algeria formed, which was September 1962, Ben Bella became premiere. That is where my film begins because that's when all the corruption began.

I could hear my heart beat but did not say anything. I could hear my heart beat but did not say anything. He ordered some more wine and we talked about love and war, about magic and life, about rivers and the fluid streams of friends who become flowers. I asked him who would be going with him. He answered, "You. And my brother and maybe his girl-friend" I gave him my address and phone number. Rising up he asked if he could walk me home. I said I wanted to stay a little longer. He smiled. "Ah yes, the wind." I will pick you up tomorrow morning around nine.

He walked away and I sailed into a dream I had a few nights back. I was walking somewhere near an ocean edged with tall stalks of elephant grass and a horse was beside me. We walked together and came to a resort like place overlooking the water. We both stopped and I led the horse to an area where he could rest as I went indoors to enquire about accommodation. After a while I came out and walked towards the water. And in the distance I saw the same horse galloping fast, looking for me. His skin glistened in the sun and his muscles sang to the rhythm of the wind. And he became the same horse of my spirit wind dream with the heavens straddled across his bare back, her robe flowing in compassion and power and protection.

I was back at the table in the café with the candle flame very close to my altered eyes. Looking around I saw my new friend running around serving other customers with a vivacity and joy. She sent me a big smile. My eyes were pulled back to the flickering flame and I watched it dance.

I slipped through and I was at the dining table back in India with my husband and mother-in-law. There was a sense of formality and tightness. I looked at my husband but he looked away as though not to confront his mother. Saddened by his aloofness in front of his mother I looked out of the window and my eyes bled with tears. I felt like the sable antelope, who was a bull among trees. He was savage, hard to catch with long curved saw-like horns capable of cutting down trees. He had long lashes that graced his beautiful eyes. My horns quivered with a silent sand impatience and I longed to run wild.

I was back through to the candle flame at the raw and open table in the café in my Paris and felt my wet eyes and rubbed them dry as the kohl smeared and my antelope lashes glistened with the sounds of the forest and trees. Taking a deep breath I realized what I had to leave be-hind and with that thought I sipped another red breath of life and dream. As I was rising to go, the woman of the cafe thanked me and asked me to please come again.

"I feel your blood,"she said.

"You feel my anerca. It is soul in Inuit"

"Yes, I do feel it. It has a fragrance. Are you married?" She asked.

"No, I am not, I chose not to live in the traditional way."

"That must have been hard." There was a sense of deep compas-sion in her words.

"It was." And I felt my words wondering free. "Something always seems to pull me back and I have to learn to be free of that. It is not going to be easy. It is bigger than I am and there is not much support when you break such a long and old tradition."

"You will be able to do it. I feel you did not leave for empty, superficial reasons. You left for more."

My eyes were wet with gratitude. I thanked her.

Returning to Central Park I headed towards Smila's apartment. The streetlights were on and evening rituals had begun. Reaching the apartment building I walked towards the elevators. In the apartment I looked around hoping that Smila was not back. I needed to be alone.

The celestial hosts gathered around me and, dreaming of opening the floodgates of the heart, I longed to look into Tobias's eyes where even birds cannot disappear. I cried for him. I yearned for him. I changed into my night sheath and felt his eyes caressing me all over. Taking the Moroccan hand weaved shawl I covered myself with it, and the land and the dust and the dance of the dry riverbeds sculpted with the aroma of grasshoppers singing to the moon entered me.

I was climbing up the winding stairs of a friend's atelier in Paris where I was staying. I felt excited and beautiful, like air washed with water. Entering the studio, I lit some candles, and finding a little traveling bag began to pack. I looked at my friend's music selection and, noticing a Jaque Brell album, put it on. The phone rang. It was Tobias.

"I am born tonight." A vocabulary of ornaments flowed through me. I felt big and alive. "I touch your beautiful soft hand with the pearl in it. The Universe was sitting in your hand. Place your hand on my heart. Good night," he whispered. Turning the light off, I lay awake and looked out at the night sky. All was still and quiet except for some voices outside. I closed my eyes and the next morning very early he called to make sure I was awake.

The doorbell rang soon after. I opened the door. It was him.

"You are early," I said.

"I wanted to make sure that you didn't change your mind."

As we walked down the stairs he softly touched my hair. I felt roses sprouting through my head, exuding wild fragrances. He compared me to earth and fire mixed together.

Downstairs in the car, he introduced me to his brother and his brother's girlfriend. And together we headed on to Orly, an international airport of Paris. As we drove I glanced at him and at the others. I felt slightly uncomfortable and wondered if I had made the right decision. He looked at me with intensity and strength. It was a silent reply to my question, which assured me that I had. The others chatted away in French. The girlfriend was a model and went on and on about some fashion show or the other. I shivered at the thought of that dry and empty world. I felt Tobias's arms around me. Time is the sensible measure in the the continuity of mediocrity.

62

We arrived at Orly airport. The bags were checked in. Walking towards the departure gates I felt elated and excited; and a little nervous as well. He made a sign for me to sit near the window. He fastened the seatbelt for me and while doing this, rested his head on my chest. "I hear your heart," he told me. "I hear the rhythms of your soul and the mad magic of your mind."

As he whispered these words in my ear, I heard the bamboo flute resonating with the breath of the two hundred year old ancient black Krishna image as it entered my eyes. And these words howled within me. They were from Rob Brezsney's book *Pronoia*, "*I love everything about me. I love my uncanny beauty and my bewildering pain. I love my hungry soul and my wounded longing. I love my flaws, my fears and my scary frontiers. I will never forsake, betray, or deceive myself. I will always adore, forgive, and believe in myself.*" Looking into his eyes, I whisper to him, "I am the vision of your soul. I am that which you always longed for. I am the feline female of your male warrior-ness. And I am the sound of your surreal mentality.

He sat back in his chair, adjusted his seatbelt and looked at me with his sea green eyes. The flight was about five hours. Looking down I saw the vast dessert and was awakened in my mythology and my dreams. The Gods laugh when men pray to them for wealth. Knowing eternity makes one comprehensive, comprehension makes one broad-minded, the breadth of vision brings nobility, nobility is like heaven. I am the instrument and the godheads are my friends.

"That is the Sahara. Isn't it beautiful?"

The plane finally landed at the main airport in Algeria. The ride was smooth and all the passengers seemed relieved at the landing.

Arriving at the airport and taking care of our luggage and equipment we walked out and met the film crew who were waiting for us. We climbed into the two jeeps and drove off. We took the route outside Algiers to avoid the city traffic and were soon heading for the desert and the little town of Taman asset, which was going to be our base. The wind was strong, and getting my orange scarf, I tied it around my head. Tobias touched my crown chakra and all the stagnant moments ripened into a phoenix like the zenith of the sun. When you trace the path of the sun you never realize its height and when it reaches the zenith at the noon hour, then you see the brilliance that shines above you. It is right there.

In Smila's apartment in NYC, stretched and strong like a wild, opened earth blossom and a feather elephant, I looked around. Touching that part of my head where the agony of breaking through personal limitations is the howling wind of growth and art and the breath of the shaman, I smiled with the satisfaction of a **champa** flower, fragrant and conscious of its very own psychological perfection. I turned my head to the love letter written of a thousand years, and I was back again in the desert that rippled within the body of the heaving dunes.

The jeeps were approaching a small and quaint town. It was Taman asset. Tobias put his branch arms around me and whispered in my ears, "I know this place has been in your dreams. You will find out. I brought you to one of your ether worlds, you who are your dreams." I smiled and melted. I couldn't believe that this person who I had met just a few days ago had entered me so deeply. My eyes drifted away. He asked me what I was thinking about.

"I am thinking of how I walk guided by beings and voices from the other world. And with them I have no fears. I don't know what an ordinary life structure means. The normal social values do not make much sense to me. And sometimes I even wonder if I am here." He laughed and sensuously kissed me on my arrow bow mouth.

"You are my connection between here and there. You inspire me and I feel alive like I have never felt before. I knew that as soon as I saw you at the café."

As the cars approached a rustic and romantic-looking hotel, everyone seemed happy to have finally reached our destination. All were shown their rooms. Tobias took the concierge aside. He was clad in long robes and spoke with a heavy accent. Tobias reminded him about the special room that he had reserved for me. He had been there before so he knew what he was looking for. The man nodded and led us to my room. It was magnificent. I walked in and stood in awe as the walls whispered simple stories with peasant dreams and earth-winged beings engraved within the dust and grain of this gentle hued surface, as my heart throbbed in recognition of a place I had been before. A low bed draped in beautiful colors and adobe floors and turquoise window frames with the light softly streaming in, leaving rainbow traces, stood in the middle of the room. I walked towards it and sitting down gently felt the dream language in all its folds and shapes. Tobias watched me as his eyes pierced through my skin. I felt myself flying above the earth, outside my body-self and becoming one with the sensual languor of all nature and all rivers and all mountains and all sinuous tree trunks. I am born again. His eyes stay walking on and in my skin, as my interior sounds echoed all the ragas and all the gypsy songs of decades and centuries. My culture was reaped and I was enhanced.

He brought in my things and told me to refresh and rest before dinner. As I began unpacking I felt a breeze touch me gently. "It is her," I whispered, "my stallion rider, my spirit footsteps." After a long shower where my feet almost dissolved into the earth floor, I placed the altar on a small table near the bed. Putting the pearl in the middle, I lay down as my wet hair fell around my face like tendrils from a stooping vine. The light from the window pulled me within, and my eyes travelled into that dream world where metaphors take on other shapes and forms. I am filled with a longing to connect and create hypnotic sutras of another language.

I close my eyes and I am walking in a dry riverbed where the water has left caved pathways towards an eternal sound. They are deep and wet and soft and warm. It is a place in a desert. As I walk I see in the far distance an adobe skyline. It looks like a little village but cannot be deciphered. I feel thirsty and am walking towards a collage of huts when suddenly I hear a voice calling out to me in the distance. "I love you. I love you." I look around but do not see anyone and continue walking. As I approach the little town, which is very much like Taman asset, I notice a mysterious looking woman. She looks Arabic and is wearing a burkha. Her eyes are like dark arrows of fire. She starts to speak and tells me about my past lives and the mystical world that embraces and surrounds me. I stop, looking at her in astonishment. Just then the woman cries out, "You do not believe me! I will show you what I can do." And saying this she disappears, as I look everywhere but cannot see her. And as my eyes look down I notice a beautiful area of green grass swaying in the breeze. Desperately I ask her to come back. "I believe you. I promise I do." And then as though from nowhere the woman reappears. Walking towards her I take her gentle hands as I kneel in front of her. Looking at me she says, "You are not alone. Remember that, and you will never see or feel age," and she walks away gracefully. I want to follow her but something stops me.

Opening my veined eyes I woke up, realizing that it was exactly here in this little town that I had seen her. I gathered the towel around me and felt the warm rays of light weaving their threads around me. I became one with all around me. A gentle knock awakened me. Tobias walked in and asked me if I would be ready for dinner soon. I nodded dreamily and whispered into his ear that this was indeed the place I had seen in my dreams. He smiled saying that he knew it.

"How?" I asked. He mumbled something in French, and looked away as the towel fell away from me, revealing my nakedness. I felt garlanded with roses and lotuses, and I breathed in deeply all the aromas of these high frequency blossoms of age-old manifestations. I looked straight into his eyes. He rose and said that he would be waiting for me. I choose a long beautiful sensual gown, which felt like it dissolved into me as I placed a drop of jasmine on the nape of my neck where Kali had blessed.

Hair still wet and falling about my shoulders, I walked. He was waiting outside. He took a deep breath and kissed me on my cheek, whispering some sensual words in French. We walked to the dining area, which was clean and well lit. Candles burnt at each table. He had reserved a special one. The waiter had the wine opened and flowers brought to the table. We sat, and looking at him, I remembered the woman in my dreams.

The flowers gave out a hypnotic fragrance. The wine was poured. We spoke about cinema and art and revolution and visions. He asked me all that I wanted to do and said that he was sure I would break many boundaries. I felt relieved. It was always hard for me to speak of myself as an artist or to define it. There was so much that I wished to explore. I did not feel the need to verbalize all of this with Tobias. He understood and saw all the layers and passions weaved into the fabric of my creative self. We spoke about him as a revolutionary filmmaker. That was his passion and he was obsessed with it. The reason for their being in Algeria was to film a political movement that he was against. He always took risks. I loved his madness and energy. I loved what he did and believed in. I said that true revolution began in oneself. He said that for him it was about getting out there and doing it. I asked him if he would like me to go with him the next day. He said it was up to me, that they would be mainly doing location hunting and it would be a hot, dusty, long day. I said that in that case I would rather stay to walk around and write.

After dining we stepped out into the night. It was beautiful. The sky was lit. The tinkling desert sounds of nomadic secret healers carrying mysterious bottles of healing balms were everywhere and the silence was strong and unusual. The night air was cool and he put his hands around me as we walked. He told me how happy he was that I had agreed to come. We walked back towards the hotel, as we both were tired from the long journey. Opening the door, we stepped in. He took me in his arms and kissed my longing face. The petals opened slightly and quivered with radiant cries and bells of anklets and wedding smoke. I touched his face and kissed his eyes, the green eyes that see my every story. He walked out of the room, his face bathed in the light of the moon. We spoke in silence, where every sound was heard and every motion and entry had been felt. I undressed and felt his winged hands on me. I lay down and placed the gardenia that the waiter had given me when I left the dining room next to the pillow on the bed. I felt the voice of the gardenia and I was back in India.

It was night and late. The moon was full here too. I was in bed lying next to my husband.

Braided in my hair was a garland of jasmine flowers. My eyes opened as though something awakened me. I touched the jasmine flowers in my hair and brought them close to my face. The fragrance was intoxicating. I looked at my husband who was asleep. Rising and lifting the mosquito net, which surrounded the bed, I carefully put it together and walked towards the window. It was dark outside, but a sickle moon lit the sky gently. I took a sip from the glass of water next to me and looked out again at the mysterious night sounds. I stood there for what seemed like a long time. My husband was calling me. I told him that something was pulling me. I looked up at the full circle of light, head arched and stretched back, sculpted by the mad howl of that magic circle. Turning around I went back into bed and lay down.

"What's wrong?" he asked in Bengali.

"I don't know," I replied. "Sometimes I am called by something or someone else."

"Who?" he asked, perplexed.

Looking at him sadly, I told him not to worry. I knew that he did not understand. I pushed myself against his strong brown Indian body. He moved closer and touched my face gently. I knew that I would always be haunted with this voice and this call because I had surrendered and given in and forgotten the wild walk of the sable antelope. My left horn felt blunt because I was not strong enough to pierce the wilderness of my own self.

A knock woke me. Tobias peeped in and said that they were leaving for the day. He saw tears in my eyes. As he walked closer I told him that I was remembering a time in London when I once had to walk for miles, as I had no money. It was wet and cold and I continued trembling in the night wind, which bit into me. The aloneness was unbearable. But I did not stop.

He sat down and leaning near me whispered that I too was a revolutionary and that politics were everywhere. I looked at him surprised and he told me that he once heard a Chinese wise woman say that the motion of the butterfly emerging from the chrysalis is a political statement. I wished him a revolutionary day. He smiled and blew me kisses. I remembered the night and felt my pores echoing the haunting sounds of India, my husband and the gentle drapes of the netting around the bed like dreamscapes embracing all circular motions and emotional spaces of the creative arc.

The gardenia was sweetly crushed from the night but still fragrant and white. Smelling it, I placed it on the altar. After showering I slipped into a white dress and wandered out to look for some mint tea. Entering the dining room I saw some tables still laid out for breakfast. Walking towards one, I sat down and looked around at the room, now in morning light. It was warm and welcoming, and the waiter approached with a freshness that was flirtatious. I asked for some juice and mint tea and toast. Finishing, I strolled towards what seemed to be the center of the village. The town was quaint and magical, with little stores strewn across vast expanses of desert. People looked as I walked through the bustling streets. They were dusty and rough with antelope hooves imprinted in them. Finally, feeling a little exhausted I saw a small and inviting café. I ordered something fresh and cool, and taking my cloth book out of my bag, I began to write.

I looked up, feeling someone's presence. A little shadow darted behind some walls. I looked back at my journal, and again the same feeling. This time I caught the silhouette of a young boy glancing at me. Leaving the table I followed him and saw him running away.

Returning to the café I pretended to be writing, but watched carefully. There it was again, but this time I kept my head down and continued to write. When I felt him very close I looked up gently and saw a haunting face with innocent eyes looking at me with fascination and curiosity. His clothes were tattered and he looked like he had not eaten for a long time. I smiled gently and beckoned to him to come and sit down beside me. The waiter, seeing the boy approach my table, shooed him away, and getting up I took the boy's hand and brought him to the table. I could tell that the waiter was not happy and he told me that the boy was a beggar and would steal everything from me if I was not careful. Ignoring him, I asked the boy what he wanted in sign language. He indicated that he was thirsty. I asked the waiter to bring him a glass of cold juice and a sandwich. I noticed he brought it in a dirty glass. Taking the glass I put the contents in my glass, which was now empty and handed it to him. The waiter was seething. I ignored him. The boy was watching me with keen interest, and after devouring the sandwich he put his hands in his pocket and brought out two beautiful stones, the like of which I had never seen before. They looked like some precious stones and yet they were simple pebbles. He carefully placed them on the table in front of me. He was like a fresh dewdrop, sitting on a leaf in the morning light of the dawn. I felt as though he knew who I was. I put my hands in my bag to find some money to give him. Finding some coins, I handed them to him. He refused, and rising from the table, he thanked me and walked away. I watched as he looked back twice and smiled. I picked the two stones up and, placing them in my hand, rubbed my hands together and kissed them. He smiled. I felt like he had just placed the pearls of his youth in my hands. His little autobiography and his story of hidden vibrations were now held in me. I had tears in my eyes as I sensed the mystery of life unfold and reassure me that being aware of the winds of birth and life are the most important realities.

"I will never forget you," I whispered as I stood up to leave the little café in the desert fields of sand and sight, where my dreams were made alive. A place where tigers ran alive and wild, and where youth came to me like a winged night and the bird of day was jeweled with earth stones of the eternal mind of a wondering mendicant who is always looking for the hidden whispers of this amazing truth.

After what seemed to be quite a while, I put the book and pen back and started to walk to the hotel, with the pebbles in my hand. The light was changing and to my surprise I noticed that the Jeeps were back. I walked towards the room where all the crew were and saw Tobias. He told me that they had achieved a lot and finished earlier than they thought. He was hot and sweaty and happy and very excited. Taking me aside he asked me if I had missed him.

"I missed you madly," he said. "I saw you in every face, every movement." And then he told me that because they were so successful in achieving all that they had, the local people wanted to throw a party and honor me.. Surprised I asked, why me? He said that they respected him and wanted to do that. So the party would be that very night, as they probably would be done by the next day and then have to leave to meet some deadline in Paris. "How was your day?" He asked gently.

"There is a poem for you."

He looked at me long, and taking my hand kissed it. "See you in a few hours."

I walked towards the room to get ready for the special night. It was going to be a surreal wedding night, a wedding of no boundaries and no structure. It was going to be a wedding of magic and mind, of poetry and soul of love and the senses, of heart and beauty. I was ready for this, more than ready.

I placed the pebbles next to the pearl on the table, and looked at what I had written. I made some corrections and placed the book on the bed next to the gardenia flower, which was now just a little tired looking, but still fragrant. Walking to where the clothes were hanging, I looked at each one and wandered which I would be in this night. I started to get ready slowly. I began lining my eyes with kajal (kohl). All came alive as inner sounds haunted the edges of sight and dreams. The five sights and five circles of the five elements coiled around me like a hooded serpent. Taking some gold dust I rubbed my face and forehead, and my lips, too, with its sparkle. Choosing a rust, golden, almost-transparent dress, I slipped it on and, hair flowing, I felt ready for an ancient known and unknown journey.

I walked to the door just as Tobias knocked.
He looked very beautiful in a long Indian silk shirt.

"I like you," I told him.

In the distance there was a light from a burning fire and people were walking towards it. Approaching the place of festivities that was held in an open area, a beautiful fire had been lit, and everywhere around were thousands of candles and trays of food and fruits and jars of wines. And in the center was a lamb roasting in the fire. We were welcomed by a brightly-clothed, smiling man, who led us to a sitting area. As soon as we sat down we were served fruit and wine, as we became the love story of Krishna and Radha. We both lifted up our glasses, toasted, and had the first sip. It was a nice local wine and had heartiness about it. Looking at me he asked if I missed India or felt out of place at times. The flames of the fire leapt into my eyes.

"There are times when I miss the simple little things and there are times when I miss the huge bigger things. There are times when I want to run back like a child to the comfort, luxury, support, and safety of it all. There are times when I miss the feeling of the sacred. That I miss always, but at certain times, the missing is an ache." I felt like Pandora's Box had been opened and I could not stop. "Those are the times when everything in the west feels like a wasteland. And those are the times when I feel like a plant in desperate need of nurturing. I am thirsty, and long for the sense of soul that is in the very air in my country. But I don't feel out of place. I seem to have an uncanny sense of universality. I don't know where that comes from. I was reading Rainer Maria Rilke's book of letters. Do you know him?"

Tobias nodded.

"Somewhere in the book he speaks that when one writes poetry, it does not matter where one is from. It is a universal language to be understood by all. Maybe I am a line in someone's poem."

Tobias held me passionately. "You are your own poem." I shivered, and with my shawl wrapped around me, we both looked up as the host of the celebration approached and told us that the men were going to do a dance in my honor. He explained that since the women were not allowed to come out, some of the men would take the part of the absent women and partner the men. I asked Tobias again why they were honoring me. "Who else?" he said. "But they don't even allow their own women to be seen in public."

"Yes, but you are not their woman," he said and added, "you are mine." He kissed my lips.

The feasting began, and according to the ritual, people danced around the fire in beautiful movements, while the musicians sang songs of love and longing. The meat was served around, and knowing I did not eat meat they had all sorts of other delicacies. After the meal all the dancers gathered and both the men and the others impersonating women did a sensuous and erotic coming together. The host told us that this was a pre-wedding dance, to hail the bride and groom. I was spellbound by the wind-like movements of the dancers. And then, out of the blue, a beautiful hand woven shawl was spread out. And gathering each corner they approached Tobias and me. They said it was a wedding shawl made by the women of the village. We were both a little stunned, and before knowing it they carried me gently, placed me on the woven fabric, and walked towards the hotel. I heard the host telling Tobias that he had no idea that they had this in mind, and that it was a good omen. The host truly hoped that I would not be offended. Tobias assured him that I would understand. He rose slowly and followed the procession a little shyly but also very excited, "My wedding night in this desert to a wild orchid flower from India he whispered loudly, "Je t'aime." I heard him.

Arriving at the hotel he noticed that the four men headed towards my room. They entered and took me in. A little nervous, he increased his pace to make sure everything was fine. Reaching the entrance of the room he watched them as they placed me on the bed, with the beautiful shawl around me. Bowing, they wished me goodnight.

As they walked out, they smiled at Tobias. He stood at the entrance, not able to move. He looked at me, entranced. I was aflame, and watched him with eyes lit by kohl and magic. There was a moment of strong silence as we looked at each other, and then he slowly entered the room and walked towards me. He came to the bed and knelt down near me. I opened my right palm and he saw the pearl again. He took it in his mouth and placed it in mine as he softly swallowed my lips of fire. We melted, and merged, and flew into the sky. Our dancing bodies entered into a ritual filled with prophecy and a secret knowledge. And through this erotic ecstasy I felt my soul. We madly embraced, whispered, and sighed. I told him about the poem I had written that day for us, for him.

"Speak it to me," he said. And I whispered in and around him, as we moved to the trembling sighs of all sensuality, ecstasy, and vibrations of the body chords of one million tunes of skin and soul.

"Veined mind
Feelings like a maddened
mendicant who has found love
Intoxicated, incensed body,
vibrating at every motion
Reeling in an obsession divine
I walk with you
Locked in youness
Erotic. Exotic. Sublime
You flow in my blood, your seed
running around in my brain
Making me heightened.
Making me maddened
You are near
You are here
I will keep you clear
like a temple bell
It is meant to be.
They are showing it to us
Smiling they watch at our
maddened desire
Let us see your strength
Change fate if you must
Your mated moment is
nigh

Death will not take
from this divine plate
Praying with you
Saying with you
The magic moment
has come
Remove your shoes
my sweet friend
and enter my temple
I open my flower
Burst and be so I can see/
Intense and trance inside
my being
Place all in me
so I can live
and breathe
I will take no less
I will break no more."

I whispered the lines over and over again into his ear as he sailed into me. The poem scattered around us like the red petals of the rose falling on the sky table and on my wounded heart, now unwounded and quivering like a peacock feather lined with wet clay. There was a sense of completion and transformation, as though the whole universe echoed in triumph. It was electric. Our eyes were closed while the candles still burned, casting beautiful shadows on the floors and walls around us. The flower petals, which were all over the shawl, now clung to us not wanting to part from the hills and vales of a rain-drenched geography of a maddened sensuality. Looking up I felt a presence in the room and half-awake I saw the woman from my dreams. Her eyes shimmered through the little etched window, as she looked at us, and I heard her whisper the last lines of the poem, "you will break no more," again and again and again. I sat up stunned. I felt like the feminine and the masculine joining into the consciousness and unconsciousness of spirit and matter. "The 'earthing' of the spirit and the spiritualizing of the earth, the union of opposites and reconciliation of the divided," said Jung. I looked at Tobias as he rolled off the bed and onto the floor to give me more space on the bed. I watched him with eyes, graced with the mythology of the heroine of a million faces. He gently covered me with the shawl and placed the petals on and around me. He whispered that he had to finish some postproduction details and dressing, he slipped out of the room and watched me longingly as he stood at the door before closing it.

My eyes opened slowly as the dawn light came in the apartment in New York. I was searching for Tobias hungrily. "He was here," I whispered to myself. Smila peeped in to see if I was awake. He was here in the room. He was here.

I could feel him.

That morning Smila and I had some tea together and discussed ideas and places for me to go for appointments. I trembled at the thought of all the superficiality and decadence that I would have to face and experience, knowing that nothing would stop me in the search for my own expressions. I am part of that world and yet have nothing of it. There cannot be fear. There can only be faith. Not a blind passive faith but that of a warrior of the spirit, walking into the mire, knowing that the Divine's will is the ultimate triumph no matter what. The banner of Sri Aurobindo and The Mother are always with me. I touched the gold circle with the Mother's blessings and took a deep and circular breath. Their work is of the integral life, and transformation takes place in the world and not in the solace of some peaceful hidden cave in the Himalayas. I will be their instrument. I am their instrument

The next evening, back from several appointments and auditions, the phone rang. It was Shane. He said he had called quite often but never found me in. I told him about all the rounds that I was making. He asked me how it was going. I replied that it had been interesting and strange. He asked me if we could meet again soon. Agreeing on the next evening we hung up.

Smila walked in soon after and we decided to have a bite, since we had not spent much time together recently. She ordered in and we settled down to a cozy candle-lit dinner. I saw the shadows on the walls from the candle flames and felt the pulsating walls of that sultry room in Taman asset, where my soul and senses howled wolf, like on the vibrating carved bamboo body of my ecstatic lover. My heart ached in longing. I missed Tobias with every cell of my being.

I told her what I felt about the calls I had been going to and added that I would continue even though some were mindless and empty. She looked at me not understanding or agreeing. Changing the subject I told her that Shane had called and that we would be meeting the next night. Smila asked if I was getting fond of him. "I really don't know him, but I do like his passion for an inner quest." She sarcastically added that he had quite a past. I sensed a tinge of jealousy in that remark.

"His past does not interest me," I replied.

"Are you enjoying and liking the city?" she asked.

"It feels like the world. Someone told me the other day that it was called the hunting ground by the Native Americans. I understand that. It seems that people come from all over the world to look for something here. It is either money, or a dream, or a freedom, or maybe to find themselves."

Smila said that she would never have seen it in that light. "I just see people coming here to make it. Money is the only motive."

"But what about the artists?" I asked.

"They just come for the same reasons. The city is the center and capital of art and culture and many other things. To me it is the world. It is global. And it all happens right here in this place and that's one of the most amazing things."

"I feel very comfortable here. I feel a kind of ease and freedom, which I did not feel in Europe even though there are other things in Europe that I miss. But because of the youngness of this country, there is a pioneer quality of beginnings and possibilities. There is space here, an inner space and that is one of the feelings that I love."

We finished eating silently and cleared up everything together. "You see everything in such a full way. You have metaphors and symbols and associations. Nothing is linear to you. Everything is layered. What a way to look at life!" Smila said. Laughing I told her how little things like eating a mango echo an awareness of all of life without boundaries or restrictions. "I don't like to slice it because that feels like a violent act. I feel it in my hands and caress it and listen to its story and then biting a tiny hole on one side my mouth drinks in all the beautiful juice. And then peeling the layers of flesh and growth the seed emerges in my hands, and I feel like I am touching its core where life first began. And that is how I like to experience life."

Smila whispered something and kissed me goodnight. She walked towards her room hesitatingly, as though not wanting to leave me. Standing in the darkish hallway, a glass of water in my hands I watched her walk away. Her back felt empty and her aura was not clean. Going towards my room, something in me told me that it was time for me to leave. Quietly undressing I sat at the edge of the bed. I lit the candle on the bedside table and everything came alive. In a prominent place sat the pearl and the two pebbles and the youth in me was aflame once again.

I was standing at the window in India on that sickle moon night. The hushed sounds seeped through with the chirping of the crickets and the haunting cries of the owls as knowledge screamed through the air. I wiped the tears from my eyes with the edge of my sari as the kohl bled beyond their almond structure and stained my skin with words of sadness and longing. I thought of the sable antelope once again, and felt my curved sickle moon horns piercing both realities: that of my journey into the wild in search of the creative forests where I had to saw off the obstacles one after the other and this one which was hushed in silence and hidden fears and hypocrisies and comfort. My antelope head stood tall, as I carried both sides and both realities within my singular self and knew that I would find that balance within and without. I would echo both selves in me and we would dream and hold and nurture each other without ever losing our selves.

75

The next day on rising I wiped my eyes again, this time with my fingertips as if to clean the dark edges left from the shadows of the night before. Taking a deep breath I organized all that I had to do for the day. Thoughts crowded my mind and I was aware of all the nuanced experiences I would have to travel through before I discovered my own personal voice and expressions.

I am an actress, I am a performer, I am an artist of movement and poetry and I embrace all of this with passion. I must always be courageous. Either we are or we are not. The word "courage" is from the French "cuer," meaning heart. To be courageous means to be heartfelt. I am developing and formulating now what I will later begin to hold and walk with. My tools will be sharpened to perfection and my eyes will be on every part of my body. I will walk with true sight. There will be huge moments of frustration caused by rejections and negations, but I will face all of this, which will be my challenge and my chiseling. Being sculpted by life itself, where all the unnecessary accessories like arrogance, cynicism and ego are crushed; after which one emerges with humility and awareness. That is when true art is born.

Quietly dressing, I walked out of the apartment, without Smila noticing. I was beginning to feel a distance from her. It was an organic shifting away from a world that cut my inner reflections and dreams with a blunt sword that hurt much more than the sharpened edge of the samurai warrior. It was a turning away from the sounds of the wasteland and false passions and the selfishness of a single human life.

I walked to an audition for an off-Broadway play. It was interesting, and I read the lines carefully and with an uncanny concentration. I felt the strength of the rendition. People were waiting outside for decisions to be made. I was nervous. No one really looked at each other as each one wondered what the outcome would be. I could hear inaudible conversations and the word "exotic," seeped through. Here we go again, I thought to myself. I looked away and tears wet my cheeks. One of the assistants walked out and told me that they were truly sorry but they would not be able to use me. I boldly asked why. He said that even though they all thought my reading was excellent, I just did not fit the look. I thought of the Navajo people who were chased off their sacred land in Canyon de Chelly, where Spiderwoman weaves the lives of people with her web that connects all humanity. I thought again of the thousands who were slaughtered at Wounded Knee and I felt humbled. I touched my cheeks to feel if the charcoal markings made when I as a child were still there. I looked for the feather in my hair. I thought I felt it. They had suffered and lost all. I will suffer and regain the beauty. And the words of the anonymous Navajo night prayer floated through my mind:

In beauty may you walk
All day long,
with beauty above
you may you walk.
With beauty beneath
you may you walk.
With beauty all around
you may you walk,
With beauty ahead
of you
may you walk.

I remembered the words of a wise Indian elder who explained to me that beauty to the Navajo was what Nirvana was to the Buddhist. I moved towards the park that was nearby. My sadness seemed to have received the many colors of the rainbow and I felt wounded and war-rior-like. I physically limped as though carrying the pain and agony of all those people. Noticing a grassy area I sat down, and slowly felt the weight bending me down. I took my head in my hands, and started to weep and cry. My shoulders shuddered. I saw nothing. I felt nothing.

I was in my home back in India. I had just had a strong argu-ment with my mother-in-law. She chided me for being out so much and not taking care of household obligations. I told her that poetry and art meant all to me and that I was inspired by the voice of the visionary. She responded stiffly that all that was secondary and that I should only be concerned with my wifely duties and chores. Arrogantly she asked me if I realized who I was married to. Everything in me ached. Lowering my head I caught the henna still vibrant on my feet, still so fresh from the wedding day where the caged bird now was losing its voice of song and joy. I was in this ornate cage of luxury and security, where the gold bars shone in victory of capturing yet another being.
The temple bell rang and wiping my eyes I straightened myself inwardly, and, walking to the mirror, re-arranged my sari and hair. I walked out, passing my mother in law. She was furious. I wanted to be with my Goddess being, and sit in front of her, and listen to the priest as he chanted sacred mantras to her. My mother in law shouted some-thing at me, but I kept walking. And as I approached the temple, I saw a beautiful elderly lady dressed in white, smiling at me with her toothless mouth. Her wrinkled face was a road map of compassion and life know-ing. She looked at me and I knew she saw all. She was beautiful. I ran to her, and stopped myself from placing my head in her lap. But then I did, and crying and sobbing loudly I melted into her earth wind arms. In the distance I heard my mother-in-law's voice as it got closer and, trembling,

77

I started to sit up.

She grabbed me from the woman's lap and scolded me violently for touching a poor beggar woman's body, as she was an untouchable. She shouted that I would have to bathe. I looked at her, stunned, and as she dragged me away I glanced back imploringly at the woman who was dressed in rags of gold, and love flamed from her eyes like a halo of a thousand arrows; and her mouth formed blessings as she smiled; the universe trembled. I wanted to tell my mother in law that it was she who was the untouchable.

In the house we sat down as the maid prepared the afternoon tea. There was a suffocating tension in the air. She watched me like a hawk without its beak. I was choking and could not swallow anything and did not understand why I was here. My husband was a warm and beautiful man but he was afraid and meek, and followed the empty rituals without truly wanting to. He was the eldest son and she was very possessive of him. At times I felt she was even jealous of me, and my heart was angry and torn with confusion. My parents had wanted this. His parents had agreed to this match. And I was there in the middle, left like a sparrow hopping about on the ground beneath the trees trying to sing my song. I stood up as he came into the room, and sensing the stillness in the air he sat down beside me instead of her. She scowled at him as he took my hands and held them softly. I felt my wings leaving a trace and a shadow on my eyelids. I was stunned at this change in him. I looked at him as my eyes stretched so wide I felt as though they had run out of themselves. In Bengali he softly told me not to be sad. She pushed her chair from the table and ordered the maid to clear the table before we could even finish our tea. But the maid liked me, and felt for me, and waited until we were done. As we walked out into the dusk garden, he did not let go of my hands. The sparrows sang. I looked up and smiled. I was sure then that the beautiful saint lady near the temple had done this for me, and I sent her my love, gratitude, and a million and one quivering red roses.

Slowly rising from the ground in Central Park I shook off grass and dust from my skirt. And rubbing my eyes dry with the edge of my fingertips, I suddenly noticed something. A flash of light sparkled from the grass at the edge of the park. Picking up my bags, shoes, pain, and sadness, I walked toward the spot and stopped. There, embedded in the earth, was a small mirror. It felt like someone had placed it there just for me. Reflected in the glass was the blue sky. It was amazing. It was the sky merging into earth. My face felt alive, as though an ethereal beauty had been given back to me to remind and reassure me. I felt the sadness leaving me. I looked in awe. As I stood transfixed, looking down again at the mirror, I saw her looking at me. My echo and dream self who had stayed within the oyster and kept all inside herself, the one who longed for expressions but could not walk away from the echoes of the screaming conch shell, the one who was always present for me, giving me the silent assurances of what I needed, because she was my other self. "All is one, I whispered to myself, never removing my eyes from my bride self.

The light was changing and some people had come around attracted by the light. As it slowly got darker and dusk walked in, I hesitatingly began to head towards Smila's apartment building. My gait was slow and measured, and I walked like an antelope, carrying both carved and sickle horns on my head. It was heavy but I had the strength of a hundred and one wild lions.

As I entered the apartment Smila greeted me warmly and asked me if I would like to join her for dinner. I agreed but then remembered that I had promised Shane the night before when he had called. I told her that and noticed that she was slightly saddened. I asked her to join us. She hesitated saying that she was sure he would want to be alone with me. "I will call him," I said. Going to the bedroom, removing my shoes and putting everything down, I wrote down what I had seen and felt. And then picking up the phone, dialed his number. The phone rang for quite a while, and I almost hung up by the time he answered. I asked him if it would be all right if I invited Smila. There was an uncomfortable pause after which he said that it would be fine. He said he thought we could dine at his home, as he had an excellent Japanese chef. He asked me if I liked Japanese food. I said I did. Confirming the time and putting the receiver down, I let Smila know that she was also invited. "It will be at his house and we will have cuisine a la Japanese." She laughed and said that he was really good. We both went to our rooms to get ready and Smila put on some music on the way to her room. Nina Simone's voice filled the air.

She was singing "Ne me quite pas."

As I rested for a moment on the bed, I was in that love room in Taman asset with Tobias. His lips whispered secrets and sounds in and around me and I was the weeping statue with the blood of the mystic and the unmasked poet. I outlined my lips to the curve of his heart as the sinuous snake coil of tantra merged and glided through every pore of my mind-soul-self. Shivering, I sat down on the bed. The polished pearl beckoned me to hold it, and picking it up I placed it in my mouth. I felt his tongue swirling inside me to find it and grasp it. I felt the autobiography of my life, and taking a deep breath removed it from my tongue and placed it back on the table. It moved slightly towards the two other pebbles and I became the curious child as I held the pebble in my hands and it skimmed across the silent lake, causing ripples of infinite circles.

I looked at the same dress I had worn on that Arabian night when I was wed to a hundred and one tales of exotic and erotic bliss. I slipped it on. I touched myself and felt the whole mountain of herbs that

79

Hanuman carried to ***Rama*** to heal his wounded brother ***Lakshmana***
fall over me. I felt the trees outside the windows touching me, like the
rugged hands of Tobias. They smelled of earth and war and peace and
revolution and poetry. In the mirror I saw Smila watching me. Her face
was reddened with a tainted longing. It was covered with drops of perspiration and her lips warped into a repulsive shape. She walked towards
me. She stopped in front and looked at me. Then she suddenly kissed me
on the mouth. I did not push her back. I touched the mountain instead
and drank the liquid juices of all its healing plants. I felt big. I felt com-
passionate and untainted and untouched, like the lotus flower.

We grow in the mire of life mud and slush. Our leaves and petals
are anointed with a special surface and all that is unneeded and not of
growth falls off without tarnishing or disrupting us. Smila stood back,
embarrassed, and said that she was sorry. Boundaries only obstruct the
flow of a woven life structure.

"You make me feel different," she said. "I don't know what it is
but I feel enhanced. I feel as though my body is transparent. I have never
ever experienced this before. It is like a state of meditation."

"Today I saw sky meeting the earth, and I know that there are no
separations. It is all one, with millions of nuances and shades of expressions forming myriads, of many textured fabrics."

I felt the moon shining through the dress and sculpting me. I felt
Smila's burning eyes walk through me as she came closer and touched
my breasts and outlined them with her fingers. I stepped back and I told
her that it was time to go. We walked out of the apartment. I looked at
my hands and saw a bowl of blossoms. A bird flew down and picked each
petal. Getting off the elevator, we walked towards the lobby where the
doorman opened the door. He asked if we would like a cab. Smila nodded
but she still seemed to be in another space. She had an uncanny expression on her face. It was of unhealthy swellings and I saw the growths on
her head caused by lies, fear, a lack of self-worth, and stagnation. I was
repulsed.

When you float through the wind you live each thought, and the
thought lives through you; and then you formulate it through word,
through song, through movement, through film. It emerges as a birth
and changes and transforms and makes you more.

A cab approached. The night was light and the sky was slightly lit with a faint sliver from the moon. The drive through the park was
silent, as I looked out absorbed with the language of my trees. Smila was
uncomfortable. She looked at me from the corner of her eyes and her
longing made me shift away from her. I saw bigger horizons where the
Avant-Garde flies, where crows bring back spirits, where the mind is a
web of light, where fear has no adobe.

As the cab approached the town house on 54th and Madison Avenue, she paid the driver and we both stepped out. Ringing the bell, we waited and looked at each other. My eyes were wide open and hers were lowered. She was about to say something when the door opened and Shane welcomed us in. He kissed us both and led us to the library upstairs. There were a few other guests sitting around and he began introducing us. Smila seemed to know them all. It felt as though they all belonged to a clique. I was introduced as her exotic princess. I was uncomfortable. They all had a similar kind of affluence and interests and seemed to be Indofiles in a chic yet empty way.

Shane looked very attractive. He asked us what we would like to have and served us wine and some exotic snacks. He enquired about my go-sees and what the outcomes had been. I replied peripherally, not being that interested in going into details. Smila joined in enthusiastically and elaborated on all the appointments that she had been setting up for me. "They really like her you know, she just has to hit the right one."

Shane mentioned that he had been talking around and thought that he could set some things up, too. I thanked him. As I looked around I felt like an exotic object being shown around. He played some Indian classical music and the sounds warmed me as I sat down. The breaking of all convention where intelligence is the breath you take. Sparks and fireflies are the fabric of my mind. The notes wonder through me like glowworms sailing through my blood veins and I watch myself watching them. Smila and Shane talked about money and business. I had never seen them together before. They seemed alike and of the same fabric. There was an attraction between them, an attraction that was small and empty. It was of sense and nonsense. It was of passion with death in view. It was of the empty howl when the orgasm is curved with withered whispers, speckled with glitter that falls away, leaving no perfume of ever having been there. They have obviously been friends for a long time, and probably lovers too. The evening continued pleasantly and when dinner was ready we went downstairs to the dining room where the Japanese chef had everything set out exquisitely. We were seated according to some plan. I was placed next to Shane and to another young man who was some famous artist. He was enamored and fascinated by my presence. I was the little Indian that night. They all seemed surprised that I loved sushi. Abundance flows like the river of all rivers. Today I hennaed my hair. Today I saw a rainbow and it became the sky.

The sushi felt like warm insides of a sultry summer flower and as it dissolved in my mouth the sea entered every pore and cell of my skin. Shane watched me. I felt his eyes. After dinner, we went upstairs to have dessert and coffee. Some of the guests told me that they would keep an eye out for me, as most of them were connected in some way or the other in the arts. I thanked them all and people began leaving. Smila glanced at me not knowing if I was staying or leaving. Shane looked at me longingly, but I didn't respond and he suggested that he escort us back to Smila's apartment. She said there really was no need, but he insisted. Coats and wrappings were found and we left. I thanked the chef, bowing before him. He bowed back as he looked deeply into my eyes. I felt a shiver going through me, like some ancient sage was blessing me silently. I knew I would see him again. Outside Shane hailed a ca, and he sat in the front to give us space. Smila quietly asked me if I had enjoyed the evening. "I did not think it would be such a large affair," I replied. She was quick to remark that there were many very influential people there and that they all had money. That was obvious.

"You have to be seen in these circles, you know. That is, if you want to achieve anything," she told me.

"You mean my achieving anything or not depends on people who have money?"

"Yes it depends on money and contacts."

It was cold and I pulled the black Moroccan wedding shawl around me. It was my earth and my song, and I closed my eyes, feeling Tobias. He was my gypsy self and Miguel was my song. They were my men, my hero's, my lovers and my trees.

Through my wet eyes I saw my trees, my silent warriors. *I want to be them, pure and strong. Their freedom is filled with quality and structure. These are my friends of the inner chord. They are the ultimate code of the soul.* As we entered the drive of Smila's apartment building, there was a strange silence in the car. Shane opened the door. Smila thanked him and, wishing him good night, left for the lobby. He looked at me and, taking my hand, kissed it passionately.

"I wish you would have stayed," he said.

"It didn't feel right," I replied.

He asked me if I was upset that he had invited all those people, and added that he had done it for me. c

"I appreciate that and understand that I will have to meet all sorts of people to be able to do what I want to do," I said. My voice was somehow cold. He asked me when we would meet again and reminded me that I was always welcome in his home.

"I have thought about it, but am not comfortable because of the money situation."

"I don't need the money. I need you," he mumbled. "There are no obligations, none, you must believe that."

"I will call you," I whispered as we headed toward the lobby.

At the lobby door I looked at him. "At times it is so hard for me to be here in the west, so hard." He pulled me to him and, taking my face in his hands, brushed his lips on mine. My petals quivered as they spread across the whole visage of the endless longing of the sacred Yamuna River, as it coils its ways through eons and millenniums of infinity and space, taking with it the wails and cries of all of humanity. I kissed him back with blood and sand and felt the grains separating and rippling into a myriad of shapes and shades in this infinite union of self and self. He is not Tobias. His hands were not of earth and clay. They were smooth and cleansed by society and security. Their elegance was of an exterior language, with the inner pushing to emerge and that is why he wanted me. I was seduced, and I hoped my compromise would be forgiven by the light holes of the universe and the strapped winds over the concrete jungles of human triumphs. He waited until I was near the elevator and then got back into the cab. I watched him. His hands were on his lips. I felt him feeling me. I waited until the cab left the driveway and I entered the elevator.

In the apartment Smila was getting ready to retire. She asked me if I would like something to drink. I got some water, making sure it was clear.

"Are you unhappy?" She asked.

"I miss India. And sometimes I wonder why I left. It is so hard here."

You know why you left. You had to. It is so clear. You just have to adjust."

"I know. But there are so many hidden nuances. Things I would not have had to face back home. I have to be strong and clear. And I don't want to just adjust. That is too simple. I have to absorb, to understand, to feel everything, to take in and change and transform it. I will not adapt or compromise or imitate. I cannot do that."

I took a deep breath and sipped some water. She asked me how I felt about Shane and if I was going to see him again.

"Yes, I think I will. I am not sure yet how I feel about him, but he has an intensity that attracts me."

"Yes, he does."

Wishing her good night, I entered my room. I lit the candle on the table beside the bed. The images shone and the faces radiated as the pearl glowed in the dark. I curled up my legs in a lotus position, took a deep breath and looked at everything. I felt my face trembling, as tears started to fall and I burst into a painful sobbing. The pillow cushioned my face as I screamed into its feathered weight and sank into its soft whiteness. Everything shook and my whole body swayed. The white wolf came closer and pushed his eyes into my raw and young interior.

Opening my eyes in India, I saw my beautifully made-up and jeweled face reflected in the mirror. I added finishing touches and clasped the ornate gold earrings, which clothed my whole ear. Standing back from the mirror with the ornate sari wrapped around me, I looked at my hands and feet reddened with henna. But as I saw myself and adjusted all the details, I felt a tremor of pain as the pollen from the lotus flower

83

slid down life and death. I saw the silk inside the ancient sea shell, which was on the sacred table waiting to be blown at dawn and dusk and I knew I would come again and again till this earth dance was completed. Moving to where the large arrangements of flowers were next to the window, I ran my fingers through the various ones, and pausing near a white lily, removed it from the rest of the flowers. I placed the single stalk in a slender vase and put it on the altar and lit an incense stick. Clasping my hands, I stood in silence. My husband entered the room and walked slowly towards me.

"You are so beautiful, my **Devi**," he whispered in Bengali.

"Yes, yours," I replied.

With a soft voice he said that it was time for us to leave. As we exited the room I looked back at the lit flame and smiled. I knew it was for my other self who was running through forests of thorns, and stepping on sharp blades to discover her core and her center.

The phone rang and I was back. I quickly glanced at the table to make sure the candle was still lit. Still sobbing but calmer, I grabbed the receiver so as not to awaken Smila. I knew it was Shane. He spoke quietly and asked me if he woke me. He told me that he could not sleep and that the sadness in my eyes haunted him. "Yes, I am sad. I feel like a slit tree as the sap drips drop by drop from its bark. I am empty and stretched out of the oasis of fragrant waters. I cannot describe it."

"You are in another culture, a culture that does not embrace warmth, a culture where myth and the sacred is almost nowhere visible, a culture where hospitality is only a manicured niceness, and not of the heart, a culture where giving is a calculated risk. And you are a woman, a woman who embraces all of this. How can you not be sad **Ondine**?"

There was a silence and I began to sob all over again.

"Would you like me to come over and pick you up?"

"No, I will be fine. I have to remember and truly understand why I am here and why I left. And never look back. I just did not know how hard it would be at times. It is the hero's journey, the rhinoceros that makes his own way, and all this has to be done without ever forgetting one's source and ground of being."

Wishing him goodnight I placed the phone back and walked to the bathroom. Glancing at the mirror I see her-and-me again, jeweled together with symbols of the ancient warriors. We looked at each other. She smiled. I smiled back. She rubbed the **sindoor** on her third eye indicating marriage and placed it on my forehead. I felt the union within me and looking at the mirror again saw the shaded red on my third eye. Trembling I walked out of the bathroom. My cloth book came towards me and unfolded its pages. Picking up a pen, these words flew through me:

Cell body of lotus and jasmine
Sometimes the walk looses the
dreamtime.
Sometimes the unholy moves
in to conquer.
Never the empty and the hollow
hole
A warrior must slay all that is
untrue
A warrior must recover all that
is beauty
Fullness has been robbed by false.
A blast of thunder sits in the sky
of my mind with the solitude of
silence in the cave of memories...

I touched the words feeling each stroke, and blowing out the candle, I lay down. I closed my eyes and entered the other reality. It was my dream world. It was my axis.

I saw a dark complexioned Indian lady with a beautifully chiseled face approaching me. Walking up to her, I showed her my open palm. We sat down. I felt I had known her. She took my hand and traced a huge circle etched in the center.

"You have to go through all this and when it is over you will be free with gold threads weaving within and without you. And you will carry the nectar from the gods in your hand. But first you have to walk through the jungle of thorns and arrows, through dark forests where light is veiled and shrouded, through riverbeds that have been abandoned by the flowing whispers of water, and waste lands where humanity has forgotten its own cry. You will have to pave your own path. You will have to walk with bare feet, in tatters, penniless with your begging bowl not knowing where you could lay your weathered soul and body, or where you could get a leaf or stalk to nourish you. You will have to weed your way through all this, until you have been swallowed and crushed and grounded and broken and stripped bare and beaten down and whipped by the blunt tongues of the little people. These people who refuse to look at a palace of pearls made by fresh dewdrops , , who never look up at the warrior sun as he glides down to rest, who never sail through the sickle moon to see it circle in its completely magical, hypnotic fullness, who close their eyes and ears to your stories of star howls in the wilderness from where you will bring down oceans of immense beauty and transformations through your significant art brush strokes. These are the people who laugh and scorn your passionate wild dreams and words because you do not conform to their small stagnant structures of fear, security, and rotten imitation. Because you are free and they are trapped. Because they cannot tame you and beat you down, because they can and could never walk with the white wolf and the fearless tiger, and because they have lost their very souls as they stumble and stutter through their pathetic gadgets and their fear of being alone." I looked down at my palm and saw an image of my sweet gentle, big, beautiful, naughty Ganesha sitting in my hand as his trunk becomes my lifeline and then the image dissolves. Elated and amazed, I asked her if my life would be short as the trunk dissolved before the end of the line. Looking at me, she said that I have a lot to do.

Still in my dream state I saw The Divine Mother's opening words from an article titled "To Know How to Suffer" as they float in front of my eyes:

> "If at any time a deep sorrow, a searing
> doubt or an intense pain overwhelms
> you and drives you to despair, there is
> an infallible way to regain calm and peace.
> In the depths of your being there shines
> a light whose brilliance is equaled only by
> its purity, a light, a living and conscious
> portion of a universal godhead who
> animates and nourishes and illumines
> matter, a powerful and unfailing guide for
> those who are willing to heed his law, a
> helper full of solace and loving
> forbearance towards all who aspire to see
> and hear and obey him. No sincere and
> lasting aspiration towards him can be in
> vain, no strong and respectful trust can
> be disappointed, no expectation ever
> deceived."

And as the stars feathered me with their lit extensions I saw myself in the midst of all sorts of people. They came closer to me and began saying that I have a mission. And that they would show me what it was. I was flying above earth, over mountains and rivers. I felt light and surreal. I landed somewhere and the same people came around me and said that the world had to be changed and helped and that I was an instrument.

I woke up. I felt as though I was still in flight. I slowly opened my right hand and watched my palm with earnest. I am sure I saw him sitting there on my lifeline. I shut my eyes and I felt his wet trunk in my palm. I arose.

Walking to the kitchen I put the kettle to boil. In the living room,

I selected some **Meera Bhajans**. Lighting some incense, I walked back to the kitchen and arranged the cups and milk.

Smila entered the kitchen.

"I was going to bring it to you."

"Let's have it here. The sun is so warm this time of the morning."

I could feel the tension as we both sat down at the table. The dream and the palm woman came back to me. The howl returned. The white wolf ran across the kitchen floor. He was winged. The tiger glided elegantly purring as he brushed my arm and feathers from invisible archangel beings fell all over my crown chakra. She asked me how I had slept. "Not too well." My dream people hushed me to be quiet and not share the magic. She said she had heard the phone ring. "It was Shane. He called rather late. He was very kind and gentle and said that he sensed my shadows. He kindly invited me to stay at his home if I wanted to and that I was always welcome." The fangs were out. They had a strange damp and murky sound. The mouth turned crooked and warped and the voice was hollow and dead.

"You never told me that. Does it mean that you might consider this invitation?"

"Well I am thinking about it since he told me that he is hardly ever there. He also mentioned many times that there would be absolutely no obligation."

"No obligation," she said viciously "you will see."

All in me shuddered.

"You know it is entirely your decision, but just watch what you're getting yourself into. As I said before, he has had quite a past with women."

"I just feel that it would be good for me to be alone and I'm sure you would like your privacy back."

The suffocating claws of the possessive concrete fingers closed in around me, and I felt as though my breath was being torn away from me. The crooked bamboo came in to give me solace and grace, and the soft and gentle leaves whispered their evergreen mantras. I sat erect and leaned back into the winds of pain as they supported and held me.

"You are never in the way, and you know I love you being here. And anyway what will you do about money?"

"I don't know," I said and I really didn't. "Do you know the origin and meaning of the word money?" I asked her.

"Money has meaning?" she said sarcastically.

"It is the primary symbol of power in patriarchal societies today. Money is a linguistic derivation from Roman worship of the great mother under her name of Juno Moneta: Juno the Admonisher. Since Juno's temple housed the Roman mint, the coins produced there were considered blessed by her and so became valuable '**monetas.**' And the Sanskirt word **arthe** also connects money with both Mother Earth and material wealth. Names for the Goddess Earth, such as **Ertha, Hretha, Urth**, and similar variants in northern Europe, came from the same root. The Goddess was the giver of all the Earth's riches: land, food, even the precious metals and gems dug out of her bowels. The Gypsies were following an extremely ancient tradition when they gave the name of 'earth' to all forms of money."

Smila smiled nervously and said that if I decided to leave she would truly miss me.

"Well, I am not far you know and we can always meet," I said.

We discussed the day's appointments and Smila reminded me of a certain one that she thought would be very important. Just then the phone rang and it was Shane. Smila gave me the phone and, taking it, I walked towards the living room where the chants were still embracing the air. He said he would be leaving the next morning and would love to give me the keys before he left. I remembered the mirror in the park, and told him to meet me there. "I want to show you something very special," I told him.

As I put down the phone Smila looked anxious and insecure. "Are you going to dine with him?" she asked.

"I don't think so," I replied

"I would love to invite you to dinner. I have a friend that I want you to meet."

We decided on the time and I went to my room to get ready for the day. And I thought of how Smila had shifted and changed since she introduced Shane to me.

The air was still soft and gentle and not too hot. I felt a bounce in my feet as I stepped out of the building. Diego greeted me enthusiastically and his warm tropical smile felt like the lush foliage of Mexico, where the Zapotech Indian women swayed in the sun with their white robes and hand-crushed silver jewelry. He was like a lion at the door of my exits and entries. I felt as though I had broken some ropes around me. *These are the plastic ones, I thought to myself. They have a false stretch and easier to break free from. There is no substance to them. They cannot protect or comfort. They are slippery and without texture.* I decided to walk through the park to get to my first appointment. On entering the park, something stopped me. My hair slightly covered my eyes and removing the strands, I looked again. The trees seemed to be swaying and bending and moving. Quickening my pace, I approached them and gently touched their rough and alive barks. Walking through the park my steps faltered. I did not want to go to the appointment.

The building loomed ahead and I felt strange and afraid for the first time as I walked in. There were people everywhere, nervous and very vocal. They looked at me strangely and I felt unwelcome. When I was called in I noticed a large panel of serious faces. The assistant told me what the part was about and asked me to do a monologue if I had one ready. I did and recited a piece that I had done before and was very familiar with. I let them know that it required movement too. They nodded their heads and I began. It was a poem by Yevtushenko called "Colors":

> "When your face appeared over my
> crumpled life, at first I understood
> only the poverty of what I have.
> Then its particular light on woods,
> on rivers, by the sea, became my
> beginning. I am so frightened, I am
> so frightened, of the unexpected
> sunrise finishing, of revelations
> and the excitement finishing. I
> don't fight it, my love is this fear,
> I nourish it, who can nourish
> nothing, love's slipshod watchman.
> Fear hems me in. I am conscious
> that minutes are short and that the
> colors in my eyes will vanish when
> your face sets."

89

There was silence after I finished. It was tangible. It was a silence like when the birds stopped singing on the cold winter morning. It was the silence of when the crickets in unison somewhere in the south of France just stop chanting. It was a silence like when an Australian aborigine forgets his song line. I felt the echo of a birthday born into a forest of bliss, a wide naked birth through a field of bamboo and sky, a birthday embraced by shell echoes, of abalone daydreams within ruptures of wasteland tremors and sighs. Walking to where all my things were, I almost fell. I was exhausted. They applauded. I was surprised. The assistant approached me and asked me if I could be reached at the number they had. I nodded and left. My seed was nurtured.

Walking out my eyes saw the youth and soul of the creative kind. And I was the song line born again of a karmic path shadowed by numerous nuances of leaf and twig. The song line, which traces the sacred thread through water and blood and breath and wine towards a found path. I felt a newness born in me, a newness given to me and I felt the custi -- kiss in Sanskrit -- showering on and around me, and I touched the union of Shakti and Shiva and the meeting of self. I saw the champa flower with its five star leaves exuding its fragrance at the birth of dusk, in the sultry night in India as it embraces its own alphabet of psychological perfection, and the love letter written of a thousand years wrapped itself all around me, caressing my awakened child. My passionate limbs were lyrical and melodious. I traced my footsteps back towards my tree place where I was to meet Shane. It was now mid-afternoon and my gait was different. Walking towards the area where I had seen the mirror embedded in the grass, I looked for it hungrily. The mirror was exactly where I had left it but without its reflection. It had lost its dreamtime. Disappointed, I sat down and stretched on the grass. My hands caressed my soft youth, fresh and alive and moist as my eyes slowly closed.

I entered my dream reality and saw two beautiful young Indian women decorating me and making all sorts of sensual sounds. They are speaking in Bengali and whisper in my ear: "It is time for your wedding day. We must get you ready." They paint my face with sandal wood flowers and henna markings. My face becomes the bride child.. My face is being transformed as they paint around my eyes and forehead. I see milk birds, a blue cow with its deep sacred eyes enveloping me. And the world was alive.

A gentle tap awoke me. Shane's face was next to mine. I felt his breath entering my face. Opening my eyes, I told him that I had been dreaming. My cheeks were wet from the red blood signs on my face and hands that India imprinted on me and I saw the tree where I began my new walk with the hands of life-sati left behind. Not burned brides, but awakened woman-wolves. The walk and the cry of the warrior woman straddled in the art of creative gold, winged with utter compassion and stretched within and without, melting all boundaries of time, space, race, and cultures, with the climate of absolute being. I told him that I was getting married in my dream. An unknown wind blew around us and fear found its space to creep in between us as all became small and linear and broken. And the superficial man-made earth was scratched and tainted. I saw something. He was trapped. I was free.

I pointed to the place where the mirror was, and told him there was something I wanted to show him. But getting closer to where it was, I realized it was no more. It had vanished. Shane smiled, and said that it was back again. "It happened while you were sleeping." He then told me about his daughter and his broken marriage. He was uncomfortable. He asked if I had been married. I looked at him from afar, through saffron fields and Vermillion Rivers where the round beetle nut represents the planets and is offered to the Goddess Laxmi who bestows us with abundance. "I have been married a million times and I still have no husband." He edged closer to me. He had a perplexed look on his face. Laughing I told him that every time a leaf emerged or a flower bloomed I wed each one, and when a leaf fell at the climax of its tree journey I married the lived veined life. I am a virgin and I am not a virgin. Excited, He came closer. He lifted my hands which were resting on of the soft green grass and kissed them. My mind wandered.

> As I see my soul reflected
> in Nature, As I see through
> a mist, One with inexpressible
> completeness, sanity, beauty,
> See the bent head and arms
> folded over the breast,
> The Female I see[1].

I moved towards the mirror and my face melted and merged into the reflection of the sky and the clouds. I felt my heart beating to the throbbing of the heavens, when Shiva makes love to Parvati. *Her sari unfolds to the winged dances of all the angels and its endless drapes of gold fall gently into the sky and dust. I felt this soft electric fabric winding within me and I melted. The musk of the male sounds touches my skin and the male-ness that I love arouses my feline being. The tiger within me is alive and his eyes are wild. I feel all sprouting as we are watched from ether caves and lavender fields. They nod in approval.* Shane took me in his arms and kissed me passionately. His tantric embrace seemed to bring art and spirit together, when its own wisdom tempts and teases the disciple to seek the undivided whole and follow its own realm of ecstasy I was making love to the curved leaf and spined bamboo, as I inhaled their

---

1   Walt Whitman, Leaves of Grass

rippled texture and my soul-sword pierced all veils of mediocrity and morality. The diamond was sliced into a privacy of green light. The cry of the howling wolves and the shame of greed and the utter prostitution of the compromised walk and Ganesha flew over me with his wings out stretched. Shane uncoiled from around me like the **kundalini** in the form of a serpent, and my energy awakened and rose through the chakras to unite with the consciousness of the thousand petal lotus. I heard the birds chirping, the crow cawing, and the fire walking elephant that eats the flames as he removes all our obstacles with his windblown trunk. He is my grasshopper elephant, my butterfly elephant, soft and strong. He is mine.

Shane gave me the keys to his apartment. And the monsoon rains fell and the world rejoiced as the dry-pressed jasmine flower from India fell out of my journal and rested on my thigh. And I caught the serpent through my eye. The tiger flower showed me my magic. The textured stone gives me my birthright. He asked me if I knew when I would move in.

"I want to do it soon."

"The sooner the better, - he replied quickly, "I just want you there."

"Smila is not too happy about my leaving."

"I'm sure she's not. She desires you. It will be good for you to be alone."

"I agree," I said and we both rose.

He carefully brushed the grass and leaves from my clothes. He was gentle. I watched him with doe eyes and saw Krishna looking at me as he played the flute and lead me into my very own magical interiors. We walked towards the place where I was meeting Smila and her friend. He was hesitant to leave me and offered to walk me to the restaurant. We left the park and dusk walked in. I heard the temple bells. I inhaled the fragrant wafts of **champa** and jasmine as they began their sweet sultry journeys into the sensual whispers of romance and mystery. And I heard the painter Gauguin's words: "I shut my eyes in order to see." Film is inside and outside of me, and will be my weapon and my samurai sword.

In front of the chic restaurant, Shane took me in his arms once again, and touched my face in his elegant society hands. I asked him to come in with me. But he said he only wanted to remember me. I watched him walk away. His long hair was uncaught. He tied it up again as he looked back and sent me a wind kiss. He faded into the distance and the bird with vibrant feathers and a jewel in his third eye flew over me. He was my muse. Taking a breath and straightening myself, I walked into the restaurant. It was called Chez Chic. How ridiculous, I thought. I entered and the waiter led me to the table where Smila and her friend were seated. Approaching, I saw the same ancient African warrior with the eyes of a lion looking at me. He had a beautiful headdress. I must have looked startled because I heard Smila's voice coming through the wild foliage of my warrior self, asking me if I was all right. She introduced me to her friend. Her name was Fiona. She had a harsh attractiveness about her and a voice to match. She looked hungry and coarse, but seemed of the obvious kind of intelligence. Her eyes were scrutinizing me. I searched for my ancient warrior. He was fading, but he left me with his eyes of power and protection. She told me how much she had heard about me and was happy to finally meet. The conversation geared around India and spirituality and her work.. Fiona spoke about how much she wanted to go to India with Smila but could not.

"I am sure it would have changed my life," she said.

"Yes, that happens," I whispered.

Smila poured some red wine into my glass and I raised it to both of them. They had ordered food and talked about their friends and business issues and I lived my dream in the park again. Excusing myself, I headed to the rest room. Walking in, I went to the mirror, almost certain that I would see my painted face like in the dream. Leaning into the mirror, I saw remnants of the red on my forehead and in my hair. I felt blessed and in unison with my India-self. I felt wholeness as her red sari wrapped itself around my flowing hips. Leaving the rest room, I walked back to the table in a dream and noticed both Smila and Fiona getting ready to leave. I wondered if they saw my stained red forehead but I knew they did not. Smila asked me if I wanted any dinner. I said I wasn't hungry and thanked her. We walked into the night air, which was warm and heady. The evening was inviting. Smila asked Fiona to come back for a glass of wine. She accepted and we walked down towards the apartment. I was silent and introspective, while the two friends chatted away and laughed about jokes and incidents that didn't include me. Arriving at the lobby I felt something pulling me. It was Diego looking at me with a strange warning smile. I was confused. The apartment was cool and Smila opened a bottle of red wine. She brought three glasses and set them on the table. Fiona walked around scrutinizing everything. I went to my room. Smila asked me if I would be joining them. I just wanted to wash and change into something comfortable. When I returned, both were seated on cushions listening to music and talking. They had left a glass on the table for me, which I took and made myself at home. Fiona looked at my altar, which was visible from where we were sitting. She commented on the statue of Ganesha and said she had a very special affinity with him. I told her about a legend which spoke of him teaching his father Shiva about OM -- the universal sound -- and how the symbol came to be.

"The symbol has five circles and each represents the five ethers," I explained.

Smila told her how much she had learnt from me. We spoke about the world of cinema and how important it was to me. "I have watched some films over and over again. They are like mirrors reflecting the many nuances within me and inspiring me on uncountable levels." We spoke about Jeanne Moreau and Irene Papas, and how their very presence on screen brought all to life.

"In a performance when one expresses an idea or a thought or a feeling which comes from a raw true place, then it becomes a phenomenal experience for the audience. It elates and transforms; as opposed to just entertaining. Great directors who work with such gifted actors produce works of profound value and it is this aspect of performance and film which fascinates me."

Listening very carefully, Fiona replied that it was not easy.

"Nothing of any value is," I echoed.

The notes of the music seeped into the room and, feeling relaxed and a little exhausted from the day, I stretched out on the many cushions on the floor. Smila and Fiona both came closer to me and they both started rubbing my feet. It felt good and I surrendered to it. They moved up to my legs and then hands and arms, and then to my face and shoulders.

I was in the porch in the house in India, surrounded by all my women friends. It was henna day. We oiled each other's hair and colored our feet and hands. Everyone was happy celebrating deep friendships. The sounds of birds and little insects, and the warm air surrounded us as we told stories and read poems to one another. We were braid sisters and we shared each other's secrets and longings, and the wrath of our mother-in-laws, and all the "dos" and "don'ts" that we had to abide by. The cats sat around purring as though they, too, were being caressed in the sun. These friendships were sacred and pure like dream streams and falling moons.

Smila gently asked me to turn around so they could do my back. Something shifted as though the ocean waves brought in another breeze. It had an impure odor, one of motivation, manipulation, and greed. I was reminded of her house in South Hampton. It felt stagnant. Everything in me tensed. My chords got brittle, I felt like cracking, and I saw the eyes of my warrior. He had entered the room and was standing with his brilliant sword unsheathed. His skin shone with a thousand eyes all over him. I released my breath, which was held captive by greed and lust. The divided longings of duality and fragmentations always have an empty echo. It was the same feeling on that first night, when Smila's moves changed and the water in the glass got murky. I looked at the wine in the glass, wondering if it too would change its hue. It smiled back at me and I reached out to take a healing sip from its liquid rivers of blood beauty. The *shamiana* tent with its appliquéd village stories unfolded itself and fell heavily around me. The atmosphere was beginning to get heavy. The

94

origin of the word atmosphere is from the Sanskrit, atman, meaning the soul. I sat up. My warrior had now sheathed his sword. Bright colored rays beamed from his eyes as they vibrated in and around me. They both seemed to want to continue but hesitated and slowly went back to their places.

I am tired," I told them. I walked to the room. After washing and changing into my nightgown, I peeped in to say good night. They were both in a passionate embrace. They looked at me and asked me if I was sure I wanted to retire for the night. I turned back, closing the door I heard Fiona asking Smila, "You love her don't you?" With the door closed I walked to the window. The streets were lit by the gas lamps.

The light of the moon in the sky was covered by a hazy veil. I missed my lovers. I missed the body of the earth. I missed my grasshopper elephant awaiting art. I missed the uncut diamond before it shone. I missed the flower with its haunting fragrance. I missed the art which will become my weapon and my tool and my power and my flight. I missed Tobias's wild eyes swallowing my whole self and feeding me back my beauty. I missed Miguel's sand body against mine on the shores of Formentera, drenched with wild sounds of *hota*. I missed the setting sun falling on the edge of my sword, so I could slice infinity with the hounding sounds of mortality's nostalgic and sentimental whimpers. All of this I missed, and the largeness and the beauty of the loss when nothing and no one ever actually leaves, and the sight which ignites the unripe fruit so every space is healed and transformed. And I missed Tobias's rugged hands on my thighs. I howled silently and felt the phoenix fly into me. I will rise again and again and again from my own ashes.

The next morning waking up earlier than usual, I put the kettle on. Fiona walked in slightly groggy. I made her a cup of tea and she took one to Smila in the bedroom. She asked me if I slept well. I nodded absentmindedly. "You should have joined us." I looked through her. She looked away uncomfortably. I told Smila that I was going to start packing so I could move to Shane's as soon as possible.

"We can both help," she said.
Wishing them a great day I headed out for my appointments. It was still early and Diego was at the door. He asked me if everything was ok.

As I was walking towards the park, which was now my ritual, I heard quick footsteps right behind me. The night had left me tight and tense. My usual wakefulness seemed shadowed and I was not at ease. My cells were confused. There was an anxiousness and a certain rhythm in them. I looked back but did not see anyone. I was distracted and not centered. My pace slowed down as I entered the park. I looked back again and I was sure I heard footsteps. There was no one in sight. Nervously looking at the time, I quickened my footsteps and headed for the first appointment. Coming out afterwards, I saw someone leaning on the wall of the building. He was waiting for me. There was something familiar in his eyes, and I felt as I had seen or known him before. He looked straight at me with an unfaltering gaze. The eyes were of a deer, wide, clear and fearless. They seemed to penetrate right through me. He knows me, I thought to myself. I mused at these encounters that come to me. A friend once told me that I was too open and that I would always be hurt because of that. I would rather be hurt than walk, wings closed with no entries. My metaphors would be dead and the wealth of life would be unwelcome in me.

I went in to my next appointment without my usual bounce. I handed in my photos and resume, wondering who this person was. I was drawn to him. It felt good. He was following me. Leaving the studio, my pace quickened. This time I headed towards him determined to know what and who he was. He clasped his hands as I approached. "Are you following me?" I asked. He nodded.

"I hope I'm not disturbing you, I saw you at the park the other day looking into the sky mirror in the grass." He said that he had been back to that spot every day since then. "It felt like a fairy tale," he added.

He took my hand warmly, and squeezed it. Energized and feeling my cells happy again, I headed for the next two meetings, one of which was an audition for a voice over. His name was Aakash. I asked him where he was from.

"I just returned from India. I am part Indian and part American. You must be from Bengal."

We both laughed. There were no restraints or tensions. We had known each other for a long time. He was in Pondicherry and spent some time in the Sri Aurobindo Ashram and in Auroville too. That was it. That was our connection. He said that he thought he had seen me there. I showed him my symbol and he smiled.

"I have some more appointments, would you accompany me?" I asked.

He was a soothing warm and healing balm. Leaning into me he said, "May the goddess of wealth appear as close and beautiful to you as air would allow, earth would comfort, water would flow, sky would loom, and may the ether world carry your spirit."

I saw my horse dream of some nights back. Thousands of horses were playing with me and then a beautiful black stallion came very close and rubbed his head against mine. His breath was loud and wet. I felt my power, and all in me re-aligned and got filled with that courage again and I knew that my concerns were with high poetry and source words that either break through commonality or take the ordinary state, enhancing it into other dimensions. It was a metaphysical intelligence, and a formal innovation of poetic beauty. I thought of the Zen saying that consciousness equals creativity in every moment.

I told him about Shane's home and we walked towards it. I showed him the little town house with its magnificent carvings on the edges, tucked in between two rather ominous buildings. I rang the bell and then slid the key in the door. I entered quietly. Aakash followed.

"This is huge," he said as we stepped in.

"Won't you be lonely? "

"I don't know. I met Shane through the friend with whom I have been staying since I came from India and he insisted that I live here since he is hardly ever here. I'm not too comfortable with the whole thing. But I need to be alone. It's getting a little crowded where I am. I need to leave."

We walked through the house. On the first floor were the carpeted den and the library where Shane had had the gathering. It looked different in daylight. It felt dark and foreboding. Aakash looked at the books and commented on how much there was on India.

"That's his big passion, especially Tantra," I answered.

"And you will be his Shakti."

We both laughed. I thought of my childhood and how often my mother reprimanded me and how I longed for her to touch me. My fears are small and they come from childhood restrictions, and not being nurtured in certain ways by my mother at the time because she did not understand. And all the wounds, and hollow cries, and feelings of abandonment that followed, and the uncanny ability to provoke life's wit and wonder, all that which makes one sager, and more humane, and more refined in his soul – life's loftiest goal.

We walked to the bedroom and then upstairs to the meditation room. It was white and bright as the sun poured through the windows. Aakash inched his way towards the altar. He lit incense and moved back. We both closed our eyes and slipped into a deep meditation. To be political is to be in action. I opened my eyes. He was still, like a rooted tree. I saw Kali slicing limbs of ignorance with power and passion. A group of Native American Indians beckoned me to join them on top of a blue mountain. Looking down I saw a lion. The women took me to their hut and painted my body silver and gold, and then drew a blue Om sign on my back. The five circular lines dissolved into me, as rivers rushed in. I held the golden snake in my hand and my back flew open. Silver braids flew through my hair and a naked body dressed in white dissolved into my sunburnt skin, and angels of one million winged desires entered me. My eyes were blue, and red, and brown, and green, and transparent as vast horizons greeted the symbol dawn of Savitri and Satyavan. He opened his eyes and gently kissed my forehead between the eyebrows in my third eye place. I shivered, and took his hands.

"You are my angel," I whispered to him.

"No," he replied passionately, "I am sent by Kali. I am your invisible sword."

We left the room and went downstairs. In the kitchen I got two glasses and filled them with water. The phone rang. It was Shane. He was happy and surprised to hear me. "I just came by to check everything out and wil be moving in on the weekend." He sounded relieved and mentioned that he would love to invite me to New Mexico.

"You would love it," he said. Taking a breath, I thanked him. He welcomed me to his home and we hung up. I noticed Aakash looking at a photograph of Shane.

"He is a handsome man," he said.

"Yes, he is," I replied. "Let this be our secret. You bring India to me. Sometimes the homesickness is unbearable and yet I know I have to be here."

"Yes," he said softly. "You have to."

We walked out and I locked the door checking carefully to make sure all was secure. He did the same. I smiled. He told me that at a certain theater nearby there was a retrospective of Satyajit Ray's films. We walked to a phone booth and he dialed the theater to find out the times. We chose an early showing. I called Smila to let her know I would be late. We talked about the appointments and she told me that there were some calls for auditions. She seemed disappointed, and asked if I was alone. She added that she would have liked to have invited me to some party she was going to, where there would be well-connected and important people.

"I feel a need to be quiet this evening," I replied. I felt like a female Siddhartha who had walked out of her father's kingdom to be a free soul, an animal soul, a breathing soul, a cat goddess, a watcher guardian, and a Sekhmet towering over waters of consciousness. And then, suddenly I felt like a useless child. I felt all the accusations and criticisms, which lashed back at me, all my insecurities, which pricked through my skin leaving scratches and scars. I was sad. Aakash noticed my distractedness. I told him how glad I was to be with him. "So am I," he whispered as he took me to where the theater was. We walked to it. The concrete felt enveloping. I looked for the steaming manholes which burnt me on my entry to this magic city, my turtle island. I told him about my feelings the very first time I entered Manhattan. And about burning my feet and how it resonated with Calcutta.

"That makes so much sense," he said.

We walked past the brass coverings in certain streets, which looked live **Shiva lingams**. I touched the tips sensuously, sacredly. He watched. He was everywhere. People looked at us strangely. I saw a little girl pulling a kite string as red rose petals fell from her cloth pouch, leaving deep horizons and imprints of a flower race. The Gods are alive, everywhere.

Taking a deep breath and looking at me with adoration Aakash said: "Thank you for all you have given me today. I have lived a lifetime in one day. This day when the sky came down to meet the earth and a garland of jasmine was strung into my heart, and when Shiva stood in front of us and with his left hand banishing all fear and with the other destroying the asura. I feel his dance right here," and he touched his heart.

In the theatre he asked me if I had seen the film. "A long time ago, and I remember how struck I was by it. It made me sad," I said. The film began without any nonsensical previews and we both got absorbed in it. Rivers flow out of my mind and I wed the banyan tree roots that grow and reach through earth's many moods.

As the tittles crawled up we stayed till the end. We were silent as we exited the theater. We walked to a simple Tibetan restaurant with beautiful warm colors on the wall. I loved it, and sitting down we looked at the menu. The waitress asked us if we would like anything to drink. I wanted a glass of red wine. He ordered a bottle, carefully choosing an appropriate one. The ambiance echoed the mood of the film. Strong Tibetan chants filled the room. I remembered why I was so saddened by the film when I first saw it.

"I think it is beautiful how the father-in-law sees her in a dream vision, but then to just prop her up and isolate her with such an immense burden was frightening. Rigidity and a blind faith destroyed her."

My heavenly bridegroom had gone crazy. But in my sanctuary, I kept the head and the arms that touched thunder and all my humming birds had alibis and a hundred profound virtues cover my body.

"To love and magic and flight," I said raising my glass to him.

We ordered a variety of things. When the first dish arrived he took a portion and placed it in my mouth. We continued to eat and talk. I asked him what he was doing in New York. He told me photography had been his love since he was very young, and he wanted to expand and learn.

"I am sure your work is amazing."

"I would love to show you."

As we finished dinner, we stepped out into the night air. It was balmy and alive. "I need to head back and prepare for tomorrow when I will make my big move," I told him. He asked me if I needed his help.

"I should be fine. But please come over once I am moved."

I gave him Shane's phone number. He was happy and we walked back to Smila's apartment. On the way he entered a store and came out with a bunch of flowers. They were tuber roses and grew wild in India and had a strong jasmine like fragrance. The flowers kissed me gently. India.

As we neared Smila's building my steps slowed down. I felt the entire weight of what emanated from inside the apartment. I shivered as we continued walking. He knew exactly which building it was. I was not surprised and thought of the cab driver that knew exactly where I was going. "I will be sure not to tell Smila about you or how we met or that you know where she lives. She will panic. I am glad I am leaving. She was the only person I knew when I came. I had met her in India, In Pondicherry. She was different there." We walked towards the entrance of the building.

He took my hands, and looking straight into my eyes said, "Devi."

I looked at the ornate mirror in our bedroom in India with my ears adorned with sacred gold, as my husband touched my face whispering the same word. I was awakened in my own mythology. And the sable antelope stood straight with his head held high, knowing that I was balancing both cultures, which fed each other as I walked into the grassy fields with my face lined with red **sindoor**, the symbol of the bride who was married to one man, while the other who was wed to every call of her creative core. I was scarred and wounded, but every line on my skin was a gift of a growth and a transformation.

Chapter 7: My limbs were torn away from me
As I see the Universe in the mouth of a beggar saint

Diego was happy and relieved to see me, and greeted me very warmly. "I heard you are leaving soon. We will miss you," he said. I thanked him and headed for the elevator. He remembered something and handed me a bunch of flowers. A bouquet of red roses, the wild fragrance of the symphony of my life. They were from Shane. There was a note inside.

On entering the apartment Smila ran to me from her room anxiously. She greeted me warmly and seeing the flowers offered to put them in a vase. After changing and washing and refreshing myself I joined her in the living room with a glass of wine.

"Sorry I missed the party," I told her.

"There were some important people, but it was no big deal. It was actually quite boring and empty."

"You go to so many parties. You must get tired of them."

"I do, but I always feel that I would miss something if I didn't go."

We discussed the move. She offered to drive me to Shane's apartment. "I will miss you," she said with her eyes moist. "And please call me if you need anything. I will keep in touch with you and forward Shane's number to people." I thanked her and told her how grateful I was for all she had done for me, and that I would never forget it. Smila blew out the candles and kissed me goodnight. She said she wished I were not leaving. It was a light nervous kiss.

In my room the already burnt and low candle sent loud shadows on the white and empty walls. I looked around and trembled at all that had happened. I saw what was to come. I closed my eyes. A bird flew into the room. I wondered if it was an eagle or a phoenix. Maybe both. I am in a pearl dress and a necklace falls into the water. A beautiful ebony skinned woman dives in and retrieves the necklace and hands it to me. Opening my eyes I search for my found pearl made transparent by the biography of weeping souls who wounded and haunted, never stopping to wear their magnificent humility like a river of all rivers. I fell asleep. I feel the body of an elephant lying beside me. I feel protected and comfortable. He places his foot on my back, pushing me slightly as though imbuing me with strength. Then he flies out of the window, and the ash of the incense on the altar enters my heart as it sweeps away fear and stagnant thoughts.

Dawn came and I saw the room dance around me in its starched and clean, sterile way. I took in everything gratefully as the fragrance of the tuber roses brought me a lush green tropical garden of morning ragas, and sacred **mantras** were chanted to all the deities who were garlanded in a hypnotic harmony of the song of the self. Stretching, I

101

glided towards the bathroom, and then towards the kitchen for some tea. The pot was already made and pouring a cup I entered Smila's room. She was in bed, but awake. She greeted me warmly and asked if I needed any help. "No I'm good." She said she wanted to return the money my father had given her. I told her that I would like her to use it for the time I stayed with her. She insisted. I continued packing and after a while she came in with a plate of toast. She sat on the bed.

"Am I disturbing you?"

The phone rang. She picked it up. It was Shane. He called to see when we were going to the house. Smila told him how nice it was of him to have me stay in the house.

"I'm going to miss her so much. I wish she wouldn't go. But I understand it will be good for her to be alone. I know I shouldn't but I'm going to be worried about her. Do you want to speak to her? She's packing."

Placing the phone down, she said that he was going to call me later that night. He was really excited about me being there. She went to her room to get ready while I finished packing up the last things, which included the fragrant flowers and the altar. Smila called the doorman to get the car ready. I stood near her altar quietly. We both got everything and headed for the elevator. Remembering the roses, Smila went to get them. "They're for you," I said. Thanking me she placed them next to her altar.

In the lobby the doorman had a carrier ready and ran to help us. Pushing the cart out, he carefully arranged everything in the trunk of the car. I thanked him and handed him a little envelope. He gave me a strong embrace. I love the skin of a graced humanity. The one's touched with simplicity. They are the fabric of the universe. Smila turned and touched my face gently.

"May the harshness of being here in the west and the difficulty of survival never taint you" I thanked her.

We arrived on the East Side and found parking right in front of the house. She commented on how unusual that was and unlocked the trunk. I stood in front of the house which was going to be my next abode, and felt the inhalations of the walls of the building. My fingers slid over their lived surface and moving close to the entrance, I leant towards it when I felt pushed by something. Standing back startled, I saw her. I heard the fast galloping of the stallion as her robe touched me in a gentle sweep. I looked up and sideways but saw nothing, and then in the distant horizon I watched her fading away with her hooded face slightly turned. It was a warning.

Smila had not noticed anything. We took the bags in and she walked up to the bedroom with my things. We both went to the fridge and on opening it found all kinds of fruit and foods and juices in it. "He must have asked the chef to take care of that. Kind of him," she said. She got glasses and said she was familiar with the kitchen. She poured some juice and we sat down at the tree table and looked around.

"I hope you don't get lonely here."

"It's a big house," I replied.

Looking at the time, she said she had better head back as she had many chores to do. She took an envelope from her bag and handed it to me.

"Would you like to meet in the evening after settling down?" she asked.

"I'll call you."

She got up to go and we looked at each other for a while.

"Thank you for everything," I whispered to her.

I followed her out and waited until she drove off. Finishing my drink, I took the flowers and went up to the bedroom. All the windows were closed and everything was very dark. I opened them,and the sun poured in. Finding the appropriate spot, I set up the altar and placed the tuber roses on the table. The cracks opened and coldness entered. I felt raw and calloused. My skin felt roughened and scarred. Was this the birth of the black Madonna within? Was this the start of the walk on the burning stone paths where the heroine of a million silhouettes walked, crawled and arose until she found all the colors of the rainbow in a silver bowl with the full moons, and their sickle births, and the stars rebirthing in the very earth of the sky? Was this the beginning of the journey? Was this going to be another death? Was this the wilderness when all must be faced and walked through, when with eyes, arms, heart, soul and limbs wide open one will have to trace the languid lines of the invisible song lines of the infinite kind? Yes. I felt it. This was where the depth of an ancient culture anchors its myriad tent of a thousand fabrics of knowledge, of relentless perseverance, and where the notes of that unique raga created by a fearless soul began its hallowed notes.

I fell on the bed and touched its well-made perfect ruffles. I felt me sinking into its language of details. I shivered, and sitting up ran my fingers through my hair. I was nervous. Like an Edward Munch painting where the surface bleeds with the inner screams of wounded humanity. There is nothing smooth or easy about his works. His definitions and details are without the ordinary boundaries or external nuances. He delved deep and the scratched surfaces were a threat to the mediocre mind. I closed my eyes.

In my bedroom in India, I was surrounded by friends, and my sweet maid was oiling and combing my hair. The sun poured in on us and the power of my dark long strands pulled my ancestry within my skin. My two carved antelope horns were being sharpened, and my sun burnt skin had dark lines as my lashes felt the piercings of my dual self

103

and my face with sickle moon eyebrows balanced both. And both cultures ran through my carved and rippled horns.

Back in Shane's very luxurious bed I touched my hair again, feeling the fingers of the comb sliding through the pathways and dream lines in my hair. Just then the phone rang. It was Aakash. He asked me if he should come over. Without any hesitation I said yes. I started unpacking. As I hung up the clothes, I came across the magic one, the Tobias dress. And I embraced and kissed it. I felt like wearing it. And the bell rang. I ran down the stairs and opened the door. Aakash was standing there with some more flowers in his hand. I asked him to come in, and offered him some juice. We walked upstairs to the bedroom and he sat down on the carpet next to the altar. He looked at all the images and smiled. I was on the bed near him and there was a silence in the room. He touched the hem of the dress. I told him about Algeria and Tobias. I reminisced about that strange exotic, erotic night of a wooded wedding, where red petals crowded all of me and where my dream people broke through the curtains to celebrate this night of ecstasy. I could see my breath leaving my body but I caught it gently and pulled it back in. It laughed and danced around in glee, like a thousand chorused symphony of a band of an invisible orchestra. Laughing, he told me that I will have a thousand weddings, and a thousand lovers.

"You are Kamala, the courtesan of the universe."

"Are you my brother, my friend or my lover?" I asked him.

"I am all of those, if you let me be them. Let's go out tonight and celebrate Tobias, who married you in the desert."

We went downstairs and, making sure the flowers were in water, I took the keys and slipped on some light sandals. It was dusk again, and the evening light touched our faces. We looked at each other and walked towards the park. We ran and stepped on steaming manholes. We burnt our feet. We laughed. We watched grasshopper elephants in human form and we saw the monarch butterfly. It was trapped on concrete and we looked at each other and felt the pain in the heart of many spaces that precedes the pain that awaits art..

In the park we leaned against trees and caressed their ageless bark. We found images in the concrete and a little sapling pushed its way skywards, surviving in stone and never forgetting its own very fertile soil. We had met again.

"You see and I see you seeing, and the rays go through and you reassure me. And I listen like a child."

As these words left my mouth, I had a dream. I am naked, watching the trees weaving into the night light of the fragrant circle of the moon.

Back at the house I made a pot of tea. We walked up to the bedroom. Washing and changing I sat on the bed and stretched out. He asked me to relax as he rubbed my feet. He lit the candle on the table near the bed. I fell asleep. Aakash looked around and just next to the bed lying open was my cloth journal. I had left it open. I heard his voice whispering the words on the page. "I am ether. A wind being where nowhere had I rested. I am the observer of tradition and familiarity, and the safeness and richness is in the magic of my own being." While he had been reading I opened my eyes and watched him. He was not aware and quietly wiped his eyes. I gently stroked his head and turning he said, "Sleep, I will be in the other room." The phone rang, but I did not pick up. I fell asleep again as Aakash left the room.

The morning light cast interesting shadows and shapes on the walls. I remembered, I remembered that I could not remember. My hand reached out for my **shamiana** marriage tent, the transparent rainbow tent where my godheads lived. They are me as I walk in mud and slush and stagnant waters and as I remember again the diamond in my nose and walk towards the water bowl in the middle of this heavy, drenched, faltering space. And in the middle of the bowl floats one hundred and one lotus flowers and, touching them, I become them.

The phone rang and I picked up. It was Shane. He asked how I was feeling. I told him I was getting used to the surrounding bigness of it. "It is a cozy home, when you get used to it" he said. He started to talk about New Mexico. He seemed very anxious and asked when he could book a flight. I told him I would think about it and call him later on.

"Have a great day and please help yourself to whatever is in the fridge," he said.

Feeling the fabric of the tent within me I arose slowly and walked to the bathroom, softly closing the door. Before showering, I lit some incense and placed it in the holder on the table. Faint refrains of some vocal Indian classical sounds filled the air and I entered the library, making sure not to wake Aakash. Going down to the kitchen I put the kettle on and looked for breakfast things to arrange on a tray. I decided to call Shane and take him up on his offer. He was delighted and said he would make arrangements immediately. I felt the trees on the table and opening the fridge, I looked for the appropriate tea, fruits and some eggs. Waiting for the water to boil I walked around. There were some amazing works of art everywhere -- Ancient Indian and African masks, miniature paintings – they were rich, and stunning. The phone rang again. It was Smila this time. She was warm, and I told her that I had had a great rest and was getting familiar with the new surroundings. "I miss you," she said. There was a silence that was interrupted by Smila saying that she hoped she would see me soon. Wishing her a strong day I took the tray and walked up carefully to the library. Aakash was lying with closed eyes. Watching him I sipped some tea and gently stroked his hair. He smiled. I handed him a cup. "Darjeeling?" Taking the cup he first took a big whiff and with

105

a deep longing sigh took his first sip. "Delicious." He noticed the tray and mentioned how beautiful it looked. " Shane called last night and invited me to visit New Mexico where he is and I decided to accept the offer. I feel I need to see that place." Aakash was silent.

"I dreamt of you last night," I told him.

He propped himself up, all eager to hear it.

"Before or after breakfast?" I asked.

"Now," he said.

"I was walking in a vast space. It could have been a village in India. There were some kids around and they came to me. They told me that they wanted to show me something. They seemed very anxious and were pulling me. We walked for a while. Some of them skipped and circled around while leading me to the place. And there in the distance, sitting on an isolated little hill, was a beautiful blue body. The sun was shining down. I stopped in amazement. They beckoned me on and I walked very slowly, almost in a daze, and approached the figure. It was Krishna in blue with a crown on his head and a flute in his hands. I could not move and then he turned slowly and, looking at me, smiled and called me to get close. It was you. We all sat around you. You asked me to sit next to you and you played the most melodious notes and then the phone rang and I awoke."

He had his eyes closed while I was relating the dream. Opening them he slid down from the couch, and sitting in front of me took my face in his hands and put his forehead to mine and looked straight into my eyes. I looked back, and all the ancient colors penetrated through every cell of my being. The isolated clouds moved gracefully within this radiant inner sky. And the chorus of crows and the peacock in all its glory cleaned the soul. And the elephant, winged and huge, broke and uprooted dark weeds of a stuttering and doubting mind, where believing was a foreign word and trust was an unknown sound, and where the child's gaze was long gone and withered into the empty nights of a vagrant and empty existence of absolute finality – a finality where there were no risks and where age and death became the only reality of a very sad and pathetic life.

The room suddenly filled with the chants of Om, and I see a million and one shooting stars as beams of light hold the sky and the earth rejoices with abundance and joy. It is the celebration of sight.. And it is the roar of the white tiger and the howling wolf as they jump through my opened third eye. My back is ripped apart and as I move carefully to make sure only the sky can enter, a black cat with a cut tail approaches and sits close by, pushing his purring body against my back, as though to shield the entrance. I am home. His eyes are my mirror. He looks deep into me and sees my bride-self, as he places the red sindoor on my parted hair line. Is he my groom, manifested here to remind me that I will never walk alone? I wiped my eyes and looked at him again.

"Are you my groom?" I whisper.

He nods. " We will dance together, and we will be born again and again. We are the ultimate twins, the echo of each other as we dream each other."

My bride-self and my warrior walk. This is the canvas and these are the colors. Pain and loss bleed on this magical tapestry. My journey has begun.

Sitting in a cab the next morning, with Aakash next to me and the sounds of Om still ringing in my ear, we were heading for JFK. I looked at him. He was looking ahead and touched my fingers. I will miss him. He will miss me. He had insisted on taking me to the airportAt the airport Aakash walked me to the airline that was heading to Albuquerque in New Mexico. I checked my bag and we sipped hot tea together. "Be careful," he said, "and have a beautiful time. Call me when you can."

In the plane, looking out with mixed feelings, the vast expanse of land opened up as the plane approached Albuquerque, the main airport in New Mexico. The earth was many shades of red. Tobias and his eyes seeped into me. Taking a deep breath, I felt the red petals that he had placed so carefully on me after we sang our ecstatic love song. I was nervous and looked again out the window. I thought I saw my stallion rider on the land, her black horse etched into the earth. We landed. I was excited.

Entering the terminal, I saw Shane and waved. He looked very brown. The sun seemed to have burnt its trace very visibly on him, shaping his cheekbones and the lines on his face. His hair was pulled back in a long ponytail. It was clasped with a silver and turquoise ring. His rugged blue jeans sat tight on his thighs, and his cowboy boots were elegant and strong. He was thrilled to see me and embraced me warmly. "Finally, you made it." He asked about the flight and if everything was fine in New York. We walked towards the baggage claim section. I pointed to my bag and he picked it up. I commented on the spaciousness of the airport. "Wait until you see the land," he said.

He had a jeep and, placing the bag in the back, he opened the front door for me. Getting in the car he took a deep breath and looked at me intensely. His eyes were taking all in. I liked the depth in his eyes. I was a little startled as he bent towards me and blindfolded me. "Just until we reach the outskirts of the city," he said. It was a silk scarf. I relaxed and leaned back and surrendered to the ride. "I am so happy to see you here." The silken darkness was opaque with some lines of light quietly seeping through. I felt a dream call and closing my eyes walked into a space of trees with their barks forming a sculpture. . The sun filters through their silent bodies and they cast magnificent shadows on the ground. All the cells of the earth dance haloed to the caress of their deep and relentless and ageless roots. The fragrant jungle of lion and tiger as they stride with grace to win their individual victory after waiting with patience for the exact moment to execute. Yes, because impatience, they say, is the biggest sin. I am quiet. My eyes are still closed when suddenly the heels and toes of both of my feet tingle and I remember that they contain the subtle channels through which the primal energy enters the physical body.

The light was blinding as he slipped off the silk scarf from my eyes. The Devi who was the enchantress of the universe entered me and I became her. My eyes opened to the mystery of life, and of the deep compassion that comes after traveling through the agony of ignorance and mediocrity and the spineless sighs of the faltered eye that pretends to be what it cannot be. Ignorance has a strange manifestation when feet are deformed and hands do not resemble the grace of the roots and their physicality howls another scream. The chords are missing and the notes are false. My eyes got accustomed to the light as the peacock danced on clay, and a silent quiver entered my heart.

I was the story of this land and many lands, where holy men painted holy women and where true art was not made for a stroll with the eyes but for screaming through, when the world was filled with glory and the third way of seeing was and will be born.

The land was breathtaking. I stepped out of the van and he walked me to a clearing. I bent down to touch the dirt. It was red in my hands. It bled through the henna markings and India and this land mirrored back to me. I thanked him for inviting me. "It is as you said: absolutely beautiful." He told me of the huge Native American presence here and that there were many areas which were sacred to the Indians.

"You look like them."

"What tribe?" I asked him.

"What comes to mind is Navajo," he said.

"Navajo, I love them. I am them."

"How do you know of them?"

"They are my warriors," I said

He told me of Canyon de Chelly, which was the Navajo heartland where Spider Woman lived. She was honored and worshipped as the goddess of creativity. We got back into the van and drove through momentous landscapes that were New Mexico, the land of enchantment. It was quiet inside the van. Shane had a smile on his face as he watched my reactions. He asked me if he was right to insist on my coming. I told him that he was absolutely right. As we were nearing Santa Fe he spoke about it and that it was much more isolated some years ago. We entered the main square when I noticed a beautiful Indian woman sitting in front of a tree, her white hair flowing. She was a vision clothed in turquoise. I asked Shane to stop and walked straight to her and sitting in front of her bowed my head. I saw the woman saint in India near the temple married to the walls with her mouth open, the universe inside. Closing my eyes, I fell into a deep meditation. The eagle flies above me as he pierces his feathers into my smoke-filled iris of spheres and fields of burning sacred sage. I feel Garuda's shiny golden body with his red wings pushing me as he takes flight. The mythic life weaves her mystery and magic in me and she touches my hand lightly.

She removed seven turquoise chains from her neck and put them on me. The street prophet with his warm face and mapped interior in the cab in New York had told me of this and here it was. I was in awe. How magnificent is this wolf wild howl walk of abalone daydreams and visions of the other reality, where all is continuous and ever present. I touched the sacred stones and felt the nape of my neck where my fingers had traveled guided by Tobias's passion, when I had felt all the symbol arms of Kali. I searched in my bag for something. She stopped me. I removed the ancient tribal dancing silver bracelet on my left arm and put it on her. We looked into each other's eyes in deep recognition. She touched the beads and said in broken English: "It is the protection for your soul. It is peace." And then smiling, she rose and slowly walked away. I sat still and watched her glide into the very same sage fields which had cleansed and healed me one thousand and one times. Shane brought me back and touching my shoulder said, "That was beautiful." Getting up I looked at him and thanked him. We walked to the van. He slowly drove around the town square on to his home. The drive and the home was magical.

"This is it."

"This is absolutely exquisite. It is earth and stone."

He said that this particular house was one of the original old ones created by the Native Americans before European-Americans settled the area and that he was very fortunate to get it. We entered and the inside was as exquisite. There was a courtyard with small windows and arch-ways. He had it set up beautifully, minimally and yet lushly furnished. He invited me in and asked me to make myself comfortable while he unloaded the van. I touched the grained walls and glanced out of the window.

The sky spoke. It was like the ocean. It had a language of its own.

Shane showed me my room and gave me a tour of the whole house. He asked me if I would like to take a shower and maybe rest. A rest would feel good, and he told me that he had arranged to go to a special place for dinner. Holding my face lightly, he whispered softly that he was so happy. I thanked him. He said he had a few things to do in town and that if the phone rang I should just ignore it. Closing the door, I looked around and started to unpack. The altar was arranged. The room felt very sensual and skin-toned. I decided to take a bath. I walked to the window and looked at the vast sky. As the water was flowing, I made some entries in my cloth journal. Closing the book and taking care of the candle and incense,, I entered the bathroom and undressing slipped into the water. It was warm, embracing, and relaxing. After the bath, walking towards the bed I noticed that it had been turned and there were some wild flowers on the pillow. I slid under the covers as the fragrant dry flowers touched my face. My cloth journal fell on the rug and opened. I felt its pages walking in me. The evening light streamed in and through my closed eyes the colors rained inside of me. I remembered Aakash. I felt Tobias. I heard Miguel's rugged sonorous voice singing to me, and I saw my groom in India soothing me by reading some of Tagore's poems after some harsh words from my mother-in-law All my lovers sailed through me and reminded me of mystics and seekers of a higher consciousness.

Shane woke me with a gentle knock and placed a beautiful glass of red wine in my hands. The soma of the gods, I thought when Garuda traveled far and wide to find it and bring it back so his mother could be released. He sat on the floor and we raised our glasses. It was robust and had a dry earth feeling to it. Looking at the time I realized it was late. Shane told me to enjoy the wine and come down when I was ready. "Smila called. She wanted to see if you had arrived safely." There was a smirk on his face. I wondered how she had known that I was here, as I did not remember telling her. He said he had mentioned it to her. I found that strange, too, but gave it no thought. Getting up languorously, I walked to the closet to choose a dress for the evening. In the bathroom I put **kajal** around my eyes. This kohl that is of nature and earth and that always surrounds my eyes like a conscious wreath of knowing and protection. It holds my sight through forest trees, whose spirits enter me and embrace my seeking. And brushing energy in my hair, I walked back to the bedroom. I wore a dress whose colors were transparent and caught the rays of the setting sun. I was glowing. Sitting down, I looked at the night table and sipped from the glass on the floor. Suddenly I felt a shiver down my spine. A little afraid I looked around feeling a presence. It was like a warning and seemed alien to this land. It didn't belong here. Walking towards the closet I got my shawl. I shivered again. I looked around again and then stood for a while in the middle of the room as though stopped by something or someone. I felt as though an invisible form was in front of me blocking my way and frightened, I walked around it.

I was in my mosquito net bed in India. Tropical night sounds filled the room. There was a magical stillness. Suddenly, I sat up sweating and gasping. My husband started up and in Bengali asked what had happened. I told him I felt some kind of danger, as though something was going to happen. He looked around trusting my intuitive nature and was concerned. He consoled me saying that it could have been just a bad dream. He said he would ask the temple priest to do a special puja the

110

next morning. I bent down to get the glass of water on the low table as he pushed himself against me and coiled his limbs around me. I curved into his limbed embrace passionately.

I stooped down for the glass of red now on the floor and taking a long sip walked towards the door, looking back as I closed it. Shane walked towards me and straightened the hem of the dress which was slightly curled. I walked toward the flowers and thanked him for the ones on the bed. He led me towards the door and we walked out towards the car. The sky was aflame like a burning heart pierced by a single lit arrow. He drove slowly on the narrow dirt roads. I loved them. I spoke about what I had felt in the room and that it was almost like there was someone there with me. He listened, and said that he knew I would feel many things as the land held many sacred secrets. "It is old and ancient and it whispers." I was uncomfortable. It was not familiar. He looked at me and said he would sage the room.

We arrived at the restaurant, and sat near the fireplace. He explained to me that desert nights were often cool. The fire soothed me with its leaping flames. He ordered and we sipped the wine and relished the dinner. The conversation revolved around tantra and sensuality.

"Why **tantra**?" I asked him.

"Because It is a practice where energy is awakened and the body travels beyond the body and becomes the vehicle to reach the soul."

"Like a cobra which has cast its coils, spiraling conch-like three times and a half round Siva, her mouth laid on that other mouth, which leads to bliss, the enchantress of the world, slender as a lotus stem, bright as a lightening flash, lies sleeping, breathing softly out and in, murmuring poems in sweet meters, humming like a drunken bee in the petals of the **muladhara** lotus and how brightly her light shines," I added.

He listened with eyes closed and told me the first time he had seen me he knew that I was the one. He explained that the reason **tantra** was so fascinating for him was because it broke all boundaries and layers of lust and greed, and that it was often misused because of the nature of its sensuality. As we continued the dinner he recited a quote from a book he had been reading, titled *Gods of Love and Ecstasy: The Traditions of Shiva*.

"The experience of absolute light, when attained through **maithuna**, or sexual union, is capable of penetrating right to the heart of organic life and of discovering there too the divine light, that primordial brilliance which created the world. The light experienced in maithuna is the Clear Light of gnosis, and of Nirvana consciousness."

He poured me more wine and my eyes wandered out of the room to the window. We finished the rest of the meal in silence as though savoring the thoughts and words. He asked me if he spoke too much and added that he was often wary of over-thinking concepts and ideas. "It is in the action," I whispered softly. He agreed, and as we finished the delicious meal he asked for the check. He asked me if I wanted to sit by the fire.

"I would love to," I replied softly. We sat on the couch and he looked into my eyes. I turned my gaze away. I moved into the fire and dissolved into the flame of one of the lamps in the temple in India.

My husband and I were sitting as the priest chanted prayers and mantras. He told the priest about my strange dream. The priest blessed me and gave me the Prasad of flowers and sweets. The image of Kali stared into me as her fierce visage filled me with strength and courage. I love her; I adore her relentless sword and her bleeding compassion. I love her skull necklace of threaded humanity and its ignorance as she slices all that shuns light. I feel the flames burning me with her gaze. I forget where I am.

Slightly disoriented I remembered where I was when Shane's hands fell on my shoulder. I asked him if we could leave. He immediately started up and helped me. Goddess **Kali's** presence engulfed me and I felt as though she had entered me.

Almost slipping, I held Shane's arm as we walked towards the car. He asked if I was okay.

Entering the house we were both very quiet. There was a musky heaviness in the atmosphere. He was anxious. I was a little uncomfortable but much more relaxed. He poured himself some more wine and asked me if I wanted some more. I nodded and walked up the stairs leading up to the room saying that I wanted to freshen up. He played some classical Indian music and I paused at the head of the stairs, appreciating the choice with a smile. Entering the room I looked around cautiously in anticipation of the feeling that I had had before. I lit the candle and incense on the table near the bed. In the mirror, my eyes looked distant, like a cat goddess purring and cleaning herself with a haunting memory of a sacred marriage in the desert dream lines of some ancient land. Pulling myself to the present I started to walk downstairs when Shane entered with some burning sage. He said he wanted to show me his room. I followed him. It was beautiful.

"A tantra tent," I said.

He sat on the floor and, looking up at me, touched my feet. He lifted them in his hands and the anklet bells sung. "Your feet are beautiful. They are erotic and sublime." He was hungry. And I felt a dawn breaking through my pores. My skin was alive and a collage of all the ragas combined within me as the snake started uncoiling inside. I was surrendering to the possibility of a very well-crafted and manipulated journey within an architecture of sensuality. A house and a structure I was familiar with. He slowly caressed my legs and thighs and placed them on the bed. I felt made and molded inside a potter's skilled hand. I felt the kiln of elegance trying to shape me into an image that was other than me, and the surrender walked in as the wild woman stretched her paws and sensed something new and dangerous, but heeded not, and she prowled on into this jungle of a calculated bliss. He kissed and touched all of me. He whispered words of passion and longing. He sighed and groaned as though lifting a hooded mountain of delight and pleasure. But he was not my **Hanuman**. I was one with my limbs and body. We were in harmony.

I have never felt a duality. Soul and body always sung within me, fearful to those to whom physicality is shunned and stamped upon inside dark and hidden caves. I am a temple of Khajurao in India and carved on my body are the stone carvings depicting the Purusha Arthas of Kama, the god of love, passion, and sensuality, and who must be transcended to reach the inner being, which is the soul. A gush of wind walked through the room and the raga took a different turn as he thirsted inside me. His gentle passion turned into an aggressive and hounding craving for more and more. Tantra and all its mysteries were lost. His hands were sticky with greed. His tongue had lost its sword. His breath was heavy and weighed down by lust and self-indulgent decadence. Magic sat sadly with her transcendent head in her hands, as she wept the tears of someone who had been betrayed and manipulated. And the carvings on the body of the temple softly shunned this invasive intruder who tried too hard, and forgot that selfishness never runs too far, and that all true seeing is a mastery of a selflessness of the bamboo flute. I heard galloping hoofs. I started. He stopped and was disturbed. I did not see her, but I felt her, and knew she had entered the room. The Indriyas, the ten senses, had been jarred and a harmony was lost. The climactic moment was thunderous and tainted. A bird flew out of my mind and entered my heart. He touched my face. I turned my eyes away from his. He was wet and hot and breathless. I was hurt and opened and bleeding with all the one hundred and eight **rudraksha** beads strung inside of me. I felt nothing except ravaged and red petals falling over me to rescue and heal me. I sat up a little dizzy and, gathering my things, started to rise. He wanted me to stay. I wanted to leave. In the room I washed carefully and going to bed lie down and burst into sobs and howling wails. I could not stop. My entire being body shook.

I was sitting alone in the temple in India looking at the image of Kali, my eyes wet with tears. My husband sat next to me. He saw my moist cheeks and asked me why. I told him that I felt that same strangeness in the night again. It was very uncomfortable. I felt like I was being used. He looked confused and asked how that could be. I didn't know. I just didn't know.

The next morning, I was awoken by a knock and Shane walked in with a superb tray of delicacies. He set it near the bed and, sitting down, said he was so sorry as he felt he really got carried away. "You took me into my senses and out of my senses. I have never felt that before. I hope I was not too rough with you."

I told him that I needed to rest. He placed a flower near me and left the room. I pushed the flower away from the bed. I was hurt and confused. I reached out for my cloth book and entered these words: *I feel vulnerable and weak and here was another death. I gave into a choreographed seduction. My regret is that I was attracted to a concept and an appearance because it was layered with sprit and depth and not true. I did not see it. But there was a reason for me to experience this, too, and maybe I was exposed to things in myself that I otherwise would not have seen. I must see. I will see.*

Finishing the tea and, looking out at the blue sky, I put the tray down and decided to have a long and healing bath. I walked to the bathroom and ran the water. Entering the warm water, I relaxed and my eyes closed. Aakash was standing there in a Shiva pose. I opened my eyes and must have let out a scream because Shane knocked and asked if I was okay. "I will be down shortly," I replied. I chose something white to wear. The room downstairs was empty, and rays of light sculpted the space. I found a spot where the sun flooded in and sat in those rays and looked out. I fell into the sun. Shane came in. He seemed uncomfortable and told me about some plans for the day. He described a place just a little outside of the New Mexico border where the dunes lay with miles and miles of endless sand. He added that there was Indian Reservation and he wanted to take me there.

"I would love that," I said.

He said that he would fix a picnic basket with lots of water. He asked me to take something warm as the evening temperatures really dropped. I ran up to get my Moroccan wedding shawl, that same shawl given to me by the people of Taman asset. He commented on its beauty. "Yes this, is my wedding shawl," I answered. A little surprised he asked me if I was married before. "Many times," was my answer. He looked puzzled. I looked back and my eyes sliced through him. Gathering my things, we walked out into the sun-scape.

The land was like a lover. He told me how beautiful last night was for him. I did not reply. We left the towns and went into the land. Coyotes were running off with amazing speed. He told me they were of the wolf family. I thought of Clarrisa Pinkola's book, *Women Who Run with the Wolves*. We were silent. Suddenly he spoke. "Last night was aflame. I felt as though everything around me and in me was touched by fire."

And I reflected on Passion and its many layers and meanings. It is like holding the universe within and without you. It is like seeing and feeling and touching all the senses. It is like the force of a huge wave which falls back into the ocean with all the white foam spreading across the waters. It is the melting and merging of all physicality and boundary into a seamless miracle. It is the ecstasy of consciousness when every cell is awake; and above all, it is the selfless surrender to all that comes to you. Passion is the essence of the universe, breathing and alive.

He told me we were nearing the Dunes. It was breathtaking. He led the way to a growth of trees before entering the Dunes. The basket was set down, and, putting a cloth on a fallen tree branch, he invited me to sit. He poured a cup of tea before we began the walk. It was warm and rich. It was the milk of a lost night. He then put his cup down and started to roll a joint. I noticed him turn around slightly while doing this and just for a moment wondered why. He lit it and took a deep breath. He offered it to me and I asked him what it was. He said it was some very good quality grass. "I don't smoke," I told him. He insisted and said that this was very pure. Hesitatingly I took a light drag. He offered me more tea. "We should walk up," he said. I got up eagerly and ran into the dunes. We walked for a while and as we got higher the sky opened up into a vastness of blue. He got very close and held me by the shoulder.

"I feel strange and uncomfortable," I told him. He got closer.

"I feel as though I cannot breathe." I started to speed up and he began to run after me, not knowing what was happening. My pace increased. I felt an eerie presence following me, wanting to trap me and suffocate me. Sweat was pouring down me. All of me was getting wet and my white dress started to cling to me preventing my run, almost strangling me. Everything was enclosing around and in me. The God heads were leaving me and I started a wild scream. The sand rippled from the sound of my wounded howl, and shapes were forming in them with strange emanations. I felt mad. I watched my mind, my very soul running out of me. Fear enveloped me and I began taking off my clothes and all that covered me. I ran even faster, stumbling, falling, rising, running, falling, crawling, and rising again. By now the sand had become my cloth. Every single grain was entering me and I screamed even louder. The only thing that I did not let go of was the wedding shawl. The history of the fabric with its rugged ancient stories was holding my sanity. I was a hunted wolf who had forgotten his way. The shawl started to leave me too and desperately I clung on to it and held it tight in my fingers. Shane was now next to me and suddenly grabbed my sacred symbol from my naked body and started to rip it off. He managed to tear it off and it fell on the sand, shining as it dropped within the folds of the ripples in the body of the dunes. I screamed and shouted and wrenched it from the sand. He caught up to me and said he was just helping me as he thought I did not want anything on me. The wind was running with me. I spoke to the wind Gods and the sand Elves and the Moon goddess and pleaded them to help me. And then suddenly something stronger than me pulled me and I fell into the hot sand and could not move. All became motionless. I tried to rise but could not. My limbs were torn away from me. The energy of the Gods had abandoned me and I was alone and empty and without vision. And then suddenly all changed and I heard my breathing soften and with eyes now shaded with sand I saw next to my face a solitary desert flower. It was pink and stood right next to my eyes. My gaze was fixed. I could not look away from it. In my hand was the necklace and the shawl was next to me. As I watched the desert flower slowly turned into a beautiful pink lotus and I knew then that all was back. Nothing had left me. In my small humanity I thought that the Gods had betrayed me because of my fear and my weakness. Looking back, I saw Shane approaching me. Fear started walking in again and I tried to rise but was not able to do it. He fell down near me and started to put his hand on me. I shrugged it off and with tears in my eyes asked him what he had given me to smoke, and why had he ripped off my symbol. He was confused and stunned and said he had just put something in the joint to give me a little boost. I looked at him, shocked. He was in tears and said that he had no idea I would react like that, and that the reason why he removed the necklace was because he saw me taking everything off and thought that I would feel better with nothing on. I continued to stare at the flower, getting calmer and quieter. Shane put the shawl over me and walked back to find my clothes. I tried to rise again but felt numb and without any power. Just then I heard that sound again. Now the galloping was muffled by the sand. Shaking within and trembling all over I looked around. Very near, almost touching me, the black shiny body of the stallion appeared. Speechless and breathless, I looked up and there she was: the winged heaven warrior, my mystic messenger. Her face was covered. Her presence tore into me. She had come to save me and this time to give me my life back, I knew that. All that I thought had left me slid back in. My limbs were being given back to me and my heart was now protected. Looking up, I longed to see her veiled face. It was not time yet but slowly her hand appeared and touched me. I tried to take it but she was gone. I started to rise as though the initiation of the mighty bird had winged my soul. The grains of the sand fell off my skin as my body glistened naked in the piercing rays of the sun. The lotus petals had wet drops on them like glistening pearls of a mirrored heart. There was no rain. These drops broke the glass of wisdom and knowledge into a transparent knowing and then the lotus once more became that wild desert flower and the leaves were still wet. I sat up. My spine spoke. My eyes cleared. My sacred triangle of gold was back on my neck. My wedding shawl was on me and I stood up in the bed of the sand as it caressed my feet and the Elves licked my sanded body with their spear tongues. The shawl fell away and my tree trunk felt soft and tight and barked and smooth. I touched me and felt the heavens sigh with relief. I was back.

116

Fear had left me. The light around was warm and dusk was setting in. Shane was approaching. I watched him and saw all the manipulation and selfish lust devouring his own interiors. He walked up to me and gave me the clothes.

"Can you please forgive me?" he asked.

I started to walk down. He was sad, embarrassed, and confused. I felt his lies. He walked back up and picked the flower in the sand. I was in the car and in my clothes. He offered me a cup of tea and the flower. My mouth was trembling and parched. The hot liquid soothed me.

I told him that I wanted to go to the reservation.

We drove in silence as the light changed. I saw his discomfort and regret. He felt my frailty and my strength. I wrapped the shawl even closer to me. He commented on how attached I was to it.

"It reminds me of Tobias."

"I am jealous of his presence."

"You should be," I murmured.

We were approaching the Reservation. I was excited. As we got nearer, he saw someone familiar and, stopping the car, got out and walked towards him. He had lost his grace. His face had changed. It was devoid of its youth and the lover in him had left him. His lips warped. I had never seen that. It was like a Smila smile, haunted by a stagnant and murky desire of the empty, ugly kind. The taking and the greed of the night before had left tracks and scars on his aquiline face, which now was distorted with regret and insecurity. I was sad. Getting into the car he said we could go in with no problems. "Some days they do not allow any outsiders." He parked the car and we entered. People were going about their business. Many of the Indians looked at me and smiled in recognition. They were of the Sioux and Crow tribes. I felt a sense of familiarity and elation. Fires were burning everywhere, and people sat around them talking. I suddenly saw the same elder woman whom I had seen in the Santa Fe courtyard. Shane was taken aback too. I walked confidently towards her. She was sitting quietly in front of her little home. She had a distant look about her and seeing me her eyes lit up in recognition. I fell at her feet and wept. People looked but kept a respectful distance. She gently took my head and face. Then she led me into her humble home and had me sit down on a small divan. She lit a candle and a bundle of sage in an abalone shell, and started to smudge me carefully. My eyes closed. The smoke filled my cells. I was being cleaned. Shane was standing outside, looking in. She leant into me and, placing her right hand on my stomach, whispered something in my ears. I started back at what she had told me and the secret, sacred message seeped into me. I slowly rose and, holding both my hands, respectfully walked backwards towards the door. Reaching the door, I gave her a last glance and, head bowed, started to walk away. Shane joined me and we headed towards the car.

There was tightness in the car as the night sounds engulfed and surrounded us. The sage was everywhere. I was carried by it. The streams of the smoke had entered my eyes and the white wolf spoke to me in the language of its tribe. I was welcomed. When we reached the house I went up to my room telling him that I needed to rest. He asked if he could prepare anything warm to eat for me. Thanking him, I told him I would have a hot bath and go to bed. At the door he hesitated and, taking my hands, asked me again if I could ever forgive him. In the room I lit incense and placed it on the little table. Sitting down on the floor beside the bed and the table, I reached for my cloth book and held it in my hands. The texture of the cover is my mind with dreams and journeys of birch trees and their barked skin. Its inner weight moistened my eyes and tears flew as my sight blurred and my limbs felt soft. My bones were weeping. My barriers were down. I was in a landscape of betrayal and abandonment and devastated by someone I thought I trusted. I felt like a defenseless infant. I was blinded and could not see the shadows, even though I felt them at times. One more death and this time it was not going to be easy to rise again.

My eyes went back to the book as I scanned all the different entries, and my fingers begun to carve: *I feel as though my sacredness is at rest. The torn bark branch staff slipped through my hands. My hands trembled and could not hold the tree. I feel grief inside my skin. My heart feels rough. I hear myself weep as I weep outside myself. I am tired. My fingers move and speak of life. I hold my dreams and cry for more. The woman in me has seen all it can see and yet the woman in me knows I have much more to see. I cry and yet I cannot cry. I laugh and yet I cannot laugh. I will survive. I will ascend. My sacredness will awaken.*

Book Two:
Sacrifice

Chapter 8: Pregnant and slaughtered in a palace of wealth

Closing the book and rising up with my liquid bones, I walked to the bathroom and filled the tub. I stood in front of the mirror and stared at my reflection. I leaned forward into the glass. I saw something behind me and glanced back. I returned to my reflection. The face was tired. The eyes were haunted. **Ondine** sees water as she swallows her eyes. The water calls her. She is the water princess and she has left her liquid earth to find herself and she knows she cannot turn back. She looks tired and worn as though she has just come through a long journey. I am Ondine. She is me.

I undressed and caressed my body with care and love. I felt all the child hood scars pricking me and I will tear them off one by one and the stem will be smooth again. The monsoon rains will fall fiercely and the world will rejoice. In the water, closing my eyes, I felt the air of my winged rider. She was very near. I *will not be disrespectful. She will show me her visage when she knows I am ready. Her hands are on my head as the light pierces through my crown chakra and a great wave of relief and peace invades me.* I felt the hands of the Mother molding my head like a clay dough ball when I was seven in the ashram in Pondicherry. It was the same tide of veined leaf ether whispers flowing down my insides. I felt the leaves prick as they flowed through my veins and became my blood.

In front of Shane's townhouse I searched for the keys. I entered warily. I was tired and sad. The place was heavy and dark. Walking in, I noticed flowers on the table and wondered if the Japanese chef had placed them there. The phone rang. It was Shane. He enquired about the flight and the house. He said he had asked the chef to have the flowers to welcome me back. I thanked him. There was an obvious silence as he asked me to forgive him once again. He wanted to know if he had lost me. How can you lose something or someone you never had? How can you possess the air and the earth and the rain and the free, fluid ocean waves and the howl of the wolves and the whispers of the birds and the quiet growth of the shaded, wandering vine leaves as they move and grow in their silent grace? How? I thanked him again and, putting the phone down, I dialed Akaash's number. I left a message. I started to go upstairs when the phone rang and I ran to the bedroom to pick it up. It was him. I burst out crying.

"I want to see you now. I could not call from there. It was impossible. When are you leaving for the west coast?"

He was on his way. Putting the phone down, I listened to the messages. Some calls for auditions and many from Smila. I picked up the phone again to call her but hesitated. I didn't want to talk to her, not yet at least. I quickly unpacked and placed the journal on the bed. I touched it. Just then the doorbell rang. I ran down to open the door, out of breath. There he was, wearing a beautiful Indian kurta and looking exquisite. We rushed into each other's arms as I sobbed with joy. Walking back into the house I offered him some water and we walked up. He was watching me. I felt his eyes walk into me. They entered with a gentle moistness, like the rose petals I once had swallowed. We sat in the library. I shivered. It was damp and cobwebbed with stagnant thoughts and desires and wants and needs. He told me how, achingly, he waited for me to call.

"I just could not Aakash. It was impossible." "What happened there?"

I began to tell him all that took place. He touched my hair and sliding his fingers through it, separated each thread of energy. He was crying. We sat in silence together for what seemed a long time. He told me he was leaving for the west coast the next day. I felt an ache inside me.

"I will miss you," I said.

Aakash stayed the night and left early. He walked away quietly. Waking up I felt unwell. I walked to the bathroom and wanted to throw up. I tried but couldn't. Coming back to the bed I lay down and closing my eyes remembered what the Indian woman in New Mexico had whispered in my ear. I was afraid. My eyes opened and I placed my hands on my stomach. I realized what she may have meant and suddenly was filled with anxiety and fear. I remembered, I remembered that I could not remember. The black stallion entered the room. He was alone. His head was bent and his nostrils wet mine. *I will transform in and with my life. I will own back myself. I will dissolve all the excess thoughts of self-lashings, of self-hatred, of self-judgment, of not believing.* I have no more time to waste. I felt like I had taken a pill or bitten into a special mushroom. The surreal ran around me and in me, and the paintings of Dali and Max Ernst and De Chirico and the metaphysical interiors and the agony of departure wrapped themselves around me like a satin gauze canvas, igniting my eye and mind. The phone rang but I did not pick up.

****

I was back in India awakened by the girl rubbing my feet with mustard seed oil to invigorate and circulate my body. Looking up, I watched my mother-in-law as she gave her instructions to prop my feet up and put a cushion under my lower back. I was surprised by her partial gentleness and care. She was hovering over me like a queen bee, ordering everyone around, and making sure I was comfortable. I was pregnant.

It was evening here in this strong iron city, a place that would become mine and that would let me enter its many moods and challenges before I was initiated. And I knew that this would be my place. The phone rang again. It was Shane. He asked how I was. I hesitatingly told him that I was not feeling too well. "I may be pregnant." There was a silence heavy with the breath of death and finality. He said he would call later and hung up abruptly. The cave inside widened. I remembered that dream at Smila's Hampton house. The snake dreams as they turned into the Shenai. The snake bit me then and I could feel its bite again now. I glanced at my hand, expecting to see blood. I was hollow within. I felt afraid, scared and alone. What are they teaching me? What do I need to learn? I couldn't understand.

The sunsets and sunrises were leaving me. I tried to catch them and to hold on to them but they fell away. I reached for the star in my palm. It glowed for a while and then dissolved into the sky of my hand. I looked for the sickle moon on my fingertips. They, too, left no trace of their visibility. I felt rotten and stale inside and I put the phone down and burst into tears.

In India, I suddenly felt a pain in my stomach and sat up as the girl propped me with more pillows. She asked me if she should call someone and I told her that I just needed to be quiet. I closed my eyes as she left quietly. My husband walked in and sat beside me. He touched my hands warmly and I asked him what he was doing back so early. He told me that the girl had called him to say that I was in pain. "I told her not to bother anyone." He said he had asked her to call him if she felt that I was in any discomfort.

"You are naughty," he told me smilingly in Bengali.

"It is nothing, just part of the experience. I will have to bear so much more, I am sure."

He very gently answered saying that he wished he could bear it for me.

The next morning in Shane's palace of lies and wealth I somehow got ready to go out. I was not myself. I wanted to leave this house but did not know where to go. I called some of the people who had left messages and scheduled meetings for the latter part of the week. The morning was gentle. I hesitated outside the building and looked around. People passed by indifferently. I felt very alone and sad and helpless. I decided to walk towards Central Park. My steps were measured and slow-paced. The bounce had left me.

In the park I glanced up at the trees as the rays of the sun slowly began to relax me. I took out my journal and just held it in my hands. It sang to me. The tunes were rare and unusual. My fingers touched its exterior as it dissolved into my lit fires. *I am in and I am out. I am a child lost in the forest, with eyes wide open. And I am a virgin woman,* big and *bold and wide open. I opened the journal and wrote with eyes closed: Do not be afraid. Nothing to fear. Nothing to lose. Dissolve like the dewdrop into the sea.* Looking up I saw a tall figure in the distance. I was stunned. It looked like the sage lady from New Mexico. How could she be here? I started to walk towards her, baffled, surprised, and elated. My pace quickened. My breath felt excited. As I got closer to her the face changed, as though in a slow dissolve, and became that of a young Native American man. He had a warrior face. He was rugged and lined as though all the philosophy of that amazing race was drawn on his skin. It exuded life and wisdom. I stopped in front of him, disappointed not to see her, amazed at seeing him. He noticed the expression on my face. I spoke about her and touched my seven turquoise chains which now sat on my neck every day along with the almost lost two gold triangles with the lotus in the middle. He said calmly that he was sent by her and Spider Woman. He told me he was Navajo. I looked at him, stunned. He asked me if I was okay. I knew I had to tell him everything. Trust was in the air. Slowly, as we both sat on the sun-drenched bench near the tree, I spoke of all. He was very silent as he listened. He did not say anything for a very long time. His hands were like the roots of the tree. He had beautiful turquoise and coral rings on his fingers, a philosophy of aesthetics. Some Inuit words entered my mind:

> *Songs are thoughts, sung out of the breath when people are moved by great forces and when ordinary speech no longer suffices. Man is moved like ice flowing and sailing here and there in the current. His thoughts are driven by a force when he meets joy and when he feels sorrow. Thoughts can wash over him like a flood, making his blood come in gasps and his heart throb. And it will happen that the words we need will come of themselves. When the words we want to use shoot up of themselves and we get the song.*

He spoke. I heard the song. He carefully asked me what I wished to do and told me in the same breath that his brother was a gynecologist in New York. There are no accidents in life. There are no coincidences. We move marked and lined by a cosmic plan that runs invisibly in and around us. We may accept this or we may not. It is. Many laugh at this. They make strange and unclear sounds but their words are not

123

songs. They do not come from their breath. These are the ones who laugh at beauty. "**Hozho**," said the great Navajo chief as he spoke to his young disciple.

We looked up at the trees. There was a depth and calmness about him, and I felt comforted. He told me to wait while he went to look for a phone booth. Returning, he said that I could see his brother that very afternoon. "I will go with you," he told me. We walked out of the park. It was about ten blocks away. "Don't be sad about your situation," he said softly. "Whatever you decide will be respected." I thanked him gratefully.

We approached the office and he led me in. The nurse greeted us. His brother looked very similar to him and gentle. The doctor asked his brother to wait outside while he examined me. I felt the pollen running wild inside me. The tree grows in me and grows and grows with a mystery of prayer and hope. Art is not ideas only, art is vision. Art is a spring festival of milk birds, blue cows, flowing water and sky body as a dream catcher weaves nights into a succulent seed of birth. He told me to get dressed and beckoned his brother in. I walked out and we sat down to listen to what the doctor had to say. He very slowly told me that I was pregnant, and asked if I had another consultation before him. My eyes went into a distant place and I spoke as though from a dream. I spoke of her and how she placed her hands on my belly and whispered in my ears words like seed: "Life. Not much pain. Water. No fear." At the time I was not sure what she meant. But this morning when I woke up feeling a little strange, I knew I was pregnant. Both brothers looked at each other knowingly and smiled. He asked me if I knew what I wanted to do about it.

My husband in India was here beside me, as I lay on the bed with the afternoon light streaming through the large windows, and the bird sounds filling the room. He spoke softly in Bengali about life and beauty, and touched shyly my now round, breathing belly. His eyes were rimmed with love and care and purple blossoms fed my inner child and we were both full.

The doctor in Manhattan asked me to think about what I wished to do and said that I had some time. Thanking him I asked him what I owed him.

"Just relax and let me know what you want to do when you're ready."

His brother told me his name. Niyol, he was called. He asked if I would like him to be with me. I was fragile and a little strange and said that I would like that. We stopped at a café on the way back. He looked at me and mentioned that he understood my connection with the Indian woman so well. "She warned you, and at the same time assured you."

He asked if I knew what I wanted to do.

"I am helpless right now and feel I cannot keep it," I said. I thought of the fertility of creativity within a grain of sand. Nothing will be lost and vision will be recaptured and embraced back in, until light glows through my fingers once more. I saw the ash of the Gods and Kali's mad dance as I felt her steps thundering inside me. He held my hand on the table and, looking at me with spears of fire, told me that I must do what I had to do. I cried.

I was waiting in the doctor's office the next day. Niyol had not arrived. I was afraid and alone. Mythology poured into me. Brahma, the Hindu god of creation, addressed **Mrtyu**, a beautiful dark woman adorned in gold who was Death, and told her to go into the world and kill all his creatures, the scholars and the meddlers. He told her that there should be no exceptions. She was shocked and gazed at him in silence. She asked him why he had chosen her to do this and he told her that she was without stain and her body blameless and that only she could do it. She refused and went to **Dhenuka**, a place surrounded by ascetics and stood there on one foot for fifteen million years. Brahma reminded her of her duty but she just changed the foot she was standing on and went on meditating for another twenty million years. And Brahma went to see her once again and asked her what was transpiring and she said that she was afraid of breaking the law and he said that no law could be as impartial as hers was. Lowering her eyes, she went forth silently. And the lotus garlanded Goddess of death with tears in her eyes, which she hid from her victims, released them from their physicality. I held on to the life in me knowing that she had come to take it. I felt small and selfish. She felt large and filled with compassion. As I waited in the room, I remembered the time in London when a strange warm liquid poured into me and suddenly I felt an agonizing pain as though an ice sharp instrument was wrenching the roots out of me. I had to undergo a similar procedure due to some complications. I felt separated from all. I saw death and blood flowing out like life pouring out of me. I was in a white bed in a white room in a white country where no birds flew. I had experienced this before. A warm female voice said that I would be fine.

Niyol's brother came out to take me to the operating room. He saw the expression on my face. I was shivering. He told me I would feel nothing and reassured me that I had made the right decision at the right time. "Sage breathes from you and guilt dusts off from your essence. It does not belong to you. Don't let it invade you," he told me. He was gentle and strong. Just then Niyol walked in and told me he would be waiting outside. I breathed in peace.

I awoke after the procedure was done. Niyol was with me. I was in pain. In the car we passed by buildings and people and somehow the city was comforting me and healing me. I thought I saw the black stallion flying across the buildings. She was straddled across him. I smiled.

Getting out of the cab, I handed him the keys to Shane's palace as I had no other options except for Smila, and I knew I couldn't go there. He opened the door, the death door We walked in and went up the stairs slowly to the bedroom, but I told him I would like to be in the library and listen to some beautiful music. He got pillows and cushions and arranged a comfortable position for me. His hands were close to my face and I felt their gentle aura and lived magic. I touched them with my lips. He smiled. The grace of a thousand lifetimes sped through me and all felt in balance and in harmony. The pain was real and it had a familiar language. I surrendered to the plan of many ages and many decades. I trusted, and the sand cloth with its grained fabric engulfed me. I asked Niyol to bring me the wedding shawl and my journal, both of which were on the bed. He walked, his feet bare, and came back with treasure in his hands. His feet spoke. They were his soul. I looked at them and he smiled. I touched them with my sickle fingertips and the full moon beams fell on his veined skin. I felt ancient and grateful as culture, and stones laced a necklace of diamonds on my now barren belly where life once was. It will be filled again with dewdrops of blood and bamboo stalks at sunset and sunrises at the hour of the temple when the gods are bathed with milk, honey, and turmeric powder. He asked me if I would like some tea and I nodded and told him where the things were in the kitchen. I touched my belly. My fingers fell through. I was transparent. I felt my soul, my **Atman**, my **Seele**, my **Ba**, my **Alma**. I heard voices downstairs and faintly thought that the beautiful Japanese chef must be in. They both came up. Hironobu was his name. I called him Hironobu san. He was shocked to see me looking so weak. I tried to get up in respect when he entered but he stopped me. He did not ask. He knew. I saw it in his eyes, they were like deep-layered pools of a knowledge which lights truth fires and holds the human race. They are of beauty and compassion. They exuded a grace of lifetimes and centuries. They melt you with humility and pain. They are as real as the sounds of the ocean waves and the deep rust red of the evening sunrise. Shiva dances inside them. He asked me if I would like some sushi, which he knew I loved. I nodded like a child waiting for that special gift. Niyol had a tray with a teapot and cups and some fruit. Pouring the tea, he handed it to me and sat near me on the couch. He asked me if I was in a lot of pain. I told him that all hurt. He said he could feel it.

The music seeped into the atmosphere. I asked Niyol if he had been smoking. He said that he did not smoke. "I thought I saw a spiral of smoke rising," I said. I pointed to the corner where I saw it. Putting his hand on mine he softly told me to relax and sleep. "What was that?" I asked him. The same thing happened again and this time I was afraid. He came closer to me and holding me assured me that he would not leave me alone.

"You are seeing his soul rising and being released. This is beautiful. He has come to tell you that he is fine and that what you did was right and that he loves you."

All within me fell into his ancient arms and nothing was mine anymore. My invisible whisper merged with his. The corners were softened and filled with raw honey where the bees sang to give us their sweet vibrant sap. Feathers fly threw me to him. I felt healed and my cells were dancing gleefully.

I was in India resting, pregnant and in pain. My sweet husband, shy and confused, sat on a chair near me. My mother-in-law was sitting a little away, looking at me. She seemed to care a little after my pregnancy but never showed any warmth. I always felt like she was judging me I took my eyes away from hers. I wanted none of that smallness and mediocrity to ever enter me. She was not pure. Her age was her shadow. She had not won it and it was slowly drying life out of her. Her lips had a strange unhealthy movement on them. "Take her away from me," I whispered to the wind.

She told her son to go to work and not fuss over me so much. "She is a woman and all this is very natural," she told him. My husband shifted uncomfortably in his chair. He was confused and insecure. There was nothing more he would have liked to do other than sit by me, his wife, but he felt obliged to do as his mother said. All these obligations and formalities and the "do good" and "look good" for society and its false attire. It was not hand-woven linen. It was a slimy, slithering, synthetic fabric which was smooth and without texture. The smoothness was acquired and unnatural. Hesitating, he finally got up and, looking at me, started to leave the room. I stared at him helplessly, wanting so much for him to be around. I was angered by his softness, his weakness. My mother-in-law looked at me sternly and told me that I should be up and about. I asked her if she would like me to lose the child. She left the room. Why does she not like me? What have I done to her?

Niyol was pouring some fresh tea in my cup. I started to sip but stopped and, placing the cup down, sank into the cushions as though a huge force was pushing me down and taking me somewhere hooded by nesting birds and winter snow wails. It was dark and my feet sank into the mud, capturing my very walk. I felt as though my steps were chained within the sticky lines of sentimentality and death. I looked up at Niyol, making sure it was not my mother-in-law sitting there. I touched his face as my fingers left the sickle moon trace of its curved shape on his sensual lips. They were alive with a trembling passion and carved trees and quivering peacock feathers. I had made love to him before. I told him about the others that I had to let go, my little bamboo souls. I spoke about the **curandero**, whom I had met in Taos in New Mexico. Her name was Guadalupe. I went to her to be cleansed and healed. She placed her hands on my then-belly. I screamed with pain. She asked me what I was holding. I told her I was not sure I could tell her because she may judge me. She said she was a healer and worked with spirits and would never judge. I told her of the five beings whom I had to release. She said I had not done that yet and that they loved me, and that I should not feel guilty.

"Release them and let them go. They will always be with you and protect you. They are your angels and spirit guides, but you must release them." I turned over and she worked on my back. They appeared in front of my eyes. I saw them. I named each one and dedicated a verse for each. She told me to write it all down on a piece of paper and place it in an abalone shell and burn it in a secret sanddune place. I did and the flames from the beautiful, Chinese gold-center paper flamed in joy and they were free. Now they are with me. "All of them," Niyol said.

Guilt is an invasion and an obstruction. It is based on fear and lies. Remember the song lines of your very being and see the path and the way that has been laid down for you. Feel these lines and see them whenever pain comes in to show you the beauty of a, rounded growth, etched by the swords of life and the way of the samurai. The selfless warrior always has his sword quietly sharp inside its holy sheath.

Hironobu san entered with a magnificent tray of sushi and sashimi garlanded with those very delicious green leaves and huge mountains of wasabi and dried ginger, all of which he knew I loved. The special green leaves were perfectly arrowed and their fragrance streamed out of their exquisitely designed complete creation. The mountains of wasabi looked like the miniature herb mountain that Hanuman carried on his back for Rama to heal his brother **Lakshmana**, who was wounded. Hironobu San brought me the mountain. He was my Hanuman. I smiled. I sat up and Niyol set the tray near me and handed me a small plate. I dipped my first piece in the warm, dark liquid soy sauce and then the wasabi and placed the collage of delicacy in my mouth. The fish flesh melted ecstatically on my tongue. I felt the universe merge into me.

Hironobu san was watching and after feeling satisfied that I loved my first bite, gracefully left the library. I thanked him. I fed Niyol the next piece. He closed his eyes. His face was my canvas. I saw the light. I see the gardens of bliss. I sailed into the face of his skin, my divine Navajo dream catcher. His dreams will be kept in my heart and I shall release his weighted ones so that his eagle feathers dance into the sky. His eyes were green and looking up from the tray he was the wolf. He shape shifted to show me his power and then he was back again. I said nothing. He said nothing. He knew and I knew that we were from the same ether world. The sushi danced between us and the sacred sounds wed us. I will have one million and one husbands and they will all be in me. I fell asleep. My eyes often opened to make sure he was there.

The next day he saw how much better I was and told me that

128

he would have to go back to Colorado but would only go if I was strong enough. I said that I was. "You must not go out for a few days. You must promise this," he said. I did. He said he would call me from wherever he was.

"You will hear me, and you will see me. I will appear to you whenever you need me," Niyol told me. He touched my eyes. He took my mouth. He caressed my transparent belly. He kissed the spirit that was released. He chanted. He danced around me with burning sage. He was her and she was him. I was filled with eternal gratitude. It was beautiful. My muses were everywhere like an army of rainbow soldiers. Their spears were boneless and their shields were pure poetry. I was saved. I was protected.

As Niyol left I felt a piercing from his wind skin. I missed him. He was my wolf who ran wild inside me. I carry him, my Niyol, my wind star. I heard his feet sailing down the stairs. I closed my eyes and piercing through the leaves were his green wolf eyes. He showed me what I needed to see,that I was not alone. The phone rang and I picked up. It was Smila. Her voice sounded strange. I almost did not recognize it. She sounded distant and asked me why I had not called her since I came back. I told her I was not feeling too well. She asked if she should come over. I told her that I just needed to rest.

"I will call you," I told her as I hung up. The phone rang again, and this time I did not pick up. It was Shane leaving a message. He said he had time to think it over and was sorry that he did not believe me when I told him that I was pregnant. He said he would like to talk with me. Another phone call and this time it was Aakash. "I am a little unwell," I said. I asked him how he was. He sounded happy and said that he was working with some photography lab and that he missed me. Slowly rising, I walked to the bedroom and entered the bathroom to take a shower. The water with its warm whispers caressed me. I started to feel alive once more. I walked to the bed and lay down. All enveloped me and flew through me, as my wet hair haloed my mind. The last days seeped through my eyes and the miraculous rain brought solace and gratitude. The forest fires devoured what was not needed, and the rest waited to begin the next wandering of a howling mendicant in search of the art wings of the soaring eagle.

There was a gentle knock on the door as Hironobu san entered. He asked me if I needed anything. I told him that I was famished. Smiling, he left and returned with some delicious vegetable tempura. I hungrily relished everything. He told me that he would stay the night. I was happy. I would sleep knowing that his presence would cloak the home and my resting soul. He was my father and his nobility was higher than the skies and brighter than the moon and wider than the stars and fertile like the red earth. He was divine, he was pure gold, and his light smiled through the human veil of ignorance and darkness.

The next day I walked to the closet and, finding a small bag, started to put certain essentials and a few clothes in. It was cloth and feather light. Now that I was stronger after the abortion, I knew I had to leave this house. I called some of the people to try to set up appointments for the coming days, but nothing was open. Disappointed, I walked through the house making sure all was in order. I went to the kitchen. Hironobu san was sitting with clouds of wisdom and serenity around him. Walking towards him, I bent down to touch his feet. He stopped me, but I insisted. I sat near him and said that I had felt I needed to leave the house. He looked at me. His eyes saw all. I trembled from its intensity. He nodded and asked where I would go. I told him that I was not sure but that I would find something. Just then the phone rang, and he picked up. It was Shane. I signed that I did not wish to speak with him. He told me that Shane sounded desperate and really wanted to speak with me. I looked at him imploringly. He nodded. He made some green tea. We sipped together and he handed me a thermos of the same. I told him that I was leaving a larger bag with the rest of my things, and would call back when I had a place to take it to. He was sad. Judgment and cynicism had never touched his shiny face skin and all that was visible was the sound of a thousand epiphanies, their ethereal whispers an unsealed symphony, free from any convention and boundaries.

I was sitting in the dining room of the house in India, feeling a little fragile. We were being served. My husband sat across from me and at the head of the table was my mother-in-law. We ate in strained silence. My husband looked at me tenderly and asked if I had an appetite. "A little," I replied in Bengali.

"You must eat for the child," the mother-in-law said sternly. My sable antelope horn was feeling heavy and blunt, my head drooped to the other side across the ocean searching for my other half, and my eyes roamed through the wooded plains of my sunny ancestry, I wept in echoed silence.

Hironobu san asked if I had any contact number. I said I would call him as soon as I had one. "I will be back for my case and will leave the keys at that point." I asked him not to tell Shane that I had left the house. I got up hesitatingly, knowing how much I would miss him. He helped me with the bag and saw me to the door. I silently asked for his blessings. He heard me and nodded. I walked down the stairs and looked back one more time to take his whole self with me. He was my wind keeper.

Outside the building I did not know which direction to go. I started to walk uptown and then walked through the park. In the park I saw a pack of wolves running with their wild, streamlined bodies glistening through the dewdrops. I saw Niyol. I saw Her. And then suddenly a solitary black stallion was galloping through. I stopped and looked again. There he was and this time he was carrying the golden warrior woman. My head was bowed. I realized I was on the West Side very close to Smila's building. Without thinking I seemed to be heading towards it. I stopped and then continued. I wanted to see Diego. Passing by the building, I looked for him and saw him opening the door for some visitors. He did not see me. I walked faster and then, noticing a phone booth, dialed Smila's number. She picked up. I hung up. It started to rain as dusk began to spread its mystery and secrets and all responded to Shiva's dance. I shivered and, wrapping the wedding shawl, close to me walked on. Smila would be thrilled to see me but I knew I could not go to her.

Now the rain was pouring. I was getting soaked. One of my sandal straps broke and removing both, I walked barefoot. The concrete was not warm or welcoming. My feet wept. My eyes wept. My hair wept. I recalled a scene from Satyajit Ray's film, Devi, when the father-in-law had a vision of the daughter-in-law being the Goddess Kali, and he set her up in the temple where thousands came believing that she was indeed the manifestation of the Goddess. Her husband was desperate and outraged. She was subservient to the wishes of her father-in-law and slowly became what he had envisioned, and finally she went mad. Her husband tried to find her and there she was in their bedroom one evening adorned like a bride, with her kohl smudged around her insane eyes. She walked towards him and asked him to take her with him and then ran outside into the misty, aged night. Her hair was wild and flowing and wet and her anklets echoed the bells of someone who was trapped in a blinded sight. Her eyes were frightened and howling as she ran into the river.

I felt the spirit of my wedding sari wrapped around me, clinging to my body with its wet grief and burning madness. I looked at my feet which were now stained with concrete lies and city dust. The henna seeped through, though fading, and the anklet bells sang as though they were on the neck of the evening cows that were being taken home in some ancient small village in Bengal. The sounds of the incense made me mad. My hair came undone and my bride red sindoor on my forehead was running and had escaped its place on my third eye. Hollow-eyed I searched for my husband. My sari fell off my shoulder and I helped it, remembering his hands on my thighs and feet on that wedding day then, in India when I was given away according to astrology and human plans. But I did not feel his hands now and, looking down, saw the concrete. My screaming feet fell through the transparency of the cement as though it was my barren belly.

Finding the canopy of a building, I stopped and, removing my little red purse, counted the money in it. Looking around I noticed a hotel. It was on the West Side near Lincoln Center. Straightening myself, I headed towards it and entered. The doorman looked at me suspiciously.

He noticed my bare feet. I looked at them. They had history written all over them. I smiled. He was confused. I asked him how much the rooms were for a night. He hesitatingly opened the door and told me to enquire inside.

I walked in and carefully wiped my feet at the entrance. Walking to the lobby desk, I saw a dark woman with a kind face. There was a silence in her. I saw pearls and brass and copper bracelets on her graceful ebony wrists. I saw five stars around her eyes for five elements. She was beautiful. I asked her the rates shyly. She told me and I was happy as I had just enough for one night. I gave her my passport and she asked the porter to show me to the room. She looked at me and I heard the surreal howls of wolf manifestations. There was art around her. I thanked her and walked to my future away from Ondine's water home and distant from the **shenai** sounds of my wedding night, on that rice grain-strewn, abundant, spine-exciting night in India. The room was 555. I was happy. Five was my birth number. I loved its shape, its sound, and its endless curves.

The porter opened the door. It was a small room, but sweet and clean. Thanking him, I gave him a small tip, which he accepted gratefully. The bed was firm and grounded. The sheets had a golden hue to them. The window looked out on Broadway, and from a corner I saw a huge collage of lights: Lincoln Center. I opened my bag and removed my portable alter and placed it near my pillow. Walking to the bathroom I noticed that the bathtub was clean and inviting. I ran the water and glanced at the mirror. I began cleaning the sindoor off of my forehead but, looking closer, realized that there was no trace of the red root powder and now my lined yinyang antelope face was leafed and veined. The third eye was untainted and open to the sounds and revelations of air, water, fire, and ether. While the tub was filling and the water rising, I walked back to the window and looked at the other side and saw a small café. I started. It looked like the café where I had dined that evening when Kurosawa's The Seven Samurai had graced and fired my creativity. It was the evening when I sailed to Paris and had my first oyster with a pearl in it, which Tobias touched with his passion tongue. I longed for him now in this place where my feet danced to unknown bark bodies of light and screaming. They missed his warm mouth and his eyes swallowing my skin.

The water had risen in the tub and, leaving my wet clothes, I entered my water earth. I am Ondine. She is me. The water awakened me with butterfly-like attempts to catch dream wings as they slide and slip through the dreamcatcher's weaved rope, and the beads turn gold with the touch of my hand. I enter the newly visioned shore of the African gypsy flower, mandavilla. I caressed the song line of this karmic path, shadowed by numerous nuances of leaf and twig, and trace the sacred thread through blood, breath, and wine. Leaving the water and wrapping the white towel around myself, I walked to the bed and lit the candle and incense. Both came alive.

I was hungry and decided to go down and get something to eat. I asked the beautiful lady at the desk if there was anything good nearby. I felt like I needed to wait to go to the Café that brought Paris and Tobias to me. She pointed to the café in the lobby and shyly said that the food was good and reasonably priced. Thanking her, I headed towards it. There were a few people, and choosing a quite table away from the others sat down. The menu was light and I ordered a salad and a glass of Cabernet. The waiter brought me the wine in a beautiful balloon glass. I held it and watched the red river forming inviting and enticing circles inside this lived glass. I raised the glass to myself and to Tobias. I looked for the pearl which was always in my wallet and dropped it in to the red liquid. It made a sound and shone through these rivers of light and water made rich by the sun's rays. I was happy. I whispered Tobias's name and took my first sip. History flowed through my veins and poetry lit my mind.

The salad came. It was green and clean and large. I was famished, and the leaves walked into my wet mouth, now reddened by the blood of life and the **soma** of the true kings and queens who live with joy and laughter and celebration. I felt eyes staring at me. Looking up, I saw an interesting male face watching me intensely. I was tired of falsehoods and tired of hungry eyes. I would not be seduced again. My guards were bamboo-soft and sword-sharp. My spine was erect and all the wolves passed by howling. I changed my seat so that my back was towards his gaze. I sipped my wine again and the warm juice of the lived and ripe grape entered the rivulets of a psychological perfection. I loved Ganesha, my sweet, brilliant beautiful, bellied one, where rubies and diamonds reside, as his trunk of knowledge writes the wisdom of the worlds. His essence came into my dreams to remind me who and why I walked this path. He was my divine one, my ruby one. I would repeat his name a million times and never stop. He was the nearest thing to a cloud and with one swish of his divine trunk he swept all of humanity's obstacles away.

I felt a presence near me and, looking up, saw the same person who had been watching me before standing next to me. A strange tiredness fell into me as my eyes met his and went beyond and beneath. I left my present space and became the blue carp swimming against the tide, effortfully and gracefully, as the sun's rays glistened on my wet scales and the light danced in motion across the skies. The water rippled around me and carried me as I glided deep into the wealth of the waves and the blue light resonated both in water and on earth. We had merged and we sang in unison the Song of Songs and laughed the laughter of the invisible ones.

I was back and he was still standing there. His voice was unusually quiet, with a very distinct accent. I asked him where he was from and what he was looking for. He asked me if he could offer me a glass of red. My eyes watched the grape glistening in the sun, as the crickets chime in unison every day at a certain time, and then stop at exactly the same time at the end of the day. It was magic as the grape melted into the blue, red, purple liquid aged in oak barrels wet with love and longing. The wine and his presence made me comfortable and I nodded my head graciously. The waiter brought me a fresh balloon. He sat down. He was from Iceland and introduced himself as Ulfhrafn, which meant wolf-ra-ven. And right there behind him was a pack of wolves, one with deep sea-green eyes, who I was sure was Niyol. He is there to assure me that I was fine and could relax. I did.

"You have a beautiful name," I told him. His eyes were that of a shifting deer. They pierced and shifted and slid through pebbles and swaying elephant grass. I felt he wanted to know my name so I whispered it very softly, "Mrinalini." I had to repeat it since he could not hear it all. I did and the sound sprouted budding lotus blossoms on my tongue, as they floated out of me and flew into the air, brushing their fragrant petals all over me. They tickled. I giggled. He asked me what amused me. I told him that the name meant a gathering of lotus flowers. He said he would like to photograph me. I looked through the Hasselblad lens and saw Lord **Vishnu** lying on the universe with a long-stemmed lotus blossom arising from his navel. He carries us and all the decades and millennium and centuries while he rests in peace.

I looked again and there curved and voluptuous, buried in the soft waves of clouds was an apsara, a female sprit of the clouds and waters, adorned with ornaments of love and a long-stemmed lotus, which arises from her sacred yoni. Ulfhrafn was telling me about a story that he was working on for a well-known Icelandic magazine. He said it was about a writer who encountered an exotic woman with whom he dined and then swore that he had been bewitched by her. I cringed at that word and asked him what he meant by "exotic."

He contemplated it and carefully explained, "It belongs to a rare and wild being or foliage, and it represents an ancient atmosphere that has existed for decades and eons, and due to its uniqueness it is often set aside and misunderstood. It is a mystery whisperer and walks away from the herd. It is not chic or fashionable. It has an elegance that is age-less and formless and does not belong to the common reality." This was the first time someone had explained the word this way. I now under-stood it's meaning in a way that I never had.

I asked him how the writer was bewitched or affected. He said that, according to the story, which was indeed true, he had dined with the woman and the next day he woke up with yellow hands and finger-tips and no matter what he tried, the stains would not leave him. Smil-

134

ing, I told him that most probably it was from the turmeric root, a spice used in Indian cuisine to both color and add a special taste to certain foods. I told him that it was also used as an antibiotic because of its medicinal qualities. We both laughed. He said that he intended to do the piece like a photo illustration with text, and that I would be perfect for it. He mentioned that the pay was good.

He noticed the pearl glistening with its white body at the bottom of the glass. I sipped the rest of the wine and the round biography slipped into my mouth. I carefully removed it from my tongue and cleaned it in the water glass. He was watching. I told him it was my first pearl from the first oyster I ever ate.. He smiled and watched as I carefully placed it back in my wallet. Its slight bulge in the special part of the leather holder felt good. He asked me if he could have my number.

"I am homeless,: I said, as the sound of it echoed in the now almost empty room. "I am here for the night, and then I do not know."

"I will find you," he said.

The sacred is art, I thought to myself. I remembered my moon meditation and how the **mudra** of the double-jointed, poised moon goddess's supple bronzed hands formed the invisible language of a dream catcher's prismed walk. I felt the smooth silver ornaments and the colored feathers, which she gave me in my dream, as my man-mate came towards me and, embracing me, chanted and danced with me. We sang together as his long black hair spoke to me of all the eagle wings and the buffalo dreams. He was beautiful.

Ulfrafhn's mouth was very close to mine and I felt its warm quiver. The magicians came to me and told me their stories. I laughed and I cried and I knew that I was theirs. I belonged to them as they weaved their turquoise beads right through my earth bed. I slept and dreamt and then I ran to the rippling river and touched its powerful body of continuous change and motion. To be moved by nature is to be in nature.

I asked for the check. The waiter brought it to me. Ulfhrafn picked it up politely. I accepted because I gave. It was the same gesture. It was true and clean and without any hesitations or barriers. We got up as he pulled my chair, so I had space. My anklets tinkled. He looked down at my faded henna feet, which all of my husbands had loved. I felt his eyes and my feet bent to his sight-sound. We walked to the reception area. The same lady was still there. I liked her. She smiled. He asked me to please wait, as he had something in his car. I moved closer to her. She said that he came there often and that he was a famous photographer and a very nice man. Nice, I thought, what a strange, nothing word. But I knew what she meant. Sometimes, a certain kind of simplicity evokes a certain kind of compassion.

I smiled and thanked her.

Ulfhrafn walked back in the lobby with some red roses. They were beautiful. He apologized and said that he would have liked to give me a special bouquet.

"Roses are of a high vibration in the flower world and they are my mythology. They have helped heal me. I love their taste."

"You eat them?" He asked.

"Sometimes," I said.

He moved closer. There it was again, that sweet, heady seduction. It felt different, and I would surrender to it always, as the male whisper strides through my open pores where dewdrops sit on many flower petals and young, fresh, green leaves. He came even closer and kissed both my cheeks.

"I will see you soon. Please leave a message for me with the receptionist. Her name is Abrihet. She nodded and looked at me once more, as Ulfrafn walked towards the main door and stepped into the dark, deep night. I asked her where she was from and what her name meant. She was from Nubia, a nomadic tribe and her name meant "the one who emanates light."

I removed a couple of roses from the bunch and gave them to her. She was surprised and happy. I felt a connection with her and white wolves danced between us. Her dark skin was transparent like the Black Sea. I felt her blood. Wishing her goodnight, I walked to the elevator and, entering the little box, pressed five. In the room the candle was still very alive. Finding a glass, I filled it with water and placed the roses into their liquid source of life. They were happy. I was even happier. Putting them near the bed on the night table, I undressed and the cloth fell around my feet. I lay down naked on the turned-in bed. It was smooth and hard and I sank into the comfort of the starchy, clean sheets. The flame of the candle sent strange formations on the ceiling. The night sounds were muffled and the roses spread their red beauty all around the room. Their fragrance was gentle and deep. I closed my eyes as my hands softly began to caress my body. All in me responded. The other half of me was watching and spreading her forked tongue across my skin and this time both my antelope horns were in perfect balance. The dewdrops of the midnight raga heaved a delicious sigh as the notes of the haunting flute and shenai refrains became my blood, and the roar of the feline tiger mad with desire walks queen-like to find her mate.

Outside the window, the trees moved and the lush foliage of the night forest opened their bodies in search of their desired one. The rose petals called me with haunting sounds and I reached out for a long stem and gently plucked the petals from the core. They fell on me like broken cloud drops and brought back the hands of Tobias as he placed them carefully in the curved lines of my draped physicality. My hands moved, guided by my lovers. My trees entered the room and their barked patina trunks fell around me. My arms sailed like freedom wings and the dream lady in Taman asset walked in with her eyes, and reminded me of my un-broken youth in the traced earth of the passion of the Kama sutra. The Gods danced. The earth trembled. The skies rained. And the clouds became surreal expressions of the artist's love song, as my hands touched my thighs and my raised nipples, and they swam down as my **yoni** resounded with the haunting sensuality of Radha waiting for Krishna in the wilderness of the forest, as her longing, outstretched hands howled for her divine muse.

In India, I was lying in the warm afternoon sunlight on my silk draped-bed as the long lush grass outside sent figures of light and shadow on the walls of the room. It was sultry. My antelope tongue was dry and desired water and more. I glanced at the long antique mirror against the wall. I saw my reflection. I stood up and started uncoiling the soft drapes of my cotton sari as it fell to the marble floor. I stopped and walked to the door with a quickened step. I locked it and made sure it was secure. The sari continued to dance on its own.

I started to unbutton my blouse. My breasts felt the burden of birth liquid. I looked again and smiled as my nipples peeped out of their enclosed trappings. I began to untie the skirt that held the sari as I looked out to make sure I was not seen by anyone. The Gardner had a way of looking in, to bring me fresh cut flowers. As my petticoat descended, I touched my now swollen and heaving belly. I lay down and my hands slid down and touched my weeping yoni but then all stopped. I felt guilty and ashamed. I sensed my mother in law's angry judgmental look. I felt shame enveloping around me. I glanced at my reflection in the ancient tainted glass and quickly covered my body with the sari from the cool floor. I began buttoning my blouse. I felt restricted and shy and insecure and scolded. I felt reprimanded by words of guilt and morality and artificial lies, by the hypocrisy of society and all its dark forebodings that make one fearful and hidden from the wide-open skies of a free songbird crying to the wind. I wept and cried, and reached out to the center of the lotus where I had begun my ant walk on the night when wedding and union melted into an arranged but beautiful ecstasy. I wanted to be mad. I wanted to drink the sap of the trees and marry their swaying trunks. I wanted the sailing sunflowers to enter me and prick me with their flower beauty. I wanted their petals to remain in me and make me the child of their sun-drenched perfection.

Where is my husband? I thought. But he will only touch me with hesitation and niceness. He wants more but he is afraid to ask for more. My heart ached. I longed to embrace my other self who had left. I cried to her and called her. I heard her sensuous voice fall all over my haunted guilty skin. "You will become your desire and your longing. You will fly and we will be one. I am growing for you and I will free you from all that stops and stagnates you."I heard her voice tell me. The cage around me began to rust and I stood up and, walking to the door, unlocked it. I limped back to the bed not wanting to see anyone and my mask of facades and formal behavior was back on. I was hidden.

Back in the warm small room in the island of Manhattan, the ancient longings filled my eyes, as my red henna hands walked into the awakened mound, and I whispered healing words to my hurt interiors and felt the soothing cries of my own feminine mystique. In leaving the confining social structures of my culture my dualities and fear and restrictions had slowly left me. I was free. I was discovering my inner eagle and with her wings I found my very own epiphany. I will give this to her, my bride-self and then we will be one and whole. All responded and the river flowed through me, vibrating its strong feline body and the heavens gave way to this absolute ecstasy. The golden hammock held me within its stretched interiors as I howled and screamed and every woman entered and became me and all my lovers sailed into me. My hand now moist with longing rested on my open skin and all of me breathed a restful sigh. My eyes closed.

Chapter 9: My lovers are with me
My feet are bloody and my bones are transparent

Reborn, I woke the next morning to the gentle light seeping through the curtains of the room. The roses were wide and open.

Remembering the night, I smiled. My lovers were with me. I was my lover. Entering the bathroom, I took a long warm shower and, packing everything, was ready to leave when there was a gentle knock on the door. It was Abrihet. She asked if she could come in. I felt ancient and whole and had a strange feeling that she knew what I had gone through that night--the night where I was in water, swimming in the waves of the cool ripples when two baby tigers came towards me and breathed into me and touched my cheek with their gentle paws. The night when I felt my bride self and her pain, the night when all women entered me. I asked her to sit on the couch nearby. She asked me how I had rested.

Innocence filled me as intuition paved its path for entry. Thanking her, I told her that I had rested well. "The roses helped," I added. She smiled and thanked me again for them. She very shyly said that she wanted to speak to me about something. I listened.

"I know you don't have much money." I lowered my head and an invisible presence moved into me. "There is a spa in the basement of the hotel," she said. I was confused and glanced at her. "It is very elegant and maybe you can work there."

"What would I have to do?" I asked. Without answering, she said she could take me down there and introduce me to the owner. She looked at my packed bags and said I should leave them for now. She sensed I was famished after the heaving night and said that I should have breakfast first. We went down to the lobby and she said that she had some work to finish and that I should have something to eat. She would come and get me soon. I will walk on slippery surfaces and stand erect.

At the café I ordered some tea, a soft boiled egg, and some wheat toast. Noticing the phone, I decided to call Hironobu san. He was so happy to hear from me and told me that Shane had called many times and that he did not know what to tell him anymore. I told him I would call him back as soon as I had a contact number. He also gave me the other messages and asked how I was feeling. I had some extra coins and I called the other numbers, most of which were callbacks and auditions, but nothing definite. I went back to my breakfast and opened my journal to write.

My hands paused. I saw another dream. A strange woman had invited me to her home. It was filled with desire and wealth and lacking any aesthetics of an inner sight. The ocean surrounded the home. She invited some guests and they were rude to me and I walked with a limp, hurt by their cold distance. We were in India. . They handed me a horse head. His face was slashed as if by a blunt, weak knife. He was bleeding. I put my hands on his face and, bending down, repeated the healing words of all time over and over again. "I love you. I love you." His skin sealed and the blood ceased to flow. I gently removed my hands. They were throbbing with heat. When the animal kingdom came to me from their green wet forest of languid light, I felt my humanity The cracks would be sealed with liquid gold dust so there would be no invasion from these soul-less beings.

I wondered what this spa was all about. I saw a cloud of ravens flying above me. I laughed at my melting mind, where visions creep in my surreal self. They are sent by my brilliant, feathered muse-bird with the jewel in her third eye and by the African warrior who stands beside me, both visible and invisible, with his sharpened spear beside him so that I never, ever forget the rhythm of the ancient love songs. I finished my tea. I found my wallet and began to pay the bill when Abrihet came to take me down to the spa. She touched my shoulder and said that I should not be nervous. As I walked with her I saw horse heads all around us. They were leading us. I also wondered why she had said that.

We stepped into a lush and exotic-looking place with an equally exotic-sounding name. It looked like a restaurant, but it was not. Abrihet held my hand and we walked in. An attractive receptionist greeted us and asked us to take a seat. She looked at me and smiled, and our eyes met. There was a recognition of something in her which made me strangely comfortable. Little water fountains and soft music and fragrances filled the air. She announced us on the intercom and an elegant woman appeared through a straw-covered door. She smiled at Abrihet and looking at me said that I would do very nicely.

What an odd thing to say, I thought as she walked us in. It was a semi-round room with little alcoves where women were sitting dressed in little outfits that looked like bikinis. In the center there was a rotating round table on which a beautiful young Chinese girl was dancing seductively. She was topless with only a transparent sarong. I glanced at Abrihet and she looked back at me with dragon eyes. In the alcoves with the women were men chatting and laughing. They eyed me as I entered, which made me slightly uncomfortable. The lady, whose name was Diana, led us to a room at the very end of the very red, ornate corridor. On the way she spoke to her assistant and told him that she would be in a meeting and should not be disturbed. His name was Percival. He was from the islands and had a gentle and caring look.

He smiled at me warmly.

Diana introduced him to me and said that he would always look after me. I wondered why that would be necessary. The room had a large hot tub and was a deep blue. It was called The Violet Dream. She asked us to sit on the large couch as she lounged on a bed covered with some sort of brocade. She asked Abrihet if she had told me anything and if she could be open about everything. Abrihet replied that she had not mentioned the details but that, yes, she should be open with me. Diana asked me if I had ever done anything like this. I answered saying that I was not sure what this was. She seemed stunned and laughed at my naiveté.

"Do you know how to turn tricks?" she asked. I told her that I was not familiar with any card games. She laughed loudly and then explained that this place was a spa that serviced men. Men came here to relax, unwind and to seek pleasure. "All final spiritual reference is to the silence beyond sound. The word made flesh is the first sound. Beyond that sound is the transcendent unknown. It can be spoken of as the great silence, or as the void, or as the transcendent absolute," says Joseph Campbell in *The Power of Myth*. And I thought of the word made flesh and the sanctuary of the flesh and the adorned flesh and the erotica of the flesh.

There was a silence as I absorbed all she had just said, and then I quietly said that I had never done anything like this even though I loved man and all his symbols. She looked at me quizzically.

"So can you do this?" she asked a little abruptly.

I looked at my hands and watched the henna dance into the night of willingness and of one thousand and one seductions. She asked me again, beginning to get into details. She asked if I knew what a blow job was. Innocently, I said that my breath was strong. She laughed again as she described what it was and added that men loved it. My snake tongue felt sharp in my mouth but I was very possessive of her and would only use her when I loved with passion.

"Does one love these men?" I asked her like a child who had just discovered how to use a jump rope, and stumbled on the rope often and fell.

She screamed back saying that was absolutely forbidden.

"How can you forbid love?" I quietly asked.

Ignoring me and getting a little irritated and cold, she asked again if I was familiar with golden showers and threesomes. Finally, after she went through everything she looked at Abrihet, not certain if I could handle all this, and asked her if I could really do this. Abrihet glanced at me with her deep nomadic eyes and nodded gently. In the **Assyrian** palaces you will see the statue of a composite beast with the head of a man, the body of a lion, the wings of an eagle, and the feet of a bull. All these will become one in me, I thought. The perfection of the opened yellow rose with each petal like a risen angel sits in a brass pot in the water blessed each night by Ganesha the lord of all who is the eternal remover of obstacles and behind this golden flower is the hand which speaks of eloquent silences of decades and ages. And behind this is his divine trunk running miles and miles to protect and to welcome a new venture.

Diana got up from the elaborate bed of seduction and showed us around. Some of the rooms needed a key. The interiors were luscious and she told me that these were the rooms I would be working in. My head was spinning. I felt I was going to lose consciousness like I did once in front of the image in the Kali temple in Calcutta. The floor was covered with blood and sacrifice and the hero's journey was never alone because there are many who have gone before and the labyrinth was well known. We had only to follow the thread of the hero's path and we would be with the entire world.

She told Percival that I would be working there. He smiled a little sadly and welcomed me. Walking through the reception area there were many more men and the young girl was still dancing and entertaining the chained human wolves. The girl at the entrance acknowledged me and asked when I could begin. I was confused and nervous. I looked at Abrihet once more. She asked me if I could begin the next day. "I will let you know," I said. She said that there were many waiting for the job and if I wanted it I needed to let her know as soon as possible. I nodded, not sure of anything. The steel blades are very sharp and there is no grass in sight. She thanked Abrihet and looked me up and down. "Very beautiful," she said, wishing us goodbye.

Abrihet and I walked up to the lobby in silence and I felt snake bone garlands all around me. They were white and prickly like the deep scars inside me. She asked me if I would like some tea. The thought of that hot, strong liquid burned my lips and the snake garland fell away and were replaced by a fragrant garland made with weaved champa flowers, symbolizing a psychological perfection. Over tea in the little café in the lobby I told her about the abortion I had just gone through. Her eyes widened like a vibrant fawn that has just seen the hunter in the forest hiding to arrow him down.

She touched my hand and said, "You cannot do this."

"I have to," I said. She had tears in her eyes and apologized for even suggesting this to me. I touched her desert skin and saw one hundred wild African elephants running in a herd in the dusty horizon.

"You wanted to help me. Film and art are my passion, I am an actress but right now there are no jobs. I have no choice. I cannot go back to where I was staying. I have to do this "

"You haven't healed yet," she said.

"My wounds are my precious jewels. They are golden amber like the rain and like the life giving rays of the sun. I wear them like precious pearls. I have no money. I will do this," I said, "I will ascend and become a tree and climb the mountain and gradually progress to the heights of my own humility. This is another sacrifice given to me and I must accept it. Thank you."

Abrihet ordered a special brew and some scones, warmed and drenched with butter. "You must be soaked with love and richness and food," she said. The tea was delicious. The scones were divine and she spoke of Kamala, the courtesan from, Siddhartha, the book by Hermann Hesse where he says that the true profession of man is to find the way to himself. Kamala was the greatest teacher and was skilled in the art of love and worshipped and honored by all who came to see her. She was an artist in every way and when the great **samana**, Siddhartha came to her after all his ascetic sacrifices and teachings in the forest she taught him what none of the other teachings did. He learned all from her and she from him.

"How do you know all this," I asked her with the curiosity of a child.

"I come from a race of powerful warrior women," she said, "we are taught all this as children. We are even taught the way of the courtesan. She was beautiful. Her eyes gave me five stars and five roses and five lotus flowers, they were white.

"Kamala means lotus," she said with that haunting child woman smile.

"How can I do all this without love?" I asked her. "Sex is sacred", I whispered. "It is", she said, "and that is what you will bring in there."

"Love them if you must, and lift them and light them and bring gold down to earth. You above all can do this. You carry the magic wand. It will not be easy but this will be your biggest learning."

Her words fell into me. I looked up because I felt a strong presence and there standing in front of me was my dream lady of Taman asset with her eyes flashing as she said, "you will break no more." I was so startled that Abrihet moved closer to me and asked me if I was alright. I smiled and said that all was good and just then I heard the galloping stallion and right across the small café saw him and his divine rider. Her cloaked head moved slightly towards me as her hand extended towards me and as though in a dream I saw her carrying the exact same flower, which was in the sand dunes in New Mexico after I had fallen.

I looked at Abrihet and told her that we should let Diana know that I would begin tomorrow.

"I will learn to be Kamala," I said.

"You don't have to. You already know," she replied.

With the ancient eyes of a dream catcher she asked me again if I was absolutely certain. I nodded very firmly and silently whispered, "I saw the sign." She looked at me as though she too had seen what I had and asked me to wait while she went down to let them know. Green eyes pierced me and I saw Niyol running towards me. He was shape shifting around me and for just one second stood in front of me and kissed my third eye and swallowed all fear away from me. I heard him whisper in my left ear, "I will be with you." And then he kissed me on my lips and the whole of humanity fell into my dream language. My strength was returning. My guides were all around me. My ashes are warm and all around me.

Abrihet returned and said that Diana was more than pleased that I had agreed. "She really likes you," she said. We spoke about the room and she said she would let the hotel manager know that I could stay there while I worked, as the spa was part of the hotel. I wondered how I had chosen this one out of all the others. No accidents, I mused. She walked me to the elevator and we went up to the room. "Make yourself comfortable," she told me and then for the first time asked me my name. I told her and she said that I would need to use another name while I worked in the spa.

"What does it mean?" she asked again.

"A gathering of lotus flowers," I replied. She then shyly handed me a one hundred dollar note. I couldn't accept, but she insisted and said that I would give it back when I could. I thanked her and kissed it as it was drenched with the still strong henna in my hand, and I watched it drip with red blood. She told me to have a romantic and ritual dinner with myself.

"Tonight you must celebrate. Be alone but never forget that you are never alone."

"I cannot forget my art," I whispered as if to myself. She heard me and said, "you never will and you will become even more because this will be the sacrifice needed for your art. These flames will burn and destroy all your doubts and fears"

I felt a warm hand touch my spine and sail through my veins. At that moment she sounded like my dream lady from the love desert of that island drenched with sensuous longings. As I glanced at her again she was dressed in a flowing nomadic gown and had symbols all over her face, neck and her bronzed back. I knew then that she was another messenger sent to me by those who had and would lead me to my sacred excavation of self, sacrifice and absolute transformation. The deep song of the duende flooded me and the feet of the flamenco dancers walk over me with their magic songs as it flew within the body of the wild dancer and then emerged through the back like the wings of the eagle.

I decided to have another one of my long ritual baths. Dusk was approaching. The gods were dancing. Night began chanting her special mantras. I took the fallen rose petals from the flower that the Icelandic photographer had given me and that had caressed my wounded body and threw them into the water. I thought of him and the meaning of his name and his strange inviting eyes and his wide and languorous lips. He will find me, I thought. The petals floated on top with their little red poem bodies. My clothes fell off me like loosened pride and I knew that

144

all would be stripped off me like the sunrays when they leave the earth. I stood in front of the long mirror and watched my nakedness. In a painting by Paul Gauguin a longing, dark-skinned beauty lies against a tree, her body stretched on the evening earth as fruits and flowers drop over and around her. Her eyes look afar as she longs for the one who will eat her flowers and be one with her. I was her this night and I would cherish the sacred prostitute in me and I would become one with every woman and every child and I would court Kamala the courtesan and learn from and with her and become the shining gold body floating in the sky, with my feet embedded in the body of the sickle moon and my head one with the rising sun.

I wore my flowing, Tobias, wolf-howl dress. The mirror came to me and the kohl painted my eyes and my loins were shaped by my lover's caresses. I threw my hair back like a wild stallion racing into the sky with garlands of jasmine flying around my horse-wolf neck. And what belongs to the golden brilliance of Aphrodite is the deep acceptance that man is made to love. I stood naked and clothed and bathed and whole and half and complete and, putting drops of my tree essence on my neck and wrists, walked out with my woven, warm wedding shawl, given to me by the male female dancers in Taman asset when the gypsy king had swallowed me.

I decided to go the same café where Tobias came to me after I had seen Kurosawa's Seven Samurai. Abrihet was working in the lobby and, seeing me, smiled. She came up to me and commented on the gypsy dress. She introduced me to the same doorman who had looked at me strangely when I arrived and told him that I would be staying for a while and that he should take care of me. He nodded. The evening air was strong and magical. I thought of Hironobu san and decided to call him later.

The café was exactly the same and the waiter remembered me and welcomed me. Looking at the menu, I saw a salmon entrée which looked inviting. I told him I would like it rare. He smiled and the flesh of the lotus flower leaf, as always, was untainted. The wine was smooth, round, and strong with the fragrance of the flowers that grew around it. It felt feline and mystical and it ran like all the women who run with the wolves, who live at the end of time and at the edge of the world and who find their identity and love for themselves. The women who know that the wild one is in all of us, as we return to our roots, unmask our truths, realize our core, and confront what we all fear the most: our own power. That is how powerful the wine is. It was a Chilean reserva from a small family vineyard, and I sipped and celebrated a new beginning and a new friend. This was the night before my wedding to the world and all was as it should be.

The waiter brought me another glass and said that the wine was on the house, compliments of the maître d'. Blood was alive in me. I felt the wounds of those who had betrayed me with lies and empty promises and false hopes and the ones who had stolen my innocence and my virginity. I thought of those who had left me after courting me with passion and I saw the tiger on my brown back and the falling child and a white dove on my breast and two horses neighing to the moon. I would become the courtesan and I would find the usurpers of my secrets and I would regain my shape-shifting power and my dream-time would be the pointing sword, and I will eat my beauty back leaf by leaf. The fish was flesh and spice; it was crisp and universal and sexy. I looked up and there, standing right in front of me, was Niyol again, dressed like a warrior, spreading his wings and drinking me in with his emerald, precious, stone eyes. He had given me this moment to prepare me for tomorrow. I was certain of this and, as he faded into the distance, I could hear his huge howl. Only I could hear it. I had my third glass of the sharpened samurai liquid and finished the meal. The celebration was dynamic as the sacrifice of the sun-lover began. My body pleased me much because it was the manifestation of the self, and the marks left by the sati wives would fall away from the walls, and all hidden desires would find the light of day, and graves would be bereft of bones, and flowers would be watered from a broken clay pot because nothing was wasted and no one would be without hope.

I asked for the check and the maître d' came with it, asking if there was anything else I would like. He said he would love to offer me some more wine if that pleased me.

"How can I refuse such a gracious offer?" I told him. The green of my wedding dress echoed the eyes of my wind-warrior, and the gypsy boy and the wind surfer were one and the same. The restaurant was getting busy and suddenly the whole building began to rise by the eyes of that same, very simple, very magical boy-gypsy who smiles because he, above all else, knows that possessions are worthless and that true beauty is in the galloping gazelle, the graceful leopard, and the brilliant white stallion running rider-less across the desert dunes of this wild world. I would marry again and this time there would be no whisperings and no empty rituals because I was my own dream and my own magic and my own mythology.

I paid and left. They all wished me goodnight and I felt the maître de's eyes on the skin of my back where all of the lotus flowers sit. I let them slide down without entering my spine. It was attractive and seductive, but of a lesser nature and a smaller vocabulary. My language must be of a metaphysical nature and not the well-made, easy paths. Since I was naughty, I looked back and sent him a flying kiss. After all, he was Spanish, and I have always been seduced by flamenco and by the wild sounds of the hota and the romantic, tropical play of love and laughter.

He sent one back and my hips swayed to the rhythm of the night-queen as the flower exuded its weeping fragrance when the sun sets in India.

I arrived at the pleasure garden on time with my weapons sharpened and hidden. The receptionist greeted me well and told me that she would help me and that she would be willing to give me some pointers. She added that I could make some very good money. She called for Diana, who was happy to see me, and took me into a room, and handed me a very small bikini-like outfit. Since it was still quite early the dancing girl was not there yet and there were not many customers either. Diana introduced me to the sitting girls, using a different name. Some smiled, while others just looked me up and down at the new competition. Diana advised me not to get close to any of them and to just be polite and do my work. She added that they could be very vicious and cut throat. Most were students and many came from very good families. She took me to a room and waited outside unitl I undressed and tried on the skimpy outfit, which was truly not me. I came out and she looked pleased. The manager whistled in appreciation. "Wow, she is going to do really well here," he said. Diana agreed and took me to the lounge area after giving a quick run-through of all the rules and regulations, and how to operate She reiterated what she had said the day before.

"You are here to please them and that is all. Give them everything they want, with exceptions of course, and be polite and treat them well. Do a good job and do not get close to them. Also, remember that you have to take the money prior to the service. Percival will always help you. Never hesitate to ask him for anything."

Just then he came out of the gentlemen's room with a customer, who looked at me approvingly. The girl with him noticed this and gave me a dagger look. Percival told me to pay no heed to her. My back felt woolly and weak and I felt myself faltering. My steps got very hesitant as Diana led me to the lounge. A huge sadness overtook me as I wondered if I could truly go through this. Just then, I felt Abrihet's eyes piercing through the walls of this fake hut of pleasure and my spine sealed itself from false intrusions and I walked in and sat in one of the little alcoves, very shy and uncomfortable. The dancing girl was now here. I liked her. She was Asian, and she was the only one who acknowledged me. The others just eyed me and then went on with their chattering. They made absolutely no effort to include me or make me comfortable in any way. The manager of the place, whose name was Brian, came to me and went over everything that Diana had told me, making sure I understood clearly. He said I would do very well and that I should not be nervous or apprehensive. He gave me a little squeeze and complimented me.

Some of the girls were smoking and the music was appropriately providing a seductive ambiance. Men walked in and were served drinks, and then they sat around and looked to see who they would pick. We were objects.

Some came for their regulars and after having few drinks walked to the back with the girl of their choice. Each time someone came in I cringed, hoping that I was not picked. As the evening proceeded it got busier and the place was teeming. A man walked over to me. He introduced himself and asked me to go with him. I looked around for help and the dancing girl gave me a friendly wink as I led the customer to Percival. According to the rules, I was supposed to go back to the lounge and wait until he called me. I did just that and just as I headed to my little safe cave, another gentleman walked towards me and asked for me. I told him that I was busy and he simply said that he would wait. Noticing the other girls already looking at me antagonistically, I ignored them.

Percival called me and I headed back. He showed us to the room and we walked in. I was very nervous and tried hard not to show this to my first client. He asked me if I was new. I nodded. Must be really obvious, I thought. I asked him what he would like as I had been told to do, and he said that he just wanted to relax and then have the usual. He asked for another drink and I went to get it for him. On the way back I asked Percival what "the usual" was and he told me that he was a nice person and just wanted some conversation and a blow job. My tongue poked through and I felt this snake entry.I gathered strengths from wherever I could and pulled strings from my own tapestry. I was reminded of these words. They helped.

"The sacred prostitute is a mortal woman who is devoted to the goddess, and her beauty, her graceful movements, her freedom from ambivalence, anxieties or self-consciousness toward her sexuality is because of the reverence she holds for her feminine nature," writes Nancy Qualls-Corbett in her book *The Sacred Prostitute, Eternal Aspects of the Feminine.*

I was the virgin woman and I entered the room with a different sway in my walk. He looked up with a start, maybe feeling this shift, and accepted the drink graciously. He spoke and told me about himself and his life and asked me to lie next to him. I listened well and responded to his confessions of the heart and his towel fell off. I slowly began my Kamala skills. Even though my tongue was faithful to her special lovers whom she surrounded passionately, I would learn to train her for these encounters when she would give part of her mastery to others, but just enough for the occasion. It worked, because the sunlit, coiled rope was right outside the palace of Eros and swayed in the wind as the drooping leaves of the window plant rise once again, erect and sighing with satisfaction. He asked me where I learnt to do this so well. My kohl eyes walked to him and I just said, "Life."

We kept on talking and as he got ready to leave he paid me the required amount. He was surprised that I had not demanded it at the beginning of the session.

"I felt too shy to do so," I said.

"That made a huge difference," he told me and gave me some extra bills. He asked if he could begin to see me instead of the usual girl he saw.

"I don't know how this works," I replied and he added that it was his choice and that he would speak to the manager. I thanked him and got dressed after washing and breathing and pulled the lit rope even closer.

I walked out and Percival said that I had another customer waiting. Mister Snake walked in again and I knew that tantra was awaking in me and that I would taste crushed humility of the unfound kind. I loved my divine beings. I sang with them and the Apsara and knew now why they threw me down to please mankind. I would and will survive.

We walked in together to the same room and I thought that maybe this would become my room where I could then bring in all my forest and ether friends to surround me as I walked within this journey of skin and flesh. He asked for his drink of choice and Percival told me that he usually took his time and liked to play and laugh and have everything. I looked at him quizzically and he quickly added that he would want "intercourse." The word was so flat and so without any music or color. I decided that I would have my own names for all these services. Names that would be mine alone and that would please and inspire me to travel with grace and art. I brought in his drink and he asked me to sit next to him and started to run his fingers over me.

I am a puma ready to run off in the barrens of Quitratue hunting the hot hearts of my tree lovers. But there is no escape and I come back covered in my own hunted and cracked nakedness.

At first I resisted this strange, unromantic touch of a non-verbal stranger, but realized that this would not work and that if indeed I could make one cup of tea with perfection, I could then conquer man's cry for his hidden soul and woman's plea to be regarded, respected, and understood for who they really are. I would become all of them and float into this seduction and show them that they needed not to be treated like objects and I would sacrifice myself for them so that they would not have to go through this exile. My mission was in motion and though the cactus plant had many thorns I would bleed and the thorns would run out of me and not stay lodged inside of me. My lover skills came into action and I maneuvered them like a skilled rider on an unknown path, like the rhinoceros tearing off all obstacles as he makes his own way. I wrapped my sensuality, this time in a brocade of gold and worked outside its jeweled cave. I would not and could not share that with these wandering wayfarers but would give them the mastery of the art of love and their satisfaction would be supreme. He was pleased, more than pleased. And after

149

taking some time he got up and paid me more than the usual amount. I thanked him and he said that by me not asking in advance he felt more human. "I am glad," I said and thanked him again.

Rearranging the bed, I walked down to the restroom to wash and take a breath. On the mirror were these words by Baudelaire: "Yet many a gem lies hidden still/Of whom no pick-axe spade, or drill/The lonely secrecy invades;// And many a flower to heal regret/ Pours forth its fragrant secret yet/Amidst the solitary shades."

How absolutely amazing, I thought and as I walked up the many stairs, nervous about the next encounter, I knew that I would pour forth my fragrant secrets amidst these solitary shades. That's what and who they were and they came for solace and a moment of triumph and victory with a stranger. I felt growth in me. I saw the gypsy women in Rajasthan painting symbols on my face because they said I was one of them. Wild, brave and bronze. Percival came to me and told me that both of the customers were very satisfied and pleased and would come back for me. Touching my shoulders gently, he asked if I was okay. Hironobu san flew in with his holy mountain and all I wished to do is grab his flaming tail and fly away.

The lounge was even busier and before I could sit down two men approached me. They were friends and said that they both wanted me and would wait for the other to finish. My feet felt wet and heavy and glancing down at their ancient story I longed for the dancing grains of sand in Formentera where my Miguel sang songs of love and wanting in his pebbled broken glass voice. "Sing to me now," I asked him, "please." I knew he could hear me and he would.

Percival greeted them and asked me to wait in the lounge.

I felt my blood enter my eyes as I lay shivering with fever and pain in my bedroom in India. Everyone was around me trying to comfort and ease me. My head was bursting with one million howls of death and trapped tigers. The physician was at a loss for words and all his examinations fell empty. Dusk approached and the night sounds haunted my soul. My husband lay beside me doing everything he could to help me. He softly ran his fingers over me. I pushed him away and told him not to touch me, as I was tainted and stained. He did not stop and pulled my whole body to him and, weeping, told me that I was his Goddess and my fragrance filled his whole universe.

****

I disobeyed Percival and waited outside the lounge and the client and I walked to the same room. I asked the new gentleman what he would like. He said it was his first time here so I went through all the services offered and the prices and he said he would like everything. The

150

yellow rose had dried in the water and sat sadly to the side of the little offering pot. Her victory had been won and her skin was now roughened by her own flowering existence. I was bold and, removing my skimpy costume, lay naked beside him.

"You are beautiful," he said as his hands travelled over me. I felt the word slicing into me like a freshly sharpened samurai sword. The anguish of the artist would always provide the artist with new seeds and my fertile creativity would never be tainted, though often challenged. I responded to his gestures and to the rhythm of his nervous touch. The lions entered the den and growled at my passive posture and they became me and my muscles were rippling as I took him with my tongue and hands and aroused him. He penetrated me and the man in me arose and all restrictions and moral conventions were thrown to the winds.

"That was amazing," he said and paid me. "I will be back," he added leaving the room.

I opened the door and his friend was waiting outside. Winking at him, he told him that he would not be disappointed. I asked him to please wait a few minutes and cleaned up the room and refreshed myself. I asked him if he wanted a drink and went to the lounge to get it. It was still very busy and, getting the drink, almost ran out before anyone could get me. He said that he had never been to a place like this and asked me if I was new. I told him that it was my first day and that I, too, had never been in a place like this before.

"How does it feel?" he asked me.

"It feels like I am crossing over a bridge and there is all this water underneath and that as I walk I try to find the body of water but it escapes me."

He looked puzzled and I went through all the services and prices with him and he chose what his friend had. He winked at me and said he wanted to experience me in every way. I was being initiated into the mysteries in order to achieve a profound connection with the goddess of love, and the sacred prostitute was also an aspect of man's anima, inspiring him to value aspects of himself that involved erotic spirituality. She was a dancing, radiant, and exciting image of the feminine. I opened my feathers like the male peacock in all its brilliance to attract the female, except I was the opposite and my erotic play was around, above, and beneath him. Niyol sailed into the room, or at least I felt his presence, and knew that I had created a dance without boundaries or restrictions or inhibitions. I threw ashes to all of the laws made by man and to the empty vacant rituals.

My husband in India was lying next to me on a misty, balmy night, with the deep and sultry fragrance of the tuber rose enveloping us. I felt liquid and whole. My fever had left me and my lips trembled at this deep sensuality of culture and passion and ancient ragas. The night seemed to enter our limbs as we dissolved into each other. My red sindoor bindi on my third eye spread all over his river mouth as he entered me and I became my male self. I spread my hands on the other side of the bed as though searching for someone. He moved his head and looked, too. "Who is it?" he asked. That other self is me, the one who left. I saw her and felt her. She is wounded and sad and alone. He started to weep and held me so hard as though crushing my bones. I sent her my red, dripping, opened third eye and caressed her trembling body of sacrifice. We both cried.

My courtesan self, in this pleasure garden in sleek midtown Manhattan, this was my third or fourth or fifth customer. I had lost count and he thanked me and paid me and said that he had a great time. He walked out of the room, closing the door. I sat quietly, absorbing all. I got up but felt weak and sat down to take a deep breath. There was a knock and Percival opened the door, making sure all was well. He told me that I had done great and that, even though some men were asking for me, I should stop. I agreed and asked if the managers would not mind. He said that he had already spoken to them and both of them agreed. Thanking him, I went down to wash and change. I saw the words on the mirror again and wondered who had written them. I climbed the stairs slowly and wished Percival goodnight. He gave me a warm hug and said that I had done very well the first night, and that he would see me the following night. I shivered at the thought of going through all of this again, but that was how it was. Brian was in the reception area and took what was owed for the house as I placed the rest in my sock and, putting up my hood, walked out of the door incognito. He told me that I did excellently and the customers were more than happy.

My feet walked on water and pistachio shells and whole almonds and walnut brains and many rose thorns and water chestnuts and watermelon seeds. I was in an altered state. I left the basement and walked up to the lobby. Abrihet was not there. The doorman greeted me. I needed air. I had to walk. My body was exhausted as I sailed through tall swaying elephant grass, as the sun entered the body of the river and merged himself within her. *You are Kamala the courtesan.* Voices rang in my head repeating these words like a chained mantra. Buses passed by. Cars passed by. People passed by. I seemed to not see or feel anything and kept walking downtown. I was the horse rider who, getting off the stallion, was slightly unbalanced and everything hurt. I saw a health food restaurant near the hotel and was pleased. I was now famished since I had not eaten anything all day. I walked in and went to the bathroom. I ran the water and washed my hands over and over again as though trying to remove some invisible stain that would not wash out. Hesitatingly, I looked in the mirror and stood back because there staring at me was my India bride-self with a huge red circle of *sindoor* on her forehead, wearing a red sari. She was beautiful with her hair braided and with a jasmine garland weaved in it and long pearl earrings in both ears. She was there to comfort me and to give me strength. I touched the sindoor and it smudged. I looked away and then back and this time it was the reflection of the gypsy woman who had just returned from a wild chase to hunt down the spit thief and soul-stealer who had not been found yet. I dried my hands, sat at the table, and ordered a glass of red. I asked for the vegetarian plate with brown rice. I needed the whole grains to burst into me and spread their complete symphony in me. The girl waiting on me was gentle and sweet and, as she brought my plate, I asked her if she had ever done anything that was very different and difficult in her life. She looked at me for a long time and nodded her head, saying that she had, and then walked away as though knowing what I had just gone through.

I quietly finished my meal and, thanking her, walked back to the hotel. In the room I ran a bath and lit the candle and incense stick. This ritual is my homage to the sacred threads of my culture and I will never forget it. The water was heaven and I sank into its longing, languid interior. I felt something on my third eye. It felt wet and, getting out of the water, looked in the mirror. There she was again, my bride-self. I cried and sank back into the water, staying there for a lifetime. She had come to soothe and heal me. Tears pierced into my open wounds and heart.

I lay down on the little bed and longed for my lovers to be beside me. Just then I felt a feather prick and looked at my little hot spot next to the alter. There in the corner the feathers were slightly flickering. Taking a deep breath, I closed my eyes and fell asleep like a newborn baby, knowing that the next day was going to be another initiation into the fire circle, the burning of unwanted things and false expectations and useless desires. I slept.

The morning was sweet. I made some calls to some of the numbers Hironobu San had given me hoping desperately that there would be a call back. Nothing was happening. All in me felt tight with fear at the thought of going in again. But gathering myself, I got ready. Abrihet was at the lobby and, seeing me, ran up to ask how I was doing. I looked at her in silence and could not speak. She walked down with me and at the entrance held me. I felt and heard the wild, haunting sighs of one million women who held and caressed me. They thanked me for carrying their burden and wounds so that they would not have to. I felt better and stepped in after thanking her. She was a shaman. I knew that. An amazing woman like the black Madonna herself. It was early so there was hardly anyone in the lounge and I quietly walked to the back and got ready for the war.

Percival was there cleaning up and seemed happy to see me on time. My feet were cracked and dry from empty eyes and a skin of peeled lust. An insect trapped in amber fell on them, deepening the now fading henna. I thought of my abortion and all the female stories of pain, abuse, neglect, and slaughter quivered from the banyan tree as the goddess was ignored and the juice of an ancient voluptuous culture had fallen to the dust, when women killed the feline story within their very own pregnant bodies. The body of life in its three-hand structure screamed in revolt as the solitary warrior, who left what were lies and hypocrisy, carried those stories into a hammock of new skin and a visioned race.

I took my place in the lounge and knew that I would recuperate that which had been stolen. *I am the Universe.* The stones given to me by the little boy in Taman asset were in my right hand and their smooth round skin licked my palm lines of fate, life, fortune and love. People started coming in and I rose to the occasion. I was in the same private room, this time with a regular client whose girl was out sick. He was very demanding and rough and did what he wanted, throwing the money on the bed when he left. Sweat was blood and blood was sweat and I wiped both off my cheeks and walked out for the next, and the next, and more.

There was a request for a threesome. According to the house policy, I could not refuse, and so unwillingly went in to a different room. The other girl was a seasoned worker and knew all the tricks of the trade. She began by asking for the money coldly and then, finding out what the customer wanted, told me what to do. I mainly watched and the gypsy queen with her fire and loud ravaged laughter rode on her stallion. I missed my divine rider. Gold coins showered from her opening gaze as she sat, spear in hand on her tiger, ready to slice the invader. The whole experience was calculated and with no emotion or care.

There were many more, and my horse head was lowered and my hooves had slowed down their throbbing, sand dune pace. I was back in the red room which seemed to be now mine, and this time there was a surprise. A very gentle man was sitting and waiting for me. As I began undressing he stopped me and said that he had watched me a few times and that he just wanted to be silent with me. I sat in front of him coiled like that very special electric serpent that has already surrounded his body around the sacred lingam in the ancient oil lamp body of the temple of Shiva and was now within me. His stealth echoed a silence and I look at this person's eyes and met his Eros, which could in turn tear into the veins of a languishing creativity. He said that he wanted to meditate with me.

A child is capable of any wonder, but I also knew that I would and must keep this a secret. He asked me if I was surprised and the sun ran through the skylight with no hesitation or shyness. He just burned through. My tongue was broken and thin flames rushed through under my skin and I was the whore and the holy one. And I cared not. We sat

154

eyes closed for a long time until there was a knock at the door. It was Percival telling me that the hour was over. Taking out his wallet, he started to bring out some notes. I stopped him and said that we did not do anything and he need not pay. But he answered saying that we did more than he could have dreamed. He thanked me and told me that he would be back to see me once a week if that was alright with me. I was pleased. He made me happy.

Sitting in a pleasure palace, I had gone in with a stranger and I decided to call him my Godot, because I waited for him each week. He broke the skin race and he was gold in my eyes because he wished to just sit beside me.

I told Percival that he was very pleasant. He agreed, saying that he was different from most of the others. Percival told me to stay with him for a while until I got my breath back. A cruise boat was softly sailing on the river and inside were winged creatures watching man's journey and whispering hopes and dreams into each one's ears so that life once again ran through their veins. The boat shone and shimmered on the rippling liquid and my muse bird tickled me in my right palm, and opening it, I saw feather imprints embedded in each cross and star. Bruce walked out of the lounge, scolding me, saying that it was very busy and I should be working.

"I was just catching my breath," I replied. "That's not allowed here," he said rudely.

I slid past him remembering the hunt of the gypsy woman for the spit thieves whose gestures and sounds were empty because they have never been on the hero's journey. They have never seen the tightrope and always stay outside the voice of bliss. My lovers were of the mythic kind and they pierced me with their language and with a fierce entry. They were the masculine in me and that was precisely why I could be the dancing warrior gypsy queen. I was male. I was female. I was balanced.

The lounge was smoky, noisy, stale-smelling, and lusty. Some men approached me and I took back at them and everything repeated itself. I worked longer than the day before and could feel my exhaustion eating my strength. My sunflower *yoni* hurt and longed for a reindeer entry. I soothed her with kisses.

It was quite late when I finally finished and grabbing my belongings, took them up to my room and leaped into the night eye. She was watching and dividing me and cleaning the crevices and then uniting me and making certain that I never had duality and separation in me. I had been penetrated, stretched, torn, pulled and widened and my sexuality was breaking all its boundaries and yet there was no conflict within me between thinking and feeling and my soul would be restored. I decided to eat sushi tonight. The restaurant was called Wind and was very close by. There were a few people. I washed and washed and washed my hands.

The headwaiter took me to a table that was low and in a corner.

"Red?" He asked.

"Yes, really red," I replied.

"Blood maybe?"

I felt blessed as this wise grape ripened with light and sun. Divine delight and burning poetry entered me. The restaurant had large glass windows and looking out I saw reflections of the horse head weighed down by old language and the tired assumptions of dead people. But the sacred prostitute is of passion and I kissed his head so he could see his next gallop onto a whole new landscape of being. My body felt used and grounded, like the black Madonna in Europe. Maybe her color is what grounds her because it is earth and mud and dust and sand. I thought of the time when I was very little and someone asked my grandmother what I looked like and she said that I was beautiful, but that my skin was tainted and of an unclean hue.

I would fly to the place where my burnt amber skin would be the delight of awakened souls, because it is indeed the color of Mother Earth. Morality cannot swing its decadent sway into my space and, like Kamala, I would take this task given to me as a found special non-object, and I would drink the hibiscus crushed juice so that I could offer my whole self to the great Kali because this flower was used for her worship.

I threw out the first bite of sashimi. It tasted like human flesh. I cleaned my mouth with blood wine, bathed my serpent-headed tongue, restored its sharpened blade, and then asked my warrior with the sickle moon sword slicer to bless my fish. I asked him to feed me with the point of his sword and, as he placed the glistening consciousness body of my raw yellow tail, I had an orgasm. That is how this dinner went as flesh fish and bled blood joined to help and heal me for the next days and months and I did not know how long. As long as it needed to be, because life is alive and the sparrow listens to my sighs and soothes my burning flesh and the eagle feather throws buffalo winds in my direction. I left the sushi house and swayed towards my feather cave to rest and sleep and swim into my dreamtime.

The monotony of a new day began. There were very few customers. The girls were beginning to communicate with me and some were actually quite friendly. They all smoked furiously. One woman in particular gave me many looks and then finally introduced herself and began a conversation. She said that she was transgendered. I didn't know what that meant and asked her. She started to inform me that she had been a man and had had several operations to become this very perfect woman. She was like a drawn design. She looked unusually pale and blood-less..

A Russian woman tried to educate me about how to catch the perfect man and said she would introduce me to her "sugar daddy," who would enjoy having both her and me. My sword needed polishing as my mind and skin wept in this hole of hell. The dancing girl was sweet like a little ripe plum, red and juicy. She told me that she was a student and was here to help pay for her tuition fees. I asked her how she felt dancing there, and she seemed very relaxed about it. The receptionist befriended me, and we decided on a code so that if she saw some very shady people, she would warn me on the intercom. I thanked her. She told me she was a musician. I liked her.

That night, it started getting busy and I was in and out of the rooms without a break. Percival was always aware of me and advised and helped whenever I needed it. He was my angel and I would bring him my wings from the hot spot corner of the studio. I loved him and his sweet ever-present smile and wise words. He reminded me just a little of Hironobu san. He told me about his family and that all his earnings from this place went to help them. He belonged to the bigger humanity and was a grace to the race. Whenever customers tipped me I always shared them with him and his face lit up.

It was towards the end of the week and people just came in hordes. One time I had to run down to the rest room to stay there and catch my breath. But then I was in the red room again and this time, just like the gypsy boy lifting the house, I left my physicality and watched myself pleasing the man. It was an out-of-body experience. I never would have thought that this could be such a sublime escape. These men were not my lovers. They were not my stallions breathing fire in me. They were the outsiders and I learnt to give them pleasure without disgust or anger and by doing this I felt the woman in me rise unveiled and stronger. And in the union of opposites, male and female, spiritual and physical, the personal was transcended and the divine entered, and there was a time when human sexuality and the spirit were one. This was my desert dune tantric tent, where sometimes this union was experienced.

At the end of the day as I got ready to leave, Diana called me and said that she needed to have a word with me. She was a little serious and I wondered what I had done wrong. She complimented me on my work and said that customers were very happy and that she was more than pleased at the returns that were coming back for me. She then added that the girls were complaining because they had heard from customers that I didn't ask for money up front. She said that it was dangerous as I "could be stiffed." I had no idea what she meant and she explained that I could not be paid at all and also that it affected the other girls, as the customers asked them why they wanted to be paid ahead of time. I replied saying that I was shy and it felt strange to ask beforehand. I also added that all the customers really appreciated this, as it made them as if they weren't an object. She replied rudely that this was a job, and I had to get that in my head.

"You are disturbing the other girls work," she finished. I allowed the asuras, the demons, to enter my space, and I fed them energy, but they would not win, and nothing was lost, and the ash of the gods would slip through my fingers, and Kali would dance all over this city, haloing it with her stride. This city was hers and she was mine, as she broke the arrogance and pride with her red tongue and they called me the flame-maker.

That day I left the pleasure dome with a limp. I walked in a mad, cathartic heat wave with salt sweat and a cleansing of sorts. Concrete cracks exuded heat and dust and breathlessness. It was survival. It was never taking anything for granted. It was a hidden jewel and the tree grew in me and grew and grew.

Abrihet had introduced me to a gynecologist who became a passion friend indeed. He asked to see him once a week to make sure I was clean. He was different. He was not Niyol's brother. I felt I couldn't see him at this time. Maybe I was embarrassed and shy and didn't think he would understand.. He was cultured and liked art and adventured in the book of consciousness while driving. He had long legs, long hands, and a very long tongue. My dreams were my warriors and my reflections and my mythmakers, and my journal was filling up and I now wrote with red ink flowing from a fountain pen. They called me primitive. I called them ignorant.

The next day, the next week, the next month and on and on and on continued in this lust palace, as I hoped my weapons of life and growth were indeed being sharpened. And then once in my very own red room a session began with a new customer. He spoke. I listened. He told me what he would like and at one point in the middle he tried to pull my sacred symbol. I stopped abruptly and snatched it from him. I fell naked on that hot sand dune day when running and desperate I grabbed the gold that Shane had torn off me.

"You cannot touch this," I screamed, running out of the room. Percival, hearing me scream, ran out and I told him what happened and knew that only he would understand what this meant. I was desperate and ran into the lounge area with only my towel around me. I was sobbing and out of breath. Percival ran to me and consoled me and told me to calm down, and, going into the room, explained what had happened to the customer. He asked me to complete the hour. I refused. He threw some dollar bills at me, but I did not take them. I fell on the bed wounded, shaking, and filled with fear. The one solitary flower on the dune which had saved my life returned, and I looked to see if her hand would be there. Right at that moment the shiny black stallion walked through this lusty red room and her hand was outstretched I cried and cried and could not stop. My veins were broken. My hair was drenched with sweat and bitter teardrops, my hands ached, my fingers had lost their tree grace, my body was folded and crumpled, and my thighs were cut open. I felt ugly. I felt split open like a fruit sliced in half, like a coconut cracked in two, one with the husk only, the other filled with the white flesh of the fruit. I was the empty one. A soft fabric brushed against my face. It was the red sari of my bride self-wiping my tears. I felt her telling me that I was there to help these wandering souls because they were looking for some joy and comfort in their lives.

In a wet bed, in my India, sheets crumpled with my tropical beads of perspiration, I awoke and watched the soft brown, humble body of my sandalwood husband sleeping. He opened his eyes slightly and I rolled into him and grabbed his shoulders, his thighs and his heaving, grass-covered chest.

"What's wrong?" he asked.

"I am afraid. I feel wounds all over and inside me I feel ugly," I answered. He pulled me to him and whispered intimate longings and desires. He took my lips where I breathed inspiration, where I breathed life itself and he thrust his long and luscious tongue in, breaking every sigh of an empty feeling. I held him as close as I could and slowly the drenched bed seemed to rise as though in levitation. We both looked around and all we could do is smile. We slept inside each other's embrace.

****

Percival was sweet and he told Brian that I was not feeling well and should leave early. Brian understood, and taking what was owed, told me to rest. Diana came in and, hastily, without any feeling, asked what had happened, since the customer had complained to her. Finding my voice, which I thought I had lost in this den of false desire, I explained what had happened. She looked surprised and sarcastically made a trite remark as to how unimportant it was.

"It is not unimportant to me," I replied.

"Did Brian take what you owe us?" she asked hastily and then added that I could take the rest of the day off. "Let this never happen again," she said very rudely and continued to mention that, even though I was good, I could be replaced.

I looked at the girls, who were all giving me unfriendly looks. They are not courtesans, because they had never learned the art of love or of seduction. Their culture stayed on their gaudy, painted fingernails and toenails. They never touched their female center. They worked from outside of the perfumed garden and their sensuality was weeping somewhere dusty and unrecognized as they pretended to be women. Kamala would have thrown them out of her flowering garden. The dancing girl blew me a kiss and I sent her back one. The receptionist told me that she would see me the next day. My divine rider had graced this desire

159

den. I walked out with something firm in my hand. I was a little anxious since I thought I might have grabbed one of the client's **lingams**. I looked again fearfully. It was a stem of the lotus flower that lay beside me when Tobias came to me in my dream. I held it tall and erect in my hand. It was my spear. I stumbled out of this spa and grabbed onto the banister as I walked up to the lobby. I was shaking. I was wounded. Just then Percival came out and embraced me. "Please rest," he said. I felt a soft hand touch me. It had the fragrance of gardenia and jasmine flowers. India rushed into my veins and there was a throbbing on my third eye. I touched it and was certain that my twin-self was there giving me her soft child-self to heal my wounds. She smelled of sandalwood and incense and smoke and I saw fire sparks all around me, like a shape-shifting deity to protect and heal me.

In the lobby, I looked for Abrihet to tell her that I could not work there anymore. I was ripped apart and my skin had lost its wild shine and my eyes were without their swords. I stopped short because there standing next to Abrihet was Ulfhrafn, the Icelandic photographer. I was speechless. He came towards me. I stepped back, almost thinking he was another client. My face burned with a lack of light and I covered it with an invisible orange veil so that he would not see what I saw. He took my hands and kissed them. "I told you I would find you," he said. I glanced around like a wild wolf, not knowing where to run or where to look. Abrihet came to us and said quietly that she had told him everything and that I should not be ashamed. I was not. A brown tiger sat on my head and a white dove drank the soma from my left breast. As he came even closer, I began crying and could not stop. They both walked me up to my room and Abrihet unlocked it. She asked me to lie down as they packed my little samurai knapsack. She rubbed my feet and my legs and my back. She then ran a bath. He sat next to the bed and said that if I didn't mind he would drive me to his apartment and studio.

"There is work there for you, Mrinalini, and you will be great. Please don't refuse. Trust me," he said.

"You are a raven wolf, how can I not trust you?" I answered. He smiled and said he would wait downstairs in the lobby for us. "Take your time." After soaking in the warm, healing water for a long time I came out and watched Abrihet drawing something. I wore a warm and healing dress and sat next to her. I asked her if she asked all women who stayed in the hotel if they wanted to work in the spa.

"Are you commissioned by Diana?" I said and realized I was being rude. Her eyes were like that of the cat goddess, Sekhmet, who lioness-like, burns the fire of the desert and breathes into the Pharaoh, and against all enemies. Without answering, she explained the line drawing she had made for me. It was shamanic and traced a path leading through a series of trials called the "swaying places," marked by water, sand, and clouds, before bringing the shaman to the radiant face of his supreme god. Certain shamans of Siberia placed familiar shapes on these maps, which guided their ascent to the upper world to heal the sick or to retrieve a lost soul. She looked at me and with her deep victory eyes said that I was on that journey and that I had seen the face of the divine and would heal and save lost souls. And then with burning eyes she said that she had asked me because she knew I had to go through this sacrifice for all women and for all humanity.

"I have never asked anyone before," she said sadly. I took her in my arms and howled and sobbed and fell into her entire nomadic race of power women, the real women, the ones who dance with their entire body and soul, the ones who eat the wild rose with no hesitation. We wept. "You did this because it was your mission." She embraced me with her entire self and my energy and light seemed to be entering me once again.

"Ulfhrafn is a great person and an amazing artist," she said. I asked her about the spa and Diana. She said that she would let them know that I was leaving. I gave her some money to give to Percival. She refused the hundred dollars which I placed in her hand.

"Just take care of yourself and come to see me. I will miss you."

I took her nomadic desert gown and kissed the hem and gave her my heart. We walked to the elevator after I said goodbye to the 555 room which had sheltered me so well. There he was. His green eyes lashed into me like huge roaring ocean waves and I felt their warmth. They were of a wild tribe. He was gentle. Walking to the desk, I asked Abrihet what was owed. She made some calculations and said I just owed one night. Just as I was about to take care of it, Ulfhrafn intervened and asked if he could.

"You can pay me back when you get paid from the photo shoot."

Thanking him, I drank in Abrihet's eyes and whispered quietly that I loved her. She smiled and we walked out towards his parked car just outside the entrance of the hotel. I glanced back at the place that had given me shelter and more on a very wet and lonely night. I was grateful. We got into his car and he said his studio was in his apartment. Silence filled the air. I remembered Shane and his lies and the presence in his room in that enchanted New Mexico land.

As we drove uptown to his Upper West Side *atelier* my mind wandered back into the streets and the energy that sculpted many shapes around me. It was a tangible energy. We approached the Park and everything danced in front of me. Ulfhrafn was gentle. His wolf self was at peace.

"I have a wonderful assistant," he said. "She is from Peru." I was happy to hear that.

Nearing his building he commented on how easily he found a spot

161

to park the car. "I usually have to drive around for hours." I smiled. As he started to open the door I hesitated and placed my hand on his arm and asked him to wait. I felt a weight on my belly, in my hurt interior. I looked down and saw the bleeding horse head from my dream on my lap. His eyes were that of an almond child. They were wet and lakes rippled in them. I entered his eyes and bent down to whisper words of love into his wound caused by man's huge, ignorant ways. He slowly closed his eyes, and I kept my red hot hands on his wound, not leaving him for a single moment. I breathed deep cloud and sang quiet refrains of the eternal mantras. All was still. Ulfhrafn was motionless and I felt him watching me, fascinated but not invasive. I looked down and the wound was healed and the stallion head dissolved inside me and the red shining blood moved within the veins of the child's universe with its eternal lotus gaze. All was clean and clear and whole. I took another full breath and looking at him. I could not stop crying. The gates were flung open.

"I know I had to go through this journey but it was so hard and at times I felt as though I was losing my mind as my body felt torn into pieces of flesh. I feel ashamed."

"You cannot feel shame, you must not. What you did was very brave and not easy but it was important. He did this for others. You will see. You must rest for a few days before you start working with me and be kind to yourself, please." He said.

> *Wounds are gateways to my own*
> *transformations and I will realize*
> *new dimensions of my own being.*
> *It is a blow to the ego. Wounds*
> *must not be neglected but tended*
> *to and healed. "I will help you," he*
> *said. My mouth was wet with the*
> *silence and humility of what lay*
> *ahead. I leaned towards him and*
> *the flowing strands of the river*
> *Ganges touched his eyes. He*
> *opened the car door for me and*
> *gently held my arm as he carried*
> *my little cloth sack.*

Ringing the bell, he was about to slide the key in when the door opened. A mountain face greeted us. He introduced her as Flora. She was from Peru. The ancient land read through her sea eyes as she looked at me with an interior gaze. It seemed as though this journey kept leading me to these magical high priestesses. It felt as though a special tribe was forming around me like a circle of fire. We just knew each other. It was a

162

gift of an ancient language and I loved it. Her face had the sensuality of a shiny leaf veined with that silent language of many mysteries and sacred secrets. Grace and power walked with her. She reminded me of the legend of the fearsome female warriors from ancient Greece. I thought of Abrihet, who had just given me the whole desert gaze. These women were trained in the art of war from childhood. They lived apart from men and went to war in their own armies as they conquered men on the field of battle. They were the Amazon women and their origins were Arabs, Berbers, Kurds, Raj puts, Chinese, Filipinos, Maoris, Papuans, Micronesians, and Native Americans. And Queen Myrna, who with 30,000 female soldiers and 3,000 female cavalry swept through Egypt and Syria, where according to legend, the Amazon woman of Libya ruled. These women rejected marriage as subjugation. When they wanted to have children they were granted a leave of absence, during which time they chose their own partners and made love to them. And only a woman who had killed a man in battle was allowed to give up her virginity. I had been surrounded by mountain women and I was filled with gratitude.

Ulfhrafn told her about the article about the man who was put under a spell by a special woman, and she agreed, saying I would be perfect. He asked her to show me a room and said that I needed to rest. He said nothing about the hotel or what he knew. She led me to a large well-lit room with sun flowing in like spears of light. She placed my bag near the bed and large couch, which was a dark-red, like blood flowing through its wrinkled exterior. I touched it. We walked through the space. The apt was large and well-lit and well-kept. They showed me around and he told me his daughter who was very young still lived with him but that currently she was with her mother.

"We share her," he explained.

There were many rooms in the apartment. After all the rooms, he took me to his studio. He showed me his work. Mainly covers for books and occasionally magazines. He said he could use me for several covers also after the magazine shoot was done. I thanked him. He mentioned that they paid quite well. We walked to the living room, which was large and spacious, and there was a wide view of Central Park from the windows. After looking at the trees reflecting the light on their shiny bark, I turned around. Flora had been with us all this time and asked me if I would like to rest for a while. Tiredness suddenly overcame me and I accepted her invitation. We walked to the room and I heard Ulfhrafn saying I would be very welcome to stay until I found another place. As we approached the room I felt my legs giving way and I held onto Flora. She carried me to the bed. I indicated the red couch. It had a language of its own and beckoned me. I lay down and placing my legs on the edge of the couch, which rose up slightly, I leaned back.

Flora unstrapped my sandals and I quickly started up, but she pushed me back with a strength that came from a very ancient place. She was the warrior woman. I wondered how many battles she had won and wanted to ask her but did not. She brought me a glass of water. I looked at it carefully before sipping from it. She noticed this but said nothing. She quietly told me that I should take up Ulfrafhn's invitation to stay. She said that he was a very kind man and that it would also be very convenient for the shoot as it might take a while to complete. All this sunk into me as I felt my eyes weighing down on me and darkness beginning to engulf me. She noticed this and asked if I was all right. I told her that I had had a surgery and though healed from it, was still weak. I wanted to tell her about the spa but decided not to even though I knew she would more than understand it. She asked when I had it and ordered me to rest. She left the room after making sure I was comfortable. My eyes lingered on her and all the battle cries of victory and triumph echoing from her beautiful sensuous back. I quietly thanked Abrihet. I would never forget her.

In India, in my bedroom, I was getting ready to go out. My maid was placing a jasmine garland around my braided hair. I took a deep breath, inhaling the fragrance. My husband came in and commented on how beautiful and vibrant I looked. I told him I wanted to visit the temple priest before we went out. He asked if I would like to go alone. I looked at him shyly and nodded. I walked slowly into the bird evening night. I danced through the flowers and leaves, some of which folded their petals and others whose fragrance breathed into the night. The evening was heady, and romance danced in the air. The temple was lit and as I walked towards it a herd of elephants led me to the entrance. The gardener had left. I missed him. He always brought me fresh flowers to offer to the goddess. "I offer myself," I whispered in the night. I wondered why I had this urgent pull to touch the temple walls.

Reaching the entrance, I looked for the priest who was offering the evening puja. Right next to the entrance a gentle figure sat shrouded in white against the temple wall. It was Her. I moved closer. She was bright and her toothless smile sang all over her lived face. She looked into my eyes and told me in Bengali that I would never be alone. I looked at her again, slightly startled, and she repeated herself. Just then the priest walked to me and blessed me as I bowed to receive his blessings and the *prasad* from the gods. I turned to leave, feeling a quietness rising within me. I walked to the woman and gave her the blessings but she refused to take it and said that I should have it. I understood and, walking in the incense waves, headed back to the house. My husband was waiting for me. He looked magnificent in his white and gold embroidered *kurta*, and tight *churidar* pants. His legs were clothed with vermillion sighs and I was filled with desire as I saw the rippling underneath the silk skin of his bronze sheath. The child inside me felt this call. My eyes ate him. He looked at me and was hooded with shyness. I grabbed him and there in the wild Indian, snake-robed night I kissed him passionately. He surrendered and I took his mouth like a wolf and a tiger and a lion as his body bent and broke into me and I robbed his niceness and he sighed and groaned into the wild sounds of the **gazals** of love. The uncoiled snakes floated around his sweat-beaded neck, as Shiva entered this realm of mad passion and he became my Krishna and I was his courtesan of the heavens. I was his eternal lover. I was his Radha.

****

Back in the room on the red couch my antelope head fell into my open lap and I noticed that Flora had lit a candle next to me. I started to get up to reach out for my altar but, feeling weak, I lay back again and, closing my eyes, slipped into my ether world of dreams, source, magic, and mystery.

I am walking through crowds of people. Some are applauding. I am the center of attention. I have a low and revealing vest-like top and a turquoise long cloak, which is on top of the vest. The seven turquoise chains shout their presence on my breasts and around my neck a fresh garland of jasmine flowers make their presence felt. Another garland is around my waist and one is entwined in my hair. I feel like a flower stallion. Suddenly looking up, I see a man. I do not recognize him. He is beckoning me. He is standing on top of a pyramid, with stairs leading up to him. I am hypnotized by his presence. He is someone from the past or many of my lovers merged into one. He pulls me to him. I remove the garland from my neck and throw it up to him. He catches it and I walk up slowly, with my hands clasped to meet him. I feel his breath caressing me. He hands me a flower chalice that is filled with a gold liquid. I hold it like a feather flower. It is fragile and strong, and it holds my finger-like wings. I walk down the pyramid as he pierces my back. It is open again. I feel all of him entering. I am opened and protected. I know I cannot turn back because the sun has entered me.

Opening my eyes, I looked around and touched my hair, missing the garland. I sipped from the glass and closed my eyes again. Feeling my strength walking into me, I slowly sat up. I was shaky but the weakness was leaving me.

Flora quickly walked in and helped me. I told her that I should have a bath before beginning to work. Ulfhrafn peeped in a little concerned and said that we would start working the next day and that I should just rest this night. He added that if I had any phone calls to make, I should not hesitate. I thanked him and reached out for my bag, and, finding my altar, started arranging everything next to my bed. Flora watched fascinated and I knew she felt the power and symbolism of everything. She was silent. I was silent. She placed the candle, which was near the couch on the table, and Ganesha was lit by the flame as was Maha Laxmi and The Mother and Sri Aurobindo. Kali stood in her warrior gaze as her red tongue dissolved all tremors of the ignorant life. Flora and I watched, and the gods danced, and the sacred was tangible, and humanity was awake, and art was clean and untainted and faith was married to true cinema.

Slowly rising, she walked to the bathroom and ran the water for my bath. This hospitality spoke of home, care, love, gentle winds, and peace. I smiled with happiness. It was a poem sung by the jeweled bird whose third eye sparkles in the grey mist of hazy nights. It was the ebony warrior-spear in hand whose fierce white eyes knife through veiled horizons. It was the sharpening of the tools and shining of the lamp so that messages can push through and all earth is fertile as the true artist is clean and humbled to carve his sight. Flora helped me to the bathroom and, disrobing, I entered into Ondine's roots. I heard her laughing and my hair flew into the mouth of her gods. She was shiny and wet and mad with desire and pain. She had traveled many long roads with dust clouds haloing her outer embrace. She had been dry and parched but relentless to touch her calling and her arrow mission of finding the seed. She was indeed the water princess and she, too, walked away from all to rediscover all. She rested in this warm liquid. I rested in her warm, sensuous, moving essence, and life came back into me and she smiled with joy. We were happy.

Flora brought in several candles and placed them around the bathtub. My eyes moved mountains and flew into all the rivers and oceans and the drenched ragas of surreal sounds left me to inspire her, my new friend. I trusted her. I knew her. I had seen her. They were all returning to remind me never to stop and never to doubt and never to fear. They were my tribe. My tears merged into the water. All was one again and the sword of duality shook in its trembling steel and moved away defeated. It was a lifetime of water birth. I had no idea how long I had been embraced. The candles were burning and the flames were shaping their selves without any stammerings or hesitations. I rose and reaching out for a towel that she had placed nearby, wrapped myself with the gentle cotton, and stepped out of Ondine's world. Drying myself I slipped into the cotton robe and India once again feathered her awareness and eternal wisdom upon me.

I entered the bedroom and Flora was busy setting up a delicious tray of various delicacies. The food collage reminded me of the café on Broadway, when I awakened back in Paris and found my pearl. A bottle of red stood erect on the table with two very round glasses next to it. The cork was beside it as it breathed air to fulfill its release.

The candle sat on its bottle body and the red liquid was mad with ecstasy. The gods were happy. Bacchus was impatient. I was full. I thanked her silently as we sat together and she poured the red and we lifted the balloons and she wished me art and life and victory and triumph.

"You will be it. You will have it. You will carve it,"- she gently whispered. I felt removed from the ordinariness of being and inhaled the extraordinary sounds of the yet uncomposed symphony where conventions, formats, rules, regulations, and foolish and useless structures made because of hesitations and haste would be thrown to the wind and burnt into the dusk-driven fire-sky. It was as though she knew what I had gone through as I felt a new self merging within me. How did she know me so well? We had just met. We sipped, and the soma liquid bent within me and my bones felt strong and my flesh was tight like the stallion's rippling body and my **athma** was visible and alive. The rebirth was here. This was the next journey and I also knew that there would be many more. And they would all be like a newborn child. And the chord would be cut. And all attachments that linger and eat and devour and stagnate would be ripped apart. And growth would dance and light would quiver, because this is the way of the spirit seeker and the true artist.

As we finished the delicacies, devouring each bite with care and awareness, I laid back fulfilled. She smiled, and removed the tray from the bed. My eyes wondered into the night sky to find the stars, and the full-bodied flaming moon flew into them. I heard Flora wishing me goodnight and the sounds of silence gave me wings as I became the Bird Goddess and the stars were already in me and I could hear the voice of the poet and I cried the song of the soul.

The next morning, I woke up slightly startled at the new surroundings, forgetting that I had already left the hotel. I remembered where I was and, taking in everything, began the day with a shower and silence. Picking up the phone, my first call was to Hironobu san. I longed to hear his voice. He was delighted to hear from me. I gave him the number and told him not to give it to anyone and asked him to tell Shane that I was away for work. He hesitatingly spoke of how many times Mr. Shane asked about me. I listened. There was a silence. I heard his understanding. He knew me. He gave me some other numbers for auditions. I took them down and told him that I would see him soon and eat sushi from his life hands. He was happy.

I called Smila. She screamed into the phone. I removed the earpiece away from me and let the River Ganges flow into the canals of my hearing water chants, as Shiva's locks poured this fluid heaven into me. She wanted to know where I was.

"I am with some friends," I replied. She wanted more. I gave her none. She spoke of a party soon and gave me the address. I asked her if it would be okay to bring a friend. She said that would be fine. She talked of all the various agents who called for me and gave me their numbers. "I will call them all, I promise," I said. She kissed me and said goodbye.

Flora walked in and asked me how I felt this morning. "Ready," I replied. She gave me a cup of tea and some toast and handed me the clothes I would wear for the shoot. I started to get ready and remembered Aakash and dialed his number. I forgot the time difference and woke him up. His warm voice enveloped me.

"I have missed you!" he cried.

"I miss you, too," - I replied.

"Did you touch the **lingams**?"

I told him that I had not. "I am waiting for you."

I spoke of Ulfhrafn and the shoot. He was happy. I gave him the number. We hung up, and Flora came in to see if I was ready. She checked everything and adjusted the makeup.

In the studio all was lit and ready. Ulfhrafn was happy to see me. He was eager to begin. We started. I floated into my creative spark, and the Hasselblad, one of the cameras he used, melted into my skin. It was a cloud choreography which shaped and formed and became me. He was awakened. He said he had never worked with anyone like me.

"I knew this the first time I saw you."

One day all this would be etched ontp my face and scratched deep into the canvas of my skin, and the geography of a gilded interior would carve its history on my then face, which would glow with the tattoos of life. They would say I looked different. Some would say I had not changed. And I would hold the shifting body of held youth, and laugh at the ignorance of permanence. I would lick the raw taste of the folds of fresh, uncooked fish as it folds my tongue sword and I would watch the ancient lines of valleys and painter strokes as I embrace my eyes with that eternal, dark, bleeding kohl which was my eye shadow and my eye keeper. I was a mad mendicant who sees the invisible, as I drank blood and spoke poetry. My cells were haloed and happy and loved and kissed. I never forgot to make love to them.

We worked relentlessly. Ulfhrafn paused only to explain to me what he was looking for. I listened and absorbed and became what he needed. The camera was his third eye. I danced to its rhythm and melted in its presence. The Greek word "to create" also means "to grow," and "to sacrifice" also means "to make holy."

"I am not a dancer. I am a priestess in the temple of art," said Isadora Duncan.

Life cracked the seed spreading the roots in earth, and tore apart any concrete walls. Birth was the silk and satin clouds, weaving the arches of that certain thrill when the I became one with a grain of sand and Shakti was given to Shiva in wedding. He who was scorned by the norm because he was one with the unholy and walked in torn clothes

168

with a bone bowl attached to his hand and laughed with all of the beggars of the world. He was the source of knowledge and creativity as he danced creation into being.

We took a break. We had worked all day and into the evening. Ulfhrafn mentioned that we should go out for a bite. Flora said that she might have to meet her man. We asked her to invite him, too. She went to call him. I changed into something comfortable. My limbs felt free. I sensed every curve of my physicality and the wounded Goddess ripped apart by man's ignorance sat in a truck as the young artist proudly completed his first masterpiece. I asked him if it was the Goddess herself whom he had sculpted. He looked at me, surprised, and wondered aloud how I knew. " Because this is me", I replied. I touched her.

"The wounds are alive and art is bleeding."

I changed and, walking out of the room after lighting an incense stick and the candle on the altar, I saw Ulfhrafn waiting at the door.

Flora had joined us and told us that her friend would be meeting us. I was happy. We were a Greek chorus that was creating a canvas of art. The restaurant was nearby and we walked to it. The night air was welcoming and seducing. The lights were lit, and through the park the liquid folds of the river peeped through. I gasped. I had not seen her before. It was a Greek restaurant and Ulfhrafn asked me if I liked Greek food.

"I'm not sure," I told him, "but I would love to try it." I ordered the spanakopita, which looked fresh and inviting. He ordered some vine leaves. I asked him where the leaves were from. He said they were grape leaves and were from Mainland Greece,.

Flora's man walked in. He was also from Peru, and had the same strength that she had. They sparkled together and she smiled gently at him. Love is so beautiful, like an amethyst stone which absorbs all negativity and attracts huge abundance. I would always wear it on my right wrist.

Ulfhrafn ordered a Greek wine called Retsina – the wine of the gods, they say. It had a strange taste on my tongue and I was not sure if it glided through like the body of a red. He told me it was an acquired taste and that it was made from Greek or Cyprian grapes, which while being fermented had pine oils added to them and that it was thought to be the tears of the nymph wood. I sipped again and the nymphs entered me and the taste changed because mythology had become liquid. We spoke of the day's work. Ulfhrafn was ecstatic. Flora echoed his enthusiasm. They both told me that they never thought they would find such a perfect subject for the piece. I was delighted.

The night wore her sensuous gown gracefully as we ate and sipped and spoke and laughed. Ulfhrafn said that I should take a day off and rest; we would begin again the day after. He wanted to shoot out-

169

doors in the park. Flora looked caringly and agreed. She said that I needed to rest. Flora and her friend left after saying goodnight, and Ulfhrafn
and I walked. back to the apartment.

The night sighed into my skin and all my well-wishers smiled.
There was fullness and gentleness between Ulfhrafn and me. The spa
and all the blood, bones, flesh and fear seemed far away, though I remembered Percival, the meditating man and the dancer with gratitude.
Ulfhrafn's satisfaction and excitement about the project was contagious
and I, too, shared all that he felt. As we walked in sync our footsteps
echoed the rhythms of art like a true painter who never repeats a stroke
twice because all of him is source-fed, and a continuous rebirth flows inside him. At that moment we both looked at each other as though pulled
by the marionette strings of the ultimate player. I felt his desire to hold
my hand and I quietly slid my fingers into the crevices of his tree hands.
His hands hesitated slightly and then entwined mine with fullness. All
these men had such magnificent hands.

We walked to the elevator and, opening the door, he waited for me
to enter. He kissed me on both cheeks and as I walked to my room, after
thanking him for his hospitality, he asked if there was anything that I
needed. I paused and slowly, with the rhythm of my heartbeat, thanked
him for rescuing me from that place.

"I don't regret it and I learnt much, but it almost broke me," I
said.

I turned my back towards him as I felt the tears starting to invade
my eyes. He came close and held me very firmly. "Take my strength.
Feel my energy," he said. - His eyes held me and I felt them enter me.
There, by the bedside, stood a jar of crystal-clear water with a beautiful
glass beside it. Flora had left it there for me. She was the woman warrior whose absolute strength was defined by her devotion and dedication
to life and friendship. She was now embraced by her lover, and I was
embraced by the five pointed voice of the stars. I smiled and heading
to the bathroom washed my face with love. The kohl had let itself run
wild around my eyes. I began to remove the shadow whispers of my
sight-keepers when something stopped me and I left them there. I looked
into the mirror and saw my sari-self, my antelope face with the other
horn. Startled, I looked again and there she was. My hands traveled to
my cloth bag and, finding the little round gold box, I opened it. The red
powder in it shifted with life. I had carried it all the way from India. It
was my reminder of the wedding night when the red vermilion screamed,
announcing the planned union.

Placing the tip of my first finger into the bleeding well of red, the
full powder scathed my skin and I carefully traced my third seeing eye.
It was a vast circle and the red was deep and dark and alive. I leant
closer into the reflection and felt myself sailing through the transparent

glass like Orpheus, the poet who was taken into the other world by the princess of death because she had fallen in love with him in the story of Orpheus and Eurydice in the Greek myth. *Death falling in love with a human*, I thought.

In my dream world I see a vision. An antelope-man is standing in front of me. He is tall and big and his breath has a forward leap in it. He is strong and gentle and as he bends into me I feel comfortable and warm. His eyes are emerald green, I feel a sharp arrow-like pain in the center of my eyes and feel gold teeth biting into me. A ball of light enters my head and travels right through me, and then, leaving me, goes bouncing along, leaving a very unusual trail of light on the streets of this city of angels.

I remember being startled and as I looked again there was a man standing in front of me. The antelope had merged and his horns were wings around me. I remember waking up and running to the bathroom mirror to see my bite. It felt wet. In the mirror, as I leaned into the glass, there was no trace of anything. I opened my eyes and now the third eye was glowing red. I felt young and childlike with a leaf in one hand and my red-tip finger on the other and I walked into the bedroom and sat down on the edge of the bed. I picked up the glass of clear, clean water and swallowed all of it and all the rivers and oceans filled me with a liquid ecstasy. If wine was the soma of the gods, then water is the life of the skies and the earth and the clouds and the hushed leaves. It is the seed bursting into life and the barren winter birch trees waiting to be licked and stroked by their first spring leaves. I saw them dancing in the whisper of the wind. Arrogance in the form of a false adult tried to invade me. I shunned him with a power that surprised me. The candle was still lit and the last coiling smoke of the incense pierced the sky. I disrobed and fell between the sheets.

The room was large and it had a cave-like effect. The red, bleeding couch was quiet. The altar surrounded me. I thought of the sable antelope and my dream and the two horns that balanced both of my sides had now become transparent wings.

The sky was shrouded and the moon was hiding. She wanted me to sleep. I did.

The next morning, I heard a gentle voice and, waking up, I saw Flora. She had a beautiful bouquet of fragrant lilies in her hands and placed them in a vase filled with water. I wanted to ask her if she had just come from the battlefield of love. I smiled. She smiled. She heard me. She said that we could have breakfast when I was ready and that I should have the day to myself.

After showering, resting and sitting in front of the alter, I put on something light and, walking to the dining area ,saw both of them at the table. Ulfhrafn greeted me with warmth and asked how my night was

171

and told me that Hironobu san had called many times.

"Magical," I replied. He is my father." They looked surprised. "His whole ambiance exudes my father's absolute grace and magnificence."

I looked at Flora. She touched my hand. They both smiled. I told them that after making calls, I would go to some appointments and auditions if possible. Flora said that she would love to drive me if that were okay with me. I told her that I did not want to inconvenience her, to which she said that it would be a pleasure. She said it would be quick as she would just wait for me and we could cover many places. Thanking her, I went back to the room and started making the calls. I was overcome with feelings and memories of all the other times when so much within was ripped and trampled on and shaken and challenged. And as I glanced sideways, I saw a lady sitting nearby. She was filled with child and talked relentlessly. Her mother sat next to her and her hands were on her swollen belly. I touched my belly which was blessed by abalone skin dreams and painted sage leaves. It was barren but whole. The belly of a shaman rope walker.

I was in the balcony in the singing, warm house in India. The afternoon was lazy and languorous. The fragrance of the flowers was hypnotic. The air itself was like the sun. The Cat Goddess whose stone is soft was my watcher and guardian, towering over waters of consciousness and the dream dog of long ago. The girls were rubbing my feet with mustard seed oil. The smell was hot and pungent and burnt my eyes. They were giggling. I was meeting birth and rebirth and the cat was scratching my heart place, as a child that I caught in a transparent milk balloon sailed towards me. My mother-in-law came in and watched the girls. She did not look at me directly but I felt her eyeing me. A throbbing pain made me sit up. I felt the world moving inside me and her cold eyes bled my interior.

I glanced at the woman and mother whose eyes held her daughter with care and love. I remembered my rounded belly and I thought of art and life as one. "There is nothing else," I whispered softly. "Life's patterns of family may or may not be. Sometimes one may feel lost, filled with a void without and within. Did I miss out on the so-called life way? Did I miss out on a life of comfort and ease? Sometimes I feel shipwrecked and remind myself that I am the pulse-holder and pulse-maker of my own life's walk. This journey is a birth of word and art and the rounded belly is the whole self and sometimes this birth can take many years and the pain of waiting is devastating and huge. But I will not stop or falter or deviate. I will not." And I saw a tall, surreal Ganesha figure as though sculpted by Giacometti himself with a beautiful yellow turmeric stone head at his feet standing next to me.

After scheduling as many appointments as I could for the day I called my Hironobu san. He was gentle and so happy to hear from me.

This time he said nothing of Shane and only asked how I was. I assured him that I was fine and that I would drop by today if he was available. He was excited and said he would make some sushi for me. I asked if I could bring a friend.

"Of course," he said, and then softly whispered into the mouthpiece, "Mister Shane did very bad thing to you." We were both quiet. The silence was full. I touched it with respect and bowed to the mouthpiece. I quietly told him that I would see him later. He said something in Japanese. I think it was something about the dance of the beetles. I didn't understand and yet I did. Looking up, I saw Flora standing at the doorway. I told her that I had tried to get as many appointments as I could and that we were invited to have sushi with Hironobu san. Ulfhrafn wished me well with the auditions and we walked down to the car. I mused at all these sudden flows of auditions now and not before when I desperately needed them. And then I remembered Abrihet's words that the sacrifice had to be made and the house had to be burnt down.

Flora was a wonderful driver. She was fast, agile, and intelligent in her moves. I loved the way she shifted the gears. She smiled as she noticed me watching her. We drove through Central Park. I thought of Aakash and the mirror on grass, of the cab driver who had seen me in his dreams and, of the turquoise chains, of she who gave them to me, and of Niyol, my wolf man.

And then I shifted myself as we passed by the building where Smila lived. I asked Flora to stop just for a second in front and I stepped out. Running towards the entrance I saw Diego. He gave me a big hug and we walked back to the car together. I introduced him to Flora and they spoke in Spanish. He asked how I was and that Smila often mentioned me. I saw my blue goddess standing straight and curved and her eyes were shooting arrows as she held a rose in one hand and a peacock feather in the other hand, and a dancing Ganesha stood on her black-blue wooden vibrating head, and I became the fifth tree. Diego thanked us for dropping by. He said something in Spanish to Flora and we headed to the first call. As we approached the building on Fifth and 55th street, Flora looked for an empty space and parked. She had that warrior gaze and told me to just be. "Diego said you are the sun," she added as I left the car. I smiled, and touching her with my eyes, walked to the entrance.

The audition was on the eleventh floor. I walked in, slightly shaky, and saw a young man approaching me. He handed me some sheets of paper and pointed to some empty chairs on the other side of the room. I glanced at the lines. I didn't recognize them but felt their shape and size and saw their motion through voice and breath. To act is to be one with the essence of the character, to go into the skin and experience every inflection and aura of that being. It is to go in and bend with the breeze of the ambiance within the person and pierce the surface.

I looked around me. The room was full. Everyone was nervous and fearful of the others. I looked through the window at the sky and, out of the corner of my eye, I saw a branch of a tree lying on the concrete floor. I picked it up and stole it away from cold carelessness and walked amongst lions and cubs.

I heard my name being called. It was mispronounced. I corrected him and he apologized and said it again the exact same way. I let it slide. A panel of people sat on the other side of the long synthetic table. They asked if I was ready. Miguel entered the room. They asked me to begin. He was standing behind the director who was in front of me. Taking a deep sigh, I began looking only at Miguel. He smiled and encouraged me on. My passion was alive. I felt his hands entering my throat and molding my words so they resonated with perfect enunciation, timing, and power. I left me, and became stronger and bigger as every word was sculpted through my mouth. I felt his wild sexy mouth eating me as his long snake tongue shaped me. I screamed and cried and howled; it was what the scene required. I finished and was out of breath. They looked back to see what I was focusing on. You could hear a pin drop in the silence. I gathered myself and got my breath back. Miguel was leaving the room and his body touched mine as he walked by. I wanted to fall into him and melt into him and listen to his scraped deep voice and make love to him. Remembering where I was, I thanked them and began to leave the room. I heard the director say that the reading was excellent and that they would call me back. I almost turned to ask if he thought that I was exotic but stopped myself. I thanked him and walked out, now running, hoping to find Miguel. I smelled him and I knew he was here. "Thank you my lover," I whispered, "as you touched me and, strumming the guitar, sang your ocean love songs to my heartstrings."

I felt intoxicated and heady and walked out to see Flora waiting in the car. I thought I would see Miguel there. I told her that my performance was strong. "I knew it would be," she said. I smiled. We went to the next and the next and the next and continued until we decided it was time to go to see Hironobu san. We found parking and Flora winked at me. I rang the doorbell even though I still had the keys. He opened the door. My heart skipped a beat. This is where it all had happened. He stood like a Zen Mountain filled with compassion, wisdom, and grace. I bowed and touched his feet. He tried to stop me but I insisted. He smiled shyly. Flora was mesmerized by his presence.

On the life table was the most inviting and delicious sushi collage. I introduced him to Flora and, removing our shoes, we entered the room. I asked if I could wash my hands. He smiled, saying that it was my home. I said nothing. He asked us to sit and started to serve. I was famished and relished all that he gave me. The green tea colored my inside

174

and felt healing and whole, as though he had put in some magic potion. I was sure he had. We were silent. I watched him watching Flora and knew that he approved of her. When we were done he asked if I wanted to go upstairs and check on my things. I didn't want to but felt that Flora did, so we walked up and after going past all of the rooms, we entered the bedroom. I saw her start. I sat on the bed and she sat beside me. She took my hand gently and touched my belly. I closed my eyes and for the first time in a long time I saw my stallion again, and the grand lady of the sky straddled across him, she who is all creation and all destruction. I saw the pink flower on the desert that dune day when I fell naked into the heaving sand, as it molded and shaped me and became the lotus and as Her hand beckoned me to awake and arise. And here she was again telling me never, ever to forget.

I was startled. It was almost as though Flora was her or that she had entered Flora. Her face was radiant and she said that she had just experienced something very special. I said that I knew. We walked to the library and there, too, we sat down. This was the place of tiger tales and elephant grass whispers where I had healed, and once again I saw Niyol with his wolf tribe and Flora became Niyol. "Who are you?" I asked her. She smiled and I knew then that all I had seen of her was true. She was a shaman, I hugged her and she held me with a power that was unbearable.

"I love you," I said.

"*Te quiero*," she said.

We walked down the stairs and my feet became Niyol's hungry wolf paws. Hironobu san was waiting for us. He had now spread out a whole array of delicate Japanese deserts. We ate the blessed food and I felt like I was in India and like the priest at the temple had done the afternoon *puja* and handed me the Prasad in plantain leaves. I told Hironobu san that I would pick up my things as soon as I found a place. Flora assured him that I was fine and safe, and that I had been working with a great photographer. He smiled and, as we reluctantly got up to leave, he handed me a small cloth pouch. I touched the sacred object with reverence, and, removing my worn-out lived wallet, I found an inner chamber and placed it in there. It sat near the pearl and now there were two little bulges. I loved them both. I told him that I would never lose it. At the door I bowed to him and he for the first time placed his hand on my head. And there it was again, that same feeling of a piercing shaft of light going right through my head into all the chakras. We got into the car and headed for the next appointment. This one was for a photo shoot. Flora said that she may know the photographer and added that if it was the person she thought it was, then it would be great.

I walked up the stairs, a little tired and a little removed, after being in that house. But I had to respect it, as it had sheltered me and led me through another labyrinth of the worn bark which was painted by seasons of growth. Suddenly, as I stepped onto the fourth floor and walked to the door of the studio, I felt like I had stepped into an unfamiliar and bleak place. There was something odd, and all of me stopped as though in front of a house full of lies and nightmares and emptiness. And then, as I opened a door that was slightly ajar, I realized where I was. It was the studio of the photographer who had tried to seduce me some months back. It looked strangely different. I was getting ready to turn and leave when he came to the door and greeted me with enthusiasm. I felt awkward and uncomfortable.

He said that it was great to see me again and that he had tried to reach me through Smila. He said that the project he had told me about came through and was approved, and that he was really pleased. I did not know what to feel. I saw the crooked bamboo shooting between the blue Goddess and the wooded electric orchid at her feet. The burnt yellow Goddess, brown and red-eyed, greeted me at the doorway I walked in to the studio. It was clean. He said he just wanted to discuss details and time frames. He said it was for a very high-end magazine. *The high end of what?* I thought and all the fallen autumn leaves flew towards me and begged me to sweep them through the cracked concrete. He spoke and I listened. He said that I looked different.

"I was away," I said. After discussing details, I told him that I had a friend waiting and that I would call him as soon as I had a number. He said he had to hear from me within two days. I assured him that he would. As I stepped out, he walked me to the stairs and I felt a tinge of anxiety but knew all was fine. I sailed down the stairs and felt Miguel's rough powerful hand walk into mine. I kissed it. "The flesh is alive. The hand is mine. He is the Song of Songs, my lover divine."

Entering the car, I thought Miguel would be sitting or standing by it. Flora noticed me looking as though searching for something. She said nothing. I told her the appointment had gone well. She asked me the photographer's name. I told her.

"He is very well known"

I told her about what happened the first time. Clouds entered me and rained inside the magic formations of my alma.

"Why are you sad?" she asked.

"He said that I looked beautiful."

She smiled. "You do look beautiful."

"I always feel as though it is a lie." I then told her about the need of this validation from my mother which I had never got.

She looked at me and touched my cheek and asked me why.

"Last night I had a dream. My beloved mother came to me. She was lying on a bed in a room, which I entered. She said something critical about how I looked. The arrow with a fire-flaming tip burnt my skin and I felt its scorching heat all over me. My entire body hurt and I lost all my self-confidence. I was that vagrant, floating leaf with a vein-less external and unpainted tip. All was like a blunt Samurai sword hidden in its sheath: shy, empty, without hope, forlorn, and dead. I had no body, no beauty, no pride, and no bones and the Maori tribe tried to show me the bone people's transformations. I was wedged within my own earth and wondered what I could learn from lizards and birds and I felt Death bowing his head and weeping."

Flora stopped the car and hugged me. Her warmth sailed through every pore of my skin. I felt grace entering me through the inner chakras, which now surfaced through the skin-self and danced with hope.
"Why did she never tell me who and what I was? That is all I wished to hear from my Mother. No other words mattered and that is when I went into the world with my brass begging bowl hungry for validation."
Flora wept. I wept. She said that my mother had a reason and did it because she thought it would help me.

"How?" I asked.

"One day you will know," Flora said.

"I will know, and I will be garlanded on a tree as a silver stallion sailing around the space between the sky and the earth; that space called Ka. Yes, one day I will know. Until then my bowl of fallen whispers and lover petals from all those amorous men and beautiful friends keeps being filled. I will eat them and smash them within the belly of my horse-, tiger-, and wolf- being, and drink the juice from the hooded daffodils and the shy budding lotus ready for its walk on the pond of eternity and mud; always untainted, always clean, and always shining. The beads of this wealth will gather on my skin and become my outer and inner layers. I will try," I whispered to her.

Flora was driving again and I was sailing inside the grape bud just under the red skin. I was the wine. I was the giver. I felt my *yoni* sprouting with light and the stems of lotuses bursting through with the fragrance of the sand. My dream lovers were standing in front of me as the car screamed through packed streets and faces and bodies. And then we were driving through the park and I saw them again, all of them. I looked again and they became trees. I looked again and they were human again. We were approaching the apartment building and, after finding a parking space, Flora took a deep breath and leaned back into the seat of the car. "You know, Mrinalini," -- this was the first time she had mentioned my name-- "you are unique and special. May all this pain and these thorns make you aware of who you truly are. This is why they were given to you, because you are not an easy human." And she continued to tell me some lines she had read from Roberto Calasso's book, Ka:

"The wives sprinkled the dead

177

horse with water from their
jugs. They said it would
purify his life breath and the
fresh drops fell on every part
of the lying horse and the wives
recited: may your mind be
magnified, may your voice be
magnified, may your breath be
magnified, may your sight be
magnified, may your hearing be
magnified, may all that has
suffered in you, all that has
been hurt in you be magnified.
May you be purified."

Her laugh rippled like a rocky river, making it textured and whole. She had seen. I leaned into her face and kissed both her soft cheeks. I thanked her. We walked out of the car, feeling a deeper bond. I felt her deep, powerful gaze. She took my hand and we walked into the building.

As we waited for the elevator, I recalled a dream where something was emerging from my left thumbnail. It was white and then it turned into a tree. There were eight of them and they had little lemon babies growing. A woman said that she had to plant them in the earth. I stood still and wondered who had given me this ecstatic affirmation. The elevator opened its doors and we walked in. The trees were in front of me. I bent down to pick them up so that I could carry them with me. They were from me and of me. Walking to the door, Flora took her keys out, by which point Ulfhrafn had already opened the door and welcomed us in. He said that he had missed us. We told him about the day and Flora mentioned the photographer with whom I had had my last appointment. He looked at me and asked me if he should be envious. I gave him a strong hug and said that he should never worry about that. He said he had worked all day with a few models and had just begun preparing a meal.

"I missed you and your eloquent motion. It's as though the camera lens melts within you." He paused and said that he couldn't verbalize it. I told him that I truly understood.

We were both exhausted and in the kitchen we looked forward to a warm and comfortable meal. I said that I would take a bath and rest a little. Flora said that I should, since the next day was going to be a lot of work. I walked to my room as they discussed the next day's shoot. My room was fragrant and inviting. Removing my sandals, I held my feet. The henna was now a pattern with slight lines and breaks. I lit the candle and the incense stick and lay down. My hands touched my belly. It felt fragile, and I breathed in all the sleeping daffodils and the awakened night queen with its intoxicating perfume. I asked my cells to accept the love streaming through me. My eyes wept as I remembered Niyol and his wolf transitions and all of the flying souls who were watching with pointed care. My antelope eyes wondered to the rising smoke spirit that I saw in Shane's library that wounded day, when I had to take away a root of my own being.

This was not nostalgia. This was not sentimental. This was that grounded compassion that comes of a lived walk through fire, rain, and sand rocks sculpted with blood and sound and red streams. I felt my breath growing heavy and wet and my eyes closed.

I see a dark-skinned sage floating above a riverbed. There are people all around me. We sing to him and praise the ether formations. He tells me that I will have what I am waiting for. Then, he descends. I run and touch his feet, I cry. He holds my head and tells me that he knows that I have gone through a lot. I am soothed. And now I see brown men in rags of gold. They approach me and tell me that Lord Ganesha is good for me. I tell them that I love Him and they say that he wants me to travel the world and spread the word. I touch their rugged feet and swim in what feels like a damp bed of glistening sand. The NYC street sounds woke me, and, slowly rising, I walked to the bathroom and ran the water.

I saw my face as it dissolved into a vermillion night sky through which Miguel's rough skin entered. I stepped back. He smiled and then slowly dissolved into the transparent surface. I heard his breath which gave off the refrains of a smoke-filled voice. I took it in and looked again at the mirror. This day he had been with me, protecting and giving me what I needed. The water rose in the bathtub and undressing I stepped into my liquid solace. I must have closed my eyes because when I opened them all the candles were lit. It was Flora and her magic.

After what seemed like an eternity, I left the liquid and, finding something comfortable, slipped into it and walked to the dining room. Flora and Ulfhrafn were at the table. The wine was in a rounded decanter and the flames of the three candles sang into it, giving light to the red poetry of all time. They both rose and drew a chair for me. Sitting down, I sighed. Ulfhrafn poured a glass for me.

We raised our balloons and caught each other's eyes through the misty glass, the glass through which, if you wished, you could just slide through to the other world and sail into the wings of mythology and magic, led by an arrow-feather princess warrior into that unknown, known reality where dreams can be tasted and licked with a body-less soul. I felt at home in the homeless garden of wild, unkempt flowers, where the exquisite gardener consciously lets the weeds grow, and where all the bent blooms weighed down by their own beauty smile at the burden of survival, and are happy that no human hands have altered or trimmed

179

their growth. The gardener just watches and only walks in if there is a need for a new path to be created. He is the eternal and absolute keeper of life. Nothing and no one is judged. Each grows according to their very own music and echo of a resounding call.

Flora and Ulfhrafn were looking at me warmly. I apologized for being silent and told them how comfortable I felt. They smiled, and we discussed the next day's shoot. I asked them where and when and Flora said that we would be in Central Park and maybe The Cloisters and other smaller gardens spread throughout the city. I was excited. Flora looked at me slightly concerned, making sure that I was ready for this. I assured her that I was and told her that I would retire early and rest and prepare. Kissing them both I rose, and they held me strongly.

I sensed Ulfhrafn. His eyes kindled and shivered through me. They felt like they were on a vision quest. His body had clean spaces around, as though it had transcended the banal and mere physicality of existence. It called for more and I was sure it was etched with his own song lines all over his skin. I smiled shyly. He saw the lines in my mind. He felt me entering him as though I was the male and he was the orchid with its flower face madly open and inviting. His breath was a loud symphony or a haunting night raga. He was excited. I was excited. Flora observed all of this and was quiet.

They both walked me to the room. He took my veined right hand and kissed it. His lips fell like those high-vibrating red petals on my skin. My hand slid through his rain fingers, leaving rivulets of opened water streams and an imprint like the crushed leaf with its embedded jewel on a sanded dune. He whispered good night. "Tonight I will dream," I whispered back.

Flora made sure that the bed was made and that the water jug was full. Then she embraced me. Her gentle feline hands fell on my soft belly. It was warm. Her hands walked right through me and touched all within, with arrows of peacock feathers whose eyes quivered. "He desires you," she whispered in my ear. My yoni quivered and I laughed out loud. She was happy and left me to change. Entering the bathroom, I looked into the mirror, waiting to see Miguel. He was not there, and yet he was.

In the bedroom I lay down and watched the night sky through the tall windows.. It was aware of my eyes, and I heaved a huge sigh as the waves of light cast shadows on the concrete landscapes of hope, greed, dreams, and more. Turning back, I saw the flame of the candle erect and proud, fully aware of the power of its presence and the beauty of its very being. My skin touched the sheets and I was cloud-kept and sky-swept. I was naked and full. I felt Ulfhrafn's eyes on me. They were like broken rustic threads of gold stars. My body was liquid. My **atman** was sculpted and formed. *They will laugh at me I am sure, but why should I care, because I will only dare.* My eyes swept and slid into that world of mine.

There he is, the four-legged one, sweeping all obstacles away as he walks grasshopper-like in and out of this world—my very own grasshopper elephant. This time he does not come towards me. He passes by. I pout like a child who does not get her piece of chocolate. I touch his ancient paws. I remembered the creases on his waving ears, freckled with pink dots. As it feathers the wounds away, my fingertips touch the flowing river and the nails fall on the belly of the wet whale and all songs have been sung once before.

And I thought of the Chinese girl in her hot, raw youth, insulting a great artist because her mind was blunt and broken by the wounds of knowledge and her soul fought to enter her, but was cast away by her inferior, stupid, mental aberrations. One day she might learn; but one day that learning might be too late because all in her is calloused and hardened, because tears of soft humility never made supple her youth of useless knowing. And her mind was embittered by love and no acceptance. *I won't tolerate such ignorance and I will carve cloud doors and open gardens of won youth within me.*

I walked away from these thoughts and felt him, the one with that all-knowing trunk through which words of wisdom flowed, and whose breathing, open tip went to the right and sometimes to the left, as he held the moon or the earth or a sweet meat of sorts. He was the one who loved sugar dreams and whose sacred belly burst with jewels of all-knowing. And then he sat on my head and graced me with his God-trunk. And he and I walked into the sky.

Chapter 10: My sandalwood husband and the birth of Savitri

The dawn broke and entered the room quietly and carefully, not wanting to interrupt my dreams. She waited patiently until all was whole and intact, and then sent her awakened, silver arrows to enter my morning stride. The sky was blue. I stretched and my warm body felt the politics of becoming where suffering had etched its markings of a new identity

Walking to the bathroom, I had a quick, cool shower. Sheathed by a towel, I came back to the bedroom and saw that Flora had laid out what I had to wear. It was a beautiful, white, long top with a gypsy feel to it. I put it on and felt the layers covering my chakras. They were hot from the night dreams and the blue-bodied beings were running around my mind's eye. Flora and then Ulfhrafn walked in. They were pleased. They explained to me why they had chosen that look. The woman who I was portraying would reflect a mystery of hidden thoughts and dreams. "Exotic," I said teasingly to Ulfhrafn. He quickly started to say something, and I assured him that I was only teasing him. He was relieved. "I love it," I said. "It is a distant love letter." His lips were trembling. Flora had everything packed and we left for the car.

Central Park was nearby so we walked to the spot that they had scouted out for the shoot. It was like a little silent forest grove. It had romance whispering through it. It was seductive and felt like a magician's choice of healing. I asked them if the male character around which the story revolved would be there. They said that they had thought of it but had instead decided to shoot me alone, as though in memories and remembering of him. Flora began making up my face, as Ulfhrafn explained what he needed of me both in look and emanation. He was always so detailed and meticulous. I loved working with him.

He bent with me and the eye of the camera truly dissolved into his eye. It was like having a blue blood, red orgasmic sky when we worked together. I was aroused. The lens touched me like a mad lover, hungry and elegant, like a rough bark of a redwood tree. Everything came from there, and was born of that texture, and the fabric of a mirrored tapestry of will, vision, and trance broke through all of myself. I walked inside the grove marking the inner and outer boundaries while they set up the camera and lights and the story from the ancient Indian legend of Savitri and Satyavan came to me. She was the daughter of a famous king and she set out on her own to find her mate, against her parents' wishes.

Riding in her chariot made of wild grass and heralded by two ivory white stallions, she travelled through vast expanses until she saw Satyavan. And when she saw him in the emerald woods she knew he was the one. On her return she told her parents what she had seen. The parents consulted the palace astrologer who spoke highly of the match, except for one flaw: Satyavan was going to die in one year at an appointed hour. Shocked, the royal couple spoke to their beloved daughter of this. Savitri was unmoved and said that she would rather be with him for one year than with anyone else for a hundred years. The saddened parents gave their daughter their auspicious blessings, and she went to unite with her man and lover, who lived in exile.

He also was the son of a king and queen. Savitri devoted herself to her new home and when the ordained time came, she asked permission of her in-laws to go to the forest with her husband. She sat against a banyan tree and watched him fell wood, and then at that ordained hour he complained of a headache and, lying down on the soft grass, laid his head in her lap. She guarded him like a lioness with eyes and heart wide open.

She felt an ominous presence and, looking up saw Yama, the god of death standing over her. He had come to take Satyavan into his kingdom. Savitri refused to let her golden man be taken from her. Death said to her that she had no choice and took the now spiritless Satyavan from her lap. She howled and cried and followed Yama. Looking back, he warned her that she could not follow him into his kingdom. Savitri didn't stop and kept walking behind him. Finally realizing how determined she was, he told her that he would grant her three boons if she would stop following him. She agreed. Her first wish was to give back sight to her father-in-law. Yama willingly granted her this. She then asked for her in-laws to be taken out of exile and be given their kingdom back. "Done," said Yama. Savitri kept following him and asked for her final wish. "I want to have children," she said. Without turning back, Yama granted her final wish. But Savitri kept on following him, now almost at the entrance of that world. Yama turned back impatiently and chided her for still following him. Savitri stared into his eyes and said "How can I have children if you do not give me back my husband?" That was the moment when Savitri conquered death.

I was in India in the bedroom with my sweet, gentle, loving husband. The birth was very close and I was uncomfortable and elated. I looked at the ceiling and showed him how beautifully the spider had been working. I told him that as soon as the web was complete I would give birth. He asked how I knew this, and I said it was a floating leaf that danced down from the heights and slid through my mental eye. He was silent. He had a book in his hand. It was pocket size. I commented on the size and he said he loved it because he could carry it wherever he went. I asked him what it was about. And he said it was Savitri, the epic poem written by the great sage Sri Aurobindo, who weaved his entire integral yoga into this legend. It was the tale of Satyavan and Savitri as recited

183

in the **Mahabharata**, of conjugal love conquering death. Satyavan is the soul carrying the divine truth of being within himself, but descended into the grip of death and ignorance, Savitri is the Divine Word, daughter of the Sun, Goddess of the Supreme Truth, who comes down and is born to save. I asked him to read me something from it. He told me he would read me some lines about when Savitri who roams the worlds alone finds
Satyavan and falls in love with him. My whole self moved towards him. I placed my head on his heart and listened to the melody of his life beats as he softly spoke:

> "Out of the voiceless mystery of the past "/"
> in a present ignorant of forgotten bonds"/"
> these spirits met upon the roads of time "/"
> Yet in the heart their secret conscious
> selves at once aware of each other"/"
> warned by the first call of a delightful
> voice and a first vision of the destined
> face."

He paused and bent down his head to kiss my forehead. He wanted to make sure that I had not fallen asleep. Looking up, I smiled at him, my eyes wide open. And he continued, saying that these were the first lines Satyavan said to Savitri:

> "Oh thou who came'st to me out of time's
> silences "/" yet thy voice has wakened my
> heart to an unknown bliss "/" Immortal or
> mortal only in thy frame"/" for more than
> earth speaks to me from thy soul, and more
> than earth surrounds me in thy gaze"/"
> how art thou named among the sons of men?
> Whence hast thou dawned filling my spirits gaze"/"
> brighter than summer "/"
> brighter than my flowers, into the lonely
> borders of my life."

I felt all in him dusk into an orange sunset and my sickle moon fingertips caressed his heart and his grass hair trembled as I wiped gold dust on his skin. With the longing of earth when the first raindrops touch its surface, he whispered in my caved ears that I was his Savitri. I wanted to triumph over all and spread my invisible antelope wings and land inside his huge self. Tears travelled down my cheeks. My mouth was full as though earth and sun had deepened its form and changed its hue. His long fingers tapered on my face and gently wiped the dewdrops away.

"You are my Sun Goddess," he said again, but this time it was loud like a bell that has been molded and carved with clay from all over the world, and when the tattered and torn and famished bell maker waited for the first stroke, it was perfect, and he crawled on wet earth and became one with the bliss of perfection and art.

Flora was done and pulled out her mirror for me to see my face. I refused. I just wanted to travel in and not be distracted when I worked and not be self-conscious of my visage. She smiled, and Ulfhrafn nodded his head in approval. I had just journeyed back from an ancient land and felt aged and strong, as though I was the long-bodied one, a saying, which I was told about somewhere in New Mexico, that meant a body filled with ancient whispers and knowing. I looked at my body, wondering if it was indeed slightly elongated. I saw them both watching me and I quietly whispered that I thought my body had stretched. We laughed. The camera began and I was present. All was alive. The horse and the rider became one as they both entered me. Ulfhrafn spoke gently, clearly, precisely, strongly but never aggressively. He felt me feeling him and it was electric. It was the wood orchid fallen on a rustic wooden floor, exuding its wild fragrance and tropical sultriness. I made love to the camera. He made love to me. My body spread like the branches of a tree and my being walked with roots spread out like the ancient banyan trees in India.

We worked endlessly without stopping, only to change costumes or for Flora to adjust my hair or face of an unwanted ripple. She flowed with us. The sky changed, as did the dance. He told me what he wanted of me and I gave without hesitation or stammerings of any kind. Culture has many hues and they are all seductive, deep and maddeningly sensuous. It speaks to a higher consciousness and a deeper seeing. Being aware of culture is being able to feel all the many myriad layers of a textured fabric canvassed within its very own depths.

The night drape was surrounding us. Ulfhrafn stopped to adjust the lights. He asked if I was okay. Flora made sure I was not straining myself. I told them both that I truly was fine and that we should continue. I felt my vision meeting all exteriors, and slaughtering all vain beauty. Ulfhrafn finally stopped and called it a wrap. I was still in flight and had to bring myself down and back. Eyes were all over, and seduction was complete in one hundred and one layers and levels. They packed up all of the equipment and I told Flora that I would change at the apartment. We walked back. We were winding down. We were very elated and excited. Ulfhrafn came near me and, standing in front of me, took my face in his hands. I felt a tree holding me. He looked into my eyes long and deep and arrowed. He brushed his mouth on mine lightly, very lightly, and told me how amazingly I had done. I whispered back loud enough for Flora to hear me and told him that he inspired me and that I loved working with him. I said he allowed my muses to enter because he did not get in the way of their dance.

"You are of the Gods," he said lightly. And then he told me of a word in Icelandic for mediocre or average: it meant, "middle lion." "You are not middle lion, he said. I laughed. "You are big lion," he added. We all laughed. Flora took my hand. I was happy.

Reaching the apartment, I went to my room to change and shower and they asked me to come to the dining room so we could eat something and sip the red, warm, muse blood. In the room I felt a deep exhaustion overwhelming me. I sat down on the red couch. I breathed deeply. My belly hurt and felt strained. I wanted to stretch and, slowly leaving the couch, struggled out of the costume, slipped on something light and lay down on the bed. I wanted to wash but didn't have the strength to walk to the bathroom. I smiled, thinking that I may have exerted myself, but I had been in another world and nothing mattered except to mold and sculpt the grace of the vine-leafed body electric.

Worried, Flora came into the room and rushed over to me. I told her that I was very tired.

"You did too much," she said.

"It was worth it," I replied. I asked her to please light the candle and an incense stick. She did, and placed her healing hands on my belly. I heard a soft thud and there on the floor was my journal.
Flora handed it to me.

"I haven't written in it for so long," I whispered.

"It is all there," she said.

Smiling, I placed the journal on my heart . The rough lines of the cloth of many sightings and emanations grew into me. I closed my eyes and faintly saw Ulfhrafn at the doorway. He had a concerned look on his face. I smiled, waved, whispered something, and closed my eyes.

I was in India. The day had arrived. All was being prepared. The child would be born in the house. The family doctor and the midwife both made sure everything was at hand. I was nervous but wanted to walk to the temple. Both my husband and my mother-in-law didn't like the idea, but I insisted. My husband reluctantly agreed and said he would walk with me. My mother-in-law was not happy. We walked together, my Satyavan and I, not to meet death but to meet life. The gardener, seeing us, ran over with fresh tuber roses. I loved these flowers. Their essence was the secret vine leaves of a golden friendship where all is understood and translated into the next level. The fragrance was heady and intoxicating, like the eyes of a maddened mendicant who has found God, and the haunted eyes of a longing Radha who waits adorned for Krishna's footsteps. I took the flowers and kissed their full blossoms. The gardener smiled and we walked slowly to the temple entrance. I saw her. She was my toothless goddess from a million decades and fulfilled centuries. She smiled, and from her open mouth the whole universe was visible. I was staggered a little by the vision. My husband held me, and she smiled, knowing I had seen what she wanted me to see. I gave her a stem from the roses. She offered it to the priest who took my offerings and placed them at the feet of the goddess. Mother Kali, who was the all-compassionate Goddess of Creation and Destruction. She was fierce to look at, because her gaze missed nothing and no one. She was all powerful. She slayed all ignorance without hesitation and walked with absolute compassion.

As the priest performed the rituals my husband and I sat, and I felt her gaze surrounding and holding me. I couldn't take my eyes off of her. She penetrated all. Finally, the priest handed me the blessed offerings and touched my head. I slipped into another realm and once again that touch of the universal mother molding my head arrowed down through me. I felt limp and closed my eyes. Rising with my husband's hands around me, we turned to leave. The priest looked at me with a warm but strange look. I gave the blessings to the white-clad, smiling one but she refused again saying that I needed it. She, too, had a strange look. We walked back and as I turned to look at them I saw both their hands raised, blessing me. I bowed my head. I felt a pain coming on and clutched my husband's strong arms and kissed his hands. I looked at him like a child with anticipation and fear. He watched me, holding me tightly and whispered in Bengali some comforting words. "Be strong," he said over and over again. They all rushed towards me. My mother-in-law, the doctor, the midwife and the maid and carried me against my will, saying that I should not be walking. It was intoxicating in its intensity. I had never felt anything like this.

In the room I looked at the web that was being created by the spider and noticed it was complete. I looked at my Satyavan and pointed it to him. He looked up and knew it was time. He enveloped me. The rest was a trance. Everything happened so fast. I surrendered and felt like I had left my body and watched from another place. I traveled far and then suddenly all was warm and wet and I heard a distinctive cry. A fragrant, crooked, bamboo-sounding squeal. They fussed all around me. All the cooing and cuddling and baby sounds and finally they gave me this new being. She was a girl. She was beautiful. My first word was, "Savitri."

Everyone looked startled and my husband nodded happily. My mother-in-law had a strange expression on her face. She was disappointed. She wanted a baby boy. "Isn't she beautiful?" I asked her. She said nothing. I looked up at the web in the corner of the ancient ceiling and startled, looked again. One thread was broken. I pointed to it. No one understood but my husband did, and he looked at it, concerned. The thread had been disturbed as though by some anger or hatred that had hurt the perfection of that creation. My Savitri was looking up at me with dark, deep eyes and a head full of hair. She was radiant.

I woke up with a start in Ulhfrafn's apartment, knowing that the seed of eternity was not the seed of the intellect. I loved the language of love, which drove me mad. Engraved in soul Maya, I listened, learned, and walked. Slowly rising, I walked to the bathroom and ran the bath. I was different. Brushing my hair, I felt the touch of the wind weaving rain through my strands. My face looked petalled, as though painted by a master painter. The tub was liquid and, sighing, I sunk into its many layers of laughter and pain. I pushed myself up and taking the journal started to fill the pages with the following:

"Imagine a dry gravel path.
Imagine a walk on this simple
way of pebbles. Imagine each
pebble opening into a play of
light and life. Imagine the dust
wings caused by your conscious
footfalls. Imagine your fingers
touching your face to set aside
your hair threads. Imagine your
fingers touching your face land.
Imagine the eyes of mountains,
of skies, of birds, of crickets.
Imagine all these simple
moments and imagine creativity
in every moment and feel the
laughter of your very being
breaking through all of you and
sometimes, and only sometimes,
the solitude of the path creates a
cry like a fake earth crust,
sometimes, and only sometimes,
the making tangible of the
intangible creates a rock hard
tremor and sometimes the
imitators spoil the milk and blunt
the sword. And I say, you fools,
you mind-trucked, heavy-headed,
thought-filled, dry-twigged
sparkling bodies, crack your
ignorance."

It flowed. I was relieved and was
assured that nothing is lost but
always forming and sculpting

188

inside the marble stone waiting
for the sculptor to release its
shape.

I placed the cloth book on a table near the tub. There was a soft knock and Flora walked in. She asked me how I was and looking at her I said, "I gave birth last night to a beautiful baby girl." She walked closer to the tub. She took my hands and kissed them gently. It went inside and the merged transparent antelope horns winged all around me. She took the loofa from the bathtub edge and pushing me gently to the front of the tub, started rubbing my back. She knew I needed it. I felt the old cells falling away and the new skin rejoicing on my back.

"You have given birth to yourself," she said, "to your inner child. You are beautiful. Your body is like the back of a tree." I smiled. She left me to soak and told me not to rush. I felt my belly. I saw my child. I embraced and kissed her and told her softly that I would not abandon her. I whispered all this into her little shell ear

In the bedroom on the now made bed was a tray with one red rose, a pot of tea, and a beautiful breakfast. She was divine, my friend Flora. She was the seeing one, my Om friend of heart and soul and pain and child and woman and culture and giving and fullness. I was proud of her. I sat down and slid a spoonful of the blood red papaya into my mouth. My tongue met the tropical breeze of India and the fragrant textured soil of that land. The magicians were alive. The yogurt smoothed my tongue with its gentle interiors and its pure white reflections. The toast spoke of wheat fields and falling suns drenched with the footsteps of the dream walker on the song lines of the ancient world and the tea was liquid warm heaven. I cracked the egg gently. It opened and I removed the top sky to get to the wet white part. I scooped the softness into my mouth and then pierced the sun ball in the body of the rest of the egg. I smiled. I tingled. I shuddered with joy. I was eating the sun.

Flora returned to tell me of the day's plans.
She said that there were many messages from Hironobu san and that I should call him as soon as possible. I smiled and leant back. I thanked her and, taking the phone, began my entry into the next journey. I asked her if we had finished the shoot. She said that we had maybe another day or two. I was happy. I didn't want to leave them.

Dialing Shane's number I waited excitedly to hear Hironobu san's deep, warm, full voice. He picked up and said "hi" in Japanese. I paused a moment before speaking. We both laughed. He asked me how I was and I assured him that I was very well. I told him that I had been working. He was very happy. He told me all the news. He said there were many calls for my appointments, auditions, and many from Shane and Smila. I noted them all down. He also mentioned that a photographer had been calling and wanted me to contact him immediately. "I will make sushi and sashimi for you and green tea.

"Soon," I replied, "very soon."

I called the photographer. I didn't remember his name. George, or Jack, or something. Not a memorable one. He sounded very relieved and said that he was about to look for someone else. I felt like telling him that he should have but did not.

"You cannot be found," he said sarcastically. There it was again, sarcasm, a way of laughing at beauty. I told him that I had been away working. We decided on a day. He wanted a number where he could reach me directly. I didn't give him any and said that I always got messages left at Shane's number or at Smila's. I was excited for some of the auditions, especially the one for the play. I remembered it was the one when I was very nervous, and Miguel had come to help me. I felt certain I would get it.

Finally, I dialed Smila's number. She picked up and, hearing me, hesitated and then screamed with joy. She repeated the same old stuff about how much she had missed me. I listened with my ears open. They flapped like the sacred elephant whose ears form the map of India. I heard her sincerity. I heard her lies. I heard her greed. I heard her lust. It all made a strange symphony of a sightless sight. We were the assassins of the shallow and the hollow but our swords were sharp only if we were full and clean, or else the strike was blunt and careless and weak. She irritated me because she always wanted to know where I was and who I was with. "Mind your own business," I wanted to tell her, "I was with fifty men, making love to all of them as they sank into every cell of my being and melted into my goddess-ness." Avoiding her question, I just went on to say that I had been working and things were good, and that I was more than well. She asked if I had been with a man.

"With many," I answered and laughed.

"You are teasing me," she said.

"Why would I do that?"

She changed the subject and reminded me of the party she had invited me to, which was the next night.
"I will be there. I will bring a friend or friends, if that is okay."

She said that would be fine, and she scolded me for not calling the photographer back, as he had been harassing her. I told her that I had and that I would start working with him soon. She seemed pleased. As we hung up, she told me how much she loved me, that word that is said to frequently in this society, until it is meaningless. I said nothing and told her I would see her at the party.

Both Flora and Ulfhrafn were in the studio organizing for the next shoot. I told them about all the auditions and about the famous photographer who had been trying hard to reach me. They were excited.

190

"I don't feel like working with him but realize that it would be important," I told them. They both agreed and Ulfhrafn pointed out that he was very good at what he did. "He has such a strange energy. It will be very hard after you," I replied. He walked to me and holding me, said that I was a natural and that he was certain that I would be excellent.

"My muses may not enter me," I said limply.

"They will, because they will hear your call specially to them."

I smiled, and Flora said that she remembered working with him before, and would be happy to be with me if Ulfhrafn did not need her. He said that he wouldn't need her, as he was going to take a day off before finishing the shoot. That made me very comfortable and I asked Flora if I should let the photographer know.

"Let's just surprise him and if he objects, I will leave," she answered.

I asked them if I could use the phone again. "Anytime," Ulfhrafn said. "You don't need to ask." I thanked him and dialed the number. The photographer picked up. He was happy to hear from me and mentioned that he had just left a message for me at Shane's. He asked if starting today would be too short notice. I hesitated and then told him it would be fine. We set a time and I hung up. I let Flora know and she said that that time would be perfect. She asked me if I was well-rested enough to do another job. "I am," I replied. I went to my room to get ready and Flora and I left soon after. Ulfhrafn was sad. I felt him. I told Flora how happy I was that she was with me. "I am too," she assured me.

We drove down through the city streets. The sky was blue and clear. The air was crisp and cool and the leaves were turning into a fire red. The sky was aflame. I had come to love those sun-filled blue New York skies, even when it was bitter cold outside. The trees were stoic and present. And here was Flora, again with her magic driving skills as she weaved through the traffic effortlessly, without any hesitation. She was a life driver. I told her that. She smiled. I was nervous about this work. I was tense and apprehensive.

"It will be okay," she assured me. We are almost there." The studio was in Soho. We found parking near the building and walked up the now familiar stairs. I knocked. The door was slightly ajar and I pushed it open gently, hearing a voice asking me to come in. The photographer, whose name was Jason, appeared, and, seeing Flora, he was both surprised and slightly taken aback. They recognized each other from a shoot that they had worked on sometime back and Flora asked if it would be okay for her to stay. She said that we had been working together with Ulfhrafn. He recognized the name and asked if he was the Icelandic photographer. "Yes I am his assistant. I take care of the makeup." Jason seemed relieved because his makeup person had called in sick. We were both happy and I surrendered myself to Flora's expert hands.

191

As Flora was adorning my face and hair, Jason started to tell me about the project. It was nothing like what I was working on with Ulfhrafn, and seemed easy. He showed us the clothes. They were all pretty skimpy and I felt a little strange, but knew I could handle it, remembering my time in London as a model.

My muses were there. They had heard me, the warrior man with his brilliant headdress and the bird with the jewel in her third eye. They danced across the room as though cleaning all the waves. I was ecstatic to see them. I slid into the first dress. He whistled. It was a dance of feathers. *A peacock dances when he opens his eye feathers and walks quivering to attract his mate and I saw the peacock dance on clay. It quivered silently in my heart and, walking in my father's hand, I was the story of this land.*

The peacock stands for the incorruptibility of the soul and I stand for the same. They can never rob me of that. I will be untainted, unmolded and not captured by non-ritual spaces, colorless skies, non-poem sounds and empty words.

We began. I gave differently. I watched myself and became the dancer in a magic-less court. My magic was my own and I walked outside and inside at the same moment. He was amazed at my uncanny skills. He did not have to speak. I felt the moves. It was nothing like working with Ulfhrafn. But I knew that this was educational for me, and I knew that I had to be able to perform in many different ambiances and atmospheres. The word atmosphere is from the Sanskrit word, "atman," which is the word for soul. And, as we weaved in and out, I was the storyteller of the invisible magic for those who could see and hear the other.. This time the rider and the horse were not one. I worked with the stallion and inhaled his breath. His craftsmanship was excellent but I didn't feel the call and I realized how beautiful it was to work with both. I glanced at Flora as we worked and she saw the difference in me; she understood. I was happy she was here with me. She surrounded me.

We worked through the afternoon and well into the evening. He asked if I needed a break. I wanted to finish so I did not stop. Finally, he called it a wrap. He was very pleased. I asked him if we were done and he said that he would let me know after he had seen all the shots. He said he did not realize how fast I worked. He said he would like to use me for more shoots and asked me if I had a direct number where he could reach me.

"I am on the move right now but you can always leave a message either at Shane's or with Smila," I answered.– But I could tell that he would have liked a direct number. "I will let you know when I have one." He wrote a check out for me and told Flora that he would send her one. We left, and I felt all the transparent foundations of a life structure given to me by my beloved parents. I thought of the uncrushed beings that had not been sculpted by the arrows of the universe.

"You were magnificent, Mrinalini." There it was again, the soft-ness with which she enunciated my name. It was like silent foot falls on an autumn, earth floor strewn with rust-hued leaves, fallen from the branches to begin their transformations. I touched her hair. I told her that I had learnt a lot, and that it was hard. "I know," she replied. Look-ing through the window of the car, I saw the faces of all the Native Amer-ican warriors fighting for their land, and Geronimo always ready to face the invaders. I must have voiced those thoughts because Flora asked me what made me say that.

"I saw them, and whenever I feel like I have gone through an or-deal or sadness, I remember what they had to go through."

Flora looked at me and her face had a dawn-dusk light of com-passion and humbleness. "You feel all," she said softly. "I do, the negative and the inspired",, I replied. The car suddenly sped and had urgency as though there was a mission to be fulfilled. The wind itself was carrying us. I glanced at Flora and her face was an arrow driving a chariot of light towards some kind of victory. I understood her and was aligned with her. She was a mystical warrior and her gentle humility was her entire lotus self. I loved her and all she stood for.

We drove in silence as I heard the cry of the howling wolves and the shame of greed and of the compromised bloodless walks. Arriving just outside the apartment building, she parked and, taking a deep breath, looked at me intensely.

"Sometimes you and your presence and what you say takes me so deep inside myself, I am filled with an unrecognizable joy. You take me to my very source and show me who and what I stand for. No one has ever done that. I feel myself and for the first time I feel nurtured and under-stood. I want to thank you for this, Mrinalini. "I took her hand and told her that she did the same for me.

"I hope that I didn't scare you just now. It was as though I was not driving. I was driven."

"I know," I replied.

I asked her if we could walk a little before going upstairs. I asked if she would be going home that night to be with her beloved man. "He is away, so I will be here tonight." Somehow that felt good, although I was not sure why. We walked through the park. It was dark but all was well-lit. The trees were silent and reflective. I touched every bark that we passed and whispered "I love you" to each one. The river body peeped through the trees, and she too was quiet as though feeling the ending of the day. We walked silently, each absorbing all that we experienced and all that was felt. We were twin souls.

Back in the building we walked up the stairs, since the elevator was broken. On the fifth floor, the door was slightly ajar waiting for our return. Flora and I looked at each other and entered quietly. It was late and all was very quiet. There was a light on in the studio and Flora and I walked towards it. Ulfhrafn was working. He was developing the shots of our shoot. He was startled as he did not hear us come into the apartment and looked up. His face was serene. He was joyous seeing us and told us how amazing the photos were. He asked if I wanted to see them, but I replied that I would rather see them the next day. He wanted to know how the work went. I looked at him passionately and whispered into his eyes that it was not him.

"She did excellently," Flora said.

"It was very difficult but I have to learn to work with different photographers and it was a great lesson in digging deep and finding more," I answered.

He smiled, and asked if we had eaten. I said that I was not very hungry and would rather just rest. He said that Hironobu san had called to say that the party had been moved to later on in the week and so was not tomorrow night. I was relieved. He added that if I was up to it we could work tomorrow, but start late in the afternoon as he wanted a certain light. "I would love that," I replied. Flora was happy too. He walked towards me, as Flora was looking at the shots and, holding me with that tree body, he told me that I would not lose anything by working with certain people. I asked him if he thought that I compromised when I did that.

"Absolutely not," he said, "you must expose yourself to many things and you will know when not to enter into certain arenas. You and your guides will show you that. But for now you must dance in many courts and learn and then later you can and will chose. You will know without hesitation because all in you will be chiseled and empowered. You don't have to worry."

I was happy and looked deeply into his eyes. He knew what I was seeing. He asked if he could come to my room that night and sit with me for a while. I nodded and whispered that I would love that. Flora looked back at me and told me how amazing the photos were. I was excited but I had to wait for the next day. I said goodnight and glanced back at wolf raven as he held me with his wolf eyes. "I am a wolf," I said to myself as I walked to the bedroom. I took a shower and chose my soft green Indian cloud cloth to fall over my body; the body of tonight. I lit an incense stick and the red candle, and looking at the night sky, closed my eyes in rest. A moment later Flora walked in with a jar of water and a crystal glass. She poured the water to the brim very carefully. Looking at the filled tumbler, I remembered the cloudy glass in South Hampton, near the ocean, where I had encountered hidden secrets and forgotten mountains, and where things were aesthetic and well-placed, but the soul was gone. My eyes filled and Flora, seeing me in distress, sat near me and kissed my third eye.

"You ran through those concrete eyes of deceit and walked through them with grace and like the lotus flower you won and are untainted. You were in a dark mire, but you left clean and whole and clear. Cry, but cry with joy and triumph because those who matter most are with you. You are held, my sweet bold child Mrina. May I call you that sometimes?" I nodded. I liked the sound. It was short and crisp and it still held the long rivulets of pulled and stretched rivers. I told her for the first time that Mrinalini meant a cluster of lotus flowers.

"How perfect," she said.

"Te amo," I whispered to her in Spanish, another language that I love. Neruda and Lorca wrote passionate love poems in that thirsty and wet language, nuanced by such erotic and sensuous details. She whispered good night and left. She glanced back, making sure that I was good and I softly said that Ulfhrafn would come. She smiled and blew me another kiss. I watched her graceful back as she swayed out of the room and I thought of all the good women and men who are and will be like little dragons, who only seven days after they are born, are already able to make clouds rise up and rain fall.

The flame of the candle was loud and still. It was upright and strong. The deities were lit, the sky was at peace and I reached for my journal. Sipping from the filled glass, I picked up the pen and the black ink painted the page, which had designs on it made by the many ingredients used to form the handmade paper. As the words flowed, I felt the snake rising from the base of my spine and pushing through the crown chakra of my head. I felt the thrust, and softly touched that center of all centers on top of my crown head. It was tender. It was time for vision to split away from its source and fly out like a baby bird to cloak the universe with its gossamer wings and become **Vajra**, the lightening flower, the ultimate weapon of the gods and the lightening flash of wakefulness. I looked up and there was Ulfhrafn at the door, waiting to catch my attention before entering. I pushed myself, and started to get out of bed when he told me not to. "You must be very tired," he said. I told him that I felt better. Sitting on the red couch, he said that his daughter, who was supposed to come back in a few days, had extended her visit with her mother. He added that I should not be in any hurry to move out or to find another place. I thanked him. We looked at each other. That **grok** look when no word is needed and when every glance dissolves into each other. I felt his body in his eyes and saw his heart in his breath. He reminded me of the Austrian poet Rainer Maria Rilke. From his book *Letters on Cézanne*, Rilke was once asked to name the informative influences on his poetry. He replied, in a letter from Muzot, that since 1906, Paul Cezanne had been his supreme example, and that "after the master's death, I followed his traces everywhere." At another instance he speaks of an insight which struck him like a flaming arrow while he had stood gazing at Cezanne's pictures: that here was one who remained in the innermost center of his work for forty years, and that this explained something beyond the astonishing freshness and purity of his paintings. For in a "conflagration of clarity," Rilke had realized that without such perseverance, the artist would always remain at the periphery of art and be capable only of accidental successes; an insight, which touched upon Rilke's painfully divided allegiance to life and to art. That is why this man who had learned to endure like the kernel in the flesh of the fruit assumed virtually mythic proportions. "For one thinks of him as of a prophet," Rilke wrote in 1916, and the same sense of something extraordinary, even enormous, is expressed in a remark Rilke made in front of a picture of the Montagne Sainte-Victoire: "Not since Moses has anyone seen a mountain so greatly." For the poet, this painter, and his work formed a unity that exceeded artistic and aesthetic criteria: "Only a saint could be as united with his God as Cezanne was with his work."

I glanced at Ulfhrafn. He was my Rilke. He was gentle and huge, a mountain of elephant grass with pearl palaces glistening on the edges of every blade. There was a throbbing silence in the room as it draped both of us. I told him that he reminded me of Rilke. He said that he loved his work.. He walked from the red couch leaving an imprint of himself on it. He came through fire and eagle feathers and his eyes bent into my very skin. My fingers like vine leaves, sang to the sun.. I was filled with desire.

There are those who would not approve but this desire united me and completed me. There were no cracks, and dualities were distant symphonies with false notes. As he sat near me he told me that I was a true artist. His voice was like a deep bamboo flute, filled and sonorous. He had seen a lot and had fought many wars against the middle lions. He then told me that in Iceland there was a lot of magic. "We see angels. We believe in them. They are everywhere." My eyes lit up. I felt the white wolf howls on my skin and my mind was sliced open and these words came to me.

Gods only laugh when men pray to them for wealth. Knowing eternity makes one comprehensive, comprehension makes one broadminded, breadth of vision brings nobility, and nobility is like heaven.

"You are noble," I told him. The flame of the candle was softer and in motion. It echoed shadows. We looked at them. He was aware and awake like an Indian rishi, burnt by the fire and consumed by the flames. His desire was contained and formed. It had no rough edges. It only had arrows sharp enough to pierce any surface. They had entered me and sung inside my interiors like a flickering light play on the glistening, swaying skin of a rivulet with its liquid form moving in the earth body. His hands touched my face and stray strands of hair fell around us. He took my hand and played with the sickle moon tips. We were like children running in a vastness of who we were. It was magical and intoxicating and sensual and erotic. Without knowing why I told him about Shane and what had happened in that land of sheer enchantment. I saw his eyes glow fierce with rage. He said nothing. He listened, and in that listening I felt all the comfort and hurt for not having had seen who Shane truly was. "I was seduced," I told him. His hands were on my belly and stayed there. I felt his whole person entering me through the hot vibrating palm of his hand. I trembled, and the entire tribe of wolves approached me and at the head was Niyol with his green eyes, smiling. I was safe.

Slowly removing his hand he handed me the glass of water and watched me as the transparent water dripped through my lips. I saw him seeing me, and my womanness was alive, and the child I had given birth to just a moment ago in India was giggling and smiling. Every single part of me was in the evergreen garden of bliss; beauty caressed me and I quietly thanked Ulfhafn for this. Rising slowly, he wished me goodnight and quietly walked to the door. Turning back he glanced at me and the pearl in the oyster shone in his mouth. I glanced at it on my table of tables and picking it up dropped it into the water glass. He saw me doing this, and coming back to the room watched me with a maddened thirst. The pearl entered my mouth and reaching towards his standing self I pulled his face towards mine. He bent down and, putting my mouth on his tree lips, my snake tongue placed the pearl in his mouth. His eyes were wild and after feeling the world ball in his mouth he gave it back to me and our mouths and tongues and lips met in an eternal kiss. It was the serpent kiss and I felt my kundalini uncoiling again as it arose, breaking through all the centers. Tantra became us. We met.

The next morning I was full and shy. *Where is he?* I thought. Entering the bathroom I decided on a bath and ran the water. I glanced at my hands. I remembered Tobias, and, walking back to the bedroom, picked up the now even more glistening pearl. Tobias's words flowed through the shiny pearl body and I heard him saying to me in French that I would always be free and wild. I kissed the pearl and heard the gypsy women shouting and laughing with me, as they rode their horses and camels with the wind flying through their brown, black, flowing manes. My gypsy tribe of many lifetimes sat me down and began etching symbols on my virgin skin. I asked them why, and laughing and giggling, they told me because I was one of them. I had been deflowered. The veils were torn apart and one single long-stemmed red rose was born in me. It was fragrant and opened with all of its petals unfurling to the inner sunlight that had filled my body. The wolves had entered and left their paw prints inside my every cell. The water had risen in the tub and, leaving my green cloth on the floor, I walked into its knowing body. I sighed with joy and then there was Flora standing at the door with a red rose in her hand. I gasped. *How did she know?* I wondered. But she did know. We looked at each other. Words did not need to be sculpted. The inner was formed and the outer resonated. I leaned forward and she unveiled my back. She left, and I stayed in for long and, slowly leaving the healing waters, dried myself off and put on something white and bright.

The day was born and I was reborn. My hair was wet and there was a smile on every strand. Once again Flora had left a tray with tea and fruit. She came in to tell me that Ulfhrafn was preparing breakfast for us. We discussed the plans for the day and I told her that I would go for some auditions, since we would not start shooting until late. She agreed, and said that she had to stay to help him prepare. I called Hironobu san, and as always he was happy to hear from me and gave me all the news and my messages. I assured him that I would see him very soon and also asked when Shane would be back. He was not sure but thought he would probably be back in a few weeks. There was a silence between us. My heart was full. He carried all the herbs to heal mankind. I walked to the bathroom mirror to embrace my eyes with Kohl. I put more than I usually do because my eyes felt that they had seen something more, something bigger and vaster. I was a bride. I was shy. I was a baby woman.

I walked in bare feet to the little breakfast table in the dining room. The song lines caught the souls of my feet and I heard the dreamscape of this new day. The little table was set and alive and smiling. The whole body was covered with hands and eyes and the head was a vibrant red lotus flower. The sky was sculpted with clouds and the park was twinkling and glistening with the morning dewdrops on their bark bodies. I felt him coming and turned around slowly. Our eyes met as he walked towards the table with delicious goodies. He said that he had prepared the food for me.

"I put every part of myself in these delicacies." It looked delicious.

"I will eat you," I told him.

"You are white today," he replied.

"I feel clean."

He took me in his arms. There was no space between us. There was only the space of us. The morning dewdrops entered and wet me. I shivered, and he asked if I was cold. I didn't answer. I became. He drew a chair for me to sit down and I asked if he needed some help. He said that he was fine. I asked him if I should call Flora, who had a room in his apartment incase of late shoots or emergencies. He nodded. I walked towards her room, where I had never been before. Knocking at the door, I heard her speaking in Spanish on the phone. She beckoned me to come in and, smiling, asked me to sit near her. The room was red and blue. It exuded her presence. She, too, had an altar and it glowed with a special light. She looked radiant and alive. She put down the receiver and told

198

me happily that her man would be back the following day. He had been traveling. I asked her if she missed him and she nodded and added that it was a missing without emptiness. Looking at me she told me that she had never seen Ulfhrafn like this.

"Like how?" I asked her.

"I am not sure," she said "all was inside and outside of him at the same moment."

I smiled because this was exactly what I would say.

"He never gets intimate or close with his models," she said. "This is very special."

"You are special," I replied.

Breakfast was ready. We walked out of Flora's room and, taking her hand in mine, I told her how beautiful last night was. "I was in India with my husband. I was here with my pearl eater. Our tongues were alive and the serpents became the shenai, the Indian instrument played at wedding ceremonies."

"He will heal you," she said.

"He already has. He is all nature, and nature holds him in her hands."

We entered the dining room and he was waiting for us. He rose and sat down after we had. The wolf and the raven were now one. My born child and I were one. We started to eat. I was famished. I was starving. Everything was an orgasm of taste, color, texture, and smell. He was watching me. She was watching us. And we were holding invisible hands and dancing on that hilltop like the last scene from Ingmar Bergman's film The Seventh Seal where only the jester, who has special sight, can see them rejoicing after death came to take them when their hour had arrived. Savitri challenged the God of Death and got Satyavan back. We would conquer mediocrity and remove the blunt arrows and sharpen them with art, sight, compassion, light, and love.

We spoke of the day and I told them that I would go for some appointments and be back in early afternoon to get ready for the shoot. *I will walk through the city and meet the angel and winged mercury who watches over the city. I will speak with them.* They both kissed me and told me not to do too much. We left the table and I walked to my room to get ready. The atmosphere was soulful. I made some calls and, taking what I needed, headed to the door. Both Flora and Ulfhrafn walked with me downstairs. He watched, and I felt his tapered look. It sailed around me. I looked back once. I sent him my eyes. I saw his raven self. He had wings and I watched them flap behind him. He smiled, and I smiled back. He was beautiful. He was a bird being, and I was the bird's nest. Flora took my hand and we walked down the stairs. The elevator was still not fixed. The stairs sang and our friendship resounded.

The morning air was chilly. I was glad that I had my wrap. The streets felt welcome. I remembered that wet, concrete walk after leaving Shane's palace that day not too long ago; and yet it seemed like a lifetime had passed. Looking at the time, I decided to go to Central Park and drink in the familiarity again. I had missed her and her shadows and all the trees that fed me and welcomed me each time I saw them. My pace quickened. I sensed the urgency to experience all that once again. Entering the park on the Fifth Avenue side I spotted the bench where I had sat on that shaded morning, lost, confused, and fearful. I touched the seven turquoise beads on my neck and sat on the edge of the bench, almost in anticipation of something. I looked around, wondering if Niyol would be walking towards me or the beautiful Indian woman who had given me the "soul-protecting" beads. There was no one, and I leaned back into the bench. The tops of the trees were a sky of green with blue and white cloud formations peeping through, like in a Magritte painting. I remembered that day when wind walked to me and showed me the way. And there right in front of me, as though sitting within the tree circle was Ganesha, beautiful, beatific, and with jewels all over him. They sparkled on his form and were of many brilliant colors. Red was everywhere and in his all-seeing third eye sat a perfect diamond. As I watched, enthralled and in awe he kept placing more jewels on himself. He was abundance and I was mesmerized. His presence shone.

My eyes stayed on this vision. I was unable to move. I quickly glanced around to see if anyone else was watching this. There was no one. The park was empty. As my eyes returned to him there was one shining stone in his hand which he placed in mine as he dissolved inside the trees. I didn't want him to leave and, sliding off the bench, fell on my knees in awe and reverence. Each jewel was a path made and a work completed. This was the message for me. Picking up my things with the sky inside my head and the elephant king inside my eyes, I walked away from the bench and headed towards the mirror. That mirror in the grass where earth and sky met and all separations and dualities were distant notes because they were out of tune and out of sync. Recognizing the exact spot, I walked towards it and there now deeply embedded inside the earth I saw the glisten and glimmer of a reflection. I was amazed that it was still there, and bending down, cleared the grass and dirt off the surface. I started. In the exposed surface of the mirror I saw Akaash's face. He was smiling. I looked again and this time he was even clearer. I looked around, but there was no one. The park was uncannily empty and quiet. I was on a vision quest and these visions were being given to me today. Patience was the gift of the gods and was the hardest to hold in the body. I would hold mine until my bones would be painted in gold leaf. And I saw her floating in the sky, my divine horse woman on an open lotus with a sparkling red necklace on her swan neck. Looking at my watch, I gathered everything and headed for my first audition. I will contact Aakash. I missed him and it was time. He had been silent and I was homeless.

It was the audition for the play and I was excited. I wondered if my Miguel, the singer of songs, would be there. I smelled him and looked around to see him. My fingers unfurled, inviting his to enter them, as I walked down Fifth Avenue. My body leapt eagerly, searching for his smile. The building was approaching or rather I was approaching it and I ran in. The audition was on the second floor and, racing up, I took a seat and waited to be called. There were a few people and some looked at me and nodded while others looked away, not interested or just engrossed in their own anxieties. I bent my head and recalled all that had come to me. I remembered the words by Andre Lorde: "While we wait in silence for that final luxury of fearlessness, the weight of that silence will choke us."

I cleared my throat and straightened my neck as though not to choke and took a deep breath. The visions given to me today were like one hundred kalpas held in one single day. I had risen and was floating in the clouds when I heard my name being called. I looked around to see if anyone had seen me falling from the sky. The assistant director, who I recognized greeted me warmly, and led me to the awaiting panel of very serious and important looking faces. They reminded me of the jury in Jean Cocteau's Orpheus, when the princess of death was reviewed by the panel of elders to determine her fate since she had fallen in love with a human. I was uncomfortable and was given some pages to read from a scene. The director asked me if I needed some time to review what was handed to me. I glanced at the lines and said that I was ready to go. They waited.

I visualized my Miguel and his encouraging smile and all that he had taught me. I thrust forth confidently and with ease. My body felt the words and echoed the presence of each nuance and motion. The timing was organic, and I took the center of each emotion and, absorbing it inside me, sculpted it externally. It was ecstatic. I was enhanced and inspired. I read the last line and stood very erect and tall as though sky hands were holding me and manipulating me like a marionette in life. I surrendered to their strings and felt the silken chords adjusting all my moves. I was in their hands, waiting and trusting.

The panel whispered among themselves. I glanced at the assistant director. He looked uncomfortable as he was not being given any sign as to what he should do with me. Finally, the director, beckoning him, said something. He approached me and asked me to wait. The still-to-be-auditioned ones watched me anxiously, hoping to get some indication as to how I had done. Looking at them, I smiled. From where I was sitting I could see the panel in a very heated conversation. I was wondering if the "exotic" look was part of the debate. I was sure that it was and knew the hesitation was because of that. Diverting my attention, I turned towards the open window, and watched the clouds floating through the apices of the tall buildings. And the slither of a cloud was slicing the shadow of the moon, just like in Bunuel and Dali's film Un Chien Andalou. A throbbing little sparrow flew through the open window. No one noticed it. I followed its flight and then suddenly it decided to sit on the crown of my head. A blade of light sliced through me. I shifted positions and stretched my legs, careful not to disturb the sitting, winged speck of life perched on my head. He then flew away and the dreamcatcher's rope entwined my spine. I felt every galloping white wolf flying through me.

The assistant director disturbed my reverie by clearing his throat. I wondered why he did not use a more gracious tactic. He said that they wanted to see me again. They said that they had been impressed by my rendition of the scene. The director said that even though they had in mind another kind of a look, they were seriously thinking of changing their minds. He told me that if they decided this, they would need me in the near future. I told them that I would be available, thanked them and left, bird and all in and around me. The assistant walked me to the door and making sure that he had all the contact information for me, congratulated me and muttered something like "these people didn't usually change their concept so drastically." I decided to give him Ulhfrafn's number, and said that would be the reliable number to call, failing which he could call the other two.

I began unfolding and then remembered the many myriad of times when it almost happened and something or someone changed. I was not being cynical and reminded myself never to open those doors, but I was also aware of how often I had reached huge heights followed by a thousand falls. I was always trying to look at the newly envisioned shore, where a playground of gifts and words were born every moment and dreams entered the barren wasteland and all was thunder and lightning in a sea of bliss. And here it was, the same song line once again tracing the secret, sacred thread through water, blood, breath, and wine.

Leaving the building, I noticed the edge of a wooden bench not too far from my mirror park. I touched the bench and sat down, gathering together all that had just happened. I placed these gifts in my inner chambers with gratitude.

I was in India, holding Savitri in my arms. She was a jasmine bud. She was the song line of my karmic path, shadowed by numerous nuances. I thought about the word "shadowed" and wondered why that word came through, but there it was and it must have a reason for being there. She was truly my ancient child. Just then, I glanced up at the spider web in that ancient corner. The thread had not been mended and hung unwanted and alone. A cold shiver entered me. Something was wrong. My eyes flew into the large dark pool centers of this now child, brought down to me with so much love and care. She was a hidden jewel.

Deciding to take her out to the light and blooming flowers, I walked out of the house. They all ran to me, making sure everything was fine and they asked if any of them should walk with me. My mother-in-law had not been the same since the birth. I marveled at this strange preference of gender and hated it–such hypocrisy, such lies. I never understood any of this in a culture that worshipped the Goddess, the milk cow, and all nature. My mind moved to Vision and Art. I heard a horse neigh. I heard hoof beats on the grass. Holding Savitri close to my breast, I turned around and there they were: the Horse and the Divine rider. As they neared me, the shining black stallion slowed down his pace. She glanced sideways, but was still hooded and veiled. Her hand emerged through. It was a hand of philosophy and of aesthetics. Every gesture indicated transparent, ethereal sounds, flowing waters and sky bodies. She pointed to the temple, where I was heading, as though to make sure I went there. Her hand touched little Savitri. I held my breath. I saw the **rishi** who was burnt by fire and the mad monk with his begging bowl, howling the songs of love. And I saw the **Bauls** of Bengal, with their one stringed instrument roaming across the land, singing songs to Krishna–– the blue one, the butter thief, the eater of egos, and the lover of all lovers. And I saw **Mirabai**. She was a princess and left her palace to wander across the land singing her love songs to her beloved Krishna. She and I were the female **Siddhartha**.

The hooves of the horse were like pearls as they dug into the body of the earth and the white-clad one who was always sitting near the temple as though she and the temple wall were one. She looked at the vision and bowed her head. She too saw them. All of me trembled. *What did this mean?* The Brahmins' curse meant losing everything. But why would I be cursed?

"Not you, but to teach ignorance what it needs to be taught," the voice echoed, "or else friends, parents, animals, all heads will be off in huge dust clouds."

I held the precious body of my doe-eyed Savitri even closer to my heart, and then out of nowhere came the gardener, this time holding wild orchids in his hand–a flower that was unique in every birth. I thanked him graciously for this exquisite gypsy plant, and whispered to myself that it had no fragrance. He heard me and replied promptly, almost abruptly, that its wild beauty was its fragrance. I smiled. Little Savitri was watching the flowers, and her face was smiling. Her little feet twitched and hit against my body. Those honey-filled baby kicks. As I neared the temple the lady had her hands held out; she in whose mouth I had seen the whole Universe. I gave her Savitri eagerly as if to protect her. The priest emerged from the heart of the temple holding a brass plate with an oil lamp lit, incense burning and flowers and fruit in it, and a little bowl with wet sandalwood paste, and with some **kum kum** and turmeric powder. He didn't see the little one at first, and then sitting down, placed the red powder and the yellow powder and the sandalwood paste on her forehead. She giggled and squirmed, as she received the blessings from the great Goddess Kali. I couldn't look at the image today. I was apprehensive.

My mind went back to that auspicious day when I was in Kalighat, Just outside Calcutta, which was said to be the most powerful Kali temple in the whole of India. It was hot, raw, unclean, and bloody. I had told the chauffer to wait for me at a distance because I wanted to be alone. He was reluctant to do so, as my husband had specifically asked him to keep a close watch. But I insisted and he listened. As I neared the image, I was struck by what seemed like an invisible blow. I was on my knees, head bent. And all else in me was hidden. She was the most powerful one I had ever seen or felt. I was captured by her and wrapped in her arrows. I could not move. Life itself had left me. I tried to rise but could not. People were helping. They were asking questions. I could not reply. Words were not being formed. I tried to point to where the driver would be and finally from a distance saw him approaching me. He must have heard the commotion above all the other endless noise. He ran towards me and, with the help of the others, walked me to the car, which was now parked right outside the temple entrance. As I was leaving the gates a woman dressed in a white sari came towards me. She pushed herself through the crowd of people and, looking straight into my eyes said, "You will have many men, many lovers and all that you wish for." I tried to tell her that I was married and pregnant. She looked right through me. When we drove into the compound of the house, I saw my husband rushing out to the car.

He told me that he was worried. They helped me out as I limped in. My mother-in-law was livid with anger, and shouted that she had told me not to go and that if anything went wrong with the baby, it would be my fault.

All this came back and now I could look at the image of the goddess kali in the temple. I was startled and looked again. She seemed alive. I shyly mentioned this to the priest, who said that she was. I looked again and this time she was smiling. I felt released of something. I heard my husband's voice. He looked happy. He noticed little Savitri in the ancient one's lap and started to take her from her. I stopped him and indicated that I wanted her to hold her longer, and relaxing, he too sat and received blessings from the priest.

As we both decided to go back to the house, I bent down to pick up Savitri but before I did that, I saw her looking down at my child and suddenly the entire Universe that I had witnessed in her mouth fell into little Savitri, and all I saw was a big ball of light. I started to weep and shake. My husband did not understand why I was crying. I couldn't explain. She looked at me and knew that I had seen what happened. She blessed us and, taking my hand, put something in my palm. It was warm and alive. She gestured to me to bend down and whispered in my ear to be very strong and trust that all that happens was for a very special reason. I felt uncomfortable hearing these words, but I knew that this was different. I saw light being exchanged. It was exquisite. When I held Savitri, my hands slid through because all I saw was a translucent being. My husband gently held us and asked me what had happened there. I told him I would try to tell him later.

We walked to the house. The gardener had a bone shine to him now. He also looked as though he too had experienced something. We all did. It was transformation. I wanted to enter my husband and swim within his calm simplicity and his honesty and his goodness. He was all of that and so gentle. Looking up at him, I whispered love words in his ears and reminded him of that red henna-stained, mad, wild first night, when he unfolded my red wedding sari as it sank into the folded floor, and touched my throbbing thighs as I wrapped them around his neck, as he merged into me and as my anklets sang and the bell necklace around my neck was drenched with laughter and longing. He looked at me, aroused and shy, like a sweet tiger lion who had won his mate. I wanted him. The light had speared into both of us and Savitri was born again. The flower child of then, of now, and of what will be.

Chapter 11: Wooden peacocks squeezing their way through narrow spaces

Back on the bench, in NYC I felt a presence, and noticed some-one sitting on the other side. I looked again. It seemed like the temple woman, except that she was now dressed in an off-white color and was in a skirt and blouse and she had short hair. They were replicas of each other.

She looked at me and smiled. I was happy that she was not disturbed or irritated or paranoid at my looking at her so intensely. I told her that she was beautiful. She smiled. I walked away, wishing her a warm afternoon. They could have been twins, and I was certain the Indian temple lady followed me here just to make sure that I had come across safely. I smiled, and now there truly was a bounce in my step. People looked at me and smiled back. When that energy exudes it is infectious. This is a wonderful infection, I thought. Looking at the time, I remembered confirming these two auditions earlier and went to them. I was close to Shane's home, I was also eager to see Hironobu San. I want-ed to surprise him. I decided to walk to both of the auditions. They were both for voiceover work.. I remembered Ulfrafhn's words, that I had to dance in many courts and learn a lot and that I should immerse myself in all before I choose what to do.

As I approached the next place, I walked in and was happy to see no other people. In fact they were waiting for me. I apologized and asked if I was late. They said that there had been some cancellations and that I was in fact early. The director seemed slightly taken aback. "Again the exotic thing," I mumbled to myself, almost irritated.

He pointed to a little airless box where there was a long stool and a make shift desk. He stuck a microphone in front of my face as they adjusted the volume and voice quality. He handed me some lines, and glancing at them, I let him know that I was ready. He signed, and I be-gan.

We did several takes until he was satisfied. I walked out of the dreadful box. He said that he really liked my voice, even though I had an accent. I thanked him and gave him Ulfrafhn's number. It felt as though he wanted to have a conversation, but looking at the time, realized that I had to hurry to the next one.

The casting was in a studio, where I walked in unannounced. I was quickly shoved out, almost rudely, and asked to wait outside. Feel-ing odd and a little out of sorts, I decided to write in my journal. Her cloth exterior was warm and nostalgia invaded me. Roots of banyan trees and a seamless awareness raced through me. I longed for all that was awake and textured. I remembered the words of Henry David Thoreau: "If one advances confidently in the direction of his dreams, and endeavors to live his life which he has imagined, he will meet with a success unexpected in common hours."

And I watched all the dream trees and the hymns that cannot be scratched and the wooden peacocks, squeezing their way through narrow spaces until they emerged and unfolded their feathers. And then I was once again the bride song of white lace and shiny hair and golden finger-tips and red feet. I was brought back by a high-pitched, vacant female voice. I looked up and a frail waif-like girl led me back to the studio. I was confused as I thought it was just a voiceover. She explained that the audition was for a very small part. She seemed to emphasize the word, 'small'. I apologized about barging in. She mumbled, and I longed for the excellence and elegance of a well-enunciated word, and the language of a formed soul and a cared living. The studio was unbearable with many large lights. It was hot. The makeup girl approached me and, scrutinizing my face, said that it was too shiny. I said I loved light. Ignoring me, she continued to dab what seemed to be gobs of some awful-smelling fake powder. She was without grace. Her fingers were dead and I wondered on how many faces she had used the same puff. I asked her that. She ignored me again. She then shoved a mirror in front of me. I glanced away. She gave me a very strange look. The director walked in and eyed me up and down. I was uncomfortable. I felt like a thing. He handed me some lines from a scene and described the part I was up for. He said that this was a screen test and asked me if I had done any before. I said that I was familiar with them.

Cameras rolled and this time I felt nothing. It was an effort, but I had to do my best and after what seemed like many takes, we stopped. He complimented me on my rendition, performance, and look. I was startled because I had felt nothing. He asked me what I thought of the lines and the part. I said, "Not much." He was silent and then asked me if I would do the part anyway and I said that I would. He said that he liked my accent and asked me where it was from.

"From everywhere," I replied.

There was silence, and he said that they would let me know. I thanked him and knew that I would not be called back but I didn't care. I rushed to the restroom, and leaning into the cracked mirror, scrubbed my face clean of all the dust, wanting desperately for light to shine in once again so I could breathe. The waif walked in and watched me doing this. She seemed offended. I was free and ran out into the streets.

I was happy. I felt strong and confident. I was eager to see Hironobu san. I needed his wise and humble stare. I walked to the house. The little door tucked between two large buildings seemed so inviting. I touched the wall, and remembered that moment with Smila when the stallion and the rider had passed by to warn me. I looked for them, but

207

they were not there and I rang the bell. He opened the door and, seeing me, was surprised and happy. We embraced. I bent down to touch his feet and he tried to stop me again but knew that he could not. I remembered my beloved mother when, as a little girl, she would indicate that I should touch some feet of an elder. I would pout and refused to touch just any feet that I did not respect. Deep down, she understood but was following social graces.

Standing up, I followed him inside of the house. He chided me for not letting him know that I was coming, as he would have prepared sushi for me. "I wanted to surprise you," I replied. We sat and sipped green tea together from two very delicate, fine little Japanese cups. He said that both Shane and Smila called almost every day. I apologized for any inconvenience this caused and he told me that he would always help me. He asked how I was feeling. I told him that I was fine. I spoke about my work and about Wolf Raven and Flora, and how kind they had both been. He said that he liked her. He mentioned that Aakash had called just a little before I arrived. Just then the phone rang. It was Shane. I took the phone. There was a silence on the other side. I said hello a few times and almost hung up when he very softly told me that he had been calling almost every day. I said that Hironobu san had given me all the messages. His voice was hurt, angry, and harsh. He asked where I had been, not how. I saw a darkness clouding me as his dry voice infiltrated the air. Hironobu san was watching me carefully. Culture and its strengths kept me from being rude to this man. I told him that I had been working and going to auditions. He wanted to know where I had been staying and if I had seen Smila. "I have not seen her but have spoken to her," I replied. The sky ocean of that enchanted land cloaked me and I could see the sand dunes where I had run naked, stripped of everything, and the vision that was given to me on those magnificent dunes of shifting sand, where I was burnt on an everlasting mountain of tears. In each grain of sand the Godheads left their imprints and sighs; it was there where the damp leaves of a manipulated seduction and a broken lust had slaughtered me.

His voice came back through the waves and I looked at my clothed self where war and warrior had met and conquered. He told me he had thought of me every single day and continued to say that my body was etched in his mind and that he could almost not touch another woman. I was glad that he mentioned the word almost. "I have missed you deeply," he grunted. I told him that I missed the red earth and the turquoise sky. He said that he would be back in the city soon and that he would love to see me, and hoped that I would be in the house. I told him that I was looking for a place of my own. He did not understand, and said the house was so big and empty and that I could stay there as long as I pleased and didn't have to pay anything. I was silent and wished him good-bye, handing the phone back to Hironobu san. They spoke for what seemed a long time, and all I heard Hironobu san repeat was, "Hai."

After he hung up, he said that Mr. Shane asked him to convince me to stay in the house. I started to say something and, stopping me, he just said that I did not have to explain anything. The winds passed by. They were raw and murky and filled with shadows of shapeless beings and haunted souls. They were without their weapons and formless. He stood up and opened the front door. I had never seen him do that. He lit a stick of incense and put it on a little shrine just above the door. I had never noticed this either. How careless of me, I thought.

Tears invaded my eyes and I couldn't stop crying. I remembered New Mexico and the sand dunes and the sacrifice. The tears were loud and without walls, and awakened even death. He sat near me and gave me a white cotton handkerchief. I opened its folded self and wiped my tears. It was fragrant and soft, something my father would have. He never used paper. I could not stop. An invisible hand pulled all the barriers down and I wept for all to hear and I know they did. He asked me to keep the cloth. I was thrilled and, folding it respectfully, placed it inside my bag carefully. "I will carry it wherever I travel. It will be my white soft fabric of truth and height and light and courage and a magic carpet that I can fly on if I wish." He asked me to go up to the bathroom and wash my face. I did not want to go up and sat for a while just seeping in all his wisdom, as the sky entered through the door and enveloped us both within the softness of her cloud body. I felt light and clean, and rising up, told him that I must go. I asked him to give Aakash my number if he called again.

I called Flora and Ulfhrafn picked up. His voice cracked through the wooden Krishna door, which is a brilliant blue as it enters me and my mind falls into one million glass beads reflecting their own true nature. And I saw the other night's dream. I was adorned in silver moon drapes and sprinkled with silver powder with a white circle on my forehead. He came towards me and said that I would be recognized. I asked him if he was Krishna. I let Ulfhrafn know that I was on my way and all had gone well and that I was just leaving Hironobu san. "I am fine," I assured him, hearing his concern. My journal had fallen out and shone on that wooden, long table. Surprised, I picked it up. I had no idea how it had jumped out of my cloth bag.

Touching Hironobu san's feet, I left as he took an ancient breath. I had met him now because I had met him then. These were my only thoughts. I thanked him for the soft white fabric and promised that I would be back soon to eat sushi with him. "Before Shane returns," I added quietly. Deciding to take the bus uptown I walked towards the stop. A golden shell formed before me and, trying to catch it, I increased my pace. It avoided my hands and floated away. It was the abalone dream

209

shell in which she in New Mexico burnt sage and smudged me. That is why I saw it. She sent it to me. Suddenly it was filled with burning sage and the smoke covered everything in front of my path. The sacred smoke was all around me. The beautiful grass essence entered every pore and I inhaled it all. Touching the beads on my breast, I thanked her. Finding a stop, I sat on a bench. There were only a few people there. I was in an altered state. I touched myself, not knowing if I would feel a body. It was there, smooth, shiny, and strong. I kissed my hands. Some people watched me doing this and averted their eyes. The bus came. It was empty. Walking to the back I chose a window seat. I love bus rides. They are slow, alive, and revealing. They are dream-enticing. I watched the streets, the people, and all the reflections on the glass bodies of the tall, elongated buildings whose ancient rooftops shelter them. What a strange contrast. I opened my journal and noted down my visions of today. Removing the white cloud given to me by Hironobu san, I wiped my face and forehead as its tulip fragrance quieted all within me. He was right here. Looking out of the window, I was startled.

I saw a noisy, very crowded street in Calcutta. I was sitting inside the car and was being driven by the faithful chauffeur. He was an excellent driver. I marveled at his patience as he weaved his way through people, cows, cars, rickshaws, and many other things. It was truly a difficult task and one had to be absolutely present and mindful. He was both. Little transparent Savitri was in my arms cooing at all the sights and sounds. I held her up so that she could see. The girl who took care of us was sitting next to me, always alert in case I should need her. Suddenly, the car screeched to a halt. There was a huge procession on the road, and he had to wait for it to pass. Someone had passed and the garlanded and incensed body was being sung to and taken to the ghats to be cremated. A cold, icy sword slid through me. I felt its sharp exterior. I gave Savitri to the maid. I didn't want to hold her right then, and needed to unite myself before I did again. I had been sliced and my two selves were disconnected. I was isolated and alone. I thought of Savitri when the Lord of Death came to take Satyavan from her. The girl said something in Bengali. I thought she mentioned that it was good luck and a good omen to see a procession like that. I didn't feel the same. I felt that it was some kind of premonition of what was to come. Looking at the little shiny one, I grabbed her back, afraid that she would be taken away from me. The girl looked at me, surprised, and I apologized, saying that I did not mean to be rude. She humbly smiled.

We finally arrived at the house and I rushed in, placing the now sleeping little one in her cot, and looked for my Satyavan. I heard wheels in the driveway and running out and ignoring all else flung myself into my husband's arms. Everyone looked a little embarrassed; as such behavior is not approved of in public. I didn't care and I told him what

210

we had seen. Taking me in his arms, he consoled me, saying that it was indeed a good sign. It meant a rebirth and a completing of one journey. My mother-in-law looked at us disapprovingly and the others just looked away. I did not care.

We walked to the bedroom. The little one was quiet and asleep. He closed the door and pulled me down onto the floral, silky bed. I melted into his arms. He whispered love words in Bengali and I wept. He quietly comforted me and wiped my eyes with a white, soft, and deep cloth. He unbuttoned my sari blouse gently and wiped the beads of perspiration on my neck and my breasts. The cloth was ancient and weathered and healing. The afternoon raga melted into the room and placing his brown, beautiful, strong Indian arms beneath me, he carried me up, and caught me in midair slicing passionately into my desired being. We made love till the dusk light entered and both Shiva and Parvati danced in heaven, and the earth trembled. We looked up at the ceiling and sadly noticed the web was still torn and unmended. We looked at each other. He placed his dark, arched lips on my eyes and inside my skin and we both cried. Savitri woke and made sweet sounds. We smiled. He kissed me again.

Back on the bus in Manhattan, the sun had left the streets of the city, and carefully folding and putting back the cloth I placed my journal in my bag. My eyes drifted and sailed to the birthday born in a forest of arrows and to another wide, naked walk where swaying eyelashes carried diamond dewdrops of early dawn. My stop was approaching and I pulled the string for the bus to stop. I walked to the front to thank the driver. He nodded in appreciation. His face was dark and worn, and caring and lived.

Stepping out, I walked a few blocks to the apartment building. Dusk was setting in and the sky was warm and lit and the last rays of the sun left its markings. I entered the building and noticed that the elevator was once again working. Relieved, I walked in and pulled the gates together. I liked these old manual gates. On the fifth floor the door to the apartment was slightly ajar. I pushed it open softly and stepped in lightly. It felt good to be back. Both Flora and Ulfhrafn were in the studio. They were happy to see me. Everything was packed and ready for our evening shoot. Flora asked if I would like some tea. I said that I was fine and would just freshen up. The curtains were open and the sky had walked into the room. Removing my shoes, I sat down and lit the candle. The two halves in me seemed to be coming together again. I took Hironobu san's white square cloth out of my bag and placed it on the table and put the pearl on top of it. Closing my eyes, I wondered what magic broke my soul apart.

I heard the soft gurgling of little Savitri. I felt the dusk hands of my Satyavan, while he spoke Bengali love words to me, and wiping my tears with that same pure water white cloth that Hironobu san had

211

given me. I saw the whole universe in a single human mouth. I saw the small-minded people whose feet were deformed and fingers gnarled. I saw the bone shine people whose souls sparkled through. I saw orchids and could now smell the fragrance of their wild formations. I saw the fierce Goddess, whose eyes held only compassion. I saw poverty, and the riches it held. I fed the little sparrows on the ground, and in my heart. I saw the limping man with a crooked crocodile cane in his hand and I rushed to help him in case he fell. I saw an aged woman hooded and stooped and I stopped to see if she needed any assistance but she looked away and was angry and bitter. I sent her my passion and my wings of desire and told her that she still could win if she could only be aware of awareness. And I looked at the young girl frivolous with her beauty, not knowing that at any moment the hawk from the sky could dive down and steal her mask. I wanted to tell her to look into the mirror of life and not the little mirror she held in her purse, which reflected back her vanity that shattered in one million fragments of lies and untruths. But she would not listen and she would not hear. So I walked on hoping I would one day wake the blind and heal the ones whose wounds scream with fear.

I opened my eyes and there standing in front of me was Wolf Raven. He was a raven now and with his wings he engulfed all of me. My eyes broke and I cried and cried. He held me and I saw the whole world in me and India around me. He took my face and swallowed my tears with his long, sweet, fragrant lips. I placed his hand on my breast so that he could feel my heart and his head entered me, and I felt the flutter of his raven wings sing with the beating of my heart.. He took my hands and we walked out of the room to start the work. Flora was waiting for us and she knew that I had seen the world today and that I had walked many paths and had become the wolf, the raven, the eagle, and the flower.. I hugged her. She was beautiful. We went down to the car and drove to The Cloisters. I was excited.

The cloister was shaded and Gregorian chants were being played. They knew exactly where to shoot and, already having all the needed permissions, they started to set up some lights. Flora started to work on my face in the unicorn room, where a large embroidered tapestry hung. I felt the difference from the clumsy, unclean fingers of the waif and my face became her canvas. She commented that my face was unusually dry. I told her about the episode with the girl. She was angry and wondered how some people even were allowed to work. I told her the puff looked dirty. "That is just awful," she said. She applied some light cream to nurture my skin before putting anything else on. She said that she was going to complain to the makeup union which was very particular about such details.

I glanced at the horn on the unicorn and his large almond eyes staring out of the tapestry on the wall. I wondered why he had only one

212

horn. Just then, Ulfhrafn came in to check how we were progressing. He approved of what Flora was doing and reminded her to make sure to highlight the cheekbones. The Bone People, a book I had read by Keri Hulme. I loved the tittle. "Bones carry us."I thought. He looked at me with care and desire. My eyes were closed but I felt it. Flora whispered words of comfort and beauty and recited a Neruda love poem to me as she painted my face. She said the lines in Spanish and then translated:

"Smile at me radiant
if my mouth wounds you.
I am not a gentle shepherd
like the ones in fairy tales,
but a good woodsman who
shares with you earth, wind,
and mountain thorns.

Love me, you, smile at me,
help me to be good. Do not
wound yourself in me, for it
will be useless, do not wound
me because you wound
yourself."

The tears were here again and she wiped them away quickly. We were woodsman and we did share earth, wind, and mountain thorns. She removed the plastic cover from the costume. It was stunning. It was a fluid rainbow, light and gossamer. She put it on me and then stood back to see how it looked. It fell all around and in me and its gentle folds inspired and moved me. Ulfhrafn came in and stopped for a moment. He came closer. His ocean waves carried me as he described the whole mood of the scene. It was the seduction scene. It was a virgin seduction. He was seduced by myth and all its symbols. She was the moon and the virgin. I thought of the lines of a poem written by a twelve-year-old girl from New Zealand:

"Here we are, in the darkness,
close to the very heart of
Mother Earth, where her
blood flows in seams of
shining coal, and our picks
beat a rhythm to her heart,
where her warm brown flesh
encloses us and her rocky
bones trap us."

213

Flora ornamented me with silver. I loved the delicate weight of this pure, ancient metal, a metal of the moon and of the feminine. It was the color of the new moon, and a recipient of other influences, symbol of new birth and purity. It had a magical quality of keeping away the negative.

I touched each ornament on my body and my dream of the other night became alive. I was adorned for Krishna and the light of the first full moon seeped through me. I asked them if I was shining. They laughed and nodded. The moon had entered me sickle and whole. My body expanded and shrunk according to her needs. I was ready.

The area in the courtyard where we were working was carefully lit and looked like a grove of wonders. In the story, this is where the two meet. I listened to all the directions and we began working. There were several locations within The Cloisters and we moved around accordingly. There were two security guards and just the three of us. I was back inside the rhythm of working with the fluidity of Ulhrafn's way with the camera and all in me responded. Everything moved without interruption. Flora was always present and ready and attentive. I was revived again. The grove was misty and moon drenched. The surrounding foliage whispered their individual shadows on the ground and the light played with each one creating an imagined forest. I sat and moved within the shaded, sculptured collage and danced to the rhythm of the clicking of the camera lens and the raven's voice.

I had been caught by the eye of my own reflection, and, looking up, noticed two lines of red blood flowing down beside the golden stars sheltering the third eye. It was blood, red, strong, sparkling, and clean. The lines were wet. I was excited. And I heard a voice. It was gentle. I glanced and saw a poet's face. I was confused and looking at Ulfhrafn realized that he had organized this intentionally so that I would be surprised and inspired. It worked.

The surprise was the male model playing the part of the writer, who allegedly had a spell cast on him by her .The article, was about a photo journalist who while doing an interview with a woman artist was seduced be her and asked her to dine with him. She did and the next morning he awoke with deep yellow fingers and could not remove the stain. He was convinced that she had bewitched him. We worked together well. Flora whispered to me of heroes and the unicorn, the wild, wooded creature that comes in a white horse body with a goat's beard. He is a symbol of purity and grace and can only be captured by a virgin. She draped me in a blood red and gold sari of six and a half yards of silken roads. We decided against a blouse and she wrapped it around me like the village women in India. And I heard the well water splashing as the bucket went down to be filled with water, and drops of warm sweat fell on my face and neck and bare shoulders, as I felt the soft silk caressing

214

my unicorn breasts.

The space of shadows was getting warmer and the night air was heated with crickets and gothic chants. The seduction was getting mysterious and almost melodramatic as we entered the pages of one hundred and one Arabian nights. Passolini would have been awakened. And now I became the warrior princess Chitrangada from Tagore's play, dressed in a borrowed beauty to attract Arjuna, the lord of love. He was seduced, but after making love to her his mind wondered to the princess warrior and her fake beauty hung around her like loosened clothes ashamed and wounded. I wondered why this story entered me now. Was it the language of the grove where we were working? Or was it the lie of a false beauty which could lead all creativity astray?

Back in this concrete, shaded grove I quickly gathered any false vanity and crude and dirty self-indulgence, which always had a stench of an unwashed and stale body and mind, and I cast it aside like some negative clothes that must not be worn again. I was afraid that the warrior in me had left, or that I had left her in search of some silly, empty, banal beauty thought. I looked at Flora, to make sure that I was all in. She nodded and smiled and I knew all was well. The fears and lies were just the clamor of dusty drapes and I shook myself free from all of that as I walked with a slight limp, divorced from what holds, binds, and blocks. It was very late and we were almost done. I felt the alchemy. There was an expansion of consciousness, purification, and a transformation in the air. It was as though the unicorn horn tipped into the atmosphere and healed and purified with each stroke. He must have walked out of the tapestry. I ran in to see if he was still there. I was certain that he had just re-entered his tapestry. Walking closer I touched him. His eyes blinked and the sun and the zenith were all one in his milk-white gaze. He was our alchemist and he transformed everything into gold and the gold in my sari border cut through my skin. I looked down to ease the crease. I felt wanted, sure, and pure and verse was sungand I would marry again on the very top of the sacred pyramid of Machu Picchu.

Ulfhrafn walked in as I was conversing with my unicorn. He said that my work this night was like clear air. "You made the dream language tangible and you sailed in with all the temple Apsaras to seduce a human," he said. I whispered that it must have been the sari. He smiled and held me, and the folds of the blood gold dissolved inside his held gaze. I gave him my mouth and he picked it up, and carved it with his Icelandic wolf raven arched lips. The gold-embroidered edge of my sari slid off slightly and with one bared bosom I was the Amazon woman warrior, with my quivering feather bows slung on my right shoulder, ready to win my victory. I ruffled my feathers against him and my one bared war breast speared his heart away and we became the sacred in art. I saw Flora's shadow in the doorway and moved into the point of the unicorn.

215

She was slightly embarrassed and, smiling, asked him if we were done. Taking a deep breath he went through all the shots taken and made notes. And I hoped that one day I could hear the sound of snow. He looked at me again, now with his lens eye and said that he needed just two more shots with me alone and then we would be done. Flora walked to me and touched my now kissed lips and added what was needed for the camera. She adjusted the sari edge as I fell into its embrace again. She told me that I was superb. Her fragrance was of all the tropical flowers.

Flora and I walked back into the fallen shadows and he positioned me to stand and look out with longing.. We worked for a couple of hours and finally he called it a wrap. We were elated, satisfied, and exhausted. It was almost dawn and a very gentle light peeped through the empty night sky. All was very quiet as I helped Flora gathered everything up She stopped me, but I knew how tired she was, so I continued to help. With all lights and cameras packed, we headed to the parked car. The streets were empty. I had never seen the city so quiet. It was a whisper of what had been and what was to come. The street cleaning cars had begun their work and the city was like a bride, waiting for all her grooms to arrive and enter. I looked up at the sky. It was waiting for the sun to touch its horizons. The streets were waiting to be cleaned. The sky was dusty and shaded, waiting for the light rays to scream through.

In the apartment we were as though in an altered state and left each other to rest. I felt his wings whisper, and I sent him my Amazonian feather arrows. No one spoke. We felt each other and basked in this triumph of what had been achieved. It was a unicorn collaboration and much had been done. Flora and I walked to our rooms. She peeped in to make sure the tumbler of water was filled. I touched her hair and flew into the mountain tops in Peru, into all the flickering fireflies dancing on earth, and into the ancient cracked skies. I told her that I would get married on the tips of sacred Machu Picchu. She replied that I had already been married there many times. We kissed each other on both cheeks. Walking into my room, I lit the candle. On the red couch, the night and all we did weaved through me. I felt the unicorn's gaze and the single mystical, mythical horn. And the sable antelope entered my mind with his two perfect sickle moon horns, and his almond eyes pierced my throbbing breasts. I stood up to go to the bathroom to wash but felt a huge tiredness overwhelm me and fell into the bed. My eyes closed and I became the instrument of all expressions and the moment of all moments as I hailed the gods in string and drum. My feet stood on lions. My sari became my sleep weapon and its shiny gold took me back to my home in India, lying beside my husband underneath the dream net which surrounded and shielded us.

216

The night in India was made vocal by the chirping of crickets and the silent flight of the eagles. I woke up to take a sip from the water glass covered by a soft rounded net cloth. The beads on the edges of the cloth clung sweetly as I lifted it and sipped from the glass. I placed the glass back and covered it and stretched my neck to make sure little Savitri was comfortable. She was very quiet and as I tucked back the edges of the net something stirred by the window. It was a flutter, and looking up there perched on the windowsill, almost hidden by the deep, dark night, two haunting eyes pierced through the darkness. I lay down so I did not want to wake up my husband. It was an owl – an Ulka – and she or he was staring at me. Then its eyes fell on the little one. The window net was usually closed but this night, for some reason, it had been left open. I was not sure what to do and waited silently.

And then, leaving the windowsill, the owl fluttered into the room and sat on the edge of the little one's cot. I touched my husband softly. He moved near to me. I pointed to the bird. He was startled. He slowly got out of the netting and slid out on his side. He walked towards where the owl was perched, now looking straight into the cot where Savitri was sleeping. I sat up. I was not sure if this was an auspicious sign or not. As my husband neared the little cot the owl once more looked straight at me and then took flight. I knew that in India the owl, Ulka is a vahana or a vehicle for the Goddess Laxmi who represents abundance, beauty, and grace. But usually the owl only visits during the day time and this nocturnal visit made me feel strange. My beloved husband carefully closed the net door and secured it, and making sure little Savitri was undisturbed, walked back to bed. This time he climbed in on my side and sailed over me leaving traces of his sandalwood body on my skin. He was bold today, a boldness that I had not seen before. He had become his height and his nobility. He had no secrets and he showed it proudly.

When we sat together at the dining table and he reprimanded his mother respectfully if she chided or scolded me. I was quiet. What had happened? He who had been so subservient and weak in front of his mother now made sure that she never, ever brought up the fact that I gave birth to a daughter. She listened and in her also there was a difference. She was paying more attention to Savitri and showing some kind of hesitated affection for the little one. He told me that a lot of her resentment and rigidity came from the fact that she lost her husband very early in life, and that left her scarred and embittered. I felt sad and swallowed her grief.

I would chant to the deities to give her back her burlap dreams and ancestor spirits. I was also saddened by the fact that he had lost a father at such an early age. My fingers slid over him and I held his heart. He grabbed my face and speeding through my eyes kissed the surrounding kohl away from the edges. He told me that my eyes were like a nomad's garden with running gypsy women, receiving the power of the sun and that he could see both day and night in them. He asked about the voice that always came to me to not forget the cry. I told him that I had become that cry and now it was in me.

"So I will never lose you?" he asked.

This time I took his face. "I too have become a brilliant bird in flight and have discovered many nuances and secrets of my inner self. My creative self has entered me.." Looking at him hungrily I told him that I was the earth he walked on, the air he breathed. "How can you lose me?" I added. He smiled.

We rested on each other and listened to the raindrops as his fingers carved my neck and shoulders. I loved him more as he broke the veils of my virgin journey and we held the fragrant lotus bud very gently in our Indian hands. His feet and hands spoke of vermillion rivers and seaweed sounds. He told me that the owl was the ruler of the night and the seer of souls. "And according to the Native American philosophy he was a keeper of sacred knowledge," I said. "But why does he come at night?" I asked him. He enveloped me in his traditional arms, clothed with his white night shirt, and unbraided my hair as the jasmine garland fell on the pillows and the fragrance filled the air. Then he peeled off his night shirt to reveal to me the forest foliage of his heart. I melted. Suddenly a streak of lightning flashed through the room and a fierce thunder howled, shuddering the panes on the windows. I walked into his strength and protection. He jumped up to make sure the little one had not been disturbed by the invasion and then ran back into my arms. His bare brown bark back glistened with drops of salt sweat. The rain drops left a hypnotic beat on the roof of the house and the wind raced through the trees and foliage. Everything was rejoicing the entry and exit of the ruler of this night's unexpected visitor. My sari had left my shoulders as I unwound myself from the rest of the many yards of hand and silk and fell naked into his wedding heart. I ate the sandalwood stick.

I slipped under the covers in my bed in this warrior country in the west as the morning light seeped into the room and I noticed that the drapes that had been open were now closed. It was Flora, so that I would rest and sleep and not be awoken by the light. On the table I noticed a flask and a mug. Opening the top I poured the warm tea into the cup and sipped the first story of the energizing liquid. I was awake. My eyes wandered around looking for the little cot and the night owl and the white cotton-clad arms of my husband. My hand reached to the other side of the bed. It was empty. The owl's eyes walked around the room. It was day now and he was welcome.

Taking my journal, I made some entries. There was a soft footfall and Flora entered with a mug of hot tea in her hands. She sat on the red couch and leaned back. The red suited her and surrounded her with

218

warmth. I thanked her for the tea. She looked tired and alive. I told her about the owl. She repeated the same story of the owl and that he was the seer of souls. I was happy. The two worlds within me were in synch and my antelope ran balanced and on fire through the forests in Africa. His eyes were on two sides of the universe and with his divine eyelashes he blinked all into harmony and balance. She told me that today I should just rest. "You have done a lot since the abortion and you must take care of yourself sweet Mrina." I shivered at the jingling sound of the name and how she said it. The word flowed out of her mouth and lips. I told her that I agreed and that I felt some pain. I thought of Abrihet and how she had guided and helped me through that journey of one million stairs of a blinded bloody walk. Flora came over to the bed and lifting up the covers with no hesitation placed her **curandero** hands on my belly skin. I closed my eyes and let the waves of her light-sight enter and heal me. I trusted her and I knew she had magic in her hands.

My inner eyes wandered once again to that night in Southampton when a friendship was cheated and seduced and tainted by pretentions and when the perfect glass of water at my bedside turned murky and shaded. Flora remained with her hands for what seemed like eons and centuries. she had filled my heart and that her face of amber reflected many cultures. She was a coral mantra, a silver aura of turquoise peace beads. Removing her hands softly, she bent down and gave me a huge warm embrace. She walked to the bathroom and ran the water, knowing how much I loved those lush, long, healing water entries. I was half and whole at the same time.

I listened to the water falling, and remembered the sharp and stunning statue at the Metropolitan museum. It was just outside of the Egyptian section. It was of a male torso sliced in half. It had an echo of both the known and the unknown, the seen and the unseen. It was as though the other half was not visible but, at the same time, alive. Flora said that the bath was ready. I pulled the sari under me as though re-leasing my magic carpet. As the red length slipped away from me, it took the shape of a shiny serpent crawling towards Shiva to coil itself around his vibrant head. It found its way into the inner sanctum of the two thousand year old Shiva temple in Kerala, where the body of the temple had oil lamps which were kept burning all the time. I was slightly unsteady on my feet. She ran to me and, leaning on her, we walked to the bathroom. The water was a liquid bed of life. It soaked in me as I rested into its wealth. Flora was concerned, she said that I looked very exhausted. "I will be fine," I assured her, "I will stay in bed the rest of the day."

Suddenly I remembered the party that Smila had invited me to and I mentioned it to Flora. "I would love for you and your man to come." She went to the bedroom and called him and spoke in Spanish. She said that he was free and would meet us there. I was happy. I told her that I would love Ulfhrafn to also come. She said that she would tell him since she was going to spend the day working with him, cleaning the cameras, developing what had been shot, and organizing everything for him for the next shoot.

The lids of my eyes were sad and hooded. I was afraid of being abandoned. This feeling was one of my biggest challenges to overcome. It stemmed from my insecurities and my hungry howl to be validated. My breath took in all the lies and falseness that I had witnessed and my heart ached at beauty given and beauty thrown to the dust and disrespected. Flora wiped the tears and said, "You will always work with him. He has learnt so much from you. He trusts you and your finer self." I shook off my doubts and taking her gentle hands told her how much I had learnt from both of them.

She kissed my head and told me to relax.

Walking on the edge of the river Ganges I saw the three eyes of the goddess Kali after she had been worshipped on the streets of Calcutta for ten days, and had now been immersed into the river, as all dissolved back in to the earth bed of wet clay. Her eyes blinked at me as they pierced all of me and I stayed with her as she slowly sank gracefully into the water with me. Her beautiful face had left me with traces of her relentless war against ignorance, weakness, mediocrity and fear.

Rising from the water, I dried myself and slipped back into the arms of the warm and clean silken sheets. Sleep invited me and took me into her arms once again.

I was awakened suddenly by the phone and, though still in the other world of dreams, picked it up. It was Hironobu san. He told me that Smila had called to remind me of the party and after a silence also said that Mr. Shane might be there too. We were quiet as we felt each other's thoughts. I thanked him and asked him how he was. He said that he was well and wished to see me soon. He said Aakash had called and he gave him this number. Thanking him, I put the receiver down and dialed Akaash's number. Hearing my voice, he shouted out my name loud. "I miss you," he yelled excitedly. We spoke, and he told me that he had not been well and had had to turn away much work. He said that it was something to do with his nervous system. I heard his tired voice. It sounded veiled and sad and a little hopeless. He was taking some medications, which made him even more tired. I didn't know what to say. Words failed me. He said that when he was better he would come to New York to see me. He asked about the mirror in the park and I told him that I saw it recently buried inside the earth, still reflecting the sky and clouds. "I saw you," I said. I felt him smiling.

I mentioned how well the work with Ulfhrafn had been and he said that he knew his work well and truly admired him. "I will call you soon." he said and he hung up. Something felt strange. I saw the turquoise ledge. I felt the seven chains always around my neck. Dust had made misty the lens. Clouds were fragmented and not part of a whole. The hare had glass amber eyes. The wasteland was sprouting dead weeds and I saw a mountain in Tibet with thirteen lamas rotating their prayer wheels, and I listened to the haunting longhorn sounds in the morning, when a spirit and body had left the earth and we sipped that very salty butter tea as my tongue cringed at the thick, hot, sticky liquid.

In this safe room I knew I was not alone. The mythic life surrounded me as the little dog walking by with his master and mistress, exuding some very strong and synthetic perfume, turned around to lick my feet and the mistress apologized. But I and the little dog had met before in physicality in another lifetime. He recognized me and I smiled.

My rest was lazy and long and stretched and soft. The late morning light was solid and had structures that were defined and knowing. The room swayed in motion. I sipped some more of the hot tea and was happy that it was not salty. Picking up the journal, I wandered through the pages. My dreams feathered and fanned my soul just like the haunting voices of the flamenco singers. Aakash sounded different. Something had left him.

There was a slight knock and, looking up, I saw Ulfhrafn at the door with a small tray. I quickly rose and sat up. He put the tray beside me and said that they had stopped for a bite and did not want to disturb me.

"You spoil me, you and Flora," I said.

"You deserve it," he answered.

He told me the shots were exactly what he wanted, and even more. He had gotten feedback from the magazine editors and they were very enthusiastic. I felt my long body pulling me and I leaned back. He asked how I felt. I said the rest was perfect and that I hoped he was coming to Smila's party. He said that he would love to. He put the tray near me and left me to rest. Outside the trees stood against the whitewashed walls as they grew bigger, bolder, and stronger. The food he had left me was a green salad with some walnuts, radishes, apples, and a cool, ginger tea. It was delicious and crisp and clean. It was only now that I noticed the blood-red, gold sari that I had worn for the shoot, which became the coiling, singing serpent, neatly folded and placed at the foot of the bed. On it, there was a note. Unfolding it I read the words written in a beautiful hand: "This is now yours. May it take you to your sati-marked freedom, seeking life of the banyan tree. The life you left to embrace more and to pierce the cries of creativity. May these golden miles only rejoice you and clothe you with the true depth of where you come from and may your ancestors hail you and honor you." It was signed by Flora. My antelope eyelashes dripped with pearl drops. I decided to wear it this evening for the party.

Looking at the time, I saw that dusk was approaching and started to get up and begin the ritual of kohl and henna. I wanted my feet to sing and the palms of my hands to leave their imprint on the human wall of flesh and soul. I had some liquid red and, sitting on the red couch, began feathering my feet. I felt weddings approaching me. I saw the ladies outside the Ganesha temple in India applying *mehndi* to women every Tuesday. My Indian friends were doing the same as they sang and smiled and that beautiful lady in Rajasthan, where gypsies stemmed from, whose name was Sita ,would have me rest as she rubbed my feet and painted them. There was a slight breeze entering the room. I walked to the windows and flung the curtains open for the evening sounds to enter. I thought I heard cow bells. Walking to the bathroom, I began surrounding my eyes with the kohl that my husband in India had kissed clean. The eyes came alive and walked out of my face. I giggled and surrounded them even more with the black magic mark of whispers and sighs and mystery. I immersed my fingertip in the copper container with the vermillion powder and put a big circle on the space between my two eyebrows. It was blood red and some of the powder streaked down my forehead. I did not wipe it off. I started to wrap the sari around me like Flora had. I decided against a blouse and tried to remember how she had done it.

Just then she came in and stood very still watching me. I thanked her for the gift and told her that I wanted to wear it that evening. She looked at my face and hands and feet. She sat down on the red couch and her silence was the keeper of my wounds. Her face was carved by ether hands. She said she knew me and that the banyan tree was rooted all around me.

"I have to live this so I can be free from any nostalgia or pathetic self-indulgence and pity. I must rip the cloth and free the red powder from any dead ritual and empty superstition. Help me, Flora, as you always do," I asked her.

She chose some really exquisite strapped sandals for me since I had left mine in the big bag at Shane's palace of lies. She was wearing red, too, and we smiled as I took my little cloth bag and we headed out of my safe, warm room to find wolf raven. He was ready and had been waiting patiently. His wings spread when he saw us. I felt my breasts exploding and unconsciously touched them. His eyes met mine. We entered the forest grove. We took each other's hands, Flora, Ulfhrafn and I. We walked to the elevator. The doors had been left open. We entered.

222

We drove down Fifth Avenue embracing Central Park as we passed by. The trees were glowing in the dusk. The mirror on the ground must have sky and earth in its seeing self. Ganesha was swinging in the swaying branches, his jewels creating stars in the green leaf sky. Niyol was shape-shifting to tease me and to ease me, and gold was on me because it is pure and constant. And there, galloping beside us was my shining stallion carrying the one who guides me on the path and warns me of the empty, hollow, dangerous human way. Her hood slid slightly as she turned towards me and my heart stopped beating because I knew that I would be gifted the vision soon. But the wild one gave me just enough and veiled my view as I felt her third eye spearing through. I was not ready yet. I had to continue and forge ahead with brave strides and limps, and be unattached. I knew that choices were being made and all had to be thrown to the winds unafraid and without hesitation. Flora, who was sitting next to Ulfhrafn, turned around because my gasp was so loud. I spoke with my eyes and she understood it all. I glanced in the mirror and saw his eyes and I gave him my bleeding, streaking, red third eye.

SoHo was beautiful with all the old loft buildings and art galleries everywhere. I gave him the exact address and, as always, we found a parking space. The doors of an ancient freight elevator were wide open as we entered. We waited for a bit and a big, husky brown man with a soft rough face ambled in apologized and took us to the top floor. He said it must be a big happening as many people had been coming. Just then, as we were riding up, both the stallion and his rider glided through the walls of the elevator. She looked again, only slightly, and then they dissolved back out as though the walls were transparent. I was sure that I saw wings when they flew out. By now both Flora and Ulfhrafn were getting used to my many expressions and didn't even say much. They just understood. I felt uneasy. I knew that the next journey was about to begin. I straightened my back. I was erect and my long body was even longer. At the floor, the elevator man unfurled the carved steel screen elegantly and showed us the way. My steps were small and hesitant. Flora took my hand and I walked between her and Ulfhrafn.

The door was ajar and Ulfhrafn gently pushed it open. It was one of those old artists' lofts, very spacious with two skylights, beautifully decorated with many plants. The ceilings were tall. Many people were mulling around. At first nobody noticed us and we stood at the entrance for a few minutes before entering. I saw white stallions running across through the crowd of people. The stallions had red mouths because, while at a pond covered with lotus flowers, they were distracted by a flashing light on top of a lotus leaf, and when they looked up their mouths were on fire, burnt by the wounds of knowledge. Why are they here? I thought and just then a loud scream cut through all the conversations and a figure came running towards us. At first I did not recognize who it was, but as she came closer, I realized that it was Smila.

The goddess was alive. The goddess was wounded. The goddess was disfigured and the goddess was dead. This was the sacrifice of the ages when the divine **yantra** is thrown to the winds and the sacrificial fires are not lit. She stood in front of me and lies streamed through her. They had formations. Her mouth curved in strange distortions and her body shook with uncertainty and desire. She looked both beautiful and ugly with silk streams flowing and startling jewelry. "I have missed you so much," she said.

Her eyes fell first on Flora and then on Ulfhrafn, jealously. I introduced them to her. She asked me where and how I had been as she grabbed me roughly. From the corner of my eyes I watched Flora almost stopping her. Smila told me that I looked even more beautiful and then whispered in my ear that Shane might be coming. I gulped, and felt a loud, screaming pain in my belly. All eyes floated within me and I felt them seeing through, and my mind, without knowledge ran to that cold rainy concrete bare-footed night when I walked on the streets alone and afraid and devastated and surrounded by emptiness. I unwound myself from her possessive hold and cut the chords of greed and attachment. She then hesitatingly took my hand and led me to some people she knew. As we walked, she asked me if Ulfhrafn was my lover. I didn't answer.

These people were all connected to the business. Some were agents, some producers, others models and actors. I recognized a few. The famous photographer was there and I saw him speaking with Ulfhrafn. I could feel them discussing me. Flora seemed to be surrounded by people she knew through business and I realized now that she was very well-known as one of the best makeup artists in the city. She was so humble and so clean and so strong and was filled with all the suns and moons and butterflies that were not frozen by nails under glass cases. She looked towards me often, making sure that I was okay. She was wary of Smila.

I walked around the room with Smila as she proudly introduced me as her exotic princess whom she had discovered in India. By this point I had no desire to comment and no energy to defend myself. *I am who I am and I will stand in that special space with one foot folded up in an asana for one million years until all is healed and the earth wounds finally rejoice at the grace of mankind.* And again suddenly, from nowhere, the shiny ebony stallion gallops across the room. His skin breathed with mine as he flew by me, and this time her hand had eyes on it everywhere and they watched me silently. I stood back to give the divine horse woman and her rider space. Smila didn't understand what I was doing. My guardian spirit had showed herself to me twice that night. As they flew through the room his wings spread and her hooded head turned again so that I could feel her acknowledging me. My eyes stayed on them until they had dissolved into the sky. Smila asked me what I was looking at. "The colors in the night sky," I whispered. She kissed me on both cheeks. I discreetly wiped off the kiss. There would be no trace on my skin of a tarnished and disturbed soul. As she led me on she quietly asked what had happened in New Mexico. I looked at her for the first time and held her eyes and told her that I was in my other home and that the Native Americans were also my ancestry. "I am mixed," I told her.

Not even hearing me she wanted to know what had really occurred between Shane and myself. Shrugging my shoulders, I just said that he had showed me around and that I loved the land out there. She asked me why I had left his house and I told her that it was too large and cold. I could tell that she did not believe me but, not wanting to lose my attention, walked with me displaying closeness, a closeness that I did not feel. My heart did not speak. The sand dunes flew around me and that one solitary flower floated right in front of my eyes. I felt sure that if I was in her home in South Hampton the glass of water in my hand would turn veiled and unreflective.

People were watching us and I seemed to be the center of attraction. *Must be my blood-red gold edged snake sari*, I thought. Ulfhrafn walked towards us and, taking me away from Smila, led me towards where the wine was. He asked for two glasses of red. He handed one to me. His fingers dissolved into the liquid and I felt their strength as I took the first sip. "You look beautiful," he said gently. I was shy and bent my head like a sunflower that after bursting forth to face the sun is weighed down by the burden of its own heavy beauty. He lifted my face gently and cut through my eyes.

"We were speaking about you," he said.

"I know."

"He thinks you are amazing in front of the camera."

I asked Ulfhrafn if we would work together again.

"Many times," he replied. "Many times."

I saw Smila watching us. I hid from her glare. I told Ulfhrafn that I needed to sit. We walked towards an area with tall tree plants and embroidered cushions. Flora and her man, who was now there, came to us. He said that Flora had shown him some of the photos. "They are powerful." Many people approached Ulfhrafn. They were curious about me and he introduced me as a very talented artist. I was happy and thought of the day when my gilded interior would be carved on the canvas of my face. They asked for my contact information and he said that I could be reached at his place for now. I noticed the looks on some of their faces but I cared not. I was almost healed and the cave was etched with ancient paintings of symbols and signs. Flora asked me if I was tired. She was so aware and so giving. I told them that I would sit for a while and relax. The trees were inviting. They walked away and mingled and talked.

I hid in the silk brocade of the tapestry of the gods. I unlaced the straps of the sandals, and folding my legs beneath my serpent sari, leaned back. Something cool and smooth on my right foot startled me. A radiant young boy had just placed a perfectly shaped stone on it and was standing shyly near me. He reminded me of the boy in Taman asset who had given me the two stones that sit on my altar on my always table. He spoke English with a gentle Spanish accent and told me that his father was a filmmaker from Mexico and that he would like to meet me. Looking up, I saw a very rugged man standing in the distance holding on to a table. My feet were back in my sandals and the stone was in the palm of my right hand now. The little boy walked to his father and brought him to me. He helped him sit down near me and introduced himself. He told me that his name was Amador and that he was in the process of casting for a very special film, and he would like me to audition for him. It was all happening very fast. In the same breath he also said that he was almost blind and that his son was his eyes and that he trusted him implicitly. "He saw you and came running to me and described you. I gave him the stone to place on your feet."

I was stunned by all this and, looking up, saw Flora coming towards us. She introduced herself to the filmmaker and they spoke in Spanish. She seemed to know him, or to know of him, and they had a very animated conversation. The little man was looking at me with his big, wide eyes and we met. He did not say much but his look was all-embracing and wise. I loved these old souls transplanted into bamboo bodies, so lithe and so profound and so open like a seamless painting of lilies in the pond. He told me a little of the story of the film.

It was the journey of a group of seekers who were on a quest to find the sacred space that would give them back their magical powers. I thought of the zone in Tarkovsky's film, *Stalker.* In the film they ,were led by a mysterious woman who was the only one who knew where this place was and how to get there. He added that the woman was very beautiful but before they go on this pilgrimage she had to shave her head. I touched my life hair and it wept but I knew each strand would understand and grow back. He asked me if I could do that. I said I would if the part was strong. Flora said that she knew the filmmaker and that she was so glad we had met.

"I told him how amazing your work is and we will meet tomorrow," she said. I was thrilled. The little boy handed me a folded note that had their phone number on it. His father looked at me intently with veiled, burning eyes. He leaned closer and gently touched my face. His fingers outlined my face and my erect spine bent slightly, a little afraid. His finger had a strange energy. I handed him the stone and he said that it was a gift from the shores of Mexico.

I saw Frida Kahlo, whom I have always admired and loved. Her screaming paintings are a mirror of an amazing wounded warrior woman. Her blue house and her reaching eyebrows echoed much knowledge of deception, passion, and a lived life. I told him that the concept of the film interested me a lot. He said that he thought that I might be just right for the part and added that when we meet he would hand me the script."Now I have to see if you can act," he said coldly. Flora squeezed the back of my neck. Her fingers slid through my spine. He wished us good night and walked away, led by the bamboo boy, who by now had stolen my heart. He looked back and Niyol was right behind him with his green wolf eyes. I wanted to see him again.

I missed Niyol's shaman hands and his tree feet. Suddenly, as though hearing my call, I saw him entering the loft. I looked again. I couldn't believe it. He walked directly to me. He looked magnificent. His long hair was beaded in parts with turquoise. His trunk neck had coral and turquoise chains and his long, strong thighs rippled with power and his cowboy boots pointed towards warriors. He sat down in front of me on the floor and took my hands. I cried. His green eyes sheltered my tears.

"I never left you," he told me, "I have seen you everywhere and have protected you with wolf howls."

He looked at the gold embroidery of the sari and began tying my sandal straps. All eyes were on us. I did not care. He placed his hand on my belly. His hands stayed on me and all the leaves of the garden entered gracefully. I was of him and he was of me. To ask him how he was would sound banal and empty, but he heard my question and mentioned that he had just come back from Colorado to visit his brother, who invited him to the party. He pointed and, speaking with a group of people, I saw his brother, who had helped me. Niyol's eyes entered me and he told me that I was healed. His brother saw us and walked over to us. He was happy to see me and thrilled that I was strong and well again. He scolded me and said that I should have visited him for a checkup.

I apologized. "I have been in limbo and have been working very hard I feel strong again, except at times." Flora and Ulfhrafn were watching me and smiled. They seemed to know who the brothers were. Niyol's brother asked me to call him so that he could examine me and gave me his number. I promised him that I would. Niyol was quiet and watched my curves. His eyes danced in and around me. He touched my feet and asked about Hironobu san.

"The last time I saw him he was fine," I said, "he always feeds me with my favorite sushi."

"He is a shaman," Niyol said, "he sees in the dark."

I looked back and saw all the wealth of my beautiful beings strung on my heart,. They came with their weapons of truth and honor and feathered me with their **trishule** tongues, guarding my every step. I was filled with gratitude and then the ones who deceived left, and the doors were sealed, because they made filthy the sacred grounds. I threw ashes on all laws made by society and man, and I stood alone on the mountain summit, knowing that the angels were all around visible and invisible.

I wanted to become a wolf and run with Niyol. He looked at me and said that the time was not here yet. "I will come for you then, when the birds will sing and the eagles will fly and the buffalos roam and when Shiva will dance and bring all into creation," he said. He took both my hands and asked me to walk him to the door, since he had to leave. He covered my eyes with his hot palms and ordered me not to be sad. At the door, as everyone watched, he kissed my red third eye, and took the powder in his mouth, and as his tongue tasted the root flavor he kissed my forehead again. This time I felt the eye open, and as he left he told me to see from the opened eye. He ran down the stairs, sending me fire kisses. I received them and held them against my throbbing lips and then he shape-shifted and wolf and wind were one singing symphony.

My heart ached and I turned around to see Smila in my face. She had that crooked mouth that constantly re-shaped itself. One part of her upper lip rose as she carved the next words and, bending into my ears, asked hungrily who that was. "I met him in the park," I told her, casually. She was shocked and warned me of dangerous things happening if I was that trusting and open. She took me by the hand, which I shrugged off rudely, and she said that there were several producers who were interested in speaking with me. She asked why I was so distant from her, and reminded me that it was because of her that I had come this far. "I have not forgotten that and I know you will never let me," I said.

I ran to the being in white in the temple house in India, who carried the Universe in her mouth and fell into her lap. It smelled of mustard oil and turmeric and tamarind and holy basil and ginger root and seeds of many revelations. I wept into the folds of her old, torn golden sari. She looked down and pulled back my hair and rubbed coconut oil into the roots so that the scalp was cool. And as I looked up at her humbly, her mouth opened wide and there it was again: I saw the whole universe shining inside. She then bent down and threw it on me and I shifted and moved to allow all this divine light to take me over. "In bliss and of bliss as we follow our bliss," said Joseph Campbell. "Your dreams are your personal myths." Lit within, I rose from her lap and bowed in front of her and touched her stained and cracked feet.

Smila took me to a group of very chic-looking people. I felt out

228

of place as they looked at me, or rather down on me. To them I was the exotic object, a strange fruit from a third world.

After introducing me to her friends she went on to tell them how she had met me. Few of them asked me for my contact information. One of them spoke about a play and a film which might work out for me. I thanked them and my mind went to the little Mexican boy and his deep eyes. Just then I felt someone pushing me. I looked around, not knowing who I would see. There was no one. But I knew it was something important.

I searched for my friends and they were laughing with some people that they knew. I waved at them. They waved back. And then I looked towards the second skylight. I saw a glaring circle of light right under the sky next to the window. Fascinated, I walked towards the circle. I saw a figure standing there bathed in that light. Her face started to become clearer and there standing in front of me was the dream lady who I had seen in Taman asset in the riverbed town; she who appeared and then disappeared because I had doubted her being. And then I saw her again at the window in that dusky sun-drenched room when Tobias and I had made love. It had to be her. She was exactly the same, only now she had western clothes and her face was not covered. Her almond eyes were the same. She came closer and, looking straight into my eyes said, "I know you." I could not speak, and all around her were the white stallions, which I had seen earlier when we entered the loft, with their mouths burnt fire red. She offered her hand and said her name was Prana. Barely able to articulate my words I said that it sounded Indian.

"It is," she said quickly. "My mother gave it to me. It means breath and more."

"Were you ever in Algeria?" I asked her.

She said that she never had been.

"I have seen you before," I told her, "both in and out of my dreams."

She walked closer and gave me a cloud hug. It felt like one of those hugs given by the wonderful Amma from India, who whispers sacred mantras in your ears while her arms surround your whole being. Everything around me dissolved into the sun. I felt my wings unfurling into butterfly whispers and rainbow sighs. I felt unreal. I felt real. I touched myself to make sure that I was present. She smiled and asked me what I was doing at the party. I knew she knew everything but she asked me anyway.

Flora and Ulfhrafn came back and I introduced them to her. They asked me if we had known each other before. I stuttered and said no. Prana smiled and said that she dealt in African antiques and textiles. "I have a store in Manhattan," she said. She seemed to know of Ulfrafhn's work, and said that she was looking for a great photographer, as she was putting together a brochure for her business called the Purana Collection. Purana means "ancient" in Hindi. He said that he would love to help. She looked at me and said that I would be perfect for the cover if I was interested. He told her that I had been working for him and that she would have no regrets. Prana said that she knew that. I watched Flora watching her and I smiled. Prana gave both me and Ulfhrafn her phone number, and Ulfhrafn gave her his, and told her that she could reach me at that number. Flora said that she would love to do my makeup if needed. Prana was thrilled. She mentioned that she almost did not come to the party as she was supposed to leave town, but plans changed and she was really happy she could come.

I was back in that dream river waterbed where she had showed herself to me. Glancing at the time, she said that she had to leave but asked us to call her as soon as possible. She left like she did in the riverbed when she vanished, and the grass swayed in response, but this time I did not call her back.

Smila rushed up to us and told me in a whisper that Shane just called and asked me to please wait for him. "He is on his way," she said. I fell into the dark well and the water was stale and stagnant. The wind was howling but could not enter the round, hollow cave and the walls of this wet, soggy interior were slithery and slimy. I felt as though I would faint and held on to Flora. She inched herself into me to support me. Smila had that crooked mouth again and stared at Flora. They took me to the seating area and I collapsed. My barren belly fell into sleep and I whispered into her not to be sad, as she remembered the harsh, wet concrete when our bare feet had scathed the rough surface while we looked for shelter on that rainy, dark, desolate night when Ondine had lost her way.

Both Flora and Ulfhrafn asked me if we should leave. I wanted to wait. I had my reasons. Smila seemed defeated and lost. I sent her compassion and knew that she could never harm me again. My ego was hurt and nothing else and I knew I would face him with this new strength. This growth and this transformation were new and bold. **Visvamitra** said, "What we thought has been thought many times and in many places, and each of these thoughts, successive and coincident, is linked together in a single chain."

I would make a statue of the goddess in the sand and dance around her wet lines. I would throw a golden jasmine braid upon her and the politics of becoming would be the roundedness of being. I walked in, raining grains of sand, and found a feather with its three-formed structure and wove it into an untold story, lost and found. I would find the delicious tastes of creativity within the spoils of my mind, and listen to the laughter of the outsiders and the cries of the waste land, and all the obstacles that came in and tried to break the unbroken wings.

Shane walked in. He immediately saw me and arrogantly walked directly to me. I placed my right hand on my sacred symbol as though to protect me. I wanted to cover all of myself. I wanted my body veiled with the soma, the nectar of the gods. I wanted to shield myself from his eyes. I looked straight into them as he tried once again to seduce me with the tantric juice bottled in his western mind. His eyes attempted to penetrate me as he wondered over my body with his lashing desire.

"You look beautiful. India surrounds you, he said."

"I am India," I replied with thunder words.

Smila rushed in and they hugged and kissed and the heavens bled with a red less blood. She told him that this was the first time she had seen me since my return from New Mexico. He seemed surprised and asked me where I had been. He walked me away from the others and, sitting down, said how sorry he was for all that had happened.

"I did not believe you when you told me. What did you do?" he asked me.

"I ran with the wolves," I told him.

The wounds in me were raw and pulled me like a puppeteer's invisible hands. It was a relentless graceless dance of a choreographed pain.

Shane was outside me, sitting and staring in to find me again. I was in a swing which was dropped down from the sky and my bright red blood feet were tingling as they reached and walked into the sky. The stone in my hand given to me by the bamboo lotus boy felt warm as I caressed the truth of its solid being. He intruded on my sky swing and his words weighed within the walls of my incense-burnt mind. He said that I was more.

"I am," I told him, "and the concrete too has wounds in it, because I left them there in the floor of this dusty, dreary, dead, wasted land."

"You sound bitter," he continued.

"I am sour sweet. I sing back because I saw the flower in the heart of the desert dunes and the seven turquoise beads are now embedded in my heart."

His face was clouded with rejection and defeat. His hatred was the gaping wound but it could not even touch me. His betrayal was complete. And I saw the shining, red, dark serpent close to me as he sang to me his flute songs. I touched his body and his notes quivered through my clay being. The lions were next to me, purring as I caressed their royal mane and they ate my golden bangles given to me by my beloved mother, because gold is sacred, as it remains untainted unlike the frail whining of human rage and the bitterness and insecurities and empty shell sounds of open wounds. According to the Chinese thought, when a Lion eats your gold you are becoming filled with abundance. *I will adorn my body with silver and gold because I want the moon to sing to me, and the rays of the zenith sun to swallow me whole and absolute. And I will invite gracefully the men of more who come into my dreams and assure me of my spirit sensuality and I will call the cat heads of Sekhmet to sit on my throat chakra*, I thought.

I was interrupted again by Shane. He told me that Hironobu san sent his greetings to me. I felt gentle and humble as I saw his divine face. I thanked him and told him that I would pick up the case I had left at his house as soon as I found a place. He asked again why I didn't want to stay in his house and added that he would be leaving for New Mexico in a few days.

"I died there and I cannot go back," I said.–

He was shocked and his hand touched me. I didn't shrug it off. I didn't have to. It fell off and I saw the skeleton shell crumple into a thousand pieces on the floor. All the wrappings had withered away. And I looked through his skin and all was hollow and empty within, and philosophy and tantra had fled like thieves who found nothing valuable they could steal. He looked old. His youth was ashamed to be trapped within such a greedy cage and I saw the white sky enter my head.

****

A gentle, gurgling sound from the rainbow crib in the bedroom in India awakened me. Reaching out for the glass tumbler with its beaded cover, I sipped the clear, cool water. Softly releasing the netting, I slipped out of the bed to check on little Savitri. Her almond eyes were open and she looked at me without blinking. I bent closer to cover her and she smiled and spoke to me from her eyes. I knew that she was saying something and it was big. We continued to look at each other as I became her and she entered me. I touched her tiny pearl feet and she giggled. She looked beyond me as though piercing into the future and I felt a flutter in my heart.

I covered her carefully, making sure her little net was tucked in so nothing could invade her. She closed her eyes and I walked back to the bed. Slipping in carefully, I took another sip from the glass and, placing it back on the little stool, started to turn on my side when my eyes fell on the altar. It was alive with the flames from the oil lamp, and the face of the goddess walked out of the image and floated across to the crib, which was haloed with a circle of light. It was beautiful. I turned to my husband and moved into his curved shape. He whispered something in Bengali and I told him that little Savitri was trying to tell me something. Her baby eyes were that of a visionary. He squeezed my hand and asked me to sleep. I walked into his dream, as dawn slowly entered the room and made all alive.

232

****

Shane was silent and looking at me said that he knew that he had lost me. "You never had me," I whispered. But he didn't hear that. And here was Smila again, chatting away about her many achievements. I thanked him for everything, for the house and the hospitality. He was very quiet as he wished me well and hoped that I succeeded in all of my endeavors. Looking at him, with all the Tantra within me, I tore his illusions into a thousand pieces like a glass door, which was created by an artist after he had abandoned his most important muse, and after completing this perfect creation while he was about to paint the final strokes it fell and all was shattered. He was shown how powerful the power of love is and always will be. Was it my imagination or did I see him pick up the torn pieces as he cut himself with the rugged pointed sharp edge of the glass? And now the wounds were his to carry.

Ulfhrafn and Flora arrived as though to rescue me from what felt like a painful and poignant prison sentence. Wolf raven took my hands and helped me rise. His tree branches embraced me and I sailed into his liquid eyes as his raven wings set me aflame. Shane looked at him with jealousy as I walked away with both of them beside me. He followed us and, as though to throw a final blunt arrow into my heart, asked me if I had seen the antique Samurai mask which always hung on the wall of the doorway of his palatial entrance. I asked him why he would ask me. He said that it was missing. The shiny black stallion walked in with his divine rider and this time not touching the ground rode on top of him. She had a glistening sword in her right hand. It was unsheathed and she raised it above her head as she and her chariot flew through the air right above Shane. I gasped. She was about to slice his head off. The sword fell and ripped through the air as she danced her dance of destruction before the dawn of creation. He was headless now. She picked it up and threaded it around her necklace of human heads chopped off for their pathetic lies and ignorance. And then the stallion and the rider dissolved into the sky, and Shane had a strange look in his eyes as he glanced at me confused, not quite knowing what had just happened. I stood watching them dissolve. And for the first time I realized that the mystery figure who rides the black shiny stallion was the goddess Kali.

I bowed down in absolute surrender as her awesome visage shined in front of me. Ulfrafn, Flora and I walked away and this time I didn't look back as I threw the keys to his home on the floor. He bent down to pick up the keys to his death palace and his soul flew out of his flesh. Smila came running and begged me to call her soon. I told her that I would. She joined Shane and slid her hand in his as though to make

233

me jealous as they walked away together and I knew that the orgasm would be pale and seedless and without any sacred tremor. It would be a lust-filled escape into the murky waters of a stagnant river. The stench of unconscious death and deception is suffocating and unbearable. All the perfumes of Arabia cannot diffuse such blindness and ignorance. Like Lady Macbeth when she tried to wash away the blood from her murdering hands and could not.

Flora embraced me and told me that she would see me the next day since she was going to be with her man this night. I told her it was the perfect night and, looking up at the sky, we both saw the moon draped in her cloud gown as she swallowed us in her full-moon-rounded light. I kissed Flora and her man as they left. Wolf Raven took my shoulders and pulled me to him and there in the circle of the moon aura given to us especially by her he took my mouth and serpent-tongued me. He traveled deep inside and I loved every thrust. I surrendered to this dew-dawn passionate kiss and the notes of the bamboo flute wailed and wept inside me. I felt the pearl running inside my mouth, as he swiveled it around and then the sun, earth, and moon all entered my mouth. Once again his tongue played with all the spheres within me. We walked to the car. I was a virgin.

As he drove up Madison Avenue, I remembered Tobias and his question to me in Café Rosebud in Paris when he asked me how many men I had destroyed. My answer was: "Not enough." Looking up at Ulfhrafn, I whispered to him silently that I would never destroy him because his art, his culture, and his rippling soul were an absolute respect of all things alive, and I knew that he could not wound. He was incapable of this. I closed my eyes and he placed his hot hand on my thigh as it sunk into every vein and each throbbing cell. The tree entered me and pushed itself into my inner space. The moon was full, unveiled by the clouds; and she shone through us. He drove with such care and elegance. He said that he was sorry that I had had to meet Shane again. I told him that it was important.

We arrived at the apartment and he jumped out of the car to open the door for me. He helped me out and smiled when he saw that I was barefoot. He took the sandals from my hand and with his other hand took mine and we walked in together. He walked me to the bedroom and I lit the candle and incense. He stood watching me and then left. I looked in the mirror and saw the red *sindoor* on my forehead spread like a bleeding wave across my face. It is a tremor of the wounds, but not the wound itself, because I was being taught to shield and heal and protect myself by the visible, invisible beings. I left it there and watched the dancing kohl shadows around my forest eyes given to me by my beloved parents. My divine father always told me of my grandmother, his mother, who rode horses in the village in India and fed all the villagers every day.

She was a poetess and he often told me that I reminded him of her. "You will continue her legend and complete her work," he said. He often told me that she had beautiful feet. I looked at mine. The sky folded in and I embraced myself with respect and pride.

"Be fearless," he always said.

"I will be and I will walk with your banner and spread it all over the tangible and intangible expressions of the Universe. I will, and there will be no shadow thieves who come in the dark night to use and abuse. They will be slaughtered before the entry," I thought

I started to uncoil the red serpent from around me but then stopped. I sat on the red couch and walked to the open night, and the candle flame now watched me silent and erect. Ulfhrafn was standing in front of me with two beautiful filled balloons of red earth. He handed me a glass, and sitting in front of me, touched mine with his and we sipped the first clean sip. We spoke about the party and all the people he had seen after a long time. He spoke about the photographer and that he had said how well I worked and that he would definitely work with me again.. I told him about Prana and how I was certain I had met her in Algeria, in a small dusky desert town called Taman asset. She was in a dream and came to me in the room where my gypsy lover and I were together. I was sure it was her. He told me that I would always have these experiences. You attract myth and miracles. That is who you are. "Remember I told you that night after the shoot that you are of the gods," he said.

He then said that he had met Smila some time back but tonight she did not recognize him. I told him how and where I had met her and how everything with Shane had happened. He listened quietly and carefully, not missing a single word. He said he would call Prana the next day and try to organize the shoot as soon as possible, since he had found out earlier that day that he might have to go to Iceland urgently. My heart sunk. I knew that something was going to happen and that knives would bleed. He told me that his mother wasn't well. I touched his hand gently. We sipped together and I spoke about all the contacts I had made, and especially about the Mexican director. He said that he knew of him and of his work, and that it could be a wonderful opportunity for me.

I felt the gold brocade pressing into my skin and with my other hand loosened it slightly. His eyes touched my skin. I walked to the bed and lay down. The candle flame smiled across me and I watched its romance dance all around me. He lay beside me, and I felt his gossamer wings slide under my head as I rested against its feathers. His hands weaved over me, feeling every nuance and soundscape of mine. He traveled with his mind and all his visions, and poetry carved his motion. His hands rested on my belly and all the elements sung their appreciation. He bent down and with his trembling mystery mouth kissed my yoni. All the gardens of orchids and gardenias and red roses and the jasmine night-queen spread their blooms and exuded their hypnotic perfumes. My yoni wept. My yoni healed.

Chapter 13: My beauty has been stolen from me
And I walk with a half-eaten language

All was quiet the next dawn as I reached out to look for my Satyavan and my hand searched for the raven wings. I heard water rippling and, getting out of the bed with the red drape still on me, walked to the bathroom. And there at the head of the tub was a collage of the most exquisite orchids and five candles lit around the tub., I stepped into its safe and surreal source, as the gold and red silk fell off me. I sink into Ondine's world and felt every woman's cry and heartbeat. To be loved and to be healed by love as Mirabai walked the folded earth, singing love songs to her beloved Krishna, and Rumi haunted the world with his passionf and all its seeds embedded into the fleshy exterior. Opening my eyes, I saw the red gold sari coiled on the white marble floor waiting to begin its uncoiling as it moved through all the chakras, opening each one until it emerged into the thousand-petal red lotus on the crown of the head. My fingers felt the head center. It was soft and alive and warm.

The phone rang and someone picked it up. Soon there was a knock and Ulfhrafn said that Prana had just called. I asked him to come in, and when he walked in he sat at the edge of the tub like a wild bird perched on the edge of heaven, waiting for any sign to fly in. My fingers reached out to the orchid at my head and I thanked him softly. His hands and eyes swam into the water and he told me how much he would miss me. My feet glistened and shone as he spoke and with tears running down my face, I pierced his sight.

After my bath, I dialed Prana's number with a strange anticipation. She picked up and was excited to hear from me. She began the conversation by saying that we had indeed met before. I was relieved and told her so. She then spoke of what she had in mind for her brochure. She was a little matter-of-fact about everything, a as though not revealing everything. I thanked her and she asked if she could speak to Ulfhrafn, who just walked in the door. I handed him the receiver and they decided on the time for the shoot. I noticed that he had brought in a breakfast tray with fruits, toast, and tea. He organized the place and time to meet and he ended the conversation saying that he would give me the message. Hanging up the phone, he said that Prana would like to dine with me that evening if I was free and that I should call her later. I told him that I would go to some auditions and set up some meetings with some of the people that we met the previous night. He agreed and sat down beside me, pouring a cup of tea for me.

The brown liquid was like earth skins mixed with baked bark, as it swiveled in the large mug. The aroma was of flowers, and a gentle breeze in some distant plantation far, far away. He told me about his daughter coming back, otherwise he would have loved me to stay on while he was away. I told him that I must find a place as soon as possible and that I would not return to Shane's place. He agreed and said forcefully that he would not let me. He also told me that she was not due back for a few weeks so I had time, and that Flora, too, was spreading the word.

"She may have to leave on a job too," he said.

"Both of you are leaving me."

"We will never leave you."

"I will mention it to Prana, too, when I meet her this evening," I said.

He told me not to worry. The blood was on the floor. The owl visited in the morning. The lions ate gold. In a small opening in the backyard of some house in one of my dreams all the deities and spirits that I had invoked showed themselves to me one by one, and a dark woman handed me a cut paper with a five and an eight on it. "Five is my birth number," I told her. Fear tried to stick its ugly head inside me. I shuddered at its smallness and pushed it away with fire force and burned it into ashes.

I looked away from his gaze and knew that every forked branch in every tree had a magnificent story, and that concrete could be turned into gold dust when consciousness was awake and alive and the alchemists were at work. I wore white this day. I felt the color and basked in its transparency. Leaving my hair wet and shadowing my eyes with kohl, I got ready for the day; the day when all would change and the moon would be fuller. Walking to the studio to wish Ulfhrafn a good day I caught him sitting at the table with his head in his hands. His shoulders shook. My hands fell on him. He looked up with tears in his eyes. I pulled him towards me and kissed him wildly and licked every single tear from his eyes. We sat quietly and felt each other's silence and strength and vulnerability.

Like the ancient banyan tree whose roots spread everywhere reaching out into the receiving earth. In that stride when all is open and child-like entries come in and fear steps out. It is a sacred gift. I touch it and feel it and I give all this to Ulfharfn

The phone rang and intruded on our privacy. I picked up and it was Hironobu san. He sounded a little sad and said that Mr. Shane was leaving in a few days and that he had my case downstairs. I told him that I did not have keys to the house anymore and would come by very soon to pick up the case. He sighed and hung up the phone. Ulfhrafn suggested that we pick up the case and bring it to the apartment as soon as possible. I called Hironobu san back and asked him to call as soon as Shane left and that I would come by. "Don't be sad please," I implored him. He was very quiet and I felt how deeply he was also hurt. The phone rang again and this time it was Prana. She asked me if I would like to join her for dinner that evening. I told her that I would love to and she gave me the address of a restaurant downtown. She said it was Arabic and was excellent.

The ways were opening. I could see everything falling into place. Like an ether jigsaw puzzle when piece-by-piece all slides into a seamless whole. A secret was being unraveled. I was sure that this reunion of sorts between Prana and me was going to be mirror-edged by the full moon and sliced by the rays of the sun and of the green, dwarfed foliage growing in concrete in this city of knives. It would be a tight rope walk with no safety net underneath, and it would carry the salted sighs of many wanderings on dried earth beds where water ripples had left their graceful waves. It would be a vision of kites flying against the blue skies with their hungry, famished tails trailing the flight. It would be stooped flowers and baby eyes staring unblinkingly into the rhythm and invocation of life itself. It would be growth. I felt the pull and the stretch as the rope cuts into my bare feet and blood drops fall onto the dry earth surface, I knew Prana had come back to teach me something. *I will be receptive to receive this knowledge. She is going to take me to strange and unknown paths some of which may be frightening, I thought.*

"I will meet Prana tonight," I told Ulfhrafn.

He too seemed to feel the importance of this meeting. Just then the phone rang again and this time it was the Mexican director. He asked if we could meet the next day since he had to leave for Mexico very soon. He gave me his address and asked me to confirm. A cold wind passed through me like pebbles falling on fragile, green leaves. I told him that I would come.

Getting everything together, I left and for the first time Ulfhrafn asked me to be careful. I asked him why he had said that and he took me within him and whispered that it was the wolf in him. I gave him back his gaze and he walked me to the open elevator. He smiled and told me that he would see me later that night. I did not want to leave my wolf raven and walked away with one feather from his wings in my right hand.

I hailed a cab on the street and remembered the mapped face of the driver of my dreams. I touched the beads around my neck. The brilliant turquoise ran over my skin like the dung-rolling Egyptian scarab beetle that was sacred to the ancients because it had emerged from nowhere and it resembled the god **Khepri** and the Sun god **Ra**, who created himself from nothing. It was a symbol of regeneration and creation, conveying ideas of transformation and rebirth. I asked the driver to please drive down Fifth Avenue. I thought of the dream of the previous night. A little boy was tracing my aura and showing me something that he held in his hand. He had a beatific face and I kissed him. The park was lit and it felt like all those who danced for and with me before were there. I felt Niyol's green eyes tickle me and I moved in the seat as all the wolf howls and wild hidden flowers sprouted through the speeding car.

239

The driver stopped at the address I had given him and paying him I walked up for an appointment with a producer I had met at the party. The receptionist was warm and guided me to the lounge area. It seemed like a long time before she escorted me to his office. He asked me to have a seat. He spoke of some parts he had in mind for me and said that they were small. "I do not mind as long as they are interesting," I replied. He asked if I would be also interested in modeling jobs. I said that I would be and told him about the work I had done for Ulfhrafn. He nodded, saying he respected Ulfhrafn's work a lot. There was an uncomfortable quietness as the wolf tail flashed by and left a shadow on the very white walls of the room. This meeting was more for curiosity. I am the curio, the strange one who bends in a different direction where the trees grow upside down, revealing their languorous roots to the sky as the clouds and the sickle moon slide through the crevices of the tree feet of life. He cleared his throat. I shifted my legs. The anklets sang and India returned to save this hollow silence.

The wooden life wheel of the ancient cow cart spiked its way into the gravel as it grunted an echo of a dusty, moist journey in a day of toil. The village homes had hand-art drawn in front of them with symbols welcoming the deities to enter and little Savitri was being rubbed with warm mustard seed oil all over her princess baby body, as her eyes reached out to caress the young, golden deer roaming the forest garden. The sun smiled into every pore of her skin and the universe and all the insiders reveled at this mysterious path. I sat near her and she stretched her little hand to play with my hair. My mother-in-law looked on but maintained her distance. Space was enlarged and I knew if I threw a stone it would disappear. Time was pale blue and all that was left was sunlight and stillness.

****

Back in New York, I handed him some photographs and told him that for the next two weeks I could be reached at Ulfrafhn's studio. There was a slight glint in his eye and I saw the cloud passing through the little white room we were sitting in, while the wild tribesmen on the hills reached out and brought the same cloud right back into my heaving heart. I thanked him as he told me that he or his assistant would be in touch. I left the room and my kite tail left a trail of dreams on the throbbing highway as my seeds spilled all over and I was raped by the sun itself. The receptionist walked me to the door. I thanked her and watched my words fall on the wooden floor making a plopping sound, and I felt my grandmother's feet entering mine, and all the crows that were fed in India at a certain time each month for those who had passed flew right through me and in front of my eyes; their eyes shone like a summer night full of stars.

Leaving the building, bruised and burnt, I walked to the other places even though I did not have previous appointments, and left my photos and resume behind. It was a zig zag walk. It was an in-and-out walk and the trees turned and bent with me as I removed the swaying elephant grass from in front of my eyes. I stopped for a glass of water at an outdoor café and sipped it as it turned milky white, not murky and stale. It was confident in its smooth liquid body. I drank it as both the moon and the river walked into the water.

After completing my mission of that day and meeting as many agents as I could, I decided to rest for a while as dusk was bending the sky with its unknown nuances. This was always a time to sleep in my little orange transparent teacup.

The sun cut its silhouette as the moon filled the glowing lines and Shiva thundered across the universe with his brass bowl dancing all to life and burning all obstacles in his path to sacred ash. The ash sang around and across me as I gathered the earth so it transformed into a bamboo flute for Krishna to play with, and all the cow girls and humanity itself from far and near would follow him passionately, leaving everything behind, and he wouldl become baby Krishna stealing the butter as his mother churned the milk, and eating it he would swallow all man's ego.

I looked at the nearby clock tower and saw that it was time to meet Prana. I was not far from the restaurant and walked with my feet and my grandmother's feet all in one towards my next journey. I entered. It was beautiful with fine mahogany tables, polished for generations, and through the tall windows the stars sailed in. I felt as though I was walking into the same restaurant in Taman asset with Tobias. The green grass dress I was wearing rustled against my body and I felt its cloth rapture holding my dreamscapes as the dusty desert wind brought back my gypsy lover. It was beautifully lit and candles were flaming everywhere. I was looking around to see if she was there when an elegant man walked towards me. He led me to a corner table above which there was an ancient Moroccan lamp, and sitting there looking almost exactly like that woman in my dream was Prana, dressed in flowing robes. She stood up to greet me. I couldn't take my eyes off her as I sat in front of her. She had ordered a bottle of red which was lit by all the candles around the room and I knew now that all the magicians were going to lead the way. The raw wooden table between us became the river bed abandoned by its water flow and I walked on its damp surface in my dream and saw her once again, standing on the grassy edge, waiting to tell me her truths.

Prana's low sinuous voice brought me back as she offered me a glass. I was humbled in her presence. She spoke about her life and herself. She never took her eyes away and said that she had come back to continue the journey that we had begun. I wanted to tell her about the

241

dream but hesitated. I felt hungry, with my arms tied behind my back. The men from the spa came in to steal me of my newfound freedom. They were scarred. I struggled and, releasing my hands from the taught rope, I looked down at them. Now they were silver – the feminine nature and the color of the new moon, receptive to other planetary influences. Silver stands for rebirth and purity and has a magical quality of protecting one from dark forces.

I felt Prana with and within me. It was as though she was speaking to me silently. My silver hands were returning to their humanity again as though to remind me of the importance of the unconventional inner life – a painful place of separation, but where one can live freely apart from the collective opinions of how one should behave. Very often this is the point where one is terrified to be alone and rejects the angel's invitation to a solitary retreat. I knew that I could not go home now, and that I had to enter into the cave of my inner being. *I cannot and will not and have not refused this call. There is nothing else to do but to continue this walk on thorns and cut glass and sharpened swords.* This is what Prana was telling me, without a single movement of her lips. I nodded and she nodded too in response. We were both very quiet as every syllable and symbol of the magic and mystery of life was forming the most beautiful and stark surreal painting in front of us. The weighted canvas dripping with raw oil paint dissolved into its own surrounding clouds, leaving us with the understanding that art opens doors in the labyrinth of the mind like nothing else, and I felt the essence of the wet canvas sitting on my eye-lids.

We spoke about India. I told her about my needing to leave the homeland. She understood everything. We spoke about my work and she assured me that I would be led and guided and I knew that the world of men and the world of the gods would be in harmony. Our language was in hidden sentences. She spoke and I took her words and completed the circle. And the red wine drew rivulets of an unseen call, and as this divine elixir flew through me I called the river to enter me and nurture all the thirsts and heal me so that I could be made fertile with the language of source and of beauty. I asked for all the dances of the Native American to be one within my reflections, and that every animal pass through my caves and that I would meditate with the moon and let her oceans remove every hesitation and faltering within me.

I asked that the peacock dance inside my clay walls, and open its feathers within my hut of vision and red memories, where the sticky sounds of nostalgia are stretched and drawn tight for the fairies to bounce upon. She cracked my vision quest of sorts and asked me where I lived. I told her all about Ulfhrafn and how we met and all that followed and that I was looking for a place as soon as possible. She mentioned that she had a friend who happened to be looking for someone to sublet his studio, as he was going to be travelling for a year. She told me that it was a small, very special place and not expensive. I was excited. She asked if I would like to see it that evening as it was close by and she had the keys to it. I said that I would love to. I glanced at my hands and touched and felt them to make sure they were back from their silver voyage.

She was watching me. I knew that I could hide nothing from her. She spoke about her work and I listened, fascinated. She began her business specializing in African, art mainly due to her fascination with the ancient worlds and their relationship with ritual and magic. I asked her why African and she said that she loved the surreal in their sculptures and masks. I saw my tribal warrior standing next to us with his magnificent headdress and his sword held in his right hand. I was looking at him and she followed my gaze and looked too. I was not sure if she saw him but I knew she felt him. We were silent as the waiter brought in all the wonderful delicacies. She asked me if I liked Arabic food. "Very much," I quietly replied.

Her elegance was breathtaking. It was of her entire self. It had no boundaries. And as we both lifted our glasses and looked at each other through that red luscious poetry river, she told me that I was both Siddhartha and Kamala, the courtesan at the same time. "You will be both in this lifetime," she continued without blinking a single eyelid. I looked at her confused. I was not sure what she meant, and yet something in me knew.

"It will be very hard but you must and will go through it and I will be there to hold you. I know what you went through. I was at the spa. You were there because you had to be initiated into the way of the courtesan. You had to help the men who came there because you treated them with respect"

"You mean the way of the Samurai?" I asked. She smiled.

Putting the balloon back on the table I felt a wave of fire fly through me. It burned me and I touched my own ashes as I threw them into the ancient, dusty river of all rivers, where the gods and goddesses are immersed after they have been invoked and hailed. Looking straight into her deep dark eyes I knew that I would survive, and more than survive and all the wolves and shining stallions would walk with me.

She spoke about her idea for the brochure and she was very excited about working with Ulfhrafn. She said that I would be perfect. Excusing myself, I headed for the restroom. It had dusk walls and large vases of tall bamboos and fragrant flowers. The mirrors were starred and glistened in the light. I glanced at my reflection shyly, not knowing what I would see and yet knowing that this time I would be covered with a mask of healing clay. It was another visage and the forest kohl had run a little, taking my eyes within their mysterious shadows. The clay on me had dreams written all over it, and removing my journal from my bag I touched its seasoned cover. I had not opened her much but I would soon because I knew that the true poet was the guardian of the archetypes.

Touching the walls, because they resonated of Taman asset I walked back to the table with the warrior and the shaman merged together. She asked if I was ready to leave and I thanked her for the dinner. She took my hand and I felt the moon and the virgin entering me and flowing through my every vein. Her hand was strong and tight and layered. The manager of the restaurant came towards us and thanked Prana. She obviously came here a lot. She introduced me as an old friend and he took my hand gently and kept it there for a while. Ah, the skin sensual and the elegance of erotica! It is rare and mad and passionate and wild and I am its very own personal rider. It is not given to all but the ones who can see and feel this ecstasy also see those invisible beings who fly in and around us every waking minute of our lives.

"He likes you," she said.

"He has green eyes," I said," almost like Tobias." Knowing that she was the one who came to us on that night when every sacred woman was none with her own feminine mystique.

She did not hear that or maybe she did. *Why did she bring me here?* I suddenly thought to myself. We walked out into the husky, dusky, sexy night and I looked back to see if those green eyes were following me. They were and my feet tingled with the tongue of silence and love. The wide almond eyes of the laying bronze horse looked at me with screams of joy and power and his gilded hooves trotted on the skin of my belly. I touched his shiny body and whispered love words in every language into his long and deep ears. He listened and licked his lips with his brass tongue and all was wet and alive and ready for rebirth. We walked towards the apartment building to look at her friend's studio. The doorman was warm and greeted us both with a smile. She introduced me and told him she wanted to show me the studio. We took the elevator to the 11th floor. She slid the key into the door and just before she opened the door I touched the exterior and closed my eyes. She did the same. The moon shone right through leaving sculpted sighs in every corner. She turned on the lamp near the door, which had a soft glow. I loved it. She watched me and said that she knew this would be perfect for me. She said how sunny it was during the day and added that because it was in the back it was very quiet, and that I would not hear all the rumble of the traffic. Before I could even ask her about the rent she told me what is was. I thanked her and we walked to the elevator. In the lobby she let the doorman know that I was very interested and that she would speak to her friend. He smiled and said that he would do the same.

The night had lifted and the moon was hiding and the virgin was at rest. I told Prana how grateful I was, for this and for everything else.

244

She was happy and asked how I would get uptown. I saw a bus stop and looking at the sign said that it would be perfect for me. I embraced her shyly as the bus approached and then I climbed in. As the folding doors began to close she sent me a wind kiss and said, "Good night Mrinalini." And out of the dark and murky waters, mud-born rooted in mire, growing upward, was the lotus opening radiantly into space and light.

In Egyptian myth, a lotus emerged out of the dark waters as an emblem of the spirit of life, luminous and fragrant, disclosing itself sometimes as a divine child or the sun god Ra.

I felt like I was sitting on a lotus throne inside a bus in Manhattan going up Madison Avenue. I looked back through the shadowed glass windows to see her again and just then her figure dissolved into the night. My heart pounded inside of me. I heard the sound of the galloping horses under the oceans and inside my belly. I felt her heave and throb and the fullness of a pregnancy of the spirit had begun its voyage inside of me. And I saw the dry riverbed in that dream village in Algeria where she had stood in her burkha and dissolved into air in front of my very eyes. It was her and this would be a silent secret between us, and she would be an instrument to show me many paths that lie ahead.

I glanced out and the streets were glistening with human light, and people were bustling and walking and holding hands and laughing and embracing. And the words from *Prayer from My Son* by James Applewhite floated before me: "Know that the psyche has its own Fame, whether known or not, that soul can flame like feathers of a bird. Grow into your own plumage, brightly, so that any tree is a marvelous city." As I grew into my own plumage the streets of the city became the green gardens of **Vrindavan**, where Krishna was born, and there in the midst of that lushness sat the divine twosome clothed in lotus blossoms, Radha and Krishna. Their erotic relationship manifesting the Indian philosophical principle that Spirit (**Purusha**, symbolized by Krishna) and Nature (**Prakriti**, symbolized by Radha) are eternal principles. They exist for one another, she for his vision of her creation, he for her bliss in spiritual union with him. And the streetlights once more returned as the bus neared my destination. As if the driver was aware of my absent presence, he announced the stop, rather loudly bringing it to my attention. Walking to the front exit I thanked him for the ride.

I walked to a bench against a tree on the street before going up to the apartment. I heard a rustling sound and, looking back at the bushes saw shiny green eyes stare at me. I looked back and I was sure it was Niyol giving me his wolf wave. I touched the lotus beads and glanced down at my white attire. The endless, undulating sands of Arabia's deserts erased all shadows and shone with newness as the briefest white of predawn yields to a rose and a saffron mist, in the resting purity of the child's gaze. I was ready to go in.

Ulfhrafn opened the door before I even slid the key in. "I heard you," he said, "I mean, I felt you."

I had come from the ether essentials and my gaze was that of the seeing bird, and all his raven feathers were spread magnificently. He asked about the evening and the dinner. I told him the food was amazing and the place was tropical, mysterious and of many languages. I told him about the walls in the restroom, which reminded me of Taman asset and Tobias. "He is always with you," he said without jealousy. I loved this so much about him.

"Prana is special and she is very excited about the shoot. She will call you tomorrow to confirm everything," I said.–

He said that Flora had called to say that she would pick me up tomorrow to go to see the Mexican director. My excitement was contained like a flower waiting to bloom with its petals neatly in place and closed. He walked me to the room and I washed and changed. Entering, I noticed that both candle and incense were lit and there were some fresh red roses on the table. My heart sang and after washing I changed into something soft and silk and brown skin and sensuous. I sat on the bed. The stone from Mexico was in my hand. It was warm and sea worn, and had an enticing shape and texture. It was in my hand when Ulfhrafn entered with two filled balloons of red fire water. I thanked him for the flowers and the candle and incense. "I had to," he said. He sat next to me and Radha and Krishna sailed in on their lotus chariot.

The time was now. I lay down as the anklets rang their India sounds. The henna had left its red gaze on my feet and fire flames walked within the skin lines. The night dress had lifted slightly and the energy of my calves felt wild and strong. I propped up the pillows and placed my head on the soft feather cushions and turned towards my Wolf Raven. I softly told him that Prana had showed me a small studio that a friend was subletting and that it might work out. He was silent and walked around the bed and very carefully and gently lay down beside me. My journal was on my left and my hand was upon it. He said that my hand looked like a tree branch as he placed his fingers on mine. The candle and the lit incense stick flickered their light into the sighing room. Turning towards him, my eyes were filled with a look from far away mountains of quiet desire as they pierced into his. His fingers wondered on my lion skin, and the strands of my hair were on fire by his wolf eyes. My surreal dream mind was sliced when he spoke poetry and my tongue remembered the silence of love. My eyes closed with his gaze on their transparent lids and we entered the forest of absolute bliss. The tree barks yielded and welcomed us in and the leaves quivered a love song of the birth of dawn. We made mad, passionate love. The earth trembled.

The next day I was awakened by the first rays of light and looked at the ripples left by both the raven and the wolf on my side. The jour-

246

nal was still there but now rumpled by the flight of erotica. There was a steaming mug of tea near my bedside table and a tumbler of clean water with the juice of one squeezed lemon in it. I wondered how Ulfhrafn knew I liked to wake up to this and as a shadow shaded the doorway I looked up and there she was, my Flora, bringing with her all the peaks and highs of Machu Picchu. I jumped out of bed and we melted into each other. She held my face and kissed my mouth. "I have missed you," I told her. She spoke of the Mexican director and how excited she was about this connection for me. The shiny black stallion flew through the room. All I felt was the wind from the robe of the holy rider and I was sure there was a reason for this. I picked up the lemon water and winked at Flora,. I spoke of the studio that Prana had shown me the previous night and that there was a strong possibility that I might be able to get it. Flora was thrilled and said Ulfhrafn had already mentioned it to her.

"He was beautiful," I said to her, "he sees me."

"I know," she replied.

She glanced at the other side of the bed and her eyes knew all and she smiled and hugged me. We were silent and Ulfhrafn knocked at the door and gave me the phone. It was Prana and she told me that after speaking with her friend this morning he said that he would love to sublet his studio to me. I thanked her for the night and gave the phone back to him. Our fingers touched and flowers and words gave birth to the African gypsy dance as a new day was born. And the beads turn into gold and the mother and the whore united to give us the sacred prostitute and the song line of a karmic path was carved in stone.

"I got the studio," I said quietly. They both embraced me, one with the pollen of the lotus in her body and the other with the love letter of a quivering symphony. I knew that a warrior must always recover all that is beautiful and somewhere I sit alone in this new journey sipping sparkling water and eating smoked raw salmon that always swims against the current and art is not just ideas; it is vision formulated through tools. I asked them what I should wear for this special meeting with the Mexican director. Flora went to the closet and selected something. It was the Tobias grass dress. Ulfhrafn nodded approvingly and I smiled and walked to the bathroom. I looked back at him. His gaze undressed me and now naked and wed I stepped into the warm water of the bathtub that Flora had already filled. I heard them speaking quietly and I felt their transparent sounds and color howls and sky bodies demanding the world alive. The water invited and welcomed and the spider plant pointed its sharp leaves at me and the blue and yellow goddess danced on the rock garden of thoughts and aesthetics and inner valleys. And the hands of the men when I was being led into the garden of Kamala, the courtesan had fallen off me.

I got dressed carefully and Flora touched up my face, almost as though we were going for a shoot. Standing back, she approved of her work and reminded me to take a warm wrap, as the trees were changing and moving into their next stage and the leaves were turning into myriad hues of reds and oranges and the air was fresh and cool. She decided to drive. Ulfhrafn said that in the next few days we would be doing the Prana shoot and some other assignments that just came in that he would like me to be involved in. I was ecstatic. He also spoke of two producers who had called and left messages for me to call them back. I asked if I should call them before we left and they thought that would be a wise idea. He gave me the numbers. One was the curious one, where I saw the wolf tail on the wall. His secretary picked up and I asked for him. She asked me to repeat my name three times and I finally spelled each letter. She apologized and connected me to her boss. He sounded courteous and told me about a small part in a film and another part in an off Broadway play. He asked me to come by in the next few days. I asked if I could drop by later that afternoon and he said that that would be perfect. The second one was for a commercial for a perfume and the receptionist mentioned that I could come by that afternoon if possible.

I was ready to go and Flora and I walked down. Ulfhrafn came with us and as we headed to the car he took my left hand and placed something soft in it. I pressed my hand into his. Songs are thoughts sung when people are moved by great forces and when ordinary speech no longer suffices. And in Inuit, the word "to make poetry" is the word "to breathe" and both are from anerca – the soul, that which is eternal. We had made poetry last night and in my hand he had placed a transparent, soft, floating feather. I thanked him and he ran his finger down my spine and once again the centers opened and all my being danced. He waited on the curb as we drove off and I waved back as my fingers became the feathers of war and of love. Flora placed her hand on my thigh and squeezed it tightly and I felt my rock garden filled with samurai sword light. We drove by the park and some falling leaves were gathering together in wind waves as they fell into the concrete cracks, and there, amidst these autumn sounds, a pink rose petal floated into the brown cluster and darkness hid beauty in its absolute intelligence.

Flora weaved and glided through all the crazy Manhattan traffic. She was calm and assured. She asked me where the Mexican Filmmaker's studio was and I told her it was on Ninth Street between Broadway and University Place. She handed me a piece of paper where the exact address of the director was and I was stunned to see that it was also on Ninth but more towards the west side. We looked at each other and smiled and I knew she was the flame-maker. We arrived at the exact place and looked awhile for parking. As we walked towards the building she told me a little about him.

"I know and respect his work but don't know him as a person."

"We will find out," I said and thanked her for coming with me. "His son is beautiful," I said holding the stone that he had placed on my foot in my right hand.

She rang the bell and we waited for what seemed to be a rather long moment. She started to press the button again when the door opened and there standing in front of us was the young stallion. He was all smiles and happy to see us. We removed our shoes and walked in. The room was all white and hanging from the ceiling were strings of mirrors all over the apartment, causing reflected light everywhere. It was as though stars were running in circles in the space. He noticed us looking and explained that the mirrors were very good for feng shui as they circulate chi energy and that his father enjoyed them due to his failing sight. His father was sitting on a throne-like chair holding court and beside him on a raised table was a manuscript. The boy announced us and led us to him. He greeted us in Spanish and the little boy, whose name was also Alejandro, mentioned that Flora was with me. He asked us to come in and invited me to sit next to him. He said something to his son in Spanish again. The son replied immediately and Flora glanced at me sideways. She had a perplexed look on her face. I was very close to him and could almost hear his breathing. He touched my face and felt my hair. My spine straightened and stretched like a tight rope that had been pulled to its maximum capacity. He asked me to relax. In an almost rude and stern voice he said that if he and I decided to do this that I would not be allowed to do anything else till the film was completed. He hastened to add in a cold manner that I had to be in excellent shape both physically, mentally, and spiritually and that I would have to shave my head. I was still and taking a very large breath said that if the part was truly strong I would do anything for it.

"Anything?" he asked me.

"Anything," I replied.

"Good."

He looked at me for what seemed like hours and then very softly asked me if I was interested in Zen Buddhism. The rope loosened and I felt its relief. I answered that I was very attracted to the philosophy. He did not ask me where I was from. I did not mention anything. There was something about him. I did not know what it was. It felt dangerous and my fingers covered my gold symbol on my neck remembering Shane when he had torn it off and the man in the spa who had grabbed it and I looked at my arms and thighs as though they would be bloody. I started to cry and couldn't stop. It was as though I sensed the entry of a dangerous dwarf usurper who was going to steal the light. Flora got up to comfort me but he stopped her. "Let her," he said, "this is very important for her." Through my tears I was eating golden sardines handed to me on a plate filled with green weeds. They were not from him. He was very silent and I could feel the young boy filling me with his deep, dark eyes. They all just waited for me until I stopped and, wiping my tears, I stroked my face with the wolf raven feather. I noticed Flora smiling. I had crossed the bridge of my own transformation and I felt the two thousand year old Tulle tree in Mexico watch my growth.

He waited for a moment and then, very slowly, placed the script in my open hands. I felt the weight. Then, almost at once, it got red hot and all the ashes of all the worlds and universes fell into my hand and the black stallion and the divine horse woman were once again in the room. They rode past me and bending down, still cloaked, she took the ashes from my hands and they galloped away. I gasped and they all looked at me, especially the director because he had felt something but said nothing. Looking at me he said that what I was holding was hot. "Sizzling," I replied. He smiled and so did his son. Flora stood up.

I told him that I would be very careful with the manuscript and read it with full respect. He was brief and with a rude manner said that I had better take care of it. I was getting used to his manner of speaking by now. He said that he would be in the city for about three and a half weeks, and that he would like to see me before he left to read some pages. "My son has marked the pages you will read so please look at them and memorize them." I told him that I would be moving to a studio apartment in the next few weeks and would contact him with all my new information.

"Yes," he said, "do that." I thanked him and he gave me his hand as though to kiss it. I pulled my hand out of his fingers and we walked to the door. There, as I slipped my boots on, I looked back at him, sitting alone, solitary and in command of all around him. His obvious arrogance and vanity were humorous. I had a strange feeling about this meeting His son walked outside the door with us and said something to Flora in Spanish. He then looked at me and his strong, deep pool eyes were warm and welcoming. He was a baby eagle and his sharp eyes sat perfectly within my nest, where the clouds leave their presence. He took my hand, the one with the stone in it and smiled as he felt it. He lifted it and kissed the roof of my hand. His lips were like tender rose buds as they fell on my skin.

Flora and I walked out of the apartment, and I waved back at him, sending a wind kiss, which he received and acknowledged. I didn't ask Flora what he had said to her in Spanish. As though hearing my thoughts she said he had asked her not to tell me what his father had said in Spanish in the room. Looking at me, she said that she needed to.

"He asked his son what your body looked like."

"What did his son say?" I asked her.

"'Like a tree,'" she replied.

His father was irritated by the reply and wanted him to be more specific. His son said that it was a beautiful tree. Flora placed her arm on my shoulder and we walked together towards the car.

That's why she came in the room, I thought.

Getting in the car, I remembered about picking up the script from the producer. Flora drove towards the building and double-parked as I ran in. The assistant was busy speaking to someone when I entered, and just as I walked in, I saw the producer in the distance. He noticed me and beckoned me to follow him. I walked into his room and he handed me the two scripts. He invited me to sit but I told him that a friend was waiting. He asked me to get back to him as soon as possible, as the auditions would be in the near future. Thanking him, I rushed out to the car.

After going to the other appointment for the perfume commercial where they asked me to come back, we drove up and Flora took a different route. She said it was quieter. She parked near an outdoor café. We walked out and headed towards it. She hesitated near a table but it was a little chilly so she walked further in. She chose a table and we sat down. I smiled at her as we sipped the full-flavored jasmine brew and I thought of the hymn that cannot be. I saw a dog and a tiger blend into one and the being approached me and bit my tongue. Flora's voice entered my dream state like a mountain chant and I heard her say these words: "You will become all. You will become your talent and your motion. You will enter this new path annihilating all doubt, all fear, and all hesitation." She took a deep breath and continued saying that I would understand the value of waiting and the importance of graciousness. "You will become the mountain."

A gentle breeze floated into the wooden walled café and we both felt the breath of the mountain itself. "Machu Picchu," I whispered. She nodded in agreement. I left my chair and walked to the other side of the round table and kissed her on the mouth. Some looked. I cared not.

Love is transparent and lush, and of the moment and fearless, and without any faltering mediocre hesitation; and time is of the present and love is the cloth of the river, the feet of the mountain and the sky of the jeweled earth. Those who fear the depth and passion of love fear all and they will never emerge and will never be the blossom on the cherry tree. They will die before ever blooming. They will be killed in their youth. They who were touched and inspired and then they think and wound the very growth that they experienced; and they fall back into the dust, crushed by the fire feet of the Goddess Kali, as she stomps the earth to destroy all ignorance and the fools who try to save their small selves from being hurt. Their strength is already blunt; their dry tongues have fallen on the dusty path as the shiny black stallion's trample all over them. They have lost their word, their fire, their voice, and every inch of sensuality that was ever in their slithering, weak souls. They are the children of the lesser gods and I walk away from them – far, far away.

251

Flora looked at my eyes. I felt fire flames shooting out of them. We drank to the jasmine tree and the beauty of the fragrance as it filled the air in the romantic nights of my land. I placed the scripts on the table. We both looked at them. We did not have to say a word. She nodded. I nodded. "I will do it, or at least I will read for it," I said. She asked for the check and as I was looking for my wallet, she stopped me and I accepted and after emptying the cups we left.

The dusk was here and Shiva had begun his dance. The sky was pink and every cloud glistened and etched in this light. It was breath-taking. We headed for Ulfrafhn's apartment and seemed to get there very fast. At the building she said she would not come up. She had to go home and prepare dinner for her man. "I will see you soon, Mrinalini, very soon. We will do some shoots before I leave for my project in Europe and the Far East," she said. I squeezed her elegant, exquisite hands and looked at her cultured feet. We embraced and her fingers ran over my lips as she wished me a very good night.

She waited until I got out of the car and was in the building to drive away. I turned and faced her before going in the door. We looked at each other and I saw a horde of magnificent elephants pass by with their pink, freckled ears flying in the light. They say in India that a freckled elephant ear is a bringer of good luck. But he is all fortune, so where is the question of even luck? He is everything. He is grand and all-knowing. I cried and she wiped her tears in unison with me. We were one, the goddess from the mountain and the wolf woman at the foot of the mountain. I walked in. She drove away gently, knowing that I was watching her. I adored her. She loved me.

As I approached the elevator I saw the doors were closed. I was happy as I wished to walk up the stairs and absorb all that had happened before seeing wolf raven. I saw my muses as they pulled and pushed me on the stairs and my army of birds fluttered around and helped me rise. The stale human dust was being bladed away as her red tongue dripped with fresh blood. My feet were shining with the henna stains that looked even redder than before. I slid the key in very softly, not wanting to disturb Ulfhrafn. I pushed the door quietly and tiptoed in and gently shut the door. It was dark with the last remains of dusk light drenching its rays inside the apartment. I walked to the kitchen to get some water and filled a large crystal glass. I watched the water flowing into the empty vessel and was reminded of the importance of shedding oneself of everything so that the new can enter. The new had begun to enter me and as the glass gradually filled I felt the fullness envelop my very being. I took the glass and smiled, remembering the murky water in the palace on the ocean in South Hampton, where hidden greed and lust had tarnished a once possible friendship. For the first time after many moons and journeys I thought of Smila. I decided to call her, knowing how much she would like this, but I was also very aware that she might quite possibly shun me with anger and jealousy for not contacting her sooner. I didn't care. *I will do what I am guided to do and I will never hesitate.*

Before entering the bedroom, my glance pointed towards the studio and I saw a slice of light streaming from it. I could hear some voices. *He must be working,* I thought to myself. Walking into the bedroom I headed towards the bed and lit both the candle and the incense, as the rhythm of the continuity of ritual made a move towards a certain kind of growth, just like a barren tree which is watered regularly slowly revives and one day may even bloom and thrive with the breath of life. Going to the bathroom, I turned the shower on and let it run. Undressing, I walked into the steaming water and cleansed myself from all that may have hindered a transformation. The warm water made love to me and I surrendered to her healing embrace. I loved love. After a long time, I finally left the water, and drying myself slipped into my silk night dream cloth. Its touch caressed me, and I was woman and whole once again. My hair was wet. I had washed every strand as I did not want the energy of his hands on them. I glanced at my reflection and smiled. The kohl had shadowed my eyes and the forest trees were swaying in the wind as the leaves bent into each other and all was harmony and grace. My fingers ran through my wet strands and I let the water drip around me without drying it. They rested on the telephone but I hesitated and decided to call Smila later.

My feet remembered Flora's magnificent stride and power, and I walked towards the studio. The door was closed but there was a sliver in the sides. I peeped through to see what my wolf raven was doing and sculpting. My eye sliced through like the moon being sliced by a cloud. There were a few models in the room and he seemed to be working on a few things at the same time. Suddenly he stopped and asked them to take five. He glanced towards the door as though he had heard something and walked towards it. I was certain he could not have heard anything as I had been extremely quiet. He must have felt something. I inched away from the crack of the door and leaned against the wall.

He opened the door and, seeing me standing there, walked to me and grabbed me fiercely. It was a passion so magnificent and so powerful I could touch it. We kissed madly and his hands touched my wet breasts. I slid out of my silk weave and stood in front of him straight, empty, full, and naked with my shining skin purified by his life breath. The rays of the moonlight pierced my skin as his mouth sent fountains of liquid fire all over me. We walked to the room and he turned down the sheets and helped me slide in. He then covered me and the nails fell on the belly of the whale and on all the songs that have been sung before. His mouth enveloped mine. My mouth was raw and cardamom-spiced, and I was mad with desire as I touched the elephant's ancient paws. He whispered in my ear that he would come back. His voice was like an ancient tree and a spirit entered my surrendered self. My eyelids closed gently.

The red sari had left me and the Indian night sounds clothed me with their incessant haunting melody. My husband's eyes were on me as I bent down to coil the sari back on to me. He smiled and pushed the cotton texture away as he touched my pulsating skin. That day of our wedding night when we had merged with the shenai sounds floated in front of my mind. That mad, soft first night when I was the ant in the lotus flower and when my thighs were tree trunks holding the first leaves of a very early spring birth. He was gentle and strong and I was a virgin, saged with the healing smoke of the Native American abalone day and night dreams, as the four corners shot their arrows around us. I felt my feet in his fingers as he played with the bells on my silver anklet. His breath was on my feet, and my toes were covered with gold leaves falling from the sky and entering his mouth. The wind stretched each leaf and, looking down, I saw the shiny sparkle of this divine, untainted metal. There was a slight coughing from the baby cot and we both looked up to see if the little princess was awake. And then I saw the owl. This time he was sitting on the window panel outside of the netting and his eyes were closed. He seemed to be guarding us.

The early rays of dawn light were falling into the room like little dewdrops on the young glistening leaves. The owl flew off and I looked up at the corner of the ceiling searching for the cobweb which marked her birth on its completion. I let out a sigh. Satyavan looked at me as he was covering my body with the sari and passion. His eyes followed mine and we looked together at the now broken cobweb. I sat up and walked to her. Her eyes were wide open and as she looked straight into mine she was telling me something. Bending down I kissed her on her forehead right on her little third eye. She smiled. It was a smile of vision and knowing. It was the child gaze which never lies and comes to us unveiled and unsheathed. It was a gaze more powerful than any knowing and any understanding, a gaze that cannot wound. I picked her up gently and walked towards the bed. We both looked at her. She had a fever and her breathing was heavy. There was a knock at the door. I was startled as I did not know that he had locked it last night. He walked towards the door, making sure that I was well covered. It was the maid with a pot of tea for us and some warm milk for the bamboo baby. I told her she had a fever and had been coughing. The maid said she would prepare some **Ayurvedic** remedies. Standing behind the door, almost hiding, was my mother-in-law. She looked at me critically and I, uncomfortable, covered myself even more. She eyed me up and down. *The ant in the lotus center falls crippled by the weight of the pollen and is helplessly crawling around trying to find its bearings again. I am this ant*, I thought and all in me felt lessened and humiliated and cheap.

The sun had fallen on earth leaving none of its rays on the cracks. I felt stripped and naked and raw like a snake without its skin and not ready to face the human or, rather, the non-human gaze. She continued to stare at me, and walking towards us, grabbed little Savitri from my arms. Tears ran down my eyes. She asked her son why the door had been locked. He replied equally angrily that we had wanted some privacy. She retorted that there was no such thing in the house and all doors should always be left open. There was a heart-wrenching silence in the room and Savitri began to weep and cry and cough. I was helpless. My beauty had been stolen from me. The middle lions had entered to rape me of my virgin sight. But I would not let them. I looked at the window, wondering if the owl was back. I looked for my black stallion and she who rides him. He was not there. I looked for my pink-winged elephants and they were not there. And there, peering through the window, her head draped in her torn white sari, was the ancient one who is one with the body of the temple. She must have felt something. Her eyes entered the room. My mother-in-law also glanced towards the window, sensing a presence, but the knowing one ducked from her gaze. After my mother-in-law walked out of the room with my child she appeared once again in the window and called me to come closer. Making sure the ogre mother-in-law was out of sight, I walked to the window and opened the netting. She whispered that I should come and see her, and that I should not be affected by my mother-in-law. I smiled and as she walked away my husband took me in his arms and held me for a very long time until the rawness seemed to be healed. I wept and howled in his dusky, strong embrace. I melted into his white kurta and walked through the lush, green elephant grass garden which had structured my loss as the swaying leaves became my music and the world would not perish for want of wander but for want of "wonder."

Chapter 14: I know that all the magicians are going to lead the way for me

Flora, Ulfhrafn, and I were at the round breakfast table going over the day's plans. It was decided that we would spend two days doing the brochure with Prana, and that it would be shot in studios and some exteriors. Ulfhrafn mentioned helping me move to the studio apartment. We had to pick up the case from Shane's and I called Hironobu san to see when we could do this. I had not heard from him for some time and his blue mountain Zen voice was the book of the Tao. And I laughed because I saw the moon reflected in the pool as the frog croaked within the wall of his voice and the rhythms of haiku were transparent and present. He was so happy to hear from me. I asked him when would be good to come by. He said any day. There was a long pause. He asked me how I was. I told him that I had been travelling a lot. He asked me where and I whispered softly into the mouth piece, which became the ear of my elephant god, that I had been crossing bridges and cultures within and without myself, and the god child had been given birth to and she had the universe within her. I knew he would understand. Placing the receiver back into its cradle, I told Ulfhrafn that we could go by any day.

The next days were spent hectically. We drove down to Prana's studio. I had to stand back before entering. It was Africa. It was exquisite in its décor with antiques and furniture and cloth and skin. The colors were strong and screamed wildness and tropical whispers. She welcomed us in and showed us around. Both Ulfhrafn and Flora scoped everything and determined situations and angles and positions for the shoot. They decided that all the shooting should be done within this space with a few outdoor locations if necessary. They discussed what the plans and ideas were, and Prana was more than thrilled because everything was exactly what she had been hoping for. She showed us the garments and costumes that she wanted me to be photographed in. I looked and touched and felt them and I became the lion in the forests of that great, grand continent. I was the giraffe reaching out with its elongated neck for some foliage on a tree. I was the one elephant within the family gracefully walking the earth like a fire walker, whispering life's truth to those who cared to listen. I was the rhinoceros finding its path through all obstacles and never walking on an already carved road and like the deer who dances the earth and gracefully runs when attacked by bigger animals, I flew with those birds of paradise who watch the world and know man's birth.

My African reverie was interrupted by Prana's strong, soft voice as she asked me if I would be comfortable in these clothes. I told her that they were a breath of saffron and my feet would be winged as my heart became the spear that she wanted me to hold. My muse walked in – the one with that magnificent headdress and warrior gaze. He was at home and stood right next to me. I felt his rough breath and the raw texture of his tribal skin garment. I felt sure that Prana saw him too, but she said nothing. This surprised me but she was hiding within her very own myth to protect and to feed it, while it enhanced and became all.

After Flora made notes of all the details it was decided to start the shoot the next day. Prana was thrilled. I asked her if I could use her phone to call Hironobu san. She pointed to it and I dialed his number. He said that it was a perfect time to come by. Wishing Prana, goodbye we left. I looked back, as something told me to, and she became the woman in my dreams. I saw the burkha and her hidden eyes. I had to hold on to Flora. I looked back again and this time she was smiling. She was tricking me and I did not understand why, but I knew it would all become very clear soon.

We walked out into the crisp, late afternoon light. Since Ulfhrafn had never been to Shane's, we told him that it was up in the sixty's on the East Side. We walked to the car, I in the middle of these two pillars. They had been giants around me. I would never forget them. As though hearing me, Ulfhrafn intertwined his fingers with mine and I pressed my leaves of grass into his. Flora kissed me on my cheek and we sailed to the awaiting parked car. He drove, and we got to the building on 64th and Madison very fast, as the traffic was light. We found parking a little way from the house. I rang the bell nervously. Hironobu san opened the door almost at once. Everything came back. On the table there was a light snack arranged. He was always so very gracious. We removed our shoes and he asked us to sit down.

My case was near the door, carefully placed on a mat. I introduced Ulfhrafn to him and he bowed. We started to sit when Ulfhrafn asked me quietly if it would be alright for me to take him upstairs. I asked Hironobu san and he quickly said that I never had to ask that. In the same breath, he mentioned that Shane left sometime back and had called several times wanting to know if I had left my contact information. I said nothing. There was a silence as we walked up the stairs. Those very familiar knife-sharp stairs where blood and water and salt had merged into one river that flows backwards. Flora did not join us. I took him up to the meditation room. We paused and I remembered Aakash and me sitting there some lifetimes ago, when my ebony face was like arrows in an awakened space, and my bride strengths were beaded with innocence and new skin. I will call him soon. We walked past the library. He took me in his arms. I felt fear shooting straight into me. It was dark and smelt musty, and I was certain that I saw the spiral smoke rising from that corner when Niyol sat in front of me, shapeshifting as his wolf eyes gave me what I needed then. I said his name. Ulfhrafn hugged me tighter and said "wolf" to me. I looked into his eyes. They were slanted and green. I wondered if he was my wolf too.

We walked to the bedroom and he and I sat on the edge. "How cold and strange and dark," he said. I felt the hesitations of afraid souls who are attracted by might and strength, and when the beauty is held in front of them to remind them of their own, they run away afraid to be hurt like whimpering dogs with their tails tucked between their legs. When they are aroused with desire and longing and when they touch the electric skin and magic mountain of the source of romance and love, they run even harder with their hands full because they are afraid to give and they hide in their stone shells with nothing open. And all cracks are covered with mediocrity and smallness, and all romance leaves them and they live each day like robots without war or passion or blood or soma. They will die while already dead; they only look like men, but they have nothing left as they take their perfumed maleness and perfectly starched shirts and pants into the dark closets of hell – locked, hidden, without breath and without air.

Ulfhrafn took my face and kissed my mouth. His long, art fingers ran on my breasts as he whispered to me that I would forget all this one day soon. My nipples were erect. We stood up and making sure the bed cover was carefully stretched we walked down to the dining area. Flora and Hironobu san were in deep conversation. We joined them as he poured green tea and we drank the mountains and trees of all the ancient sounds as we flew with eagles. We were quiet. Ulfhrafn thanked Hironobu san for taking care of me. He was silent as crescent moons sculpted our presence. As we were about to finish, the phone rang. Hironobu san picked up and then turned to look at me. I knew that it was Shane. I shook my head and we heard him saying that he had not heard from me yet. No one spoke. We glanced at each other and we rose slowly. Hironobu san walked to the door and held it for us as Ulfhrafn picked up the case. They walked out first and I stood in front of this great saint sage, and bending down, touched his sacred feet as he blessed me. He held me, and my autumn skin carried the load of salt and pain, and the butterfly flew out of my mind and entered my heart. "I will call and give you my number very soon," I told Hironobu san. He softly replied that he would not be working there much longer. I was happy as he told me that he did not want to be here anymore. I embraced him and told him that he would always know where and how I was. He told me never to give up. I said that I would soften the hardened and that I would carry the day. He smiled, and I knew that he was the soul keeper, and that he followed the mystic path and his hands held the sutras of silence and sound. He was the spirit seeker.

He waited at the door until we left. That rough, huge blood door where I had entered to discover what birth and death was. Reborn into rebirth as the chained elephant walks on the howling screams of the ignorant man, and he crushes and destroys all that is blind and deaf with

258

his beautiful, magic paws. He is mine. He sits on my head. He walks into my throat. He removes all obstacles in and around me as his wisdom trunk becomes one with me. I worship him, my divine Ganesha.

Flora and Ulfhrafn were waiting for me. They both smiled and we walked towards the car. He placed the case in the trunk and we got in. I remembered that I had both the scripts with me and had prepared a few scenes. I told them that if they did not mind I would like to go to the producer and, if he was available, get the reading over with. They both agreed and Flora suggested that I call first instead of just appearing there. We noticed a pay phone nearby and I ran out and dialed the number. The same assistant picked up and once again I had to repeat my name three times before she got it. She told me that I was in luck, as just a half hour ago two people had cancelled. I told her that I would be there in few minutes. Running back to the car, I told them that there was an opening.

We drove to the building on Fifth Avenue and 55th street. Walking out of the car carefully, I told them that they should not wait as I was not sure how long it would be. They looked at each other and he said that they would just work on all the details for the shoot until I was done. He double parked as I walked into the building. I felt uninterested, as the script was quite ordinary. But I knew that the experience would be helpful and, of course, I needed all the resources I could get. At the reception area there were a few men and women waiting. I sat next to a window and the receptionist acknowledged my presence. She came over to me and let me know that I would not have to wait too long. I thanked her. The others were called in and I noticed that this time I was not as anxious or nervous about the reading.

The sky beckoned me and my eyes fell on the clouds and the sculptured formations of each one. I felt the pearl in my mouth and the wild gypsy eyes of Tobias with his fevered sensuality, and the woman in the café in Paris who sat in front of me as she placed the large round tumblers of the red grape on a table that had seen and felt everything. I felt my art growing within me and I thought of André Malraux who had sent me a letter after he had heard a recording I had done in London. I felt Tobias swallowing that very pearl from the center of my hand and then placing it back in my mouth in Taman asset, on that fire-flamed wedding night.. He was the wild one. One of the few men who truly walked the path of Eros and Pathos, and through the art of Tantra, knew it was just a natural presence. *Why Tobias now, today, this day when all is in flow?* I wondered. They were my heroes of a thousand faces who walk the path of bliss and always remind me to never jump off that tightrope, because there would never be a way to get back on. And thus far had I walked, sometimes almost slipping off and at other times trying to be pushed off by those who could not get on or chose to fall off. They never succeed because their safety and fear softened their skin, and their feet had no sole to hold on to the rough texture of life. And in my mind and heart Tobias and Miguel and Ulfhrafn and my very own wolf man king, Niyol walk with me on this coconut fiber rope of texture and bliss.

The assistant called me and I noticed she finally pronounced my name correctly. We walked to the room where the auditions were held. The producer asked me to sit down. He was in a panel of about five very austere-looking men with one woman who was sitting on the side. She was very thin and vacantly elegant. She glanced at me with one of those obnoxious, non-smile smiles. I wondered why they even bother curving their lips so effortlessly. They asked me if I was ready. I nodded and began. Opening one of the scripts, I read carefully and with confidence. I asked if I should read from the second script. They nodded again. I felt much more comfortable with this one and the read went very well. Putting both scripts down I looked at them shyly. There was a pause, and the producer asked me to wait outside for a few minutes.

Walking out I took the same seat as before and thought of Hironobu san. I remembered his words as I was leaving and felt refreshed and strong. The assistant came and told me that they were ready. As I walked in, I was sure I would hear the same repeated remarks about my exotic look. Instead they told me that they were almost sure that I had the part for the second one. Thanking them, I asked them when it would be. The producer told me that he would let me know. He asked me if I could still be reached at the same number. I told him that I would be moving to a studio downtown and would let his assistant know my new number as soon as I did. I left the room and was surprised when a hand fell on my shoulder. It was the producer. He told me that they were very impressed by my reading and that he especially liked my voice and its many inflections. He looked at me for a while and added that he was certain that I would do well in what I was pursuing. I thanked him and, as I started to walk out of the building, I heard someone calling me. It was the assistant running after me with the script. Her boss asked that I keep it and get familiar with the part. Thanking her, I walked to the car with my people waiting for me. I had a bounce.

Getting in the car, I told them that I most probably got the part. They both held me and kissed me. Ulfrafhn's nape was a shiny column of many-hued rainbow beams. I could not take my eyes off the elegant pulsating shape and my wet lips flew to it. Our eyes met in the car mirror and I made love to him with every thread of my being. His mouth formed my name and my whole body had hands and eyes and I would be youth forever and the sky and earth should meet and I saw the *yoni* tree and I would write from other realms and I would love and make love even to the one's who did not see and I will always learn how to be.

We drove past Ulfrafhn's building to drop Flora, as she had a business meeting. She stepped out and waited for me to get in the front seat. Looking into her hazel eyes I remembered many dreams that had not been recorded as they floated within the stars of my mind. We embraced and I got in. She told us that she would be there in the morning, ready for the shoot. Her walk was like a lioness. One could almost hear her roar as her calm confidence enveloped all around her. We watched her before driving off. She looked back and waved to us.

Ulfhrafn suggested having dinner at a Japanese restaurant nearby. I thought of Hironobu san and smiled with joy. Ulfhrafn told me it was very Zen-like. The sushi was spectacular. There was a silence as we drove back down, with the silhouette of the trees casting shadows on the streets. And on the passing stone pavement I saw "hope" written in large, fleshed out, red letters. His hand was on my thigh and I was carried on ancient journeys. My tongue crushed raw almonds as it felt the silence of love.

We parked near the restaurant and walked in. The tables were low and we had a choice to sit on the tatami mats. We removed our shoes and sat down. He asked me if I would like some warm sake. I looked at him, not sure, and so instead he ordered a dry, full-bodied red. "This is your poetry," he told me. I nodded and told him the story of how I was first introduced to this divine liquid by Miguel when I was in London.. "He was a friend for whom wine was a philosophy," I said. "He educated me and introduced me to the elegance of this nectar."

Ulfhrafn was silent and watched me with care and a rainbow intensity. I felt all the colors and saw the seven lines echo through his translucent neck. It throbbed with life. His feet touched mine and the avant-garde flew, the crows brought back spirits of those who had left and the mind was a web of light where fear had no abode. All conventions were broken and confidence and strength began to step in. And there was no need to be defensive because all came from that one rich source where freedom is filled with quality and structure. The waiters brought a huge boat with all kinds of sushi and sashimi spread on it with those amazing green leaves all around. He started to feed me and raindrops fell inside of me. I knew now that one day I would feed sushi to the man whom I would marry, a man I would meet on the street who would approach me with broken English and would be carrying Red and White by Stendhal and would have a green skull cap and tight red trousers and with the most intense green eyes would look at me, and five days later would ask me to wed him and I would say "yes" because art is the greatest seduction and seducer of all and I would always be seduced by it.

Ulfhrafn fed me again and I wondered how I knew all this. It was given to me and I simply knew it. Maybe in a dream that I had some time back when an wolf bit into my third eye and then became a man and I

261

awoke and ran to the bathroom mirror to see if I was bleeding. Maybe on that night in that dream my three eyes had been unveiled and maybe that is when I began to see from inner and higher realms.. I laughed loud and others in the room looked at us. Ulfhrafn just smiled and continued to place pieces of succulent flesh-life into my mouth. He then began to speak softly and slowly, enunciating every word clearly like a special mantra. He told me that he would be gone and for how long he did not know. He said meeting me was his falling in love with himself. He told me that he had sort of died and had lived a sad and detached life shunning everything that made him sing. He said he had read the Tao Te Ching and that it had helped him, but he had taken it too literally and there had been no space left. He had been trying too hard and was losing everything. "You have given it all back to me, Mrinalini, I feel my art and my sensuality again like never before. You must know that this is what you do for people and this is also why they hurt and deceive you because those who do are fearful of the power within and around you."

"You came to show me the wind. You came with a bowl of blossoms and a bird flew down and picked each petal. You showed me the now, and the mad beauty of ecstasy and touch. Mrinalini, you set me on fire and lit every candle in me, and romance has run back into me like a silent monk who had left his unlit cave of dreams."

He touched my hair and my child gaze was awakened. He thanked me. I wept with rain and the drops flooded the wounds and scars made by broken souls. He continued feeding me and told me that no matter what transpired, I should never lose my gypsy laugh and my virgin sight. "I promise," I told him. We touched glasses loudly and the clink created thunder. I heard **Shiva** and his consort **Parvati** making love as the earth trembled. He told me that even though I had seen and experienced much, there would be a lot more. I saw sharpened knives spread across the earth and as I walked on their shining blades my feet bled and my soul transformed.

"It will be very hard," he said again, "but you must go through all the caves and dark tunnels where you will meet enemies and allies. You are the hero and the journey has begun. And there is no stopping or hesitating now. You are on the tight rope and you cannot get off because if you do you would never be able to get back on. You will reach the grail, and you will return to give the nectar to all. This is your mission and you cannot refuse the call."

He took both my hands in his tree fingers. He kissed every line, and looking at me with those eyes of love and desire, he said that this was why I would never lose my child's gaze, because I walked and would walk the flower path of pain and pollen. I thought of the samurai sword, which is polished only by a very special sword smith because it is the soul of the warrior.

262

We finished the rest of the succulent meal and as the last drops of the red river entered us I thought of the owl on the windowsill, the golden purring cat, the hungry eager eyes of the bronze reclining horse head, and my magical divine horsewoman who comes to warn and protect me. I touched myself and Wolf Raven smiled, as his passion eyes followed my fingers. I wanted him, and my petals trembled and opened. We rose slowly from the mats and I put on my boots as he laced his shoes, and we walked outside the Zen temple. He took me in his arms and all the shiny black stallions danced in and around me and my mouth became his and my snake tongue slid across his inner landscape and the trees around us walked out of their bark bodies and melted into this union of skin and wind and earth and rolling, sculpted sky.

The next days were spent working and shooting and moving into the studio apartment. In between I was called once more for another audition to confirm the small part in the play. The Mexican director's son also called to set up a time and day for me to read for his father. I called him back and told him that I was in the midst of moving and would call him as soon as I had the new number.

The work at Prana's studio was amazing and she gave me something each time I saw her..She did not say much but sent me invisible messages and I felt it all. Ulfhrafn was in his element. We worked long hours into the night. The three of us were aware that we would be separated soon and there seemed to be a strange urgency in this work. My heart hurt knowing that both Flora and he would be gone and I would be alone. I knew this was a very sentimental thought but I remembered Prana once telling me that there always would be cracks and I must never forget to seal them with gold dust. I laughed loud. They glanced at me and the shaman marriage tent flapped its drapes over me to reassure me of an inner wedding of the found self.

That special evening after we completed the African shoot, Ulfhrafn drove Flora and me to the studio apartment with the suitcase that I had left at Shane's. He helped us to unload it and the doorman rushed out to help carry it in. He said that he would pick us both up in a few hours, as he had some work nearby. The doorman was pleasant and welcomed us in. He pointed to where the elevator was and we pulled the case, and entering the elevator, pressed the eleventh floor button. The studio was empty with just a few essentials and had been cleaned meticulously. Flora helped me unpack after we had removed our shoes. I found a small table and set up the altar near the little bed which was next to the window. She smiled, and we unpacked and hung the clothes up in the small closet. I found my sage pouch and, removing a handful of the ancient leaves, took my abalone shell and burned the fragrant cleansing leaves. The smoke was heady and strong. I opened the windows so all unnecessary vibrations could fly away. The bathroom was small and cozy and I decided to take a shower.

The phone had been connected and Flora said that she would make some calls. The water felt warm and strong. I could sense change and suddenly a cold breeze touched me. I shivered, and getting out of the shower, draped myself in a large towel and walked out and sat on the bed. Flora looked at me and came closer. She put her arms around me and whispered softly that I would be fine. Tears flowed, and I knew that this was going to be the beginning of the hero and the god, the meeting with the goddess on the road of trials.

It would be a departure into the belly of the whale, the crossing of thresholds where there would be supernatural aid because the call was not refused. It would be of myth and dream and of the virgin birth and the virgin motherhood, and the transformations of the hero. And I would see the peacock that signifies the golden dawn, who is the bird of immortality and who enthrones mortals with his multiple eyes suggesting their surpassing vision and the all-seeing eternal. I remembered that according to a Hindu saying the peacock has "the feathers of an angel, the walk of a thief, and the voice of a devil." his stunning tail is a courtship display, making it vulnerable to enemies and moralizers who see this as an example of pride and vanity. I was reminded never to be lost within the dark, deathly prison chambers of vanity and Ganesha loomed ahead and was the guardian and the watcher at the threshold of sacred space as he emphasizes the danger and the opportunity to cross over between the human and the divine worlds. And I was reminded of the **Dakini** whose symbol integrates traditionally masculine attributes but her action is of passion and yang energy and her feminine manifestation is playful, wild, mercurial, creative, and deeply wise and is sometimes referred to as sky. One could summon her but the Dakini would arrive only if and when she wishes.

One could beseech her with longing and reverence. She could bring fear, delight, awe, and great challenge when she appears. But she cannot be pinned down nor made subject to the ego's demands. In her sky-dancing form, her garments speak for her; they flutter around her on her little cloud of bliss. Beware never to grasp at her, nor ignore her because she vanishes leaving a faint scent, and an ashy dusting of once brilliant possibilities in your empty hands.

I thought of Shane and his parched, desert, dead, empty, scorched palms. Smila came in too, with her crooked mouth and her scornful gaze. She walked out limping as she had lost a friend, because she grasped and clung and tore the gossamer wings of this female bird and now the howl was hollow and empty. I am one of the Dakin's *manifestations*, I thought.

My body was dried by the sage smoke and moistened again by the fresh wind that had danced in. I rose from the bed after kissing Flora's shoulder. The towel fell off and my nakedness was alive and new, as Flora's eyes moved around. My skin had veins etched through sunlight and angel dust whispers. She walked to the closet and removed a dress and said that this was what I should wear this night. And the shell and the seaweed danced a symphony of melodies.

The bell rang. It was the doorman. He said that a gentleman was waiting for us. We looked at each other. We smiled. We walked to the elevator. I smelled of jasmine. Flora exuded the mountain lilies. We were women.

In the lobby Ulfhrafn was standing dressed in his elegance and charm. Walking towards us, he said that he had spoken to Prana and we might have to shoot just one more day. I was delighted to be with them just a little longer. He said that it might be wise for me to just stay this night at his studio so Flora could prepare me the next morning. He wanted to take us for dinner. I was famished and we walked to a wonderful health food restaurant a few blocks away which Flora knew of. It was called East West.

The restaurant was simple and warm and the food was wholesome and clean. We discussed the shoot at Prana's. Ulfhrafn felt that he could do some things in a different way to emphasize the quality and essence of what she needed.. He added that she was thrilled with what she had seen so far. We were quiet. We all knew Prana was a very special woman. I nodded, and right then she appeared with her burkha, with only her eyes in sight. I decided to tell them both about the first time I had seen her in Taman asset. This was the first time that I had described what had happened in such detail. Flora took my hand and told me that she was not at all surprised. She added that she was glad that I would be near Prana when I moved. "She will be a guide for you," she added. Ulfhrafn was looking at me and I was the walk of an Indian soul and the two women in me, **Ardha** and **Nari**, female and male, yin and yang, the one who stays and the one who leaves, both walked with anklets around their hennaed feet, sinking into the ripples of shades as the youth child pulls the kite strings.

Looking up, I saw a huge Kali face dripping from the sky and that same girl-child who runs in the grains of sand, as red rose petals fall from her waist pouch, leaving a trail of truth and longing, as all the names of soul in all languages echo in the heart beat of her musical breath. I picked up the rose petals from the nuanced sand and begin to eat them as my tongue was collaged with broken red formations. And I call my beloved father, the "rose man" because he loved this flower of a million superior vibrations.

I felt Ulfhrafn pulling me back to his eyes. I swept all the leftover petals and the water drops left from the potholder that had walked with two pots to fetch water from the riverbed. One was whole and the other

265

was cracked and as he walked back with both pots filled he explained to the cracked one how important its existence was, and that because of his cracks and holes made by time and lust and dust, now it let the water trickle to feed all the little wild grass growths that would be otherwise neglected if not for him. And I thought of the woman in London who hated herself and felt ugly and I hoped that she had understood her importance in life and hoped that I would also accept the beauty given to me.

My eyes were back with my wolf raven and we sang our love song of art heart and love. We smiled. Flora laughed and, finishing the very nourishing meal, we headed for the car. I paused and wondered if I should get the altar for tonight and decided to leave it at the studio, so all there would be held by the body of its divine melody. Flora opened the front door of the car for me and I asked her to sit there as I slipped into the back.

The night was glistening. It had rained while we were inside and everything was wet and ripe and ready to receive. I saw his rainbow nape again and once more learned that structures, rigid formations, staying within the safe and secure mind and mental absorptions, are imitations where the real walk never happens. I floated in the wind. The car raced through the streets. We were quiet and still. My eye fell in the mirror of the car and I caught his, and the yantra of the goddess Bhuvenesvari, who rules the three spheres of the earth atmosphere and the heavens, painted itself with our eye gaze. His eyes were the psychic energy of the yantra itself. Tears filled my eyes. Flora reached for my hand. The three of us were like the **trishule** held by Shiva and Durga. The weapon has three points representing creation, maintenance, and destruction. It also represents the past, present, and the future. It stands for the third eye. And as my eyes travelled back to the mirror of myth and magic, I felt Ulfhrafn's eyes piercing into that middle power point. It stung. It was bleeding.

He smiled, and the whole ball of the sun entered my feet and travelled through me. I sat up erect and let the warm glow fill every cell of my being. I was lit. We arrived at the apartment and after parking we went up to the place that had sheltered and fed and nurtured me in more ways than I could even conceive. I was filled with gratitude and, turning to both of them, clasped my hands together and bowed to them, whispering, "Namaste."

We walked quietly in. Natural and mystical things were happening. Our nature rejoiced in each other's nature. Ulfhrafn went to the studio and Flora and I walked to the bedroom where I would rest and dream one more night – one last night of alchemy and magic. On entering the room, I missed the altar but burned an incense stick and lit a candle. The flicker of the flame brought back the images and they floated across the room in between the shadows and light from the street lamps outside. I noticed that I had left my journal here.. It was hot. I thought of the Mexican director's script, which fell into ashes as I held it. This was different. Opening the textured pages, I picked up a pen, but my hand stood still. I closed the book and decided to have a warm shower. The water poured over me like an elixir that is fiercely guarded by the gods and held safely within a fiery ring that covers the entire sky. I felt elevated as though my wet hair head was touching the ceiling of the room. I walked out of the room and saw that Flora had left a robe on the bed since all of my things were in the studio – my new nest where Uluka, the owl, ruler of the night and seer of souls would keep the sacred knowledge intact. The robe was orange and red.

Just as I slid into the sheets, she walked in with a filled tumbler. She sat in front of me on the red couch. We looked at each other and said nothing. All was whispered in and around us. Words were not needed. The silence was sculpted with a hidden mysterious vocabulary, visible and invisible. There was a soft knock and Ulfhrafn entered also with a red rose in his alive and exciting hands. Here we were again, us three. He spoke about the next day and all that had to be accomplished. He said that we had to complete everything as he had to leave the following day.

A pang floated within me, and I touched my heart. I took a deep breath. "We will start early," he said, and getting up, he wished both of us a well-rested night. At the door he turned back and walked into my breath and mind waves. I watched him and felt his shiny golden body. It was big enough to block even the sun. Flora kissed me on my opened third eye. She whispered something in Spanish. I didn't know what it meant, but in its silence it whispered all the languages of the world of love and passion. It was beautiful. Before leaving the room, she covered my tired body and spirit and left the candle burning. The flame was my night companion, the night when the sky and earth would merge and reflect each other, and the soft body of the River Ganges would run eternally and endlessly.

****

My Satyavan walked into the room holding little Savitri. She had stopped coughing and was sleeping peacefully. I noticed the shadow of my mother-in-law outside the room. She did not enter and I was glad. I whispered to him quietly that I would take her to the temple. He nodded and made sure his mother was not watching so that I could go without being reprimanded. As he handed me the beautiful child, he took me in his arms and I felt the embrace of both, husband and universe child. She was beautiful as she slept and made those adorable sounds – so brave, so huge, so small, and so vulnerable.

Covering my head as was customary with my fresh morning sari,

267

I quietly walked out from the back entrance. I didn't want to be noticed by my ever-watching mother-in-law. I slipped into the morning dew-wet grass and my feet sank into the refreshing moisture. I saw my husband looking at me. I looked back and smiled. The temple was being cleaned and the priest was preparing for the morning *puja*. The flowers had just been plucked and placed in front of the image of the goddess. Her fierceness felt very alive, as I bowed in front of her and sat down with the still-sleeping little one. The priest smiled as he came near us and peeked at her. I told him that she had not been well and had a high fever and a prolonging cough. He walked back towards the image and began the morning ritual. There were prayers and mantras repeated in Sanskrit and a few other people came by. I glanced nervously to see if my mother-in-law was present, knowing that if she saw me she would be very annoyed that I had brought the little one when she was not feeling well.. I was happy not to see her.

The morning prayers were usually long and heady. The bells and the incense and the melodious chants gave me peace, and looking down at Savitri I saw her eyes. They were wide open. She looked at me and I raised her a little so that she could get a glimpse of the priest and the divine image. Her eyes wandered in that direction and she watched him knowing exactly what was going on. Her eyes came back to me and she smiled intensely. I bent down and kissed her little forehead, which was now not as warm as it was before. She kicked her little feet into me. I felt the world heart beating within me. I adored her.

After the long worship, the priest approached us and placed blessings of turmeric and sacred ash on our foreheads. It tickled the little one, and with her tiny hand she rubbed her forehead and the red powder smudged across her face. She looked like an abstract painting by Max Ernst and I left the red streaks on her face. Her eyes were wild. It felt as though the goddess herself had entered her. Rising from the ground, I thanked the priest who came back with some fruits in his hands and told me not to worry. I asked him about the woman in white. He said that he had not seen her in a few days. My gait faltered as I walked away thinking of the Universe in her mouth when she had sent it to me and dropped it into Savitri.

We walked back slowly. She was now awake, smiling and wriggling in my arms. I propped her up and carried her so that she could see the garden. We walked through all the flowers, the orchid trees and the little lotus pond. I decided to sit by it. The sun was gentle and kind and had not entered my feet yet. I smiled as though in a dream or from another place, and watched the dragon-flies squirt about on the water, chasing each other and then flying from one lover to another. Savitri was watching, too, with captivated eyes. Her gaze followed flies and she giggled when the sunlight reflected on their wings carrying the rays on their winged bodies.

I looked at the nearby floating lotus and became the ant inside it on that day when we were wed. I started to weep quietly remembering all that happened since that day., She felt the shift in me and her eyes came back and we held each other. Who is she? I wondered. I pulled her tightly to me and told her never to leave me. I was certain that she had understood, and she continued to look at me as though from another plane or another world. I heard a noise and, starting up, looked, and there was Satyavan. He said he did not have to go to work today and wanted to see what the priest had said. He looked at her red streaked face and smiled. I told him that the priest had given us blessings and told me not to worry. He asked me if the lady in the white sari was there. "She was not," I said. He sat down beside us on the dew-dropped grass and watched the sunlight play on the rippling water and on the transparent wings of the messengers in flight. We were silent, together, and blissful. Nature enveloped and embraced us.

Suddenly we saw the gardener walking to us. I had not seen or heard him. He had some fresh flowers in his hands. He gave them to me. They were roses, and the red screamed through them. The fragrance was strong. He handed me a pinkish white rosebud and said that he had picked that especially for the little one. I placed it in her tiny hands making sure that there were no thorns on the stem. He had already removed them. She gracefully held onto the stem and very slowly plucked one petal, and then another, and placed them in her little mouth. Satyavan started to remove them from her mouth, but I stopped him, saying that she knew exactly what she was doing. He looked at me but was not sure, and looked at the gardener who nodded in approval. She smiled and looked at us. My legs shifted. I felt the seven chakras shiver and tremble. The subtle body echoed a tremor, and the wounded bird fell from the sky next to the little one.. The warrior was limping; the painted art on glass had broken and fell shattered in one million and one pieces. The lover had left his bleeding space in my heart and the purple lotus had begun its blossoming. I looked at them and handed her to my husband. I had to leave now.

Chapter 15: My tongue crushes raw almonds as it feels the silence of love

Prana had become large. She now began to come closer to me. It was as though she had given me the time and space and felt that I was ready to be guided. She told me a little about her friend who owned the studio and that he was glad I had moved in. She also mentioned he had reduced the rent.. I thanked her and felt very relieved. Ulfhrafn and Flora both embraced me. This was the last day of Prana's shoot.

While we were in her jungle her face became Ganesh's round, proud, ornamented, and winged exquisite head. Looking at my right wrist, I saw him sitting there. I kissed his coiled wisdom trunk and felt the quiver of the petals on all the inner centers. We started to work. I moved in and out of tree barks and saffron robes and held ancient spears and swords in my hand. I was the instrument of all expressions and the moment of all moments. I hailed the gods in string and drum. My feet stood on lions. My warrior muse was on my right. I felt his breath. I heard his cry. He was powerful. He was mine and in flight.

This next morning I awoke in the studio apartment. The walls walked around me. The table wept. The angled sofa was not red. And the windows were small, but light did seep through. There was a sense of insecurity in me. Fear began to creep in like a coward and a beggar stealing into the back door of my vulnerability. I felt the blunt arrows of mediocrity bumping against my skin. They thud and fell on the wooden floor and made an empty sound. They tried to pierce but they could not. I was alone, and the cracks were opening as I tried to close and seal them with gold dust. I was naked and didn't feel the sky near me. The earth was far away, but I knew I must place sugar crystals on her every Tuesday before noon so the ants were fed and Laxmi was happy.

As I was still in bed, I heard the whispers of my men and lovers. I tried to touch and feel them. I could not. My hand went to the phone but I stopped. My lion had to enter back in. I longed to hear his growl and touch his warm mane. I wanted his paws to leave an imprint on my burnt, brown ancestor skin. "The leaves are my angels," I whispered to myself. "The vines are my soul keepers and the red lingam flower is my companion of eons and decades." The book of symbols fell on the floor. The owner had left some of his books on the shelves. The page opened to the dove and on the top was written these words from the Song of Solomon 2:4: "O my dove, in the clefts of the rock, in the covert of the cliff, let me see your face, let me hear your voice, for your voice is sweet, and your face is comely."

The phone rang. It was Ulfhrafn. He asked me if I was okay. I hesitated only because I let mediocrity and shame come close, and I told him that I was filled with fear. I remembered the fog and the cloud and the salt stings and the stone, the deer and the kiss of longing. He was very quiet and I saw the spaces of his body behind his sealed lips, and I saw the erotic statues on the temple walls in Konarak passionately melting together in a union of the self. And the supreme and the bow and arrow became one. He told me that I would be fine and reminded me of the journey. He said that he loved me and I rose from the bed and walked to the window. The sky was sculpted in front of my eyes. I felt my tongue playing with his and told him so. I heard him take a deep breath and felt his tree hands covering every part of my wed and married nakedness. He was never afraid of my wild openness. He never ran away like many cowards I knew. He received and responded. I was full-filled again. My skin was alive and I called the clouds to wipe the fear and the sadness away with their soft sculpted bodies. And I saw the sun giving light to the moon. The journal of circles began as each one was holding all positive energy.

Intuition is the affirmation of all that is alive and tangible, I thought. On the phone Ulfhrafn whispered soft and sensual words. I became the warm, curved sinuous statue on the temple walls.

"I will call you from Iceland," he said, "and I will see you soon. Please don't forget anything. I carry you with me," and he hung up.

My breath began to flow and whisper again, and very slowly the rays of the sun made their way into me. I walked to the bathroom and decided to take a bath. I lit a candle and waited. I was Ondine again. I would survive. And the sacred prostitute was there as the courtesan of the gods entered and the fools walked away, far, far away. The water had risen and the moon was reflecting in it. I merged into the liquid as all falseness fell away. The phone rang. It was Ulfhrafn again. He wanted to know if I had all the numbers of the producers. I thanked him and told him that I had everything and would call them and make appointments. He was silent, and the five oceans met in a sacred place in the land's end in Kanya Kumari at the tip of Southern India, where people go to touch the healing waters as the *Vivekananda* rock looms in front. I touched his longing with my eyes as he put the phone down. He called back, and I lifted the receiver as though sitting on his rainbow transparent neck. He softly whispered, "We are all with you. Feel us."

I was in a painted forest, holding the world in his enticing gaze, and I told him that he made all things moving and motionless shine. "Give my rays of sun to your mother. She will be well. I am sure," I said to him. He thanked me and hung up. I stood in awe as the water pearls sat on my body, and the oyster gave birth to a pearl – its very own auto-biography. I was certain at this moment that love is art.

In the bathroom I stepped into the warm water again and knew that I had flown with eagles and was held by the gods. Men have jour-neyed through time, and this was my destiny. I stood alone now – my sol-

271

itude and myself. In the water the dreamcatcher entered me as I watched the ones that had been held. I would try once again to walk on concrete engraved by the crescent moon, and all the wounds and obstacles would become jewels on my naked body.,. I would burn the minutes and hours with its ancient smoke, and they would enter, Niyol and she who bequeathed me with those seven turquoise chains to protect my soul.

They had never left me. They were always watching.

As these thoughts were caressing my mind, I saw fear losing some of his clothes like shame, as he began to stumble out slowly, frightened of the power of the rolling sun and of the silent moon and of the shooting stars. *The petals that I will take in my mouth one by one as I will swallow my grief will be eaten. And they will float inside of me.*

My eyes closed in the water of rivers and I trembled at what lay ahead and could still feel some of the clothes that fear had left behind.. I stayed in her liquid and moist embrace and breathed in every grain of sand and truth and blood. Leaving this reflected warm water I chose what I would wear this fallen, risen shadow day. I missed Flora. I missed her touch, her beauty, and her warm sensuality. The phone rang. It was her. I was not surprised because when I was clean and clear I could see all. Picking up, I said her name. She didn't ask because she knew that I knew. I told her that I was picking something for today and she told me what I should wear. She was leaving for the airport for her project in the Far East and Europe and wanted to hear my voice once more. I told her something she had taught me in Spanish. She laughed and the sound of her voice rushed through the phone. I felt her love and care removing all the ripples of unwanted sighs. I adored her. She told me to be careful with the Mexican director. "He can be very brutal," she added. I felt a pain and sat down. "I will call you whenever I can. Don't ever forget your talent and your uniqueness no matter what happens. Feel your beauty as you touch the trees and see your dreams because you must claim it now." She repeated that she was more than happy that Prana was close to me. She also told me that Ulfhrafn showed her some of the shots from the photo shoot.

"They are amazing," she said.

"He called me a little while ago," I said.

"He loves you, Mrinalini."

I thanked her and wished her a wonderful trip. "I will miss you, Flora. But I will feel you," I added. "It will be strange to be made up by someone else but I have learned so much from you that maybe I can direct some of them at times." With a firm voice she said that I absolutely should. "And don't forget your mirror and your earth soul," she said.

She hung up. I wore what she had asked me to; it was just perfect. Alive and full of light once again I called the Mexican director and his son picked up. He was very happy to hear from me and told me that

272

his father was getting slightly irritated and annoyed that I had not called. I told him that I had been moving and gave him the studio's phone number. I asked him when they would like me to read for them. He covered the mouth piece and asked his father. After a long pause he asked me if I could come in two days. I said that that would be fine, and we decided on a time. I asked him if his father would need the lines memorized. He replied that that would not be necessary. Placing the receiver down, I was relieved. I decided to call all the other directors and producers.

The producer who had said that he was more or less sure that they would want me for the part was out, but his assistant told me that I should call back in an hour. I called the others, one of which was the photographer who Smila had introduced me to. He was surprised to hear from me and sarcastically told me that he thought Ulfhrafn had stolen me away. He told me of an upcoming project and I gave him my new number. In the back of my mind, I heard the Mexican director telling me that if he decided me for the part, I would not be able to do anything else.

I was in Paris in that quaint atelier with Brell's sultry voice and Tobias on the phone telling me how he had dreamed of me. The phone rang and it was the assistant of the producer. She had him on the phone. He asked me if I could come by in the afternoon to do one final read and then meet the rest of the cast. Hanging up, I called Hironobu san. I wanted to give him my new number. His calm voice relaxed and strengthened me, and the mountain that Hanuman carried floated through the window as Hanuman's tail painted the brick walls with love, which was in eternal conspiracy with art. I told him that the atelier was gentle and in a very special street.

"The number of the street is nine," I said.

"It is the number of the Maya," he said. – It stands for patience, harmony, and perfection of ideas, many talents and rewards from passing the tests. And it symbolizes creation and life, and is considered sacred in Egypt and in Greece."

All these words came from him, my very own Hanuman. He told me he would not give my number to Shane. I thanked him. "Smila also calls a lot," he said. I told him that I would call her. "I need to," I admitted. He agreed. As we parted my ancestors smiled. They held the soul and the presence of the present. Standing at the window, I watched the white bird fly across my Manhattan. And I was made aware of the essence of the center and the core. I remembered flight. They manifest as animal and human spirits of surpassing intelligence. They are the stars in the night sky of my subconscious being and emit the light of millions of years ago. Hironobu san was my rain light.

Suddenly, I felt a shooting pain in my stomach and lay down. My hands were on that wounded place and I breathed every vibration of river love to heal that space where that wound was an opening for my transformation. I hailed the sharpened life blade of the sword that caused the slit. I rearranged the altar and lit an incense stick. The smoke coiled up to the ceiling and seeped through to the sky, merging the tangible with the intangible, and my pain uncoiled like the body of the snake, and the divine howl cradled every agony and cry of the human soul. Being alone is like Parvati who wants to be with Shiva, I thought, and s*he does penance by standing in the forest on one leg for decades and centuries until all was ready. The bliss of that solitude will be mine.* I unlocked the many crevices of my mental being, as some strange formations entered in the night to try to take away the prism of light. I burned them away with the song of myth and magic and they fell away unborn and unrealized.

The pain was leaving me as I watched it slide through the locked door of the studio. My hands were warm and the rays entered my belly. When I was a little child someone told me that I had healing powers. The shadow of the sun sang its melody on the brick walls and guided the wandering mendicant who may have forgotten his purpose in his now birth. My journal fell on the floor with a resonating thud, reminding me not to forget her parched pages. I touched her, and I saw what my face looked like before I was born. I felt and heard a rustle. I looked around. There were only a few flowering pots. A Noh theater mask danced in front of the reclining sofa bed where I was, as though to shift and change my solitary reflections. I began to rise and tried to touch the moving, dancing mask of shape- shifting and transforming qualities.

Lifting the script, I glanced at the pages I would have to read that afternoon. The Mexican director's manuscript had an ominous presence. I placed it on the table and remembered how it had burned to ashes in my hands when he first handed it to me. I wondered why my divine horsewoman on the shining black stallion had not come to me. I knew they would come when it was time. I longed to see her face.

Looking at the time, I started to get ready for this new walk of a new journey. I decided to take my Moroccan wedding shawl with me as my shield, and I laced up my tall warrior boots. I loved them. They had a male and female quality to them – an elegance of the real kind. It was getting chilly outside and, making sure the incense stick was straight and safe, I walked to the door. I missed Flora and Wolf Raven deeply. I was sad, and the Noh mask once again glided in front of me as though to shapeshift my melancholia. The corridor outside the studio was carpeted. It was a long walk to the elevator. The door opened and some people walked out. No one seemed to notice me, except for a little girl who looked at me through her hazed glasses and her missing tooth mouth. I thought of Wim Wenders' Wings of Desire, where only the children can see the angels who weave through the human crowds to help and save. Our eyes molded each other and I stayed with her until she and her mother turned the corner. Maybe I was invisible to the others. In the lobby the doorman was the one who had greeted Prana and me when she first brought me here. His name was Reynaldo. He had a warm and caring smile. He said that he was happy to have me in the building. I thought of the ants in the earth and in the center of the lotus. He opened the door for me. I felt humble, and bowing to him, walked out.

Out on the streets, I felt disoriented and, seeing my confusion, he asked me where I had to go. I showed him the address and he told me the bus right in front of the building would take me there. In that moment the bus roared by, and he ran out to hail it. He asked me if I had exact change. I realized I did not and he quickly handed me some coins. I could not thank him enough. The driver was anxious and, placing the coins in the slot, I walked to the back of the bus. I looked back. Reynaldo was standing as though to make sure I was okay. I waved at him.

I have always loved these slow bus rides. I loved looking out, watching all the light play and the bustling of humanity. I loved the fact that in so many myriad ways, New York City reminded me of Calcutta, where the goddess Kali is manifest in every nook and corner of the huge, crumbling, mad, alive, and sizzling metropolis. And in this concrete-carved jungle the tall, elongated buildings looked like mountains in flight. The fine blade of steel and glass played with the sky and the clouds wondered what these tall, sharp formations were as they slid and sliced through them without a care, and the sky became water. The bus moved uptown. I saw the street sign and realized that it was my stop. Ringing the bell, I left from the back exit this time. I walked to the building and went up to the right floor. I felt a slight breeze on my left cheek and removed the strand of hair fallen on it. I wondered who was present.

At the door, the receptionist approached me with a warm smile. She even said my name right and I commented on it. She smiled and apologized for taking so long. She added that Americans are very bad with new and foreign-sounding names. I nodded and replied that I was definitely foreign. She responded saying that I spoke such good English. I told her that I had been taught by the best. Yes, I was a stranger in a strange land, sitting in the land of grok and intuition and empathy and magic. She took me to a room which looked like a studio. Both the producer and the director and some members of the cast were sitting around, as though waiting for me. I apologized for being late. We all sat around a table and began reading our lines, after everyone had been introduced to each other. The director was also the writer. He listened carefully as we gave his words voice. I liked him. He sounded European and had a very soft and distinct accent. I was attracted to the way he spoke. Immediately I was reminded of what Flora had always said to me, that I ate life and walked like a wild tiger in the jungle, sensing all and holding back nothing. I love beauty. It stands on my lids and walks around and through me like the ancient Navajo poem.

We read for more than two hours, and I felt and enunciated every word as they throbbed into life. The director's eyes met mine. I smiled. He was watching my every move. The other actors seemed very professional and sincere. My part was small, but it was strong and I felt all my tree friends entering me. Looking at an empty chair in front of me, I sat back. I was sure I saw Miguel there. I looked again but he had left. I knew he had come to assure me that he was always present. I saw the director following my gaze. I looked down and my eyelids had butterflies on them, and every blossom and leaf was perched on my arched lips. I felt them flutter. As the afternoon ran into evening, we finally stopped. The director gave us directions and told us to meet at the same time the next day. We dispersed, and he walked to me. He asked me where I had studied. He said I had an excellent diction.

"Your words are molded with emotion," he told me.

I replied that I always feel every word I speak. He said that he was very pleased with the cast. Thanking him, I started to leave. There was a pull from him. I could feel it. "I will wait," I told myself and with my longing dreams written on the canvas of my face, I told him that I would see him tomorrow. He walked me to the door. "I'm from Ireland," he said. I was surprised.

Miguel's hand slid into mine as we walked out into the symphony of dusk. The night was young and brisk. I pulled my shawl around me and every desert sand grain from the land of the Bedouins surrounded me. I decided to walk down to my apartment. It was a long walk but I felt the need to touch everything with my feet and hands. I thought of the afternoon, and I felt happy. I wished I could share this with my friends, and sadness invaded me. But I knew I had to push forward with no hesitations or shadows of untruth. I had given my word. *I will not get off the tight rope*, I thought with all my heart. Pulling the Moroccan wedding shawl even closer, I took a very deep breath and quickened my stride. Aakash entered my mind, and those first new, raw days when he and I had walked the streets with passion and love. I had not spoken to him for a very long time. I made a note to call both him and Smila. It was time.

I was downtown when I saw those Shiva Lingam formations that I loved so much. I touched a few as I walked past them.,. I was hungry and noticed the health food restaurant that Ulfhrafn and Flora had taken me to. I walked in and the waitress sat me next to the window. It was beautiful. There was a slight drizzle and the pavement was moist and glistening, and I saw the serpent uncoiling on this manmade surface and all was in harmony and in balance once again. I ordered a house cabernet sauvignon. I remembered the taste when we three sat together as it flowed and grew in my mouth and we raised our glasses to art and creativity. The glass was round and large; the red river was happy to be caught in this shape. I ordered some wild salmon, a salad, and some brown rice.

I reminisced on the spirit of surrealism and how it had become the soul of modern poetry, always in search for the marvelous, and its desire to break through boundaries between subject and object, between desire and reality – the need to create a superior vision. The salmon was burnt on the outside and raw in the inside. I loved it. The rice was bursting and each grain was covered by tahini sauce. As my fork lifted some of these luscious grains, one fell from my fork, and I saw them thrown all around us on that night in India when I was being united with a strange man for my wedding.

My glance swayed outside and now the pavement was transparent. Some reflections from the lit lampposts fell on the surface and the earth breathed through the concrete. The sounds of the *shenai* seeped through my mind and my eyes fell on the imprints of the hands on the wall left by the sati wives, and the tree where I had begun my new walk. It was marked with hands of life and woman-wolves, and not with burned brides. This was the cry of the warrior woman straddled in the art of creative gold, winged with utter compassion and stretched within and without, melting all boundaries of time and space and race and cultures, and with the climate of absolute being.

After paying for the meal, I walked out. The air was silent and still. I felt the sculpted trees swaying in my mind's eye and I was reminded of the words whispered in my ear by that magnificent Native American lady in New Mexico, who had said that I was in sync with nature, and that every tree and every swaying leaf of grass held me in their gaze. Tonight I felt them stretching my spine and aligning every wave in my being. I took a deep breath and the horses galloped in. Looking up to the steel and glass etched sky, I saw Hanuman once again, now with his tail on fire, setting flames to all greed and hate and petty reflections. I reached out my hands to touch this divine monkey. His tail was a sharp arrow and scathed the skies of the ordinariness of time, and the fake obsession of age, and the tinsel reality of the masks of beauty and the ignorance of an unaware existence. I thanked all the beings earthly and celestial for gifting me with this sight, and I promised in blood whispers that I would love everything about me – my uncanny beauty and my bewildering pain, my hungry soul and my wounded longing, my flaws, my insecurities, my fears, and my scary frontiers. I would never forsake, betray, or deceive myself. I would always adore, forgive, and believe in myself, and never refuse, abandon or scorn myself, and would always amuse, delight and redeem myself.

My steps felt heavy as I approached my building. The doorman briskly opened the glass doors. He was different from the day person, Reynaldo. Thanking him, I walked towards the elevators when he called out to me and said that he had something for me. He handed me twelve red roses.

They were absolutely perfect in their formations and fragrant to boot. He smiled as I merged my face into their lush petals. Looking at the card, I saw that it was sent from Ulfhrafn, and my mind travelled to that first night when I had met him and how the petals had become my very own healers and lovers.

The elevator doors closed and went up to the eleventh floor. I mused at this motion and felt the golden descending and ascending triangles, which are Sri Aurobindo's symbol. The descending triangle represents **Sat-Chit-Ananda**, meaning truth-consciousness-bliss; and the ascending triangle represents aspirations from matter. The square between the two triangles is the perfect manifestation. At the center it has the avatar of the supreme, the lotus floating on water, signifying creation itself. I touched the symbol on my throat chakra, and I reflected on the cab driver who had seen it in his dreams. The elevator stopped and the doors opened after a slight hesitation. I could sense a tension in myself as I waited. Stepping out onto the carpeted corridor, I smiled knowing that I had many floors to ascend. The key slid in smoothly, and just as I opened the door, the phone rang. Peeling off my boots, I ran to get it and, picking up the receiver, I heard Prana's voice. *It had to be her*, I smilingly thought. She was big and I had just experienced a rather large feeling. She sounded warm and close. She asked me how I was. I saw the Burkha woman standing in the desert in Taman asset. Her eyes pierced through all the veils.

I told her what I had been doing. I mentioned that I was feeling very comfortable in the studio. She said that it was a very creative space. I saw the Noh dancers with their masks prancing in the warmth of the room. I agreed with her, as I placed the roses down. She told me that the photos from the shoot were amazing and that I had done a great job. I thanked her. She kept on saying how brilliant Ulfhrafn was and what an excellent eye he had. I saw his tree hands holding the camera as both their eyes entered me; I felt his very sensuous full mouth on mine, as his tongue found all the hidden secrets inside of me. She paused for an instant. Then she invited me to have lunch or dinner in the coming days.

"I would love to," I told her. We hung up and I felt warm and safe, as though a tent of a million bright colors had just risen all over me and was sheltering me with its absolute magnificence. Removing the street clothes and all the hesitations, falsehoods, and middle lions behind, I opened the card nestling inside the roses. He had written You are bliss. I felt the fairies dancing all around them. Removing the long stems from the paper, I walked to the kitchen to see if there was a long vase. I noticed a tall and elegant one, and filling it with water, plunged the stems in. I placed them on the wooden table. They were magnificent.

Deciding to run another bath, I walked to the bathroom and noticed several red candles on the shelf. I was certain Flora had left them there. I lit them along with the one on the altar. The nighttime light in the room was mysterious and I refrained from turning any lights on. The incense, which was called white lotus and the fragrance from the roses filled the studio and creativity made her sensuous dance. As the water ran, I called Smila. She picked up immediately. I was startled; I was sure she would be out. She was cold and distant I knew she would be. I almost hung up, but she changed her tone. She said she was very happy to hear from me. She asked me if I had forgotten how much she had done for me and helped me. I listened to these vacant, stagnant repetitions and said nothing. There was a silence between us.

"How are you?" she asked.

"I'm fine. I just moved into a new studio. It is warm," I replied.

Immediately she wanted to know how I had found it.

"Some friends helped me," I said coldly.

"Of course," she replied. Her sarcasm was offensive, and now I realized how far away I was from that language. She asked me about Shane once again, and what had happened in New
Mexico. She just couldn't help it. I replied that it had not been a pleasant experience, and she was very quick in reminding me that she had warned me about him.

"You did," I agreed, "but I learned from it."

"Oh yeah," she retorted.

Ignoring her tone, I thanked her for all the people and contacts she had introduced me to. "It has been very productive," I told her. She said she was glad and asked if we could meet soon. We hung up. She called again and apologized for being so distant.

"I miss you so much," she said.

Wishing her good night, I placed the phone down. I was glad I called her because she had helped me and I would always remember that, even though I had no desire to see her.

My nakedness pleased me and my skin was electric with the quiet flashings of the ether sounds. Everything was alive as I approached the now-filled bathtub. I played my messages and slipped into this welcoming liquid. The first one was a rough voice with a strong accent. It was the Mexican director asking me to call as soon as possible. I realized that I still needed to read the pages. The director of the new play called about some corrections and the photographer also needed me to call him. Ulfhrafn asked me if I had received the roses. He left a number.

I closed my eyes, and my mind travelled to the space between earth and sky. First among the Apsara was Urvashi with her swan-like elegance. The gods who sent her down to earth to satisfy the pleasure of human beings cursed her. And it was then that she discovered what it was to fall in love with a man who was a prince among princes and a

279

seer. His name was Pururavas. She heard his roaring through the clouds and found him dark, compelling, and more wild than any of the gods she had been with, who were all too similar to each other. They bored her. Man was earth and adventure and unpredictability and an ever-changing creature. This would cause her pain and suffering. She knew it, but she went on without hesitation. This is why the gods threw her down into the forests. But Urvashi took this as an exciting challenge, which would enable her to feel and breathe and be touched with her skin of sensuality. She was a fallen goddess who came to earth to give man joy. I was the fallen Apsara.

The water was getting cooler so I got out. Drying myself, I slipped on something soft and decided to start reading the Mexican script. The *Sacred Mountain* was the title. It was about a group of people who had been told about some valuable knowledge that lay in the heart of Machu Picchu in Peru. The only person who could lead them to the source was a young shamanic woman. She was a seer, a prophet who did not know that she had these abilities, but was being initiated by a priest who had chosen her. The group of people going to Machu Picchu consisted of five men and three women. They had to take certain vows before the beginning of this arduous and dangerous journey. The young woman had to be ready. I put down the pages and took a deep breath. I felt the Apsara holding my head. I wondered why she was with me and not with her human man. I could feel her transparent, warm, ethereal hands all over my hair and face. My blood rushed through me and I moved my body. My feet had some residue of the henna from India. I watched them. I love their ancient beauty.

The script fell to the wooden floor.

Closing my eyes once more, I touched my hair and felt a human hand. It was my husband in India. He was holding little Savitri and they were soothing me. He told me that I had fallen asleep and that I was groaning and restless while sleeping., I shivered and pulled the cotton sheet over me. Little Savitri was watching with her deep, strong eyes. She became the Apsara as she saw all. Pushing myself up, I took her in my arms and kissed her longingly. She was hot and cuddled close to me, as her little body melted into mine. My all-loving husband whispered in my ears that her fever was not going down. I looked up at the spider cobweb. It was still tattered and torn. I knew something was wrong. I wondered if the woman with the universe sitting in her toothless mouth was at the temple.

It was dusk and, pulling my sari together, I looked at my husband and told him that I would walk to the temple with the little one. Dusk was magical. Temple bells were playing everywhere, cows being led home, fires burning; the haunting whiffs of incense filled every cell in the air. He told me that his mother might be there for the evening prayers. But

I didn't care. I wanted to see my lady in tattered white robes. He agreed and, pulling the sari over my head, we walked out through the back entrance. It was hypnotic outside. My feet felt the red earth and, looking down at them, I remembered my grandmother and her poetry and her divine sophistication. I peeked at my hands, which were holding the little one, and as though reading my thoughts she grabbed my fingers in agreement. The gardener appeared as he always did when he saw us going to the temple. He had some fresh flowers in his hand. I thanked him.

Outside the temple some people were chatting together. But I didn't see either my mother-in-law or the lady. As we neared the entrance, I stopped. There she was, sitting with a fresh new white cotton sari. She looked new and reborn. The golden border of the sari framed her ancient head and her face glowed with the reflected light. She saw us and, running to her, I sat in front of her. She opened her arms and I gave her my little one. They looked at each other. The, little one kicked into her with her baby feet. The priest approached us with all the evening blessings. Seeing the little one he placed some turmeric and kum kum powder on her forehead. He said some special prayer. I asked my lady of the universe where she had been, and in Bengali she replied that she had been on a pilgrimage to the ancient temple of Tiriputi in South India. She said that it was a very long journey, but powerful. We sat next to her for a long time as the evening light began to dim and night flowed down in its starry gown. The air was slightly chilly and she handed Savitri back to me. I told her that she had had a fever for a while and it didn't seem to be leaving her And the doctor had no idea what had caused this.. She placed her hand on the little head but said nothing.

Getting up with the blessings, I told her that we would see her very soon. She nodded and there it was again, her lit face. The universe itself was smiling through that ancient, young mouth. I glanced at my husband to see if he noticed this, but for some reason I knew this was meant just for me. We walked away and I looked back to get another glance of her. Her right hand was raised as though in blessing. I bowed to her and she became one with the temple. Suddenly, a shrill voice jarred us in our silent threesome reverie. It was the ogre. She screamed at us for bringing the child out in the night air and, looking beyond us, she noticed the lady. Her screams got even louder. She said that she would throw her out because she was a witch and was casting a spell on us, and that was why the child was still sick. She said that the beggar woman was not welcome to the temple because it belonged to the family house. I felt like hitting her but such behavior would banish me from all of her good graces, if there were any. My husband tried to calm her down but she was livid and ran to the temple to reprimand both the priest and the "untouchable." We walked on as I squeezed my child even closer to my body. My husband put his arms around me. The maid who followed my mother-in-law stopped and watched us. She was secretly smiling as we walked back into the bedroom.

****

I picked up the sacred mountain again, found the page where I had stopped, and continued reading. The night was very still as I poured through the pages. My fingers reached out to my hair. In the script the girl would have to shave her hair in order to be initiated. Tears filled my eyes as I realized that I had to do this part and all that was required, including a retreat to prepare myself before the filming began. I couldn't stop reading. It was magical and powerful. I remembered the little boy who had handed me the stone from Mexico. I felt I identified with the character completely. It sat on the altar and, picking it up, I held it in my hand, until it got warm. It was very late and sliding under the sheets, stone and the Mexican sun in hand, I closed my eyes and fell asleep.

The ring of the phone woke me up with a start. It was the warm gentle rippling voice of Ulfhrafn. He whispered "Mrinalini" softly and I became the apsara in love with an artist prince. He apologized for waking me and said that he wanted to be the crumpled cloth of any and everything that covered me. He spoke. I listened. He said that he felt lessened and alone without his firebird muse. I saw blades of light all around us pointing in many directions. I told him about the script and the part. He was silent. I sensed something and told him that I would be seeing the director the following evening, and that the girl had to sacrifice her hair in order to be initiated. He gasped and asked me if I was sure I would want to do that. I said that I had to. He asked about the photographer and the play. He listened carefully as I told him everything. As I was recounting my last days, the stone dropped on the wooden floor with a bounce. He heard the sound .

"The roses are beautiful. They are watching me," I said,.

"I know. Every petal was born for you."

He kissed me and the prostitute was sacred and my hands fell on my breasts and the wild wolfs tore all the veils of the illusion of love and pain and longing and suffering. The shreds fell around me like white feathers, slowly floating down on my hair strands. We hung up and, looking at the time, I cuddled back into the sheets.

The next morning, waking with the residue of burning flames in and around me, I heard the voice of the **Gandharvas** saying that all men on earth are lacking fire and that is why the earth is heavy and dull. "But I will not live without fire," I said to myself, and walking into the forest of my still dreaming world I saw a fig tree stretching its branches towards me. I broke off two twigs and rubbed them together and sensed something rising from each branch and within myself. I felt Ulfrafhn's skin brushing against mine and a light burst and it was a fire flame, and I know now that my fire would never leave me.

My last reverie was interrupted by the phone. The producer's assistant called to remind me about the afternoon rehearsal. I then confirmed the meeting with the Mexican director and told his son that I had read all the pages and was ready. Remembering the photographer, I also called him. He asked me if I could be there in a few hours. He added that we would not be shooting anything but wanted to go through a project with me. Opening the window, I stuck my head out. It was cooler and I decided to wear something warm. I took the stone with me today. *I will need it*, I thought. Walking out of the studio, I headed to the elevators, which opened as I approached. Stepping in, I remembered the night thoughts. Nothing was lost in an awakened journey and all was observed, absorbed and taken in. Reynaldo was at the door and I looked into my purse to give him back the change he had given me the other day for the bus. He did not accept it, and I saw sugar grains thrown on earth every Tuesday before noon to feed the ants. The goddess Laxmi was pleased, and the elephants were rejoicing with their divine trunks lifted up, and the tiger is ready with his tight body for the approaching moment.

The bus arrived and I gathered the shawl of Morocco around me. I felt beautiful and my gait had a bounce. I waved back to Reynaldo as he watched me. I liked his gaze and I stepped into the bus with the right change in my hands. The sun was shining and the tree barks were glistening. The bus drove up Madison Avenue. People were everywhere, bustling and running about their business. I felt my stone and caressed its rough and smooth body. Lifting my head to look out I started: a huge image of the goddess Kali was being carried on the streets of that hauntingly impossible and magical city. I was in Calcutta.

****

It was Kali *puja* time, where on every street life size images are worshipped for ten days, after which they are carried ceremoniously through the bustling streets to the Ganges, ready to be immersed in the sacred waters. Her face was so near I could almost touch it. She was alive and from her third eye fire flickers streamed out. She was assuring me that my fires would never die. I watched hypnotically. I was sitting with the maid as the car weaved through all the impossible traffic. Horns were blowing everywhere, as the driver avoided cows and rickshaws and people. She was holding the little one and I noticed that she was sleeping peacefully. We whispered about what the doctor, who we had just seen, said. We were both relieved. He told me that she was getting better. At that moment she opened her eyes and looked straight at me. She was

283

telling me something.

The car came to a sudden stop. We were surrounded by a whole crowd of people carrying the worshipped image. Suddenly something fell onto the bonnet of the car. There was a big thud. The people carrying the image had lost a grip of her. They were all carefully pulling her back onto the stand that she was erected on. As she was being straightened her face passed by us. She was very close and she looked right into the back seat of the car. Little Savitri gave a loud and happy scream. She reached out her little hands to touch Kali's face as she glided past us. I felt as though she had entered the car. I looked at the little one and caressed her face. She smiled.

****

The bus in Manhattan jolted as though avoiding some construction on the road and, looking out, I saw that I was close. Ringing the bell, I got out from the front and thanked the driver. He responded with some sort of grunt as I stepped onto the pavement. The air was brisk and, pulling my shawl even closer, I walked to the photographer's studio. I was not nervous or intimidated this time. My fires are burning, I thought. He opened the door. He looked surprised.

"You look different," he said.

"I feel different," I whispered.

I thought of all that had happened since I had last seen him. I felt as though I had stolen the magic from every broken and dying leaf so they would never die. I heard the homeless blind man thanking me because I had brought him some food. And I saw all the sad men who had lost their desire to love and live come alive again because Kamala, the great courtesan had initiated me so I could share my gifts with them in the garden of pleasure.

"You are even more beautiful," he said.

I thought of the danger of vanity and the bliss of the heart which sculpts the face. We began to work and he showed me the project. It was a typical rendition of what exotic looked like and, though he was very excited, I wasn't thrilled. He told me the pay was very good. He showed me what I would have to wear. I let him know that Flora was not in town. He seemed disappointed and mentioned that he would have to look for someone as good. "I agree," I replied. We set a day and a time and, thanking him, I left. Walking out of the studio, I felt his eyes watching me, but this time I had no fear. "You look beautiful," he said again.

Back in the crispy air of morning sun I touched the tree on the sidewalk. It was full and large. "You are beautiful," I whispered looking up at the branches stretched up to the sky. My hands ran across his body and I told him that he was a giant; he was the most magical thing

284

on earth, because his roots were in earth and his branches in the sky. "I love you," I said.

I glanced at my watch. I had a little time before the rehearsal and walked towards the building. I was looking forward to the afternoon. I felt a connection to the part and felt the director had culture. He came from a strong theatre background. He reminded me of Miguel, but I also knew that no one could ever be like Miguel. The assistant greeted me warmly and led me to the room. Everybody was there and we began. I let them know that I would have to leave around seven to go to another read. The director asked me what it was for, but immediately apologized for being inquisitive. I told him the Mexican director's name. He knew him and was very impressed. Some of the other actors also knew of him and congratulated me. I told them that I was not sure if I had the part, but that I should know that evening. They all wished me luck.

After our reading, I decided to walk. I wanted to absorb all that I had read of the Sacred Mountain. The air was brisk and even a little cold. My pace quickened as I felt the wind cutting through me. I was tempted to take the bus downtown, but decided not to. At the apartment building I paused. I took some deep breaths, remembering the last time I was there with Flora. Gathering myself, I rang the bell. The son opened the door. I realized there was no doorman. Approaching the elevator I pressed the button for the eighth floor. I closed my eyes and felt the ascension. The elevator came to a stop. I stepped out and standing right in front of me with a warm melting smile was little Alejandro. He took my hand and gave it a tight squeeze. He looked up at me and smiled as he felt the stone in my palm. He whispered something softly and said that his father had been anxiously waiting to see me. He also added that they had been seeing other actors for the part, but no one was right. I smiled, feeling a slight pang since I thought that he had felt sure I would be perfect for it. The door of the apartment was slightly ajar. I decided to remove my boots outside, as they were a little wet and muddy. I took my socks off too. Little man looked at me feet.

"They belong to the long body of all my ancestors, and carry the language of an ancient red road," I whispered in his soft ear.

His eyes smiled, filled with enthusiasm. Walking in, I saw the director. He was sitting on his throne and beckoned me towards him. I gave him my hand. He pulled me down and kissed both my cheeks. He reprimanded me for not contacting them earlier. I told him that I had to move and organize everything before I could enter this journey. He asked me if I had read all the lines. I said that I had almost completed the entire script. They were both silent. All was still, and after taking a deep breath, I told him how powerful the part was, and that I felt aligned to it in a way I had never felt before. Raising my eyes, I added that I had been waiting for a part like this my entire life. I knew I was being too open and disclosing my vulnerability, which may reflect as weakness, but I did not care. They were both silent and I continued.

"When I was in London, I played many parts, some of which were empty and superficial. Once, after being an extra in a very large production, I made a vow that I would never do that again and that I would wait for the right part however difficult and hard it may be," I told them. He asked me if it had been hard to find good parts. I nodded. The son said something in Spanish to him and he asked me if I was ready to read. I sat down on some cushions on the floor very close to him. He wanted to see me as much as he could. We almost touched each other. Removing the script from my cloth bag carefully, I began.

I went on and on, and he just listened without stopping me even once. And then, after what may have been fifty pages or more, he touched my head, and looking up, he nodded, asking me to stop. Lifting my eyes, I saw a golden swing. It was the sun on the rock, and I felt that something was about to happen. He who was born of the seed flying in the air entered the space of vision and clairvoyance. He was the rishi who unleashes a friction causing heat. I felt as though the whole room was on fire and that the words I had just read were like Vedic hymns not of human origin, not from man. They were like exhaled breaths, and I felt like I was being watched. I was certain that my gaze was born before me and the sensation of being alive filled each part of my body. I knew now that I was awake. And right there in front of me I saw Vajra, the lightning flower, the ultimate weapon of the gods and the lightning flash of wakefulness.

They were both watching me, he with his inner eye and the little man with his ancient gaze, which was the horse eye, the horse that never ages and remains in the child state all his life. We sat still and I felt the sound of the syllable of beauty and the carefully sharpened samurai sword. I wanted to ask him who had written the script, but I refrained and, as though hearing me, he very quietly said that it was written by a very special person who was a shaman in his own right. "It felt like it," I whispered to myself. He said that I had read very well, and he would let me know in a couple of weeks before they left for Mexico.

The surface skin of my wakeful mind trembled like the surface of the water that had been disturbed by a pebble, and I felt seduced by all those creatures who could lead me to madness. His words felt cold, as though he was shielding what he truly felt, trying not to reveal too much to me. I felt wounded within my own waters and fell back, caressed by petals and lotus flowers that were holding me and I knew now why my divine warrior, spirit guide had appeared on that very first day when he had handed me the script as it burnt into ashes in my hands. I would emerge from these fires unharmed and unscathed.

I tried to rise from the soft billowy cushions but was not able to.

286

Little man came to my side and gave me his hand, open and wide, and I noticed all the engraved lines on it. I stood up with his help and, thanking him, started to walk to the door. The director loudly reminded me that after he made the decision he would want me to prepare and not to take any other parts. I stopped because there was a strange underlying nuance in his voice as though a dark shadow was lurking somewhere. I saw the horse's head falling, and the mask that man wears to protect his empty values and foolish pride laid tattered and torn on the white carpet. My feet stepped on all these fallen untruths and, limping, I walked to the door. Just then some young girls entered. Ignoring me as though I was invisible, they gathered around him like hungry disciples, listening to his vain and absurd words about Zen. I looked back as he was lost in their adoration, and tying up my boots, started to walk to the elevator. He looked up at me one last time and nodded, as though to show me how powerful and adored he was. And I knew that one day the horse would reappear intact as though it had never been separated from its origin and the priests would welcome me into the hut that that they had built on the sacrificial clearing. I felt a soft, small hand enter mine as though little man was assuring me that all would be well.

As we both reached the closed door of the elevator, he apologized on behalf of his father and added that he knew how moved his father was when I read.

"He always hides his feelings," he said, "because he is afraid of being hurt."

I asked him who those girls were.

"No one," he replied.

"What a wise young, old man you are," I said.

The script was in my hand and I gave it to him. But he told me that I should keep it, as I would need it when I started reading and preparing. Looking at him, I reminded him that his father was not sure yet.

"He is, he just didn't tell you. That is his way because he does not want you to think it is that easy."

"It has not been easy," I replied.

He told me that they would be leaving in a few weeks and he would call me.

The evening had lost its light. The streets were still wet and the air felt cold. I had put too much into this part and I was very attached to it. My heartstrings felt knotted. I cried for Flora; I wished to sink into the rippling soul of my wolf raven and feel his sensual arrows piercing my flesh. I wanted all the red rose petals from the whole world to fall over me and enter me, and I wanted the stone soft walls of the statues of the temple carvings in India to dissolve into me. I looked back. The little man was standing like a half-grown tree, rooted to an ancient mountain of knowing. I waved back and sent him a flying kiss. He sent one back. I felt

287

his eyes protecting me with a lit oil lamp, which he was carrying to shield me from the scales of death and blindness and from the thieves who steal the soul of the trees.

I pulled the wedding shawl around me and touched Tobias's green gypsy eyes, as he swallowed the pearl from my tongue. I wanted some food. I needed some food. I was famished. I felt as if all of the nutrients in my body had been robbed from me. I wanted to eat raw flesh, and, remembering a sushi place nearby that Flora had told me about, headed to it. I checked my wallet. I had enough money. I thought of calling Prana to join me but changed my mind. I wished to be solitary. I knew that the sacred prostitute is the spiritual and erotic feminine, and she is of passion; I knew the moon goddess and I was conscious of my moon phases. It was time for the bloody part of the sacrifice and I would be ready.

My pace quickened. The concrete felt my steps as every footfall trampled on empty arrogance and the cynical mind and the tired sarcasm that pollutes and contaminates the virgin forest. I was free and unconstrained like the virgin goddess, existing in her own right, one in herself, not belonging to any man. My spine was straight and all the centers felt an awakening. I touched my hair and each strand responded. I spotted the Japanese sushi restaurant from afar. I was happy that I remembered where it was. It was called Wind. I walked in. There were not too many people and the maître d' asked me if I would like to sit on a mat as opposed to at a table. I chose the mat and, removing my boots, sat down. All around me were tall bamboo trees, gentle and strong like a human spine. There was a tall one right next to me and I felt its stem body. It was smooth, and I remembered the wet and glistening bark body of the tree that I touched this evening on my way to the director's place.

The waiter asked me if I would like something to drink and, remembering Ulfhrafn sipping sake, I decided to try this warm liquid. The waiter brought a slender container with a neck, and poured some into the little cup. It was warm and I felt the rice juice entering and flowing in me. It was not my red wine poetry, but it had another language and I liked the slight, almost fermented, flavor of the grain and the sea green fields of rice paddies, swaying in the tropical skies in the villages. The words of the script echoed in my mind and the lioness sat still and proud on the grassy edge of the river awaiting its prey. Every muscle was tight and ready. Tears filled my eyes as I realized how much I loved this role. I was not sure if I trusted the director, though. He was a game player and he knew how he could manipulate me. I thought of Aphrodite who was often referred to as the "golden one," as goldenness defined her radiance. She was also a symbol of freedom from pollution. I touched the golden bracelets on my left wrist. They shone, and I remembered the letter written on Monday, September 16, 1907 on Rue Cassette in Paris

288

by Rainer Maria Rilke, the great Austrian poet put in his book *Letters on Cezanne:*

> "In all things, I am disposed
> to that patient waiting,
> that improvidence, in which
> the birds surpass us,
> according to Kierkegaard;
> the daily work blindly and
> willingly performed, in all
> patience and with the
> obstacle qui excite l'ardeur
> as its motto...this is the only
> kind of providence that does
> not interfere with God's wish
> to keep us in hand, night after
> night, that we may cover these
> pages without leaving a gap
> and without taking thought
> of others who are held in that
> hand as well."

Impatience is a sin, I thought as I ordered sashimi. I needed the soft, succulent protein flesh to give me with strength. Ulfhrafn was sitting in front of me, feeding me sensuously, and his hands became mine as I fed myself with this life from the ocean. I was unfamiliar with chopsticks. I preferred using my hands. The green wasabi burnt my senses and opened all in me. Some people glanced at me, maybe because I was using my hands and my eyes fell on the night sky through the window. I was sure that I spotted a star in the sort of foggy Manhattan sky.

The sake was singing in me and I decided to have another small one. The waiter said that it was on the house. I thanked him. I sang the hymns of life and walked the body electric.

I will wash the fallen leaves and touch the wounded homeless person and wait and watch to make sure that the bent old man has crossed the streets safely. I will watch the animals on a leash look back at me when smell my soul. I will not miss anything as I walk on this path and every drop of blood fallen will be from the wounds of the middle lion. I will be afraid and I will walk into its horrifying trenches and somehow transform the quivering, wet child into manhood. I will not stop or hesitate and even when doubts invade me like hungry uncultured thieves, I will slay them with my always sword. And if the edge has been blunted by a lack of passion, I will travel far and wide to find the right swordsmith who will bring it back to life and, sliding it in its sheath, I will walk again and this time there will be no doubts or hesitation. And I will look at age and find her beauty and respect and love the life map of many journeys and many suns and one million moons. Because the time is the present and every journey that has led to this thriving moment has been one of purpose and reality and nothing has been wasted and nothing is regretted. It is beautiful to be aware of the present soul and nurture it and care for it so that it in turn will do the same. And every phase, every decade must be honored and loved so that the virgin is always untainted and the feminine is alive and no vain youth can surpass the magnificence of growth and the fresh dew of true passion and the palace of pearls on a blade of grass is right there in front for all who can see.

I asked for the check and, taking care of it, tied up my boots and walked back slowly to my new abode. The doorman was the same as the night before and I asked him if there was anything for me. He shrugged his shoulders and I headed for the elevators after checking the mail. The studio felt warm and cozy and, removing my boots, I changed into something soft and Indian. The phone rang and a whisper greeted me. It was little man. He said that he did not want his father to hear him and told me that his father was very excited and had spoken to him several times about what he felt after I had read the part. I thanked him.

I felt my heart fly, and I had to catch it, just like Krishna as a baby would crawl around and steal the cream that his mother was churning to make it into butter and eat it. He was eating the ego of man. I was holding my heart so it wouldn't leave me. I lay down on the narrow bed with the lit candle and placed the script close to the altar. My journal beckoned me and I held it in my hands, placing that Mexican stone on it. I waited for the muse and the jeweled bird and the *massai* warrior man to fly into my heart and my hands. The pen point was angled and sharp. The children of the new earth had arrived as the blue-bodied Krishna knew who he was even as a baby, and took many forms and destroyed many demons as his bamboo flute attracted all from far and near. I thought of the baby in my dreams, who I was holding in my arms and who uttered my name and would not leave my clasp, and whose mother came and snatched him from me and said that I had poisoned the child. No, I had not poisoned him. He was poisoned by her lust, greed, and unclean mind and that is why he left his body. I would defy death.

290

Chapter 16: The blood is on the floor, and the owl visits each morning, and the lions eat gold bangles

In India, the car ambled into the drive of the mansion. The maid and my mother-in-law came running. I did not see my Satyavan. He may be still at work, I thought. The mother-in-law ignored me and grabbed my little sleeping Savitri from her arms. She woke up from the rude jolt and started to cry. I took her in my arms again, from that dark ogre, who was reluctant to let her go. She stopped crying and I told my mother-in-law what the doctor had said, to which she rudely replied that if I kept exposing her to the evening air and untouchables she would never get better. I walked away, respectfully and thought again of the legend of Savitri and Satyavan.

I was exhausted and asked the girl if she could run a bath for me. She said that I also needed a long and relaxing massage and I agreed. She went to find the family masseuse while I changed my sari into a fresh one. Its folds and starched ripples felt holy and healing. The girl came back with the masseuse, who organized the bed for me. The little one was in her cot and fast asleep. I could smell the mustard seed oil. It relaxed my nerves. It was very quiet and still with lazy bird chirpings. His hands were strong and knowing, and my muscles surrendered to his touch. I went into my dream space and a friend entered with a Ganesha mask and lay beside me and held me. My ancient wooden Ganesha sat on my head and I knew that he was alive. I was leaving my body and from that place watched the one in me who had left to live her call and follow her voice and art. I wanted to touch her and protect her with my ancestry and culture. I descended and placed my hands over her. She was resting in her little studio in New York city with her cloth book in her hand, with the flaming candle and the red roses nearby. I smiled and came, back as I felt the warm, hot hands on my head rubbing into my scalp and pulling my hair.

I asked the maid if the door was locked and sighed with relief. I did not want my mother-in-law to come and spoil the peace. I would forgive even her distaste of me and her hatred towards me because I had to rise and be more, and not sink into the mire. Transformation is constant and an arduous task but it must be an ongoing process without stopping so that true youth can reign forever. I melted and fell asleep.

My husband woke me up to tell me that it was time for dinner. He had bathed and changed from his office clothes. He smelled of sandal-wood. I wanted him and I touched his skin. I told him about what the doctor had said. He said that he knew, and was happy I had had a massage. . Glancing sideways, I noticed that little Savitri was still fast asleep. Getting up with difficulty, as I had to gather my melted bones and dissolved skin, I changed into a silk sari. I decided on red, and walking to the mirror, surrounded my eyes with the kohl of the forests and put a very large red kum kum on my third eye. "You are beautiful," my husband said, holding me in his arms. He took my face and my lips parted, inviting him to enter. True Passion is supreme and the gods are alive and the spirit is in harmony because there is no separation.

We walked to the dining room. He led the way, as is customary in this culture. I followed, my head covered with the sari. I felt the golden embroidered border of the sari adorning me and I was rich and strong. We sat around the table. The dinner was served ceremoniously. All was quiet. The food was warm and delicious. My husband told his mother that the little one was doing better. She grunted in response. Not hearing her, he asked her what she had said. She frowned, saying that I was careless to take her out, exposing her to the cool evening breeze, and giving her to filthy untouchables, not knowing what disease or germs they carried. Something unexpected happened next. My beautiful husband, freed from the lashes of quiet obedience burst out loudly asking his mother if she was accusing me of trying to harm my own child. She replied, retorting that I did things that no other mother would do. The face of my beautiful lover and companion and mate of my soul was filled with anger. He asked why she hated me so much and what had caused this anger in her. He went on to ask her if it was because the color of my skin was not a sickly white, or because I had given birth to a girl and not a boy. She was still. Her face moved to the plate in front of her, not saying a single word. She continued to eat and said nothing. He repeated the question but she was silent. I lost my appetite and wanted to leave the table.

Just then, I heard Savitri cry loudly, and, pushing my chair back ran to the bedroom. At the entrance I stopped, shocked. There sitting right next to the crib with her hand outstretched, was an apparition in black. Even though her back was towards me and her hooded head was bent close to the edge of the crib, I knew she was from another realm. All was still. I looked around and heard the quiet breathing of a stallion, but I didn't see him. I did not move. I could not move. And then her right hand gently touched the little one's face. Baby Savitri was looking at her with eyes wide open and had a beatific smile on her face. Slowly rising, her back towards me, she vanished without any sign. I felt certain I heard the fading footfalls of the stallion. I quietly walked towards the crib. The little one seemed to be in a trance as her eyes remained on the now vanished mirage. Her face was lit and glowing, and as she slowly turned her head to me, she giggled and kicked her feet. I covered her carefully and sitting beside her could not stop crying. I heard footsteps as my husband asked me if everything was okay. I was in shock and just nodded and said that she was a little cold and I covered her with he little blanket. By now little Savitri was already asleep. Fear entered me and, looking up, I noticed that the tattered cobweb was still hanging in shreds. I knew something was going to happen and shivers stabbed my open back. I leaned into his sandal-wood body and, looking up at him, asked if it was okay if I did not go back to the dining room. I told him that I had to lie down. He understood and told me that he would excuse me.

A few minutes later, I heard loud arguing between my husband and his mother and, gently closing the door, removed the red sari as the blood of the fabric stained my heart. There was going to be a lot of pain. I knew it and I felt the invisible wounds scathing me. My feet had lost their henna stains and I remembered with some elation that tomorrow was the day of my beautiful Ganesha, when the women from the village would come to apply henna to our feet and hands. I adored this day and, as I lay down in my changed, fresh white sari, I was happy that my feet would be red gain, and I would walk with the blood of life on the brown dusty earth bed.

Just as my eyes began to close, heavy with sadness, I heard the little one calling to me in her baby language. Getting up, I noticed that she was awake and restless. Lifting her from the crib, I carried her to the bed and placed her beside me. I spooned her warmly and she melted into my body.

A wave of light entered me. We both fell asleep.

Soon, my husband was lying beside me, and all three of us were in a harmony of love and softness. The night was happy and my heart beat silent and strong, like a bird that had flown away from its rusty steel cage of years and eons and decades and centuries, and my wings were heavy at this new sensation of freedom, so I adjusted my feathers accordingly.

The next morning, the three of us were refreshed and happy. The maid came in with a hot pot of tea, and some warm cinnamon milk with some **Ayurvedic** herbs for the little one. I decided to have a bath and she went out to have the helpers bring in hot water in large buckets. I wanted to bathe the little one, too, since she loved water. She was a little glistening mermaid of the stars. As Gauri adjusted and regulated the water, I massaged little Savitri with some mustard seed oil, carefully avoiding her eyes. She giggled. Gauri scrubbed my back and oiled my hair before washing it.

My Satyavan was getting ready for the day and I was happy that he was not going to work today as it was a special day for Ganesha.. We got ready and walked to the dining room, where breakfast awaited us. I greeted my mother-in-law warmly and showed no anger or discomfort as we all sat down. *I must be the bigger one and must never stoop down*, I thought. We ate in silence. The little one was hungry. I fed her some soft rice and molasses, which she particularly enjoyed. She had an appetite and I knew that she was feeling better. Preparations were being made for this special day and there was bustle and noise as all was made ready. We left the table and headed out to the verandah. The sun was streaming in and the shades had been pulled down and watered so that the heat was not too harsh. The women who apply the henna and mehndi were arranging their powders and mixing it with water. The henna was cool and welcoming and little Savitri was watching everything intensely, with the world in her two almond-shaped eyes. Her eyes felt like they were made from the very tears of the gods, retaining their magic aura. She was born with her eyes open, ready to illuminate and understand and protect and annihilate. She was a third-eye baby born with the opening of clairvoyance and of inner sight. She turned her head, feeling me watching her, and her eyes became two oval mandalas, shining with the secrets of her soul.

Suddenly and with no reason, she began to cry. I took her in my arms and her tears fell on my breasts and neck like a chain of pearls, and my mind wandered to the sap of those beautiful trees from which incense and myrrh are made. On my skin her warm salt drops felt as though they were made of dreams and myths and precious jewels and rain and sun. And I knew that her tears would melt any harshness and bitterness that might have entered me. She cuddled into my body and I held her tightly, never, ever wanting her to leave me. She was my diamond, heart, soul, feather, vision, prism baby-child. She was mine, and as I felt the attachment, I was pierced by the pain of our possible separation.

Under the warm and filling light of the morning sun, the women began the application of the dark earth paste on the little one's feet. She giggled and wriggled as they made little designs on her feet and palms. Then they began on my feet and I loved the sultry and pungent scent of these crushed leaves. The sun streamed in through the straw mats, creating magical shapes on the cement floor and the white walls behind us. The afternoon soft breeze slid through the winds. The air was drowsy and wet, and everything around felt lazy and sleepy.

My eyes fell on my beloved husband who was reading his favorite book of poems by Tagore and enjoying this day of celebration. Our eyes met, and my body shone as his shy Bengali Indian eyes traced its shape. His sultry, large eyes with the whispering lashes like the waves of the Indian Ocean took me to myself, and I honored the gift given to me by my parents. My glance moved to the little one who rested close to me. The henna had left stars on her feet.

The women were now on my palms and as they traced designs meticulously I was reminded of that dream when the dark Indian woman with chiseled features looked at my palm and saw Ganesha sitting on my lifeline. I felt his wet trunk in my hand, and I closed my eyes in adoration and wonder. My Savitri seemed to fly into me as we fell into a light, warm summer siesta with the humming of bees and cawing of crows, and the dull repeated drone of those transparent, winged creatures, flying into the burning rays of the zenith sun. I felt the little one's skin catching mine, and I saw us travelling somewhere strange and reminiscent of my birthplace.

She was older, and we were walking into wild and wide areas of green and brown landscapes. We took each other's hands and moved into isolated and empty architectures of concrete and black soil. At first there were no people but when we finally saw them they were against us and didn't want us there. It felt as though we had been trapped. I heard some bizarre-looking man saying that we had been there for seven years. and that now we were not welcome anymore and he pointed to a way where we might be able to escape. I looked around but all I could see were huge hollow valleys with no end in sight. I was afraid and desperately wanted to leave this foreboding landscape of nothingness. At that very moment, clasping Savitri's hand I looked up, and chanted some mantras invoking Ganesha and Laxmi and all my deities, and then I felt myself being lifted and was in flight with her by my side. We rose and soared above this soulless visage and we were in flight, my daughter and I.

My little studio on Ninth Street felt warm as I woke up. I threw the cotton quilt aside. The sensation that something had entered me overtook my whole body. The candle was still lit and flickering slightly. I tried to blow the flame out. And then I saw the red markings on my hand. I didn't understand how this could have happened, as I remembered clearly looking at the faded stains only the day before. Shocked, I looked around, sensing a presence. I was afraid and stealthily walked to the bathroom. I turned the light on dimly to avoid its harshness. I ran water over my now very red, beautifully designed palms. I rubbed them to see if this was not just a dream, but the red got even stronger and more vibrant. I felt as though I was in an altered state and, stumbling, decided to return to the bed. It was still dark outside, with the night sky lit from buildings and signs nearby. Nervous and baffled, I looked at my hands again, amazed at this miracle and, taking a deep breath, I lay down. I burnt some sage and smudged myself. The smoke coiled and burned, and I remembered the Native American lady in Santa Fe. Her wise face was in front of me, as the essence of this cleansing and healing herb soothed my nerves. I felt calmer, and with the fingertips of my adorned hand, I touched my hair. I felt the thoughts and longings and visions in each strand. I slipped into my dream language. I saw a young boy approaching with his fingers pointing to the top of my head. As he came closer he whispered into my ear, saying that there were things flying over my head. I asked him what they were and he said that they looked like light beings flying around. "Like angels?" I asked him. He shook his head and walked away when someone shouted out that he was my son.

My eyes opened with a start, and my hands reached up softly, afraid to disturb the flying wonders. I left my right palm on my head and felt the inside getting hot. I pondered on this round shape, which was the vessel of transformation and wholeness, and its alchemical qualities symbolizing seeds of new and immortal life. As my palm got even hotter, I felt the dragon's fire tongue piercing through my skull, breaking any obstructions and obstacles. I was watching the external and internal parts of my mind, as the tongue sliced through. Now it settled in the throat chakra in my neck, connecting the body and the transparent mind, which contained the psyche and the essence of the incorruptible life. My voice felt as though it was edged and parted by the floating gold leaves used by renaissance artists and antique restorers, who after placing each delicate page on the needed area blew all the bumps into a smooth golden liquid of aesthetic wonder. My fingers glided over my throat and a blue light filled my head and the room. I felt circles of sound resounding around me as the notes from Krishna's flute haunted the studio walls and everything in it.

Dawn light finally walked in. I sighed with relief; it had been a difficult night. And the soft rays comforted my still-shaking spirit. My fingers left my neck and, uncovering the cotton blanket, I slid onto the floor feet-first. My eyes fell on my feet, the extension of my soul, and I gave out a loud scream, which flew through the window so the whole world could hear. I looked again and painted on both of them were red flowers and intricate designs. The sole was immaculately painted with a red dye, which in Bengali is called *alta*. It was made from a plant and used when women are married. I was trembling and a little afraid. I lay down again and everything in me ached for my beloved parents. I heard my older brother, who left earth too young, saying in his very deep and distinctive voice: "Remember the still point." He repeated the lines very slowly twice. And that was the very last time I heard him speak. He was my creative other and I loved him.

The tent was empty and the appliquéd patterns on this cloth marriage roof were slack and drooping. I didn't seem to have the strength or the will to lift my falling soul. I felt the breath of the cotton enveloping me. I looked around for some solace and hope, and I touched the altar. It resounded like waves in the lake, and just then the loud shrill of the phone startled me.

Clearing my voice to disguise the ethereal mystery that I had just emerged from, I picked up the receiver. It was the director of the play. I sat up to straighten my threaded spine, answering with a sort of trembling voice. He asked me if I was okay. Maybe my voice sounded a little distant. I quickly answered, saying that I was fine and was about to get ready. He talked about the play and how happy he was with all of the actors. Then, after pausing for an eternity of falling stars, he said that he was especially pleased with my work. I told him that it gave me a lot of joy to do the part, and that I was learning a lot from him and all of the others. I thought of all the many lessons given to me by people, trees, children and seers.

As he continued speaking, I was reminded of one Native American elder who had once whispered in my ears the purpose and reason why tobacco is offered and used in peace pipes. It was used in ceremonies and religious observances and was the unifying thread of communication between humans and the spiritual powers. Many believed that tobacco was received as a gift from Wenebojo who had taken it from a giant and then given the seed to his brothers. He had also mentioned why at times shamans had to partake in these substances in order to be anchored to the earth. As he spoke I felt as though he might be an anchor of sorts for me. I needed something to keep me rooted. I thanked him for calling, and hanging up, said that I would see him soon.

It was still early, but I needed to regroup and align myself before the birth of day. There was a lot to be done and my center felt jarred and frail. The water in the tub healed and soothed me as always. The phone rang several times and with each ring I felt the silver weight bringing me down. I touched my body to make sure that I could feel the solid tree trunk that was my physicality.

I remembered a special friend, Millie Blanke, who lived in a little town somewhere in Germany. Once, when I was invited to show a film there, a young girl from the audience came up to me and said that her mother wanted to invite me to her country home and that she would drive me there if I was willing. I went with her through the lush tree roads and we came to the house. It was spacious and silent. Millie ran out and embraced me. Then she led me to her garden, which she had spread with a vibrant blue powder. It was her art piece; and against a huge center tree she pointed to a trunk, which was leaning against it. She said, "That is you." I slipped my hand into her blue-stained hands. She looked at me and said, "I Know you".

In my world of water, I could feel the tree trunk and the rough and wet bark speaking to me. Getting out of the tub with my towel around myself, I sat and lit the incense and candle. I saw the forest of bliss and in it Niyol, my sage lady, Ulfhrafn, Flora, and Prana. They were looking straight into my eyes to show me the way and let me know that what had just happened with the fresh henna on my hand and feet was a miracle, and that only a few are blessed with such wonders. Waves of gratitude streamed through me and the fallen lazy tent began to rise once more, as my very own people held every corner up to protect me. I stretched my legs with glee and massaged my thighs with lavender oil.

297

And I looked at my now red-fire feet awakened and glowing, fearless and flowing. And once again, I was ready.

Preparing for the day, I shadowed my eyes with he same forest whispers and made certain that I had the script and everything else. I listened to all my messages – Smila, Hironobu san, the photographer and Aakash. Deciding to call Aakash first, I dialed his number in San Francisco. He picked up and I greeted him. He asked me how I was. I told him about all of the projects I was involved in. There was a lot of hesitation and faltering in his speech and I was sure something had happened to him. He said that I sounded different. "So much has happened, Aakash" I replied.

A cloud entered in our conversation; it felt weighted. I asked him why he had so much hesitation in his voice and he said he had had complications with his family and things were not good with him.. He spoke about his sister, who was also in California and that he had to take care of her due to some medical problem she had. He also mentioned the fact that he had distanced himself from the rest of his family because they did not approve of his homosexuality. A cloth fell on my head. It was not the saffron veil with the Om signs on it, the one that priests or seekers wrap around their shoulders, it was dark and heavy and wrinkled and un-textured. I bent with its valueless weight as it drooped around me, limping and empty. There was a silence after which he very quietly questioned my love for him. He asked me if that changed anything in me. I assured him that my love for him was deep and that nothing could alter that and that so much transpired since they last met.

"So you still care for me? "He asked again.

"Of course I do but time sculpts and molds and our shapes change. But the essence never lessens", I replied. The sable antelope came in and I watched the beginning of this solitary journey of a woman leaving her roots and safety to find her art and calling and all the sacrifices that had to be lived and learnt from.

I was the female Siddhartha born to be maintained by the child's gaze and I was Urvashi, the first of the Apsara thrown down by the gods to please man on this barren, dusty, crusty earth surface, where even lions walk with stealth, afraid to disturb the artists of the Universe. They who tend the lotus flowers and protect the visionaries who have to walk on sharpened knives and bleed and sacrifice before they can sculpt their language of sight. Just as in the great Russian filmmaker Andrei Tarkovsky's last masterpiece The Sacrifice, where the main character – the wounded hero Alexander – makes a pact with God that if the ecology, which was out of balance, could be brought back into the world he would sacrifice everything: his beloved son, his wife, and his house. At the end he burns the house he loved so much and is taken away. He sacrifices everything. And I sacrificed all by leaving my culture, my home and my country to find my

298

art and myself. I too burned my house and left my beloved parents and my familiar protected surroundings.

As we were about to hang up, Aakash mentioned that his parents had found out about me and him, and accused me of being the one who had spoiled him and exposed him to wrong ways. My heart was wounded. I asked him what he had told them He said he didn't say anything. "I thought that we were echoes of something more", I said softly. My eyes watered. I said nothing as he continued to speak, telling me that he was coming to New York for a shoot.

I felt like he had forgotten his source. He was not the same. I was in a motionless circle of sorrow and love. I listened to the rest of the messages,. The phone rang again. I did not pick up. He begged me to, asking to forgive him for not defending me to his parents. I called Hironobu san, my Hanuman mountain. He was still at Shane's ,where another bloody sword had slashed into me. I felt his face lighting up as soon as he heard my voice. He quickly told me that Master Shane was in town. I told him about Aakash. He was quiet, and all was hushed. Then, very, very slowly, he said that he felt there would be a change. I was shocked and asked him why he did not warn me. He replied that I had to find out by myself. I asked him why I had not seen this other side in Aakash.

"You are very open," he said, "and you trust, and you get hurt."

"But I cannot walk around with my doors closed," I cried to him.

"You will learn with life, to know and to see the difference between absolute truth and a half truth," he said very calmly. "There will be mistakes, because the common man manipulates and knows how to play the game, and it is very easy to not see through," his voice was the whisper of an old samurai. "You will grow with each blow," he repeated, like a saged mantra in his deep sonorous voice and very special accent.

There was a wind chime silence on the phone as we listened to each other's breath, and I felt the mountain of herbs once again, feeding me as he wished me a wonderful day. I wished him the same and asked him when I would have the pleasure to see him again. "Soon," he said.

Then I quickly dialed Smila's number as she had left many messages. She picked up immediately, and said that she was hoping it would be me. I told her that I could meet her for dinner after my rehearsal. She paused, and I saw that very crooked mouth, which warped and moved like a strange writhing worm. *Why do these women have to distort their faces with the unknown sounds of a synthetic language which only imitates feeling and no more?* I thought. She said she would call me later and let me know if she would be free then

Putting down the phone, I began lacing up my very high green boots, which I loved and which a very special friend had bought for me one day in Rodin's and Brancusi's and Picasso's Paris. We walked by a quaint shoe shop and I pointed to them in excitement, like a little child first discovering something that had caught her attention. My friend immediately walked in and asked for the boots and the assistant, who was wonderful and male and beautiful, began lacing them up my legs, as he touched my left lotus calf and made my skin sing. They were called Palladium. Feeling the touch of that young Parisian man I smiled, and just then the phone rang.

This time it was the little Mexican prince. Happy to hear him I said something in Spanish. Gently, as though not to hurt me, he said that his father would like to see me one more time with some of the lines memorized, so that he could also feel my movements. I felt death near my door, as the helm of a large dark mechanical boat was pushing its way into the still waters of the river and me. I asked him why, thinking his father had made up his mind. He said that I should not worry. He assured me that his father truly liked me, and that he just wanted to be completely certain. I looked at my feet, hoping that the Alta and the henna stars had not left them, and that my hands were still red. They were. I asked him when he wanted to see me. "By the end of the week," he said. "But only if that is enough time for you to memorize the lines."

Hironobu san's words of a little while ago rang through my mind. "There will be mistakes because the common man manipulates and that it is very easy to not see through. You will grow with each blow, learn and become." *There is no other way, I thought, and the full moon slices barren trees and the leafless branches howl, and two eyes race by in a silent star, and every stride of the wounded warrior is felt. Never close anything. You will be sharpened and chiseled by life and you will blossom like the cherry trees in Japan. And in that special season every child will weep with your flowering beauty.*

Thinking of this, I realized that Hironobu san was my very own sword sharpener. The phone rang again. This time it was the photographer. I shifted gears. He asked me if I could come by for a little while. I told him that I would be there in an hour. I knew that I had to be careful with this one. The phone seemed to never stop ringing. Smila called to confirm dinner that evening. I agreed. I told her when and where the rehearsals were, and she decided on a place.. She mentioned the place where I had met her with her friend. I agreed since it would be convenient and we decided on a time. I also gave her the studio number where we would be rehearsing in case she had to change her plans. She asked me to wear something stunning. I laughed, and told her that she had not changed.

"I am not your prize possession," I said teasingly. We hung up. I was calm and looking at the voice mail, saw that someone else had called. It was the little man. He said that they had extended their stay for a few more weeks and that his father could see me at a later date if I needed more time. I called him and said that that would be fine. I sensed

300

his tension. I was sure his father was right next to him. Hironobu san entered my mountain sight, and I knew it was going to be a bloody path, and I knew I had to take it.

The safe life would have been so easy and painless, I thought. But this is the way of the falling fruit, which I have to pick up and walk through. I have to reach the golden bowl in the middle of the desert sand dunes where a flower blooms, and in that bowl I will drink the elixir that will quench my maddening thirst, and I will be the mendicant who has found god, and I will walk back with this begging golden bowl and offer the water to all who are willing to drink it and become their own truths and their own art; I will remind them of the beauty that they had denied and all my wings will be on fire and out stretched, as my created child will be born and will see the light of day.

Making sure that all in my apartment was aligned and that the candle flame was not lit, I closed the door of the studio and walked to the elevator. The carpeted corridor was like a long avenue of hidden secrets and hushed lives. I wondered what lay behind each secure and locked door. The elevator opened and that same little girl who had looked at me the first time came out with her nanny. She gave me the same recognition again, and I responded with a smile and a nod. As the doors closed, she looked back again as if to make sure that it was me. I was happy. I made sure I had the script and the addresses for my appointments that day in my flower-covered daybook which read: "Resistance of the heart against business as usual." Reynaldo, my favorite doorman, was at the door. He greeted me warmly, and before he could ask I told him I had the exact change I needed. Wishing me a beautiful day, he opened the door. I wished him the same.

The bus arrived and I climbed in and walked to the very back where there were some empty seats. The sky was blue and the clouds seemed to have a story of their own. I remembered the words from Odillon Redon's book *To Myself,* when his father pointed to the clouds and asked him if he could see the moving shapes in them. My stop arrived quickly, and, climbing out of the back exit, I stepped on the concrete, feeling the fire red of my henna feet flaming through my boots as the ancient ancestry screamed through breaking leather walls of captivity and duality.

As I approached the building where the Jason's studio was, I could sense the sharpened sword edges under my feet. I slowed down and took deep breaths before going up to the photographer's studio. He welcomed me warmly. He commented on my outfit. I mumbled something and walked in politely. We walked to his office area and he started explaining to me the project that we would be working on. He told me that it might take a few days or even longer because we would have to travel to the Dominican Republic, where some wealthy Americans were building a resort on the waterfront and needed all sorts of posters and advertisements. He asked me if I had ever been there. He said that it is very colorful and fun and sunny. I saw the peacock with his full plumage spread out as he danced, waiting for his partner. In India the peacock is the national bird, as it symbolizes the incorruptibility of the soul. I told him that I had been there for a film shoot and loved it. "There is a lot of magic there," I said, "and the people are warm and welcoming."

I missed Ulfhrafn and Flora immensely, and just as my mind was caressing their eyes, he asked me if I knew when Flora would be returning. I told him that I had not heard from her for a while as she was traveling somewhere in the Far East. Looking at the time, I realized that I had to rush to the rehearsals for the play. He told me that Smila had called him and mentioned that we would be dining this night. I wondered why she did that and the echoes of Hironobu san's words rang through again. Thanking him, I gathered my things as he told me that he would let me know very soon about the shooting schedule. I rushed down the street, knowing that some very strange and unpleasant things awaited me with this project. But I needed the money and knew I had to do it.

My feet hurt. My soul hurt. My heart hurt. The concrete gave in to the stars on my feet and as I walked fast and stallion-like I saw a fallen, solitary red rose on the filthy street. I picked it up and placed it within the pages of the script. "I will heal you," I whispered to its trembling petals, thrown by a careless hand.

In the theatre they were waiting for me, even though I was on time. My heart skipped when I saw the director. I saw Miguel's face in his.. We rehearsed for many hours. I forgot some lines and scolded myself for making mistakes. But I kept repeating them until I had them memorized. Each actor was giving and there was a loyalty within the group. It felt good and comfortable. Even though my part was quite small, it resounded with a power and femininity that I felt aligned to, and I gave it my all. I thought how art and creativity always brought back my truth and my confidence.

As the rehearsal went on I felt my voice growing and my weapons sharpening. I was certain that Miguel was watching and guiding me in every detail. Finally, when we all were exhausted the director called it a wrap. I sat down to catch my breath and, lacing up my boots sensed the director, watching me. His name was Johann, with a soft "j." I missed Ulfhrafn and felt his tree hands touching me.

The creative walk of art is always drenched with mystery and inner sights that fired my passion and made me mad and wild. It is the juice and very life of all living things.

Looking at the time, I remembered my date with Smila and reluctantly made my way to the door, wishing everyone a good evening. Johann walked with me. He praised my performance. As I thanked him he politely asked me if I was doing anything that evening. I told him that I had a dinner appointment. and that it was because of her and her many connections that I had been introduced to the producer of the play.

The night was cool and crisp and, wrapping myself in the never-leaving Moroccan shawl – my shield of warmth and protection – I decided to walk up to the restaurant. I heard the tinkling of the cowbells as they return home from the fields, and saw the blue evening light. Baby Krishna was playing with the other little ones when his mother drew him to her and as she opened his mouth to look inside, she saw a starry universe that pulled her in and suddenly she was flying and travelling through endless forests and oceans and lakes and then finally she, **Yasoda,** breathed calmly within her son's mouth. She saw the wheel of the zodiac and her mind jumped back and forth from branch to branch with the changing moons until finally she saw the village of **Gokula** where he was born. She saw all this in her divine son's mouth.

The restaurant was very full. I was a few minutes late and felt slightly nervous as I walked in to be greeted by the maître d'. He greeted me warmly, then took me to the table where Smila was sitting. On the table in front of Smila an opened bottle and a glass sat knowingly. She did not see me at first, and watching her, I felt like turning around and leaving. But I knew I was coming to meet with her.

She got up screaming. Bringing all attention to us, she embraced and kissed me, and made a big self-conscious scene. I felt shy. She was very loud to make sure that everyone in the room could hear her. She looked me up and down and asked me to sit. The waiter poured the red into my glass and I slowly took a sip and breathed the fragrance of the wine. It was dry and full and mysterious, and I now remembered her good taste in wines. "How are you?" she asked, looking at me very intimately, and adding that I looked very well. I told her everything I had been doing, except for the Mexican director and thanked her for all the connections. She asked me about the play and the director and wanted to know everything. She then questioned me about the studio and how I had gotten it. I told her about Prana. She sarcastically asked if it was "that strange woman from the party." I said that it was she. Smila immediately wanted to know all about her. She just couldn't help it. I didn't say much, except that she had an antique business and specialized in African art. We moved on to Shane and there again she insisted that I tell her all that transpired in New Mexico. She added that she had seen him a few times, and he always wanted to know about me. I told her that it was a difficult experience and that I did not wish to talk about it. "I warned you," she reprimanded me. Then she asked me why I always had to do things the hard way.

"I just do it the full way," I replied.

"I'm sure you do," she said with the cynical tone of mediocrity.

All the knives and thorns that paved the paths of the streets of warriors and artists cracked and broke with the dry dust of the absence of true compassion. We ate silently. I felt uncomfortable as she told me that I had changed and was different. You seem older and wiser.I said nothing and she started to talk about all her many successes and how well she was doing. "My business is booming," she kept on repeating. "I am making a lot of money," she added. I told her that I was happy for her and she quickly retorted that if I needed money she could lend it to me.

An eagle perched on the chair next to me, as though emerged from the dark rippling waters. She was the partner of the red sun ball and with him they evoked a higher ascent. I felt that she had come to show me the ferocity of the natural law, and the hero's struggle against the limp powers of separation, duality, and dissolution. She was beautiful, and I could not remove my eyes from her, because she soared higher than any other bird in the sacred form of the circle and I remembered that the wings of angels, those messengers of unflinching gaze and transcendent vision, are the wings of the eagle. I knew she had come to carry me through the clouds from the brush fire of mediocrity. My soul lay with her as she left her perch and soared through the room without anyone noticing her. The sound of her rustling feathers were a sweet sonnet and, taking a deep breath, I was back in the restaurant, with the soft liquid poetry flowing through my veins.

"Where were you?" Smila asked me. Startled by her high-pitched, nasal voice I flinched and told her I was just remembering the words of the play I had to memorize in the next few days. I did not mention anything about the Mexican director and the film. She asked me if I wanted some more wine and I told her that I was slightly tired and would like to leave soon "I have a very early call time," I said. She said that I could spend the night at her apartment since it was right there. I just looked at her and said that I would have to prepare my lines this night. Her mouth had that sneer again. It was warped and looked like a demon mouth, capable of swallowing anything conscious and alive. A shiver ran through me and I tried to touch the starry sky within the blue-baby Krishna's mouth. She did not like that I had to leave and asked for the bill with a rush.

I thanked her for the dinner and told her that I would walk her to her building and then get on the bus going downtown. We walked down in silence. I thanked her again. She grabbed me and held me tight, whispering that she had missed me so much. I pulled away from her and right then I spotted the back of Diego. My face lit up. She noticed that. She looked offended, and turned to leave, reminding me once again that without her contacts I would be nowhere. I told her that I would pay her back sometime for all that she had given me. But her reply was a laugh full of sarcasm. Her darkness seemed to pull everything in, including

304

myself. I shivered at the feeling. Diego walked to us and greeted me very warmly. Smila complained to him that I refused her invitation to stay the night. He looked at me and I knew he understood all. I wished them both good night.

"Don't forget to call me," she mumbled.

"I will," I replied almost automatically.

I waited until she walked inside and then headed towards Broadway looking for a bus stop. I heard running footsteps and turning I saw Diego. He said that he had hailed a cab for me and before I could say anything told me he had already paid the driver. I asked him how he knew where I was going. "He has enough," he replied with his beautiful smile. I hugged him and thanked him.

He hugged me back. I knew he was happy I had not stayed. He opened the door of the cab and told the driver to take me wherever I needed to go. We drove away and, looking back, I sent him a kiss. I relaxed into the seat and closed my eyes. I felt drained and alone and aware.

As the cab was speeding through lights and buildings, I remembered the shamanic line drawing I had seen in a gallery in SoHo, which looked exactly like the one Abrihet had drawn for me on that day when my wounds were raw like a diced and bleeding pomegranate. I sent her all my love. I would see her soon. I remembered the traced path leading through a series of trials called the "swaying" places marked by water, sand and clouds, before bringing the shaman to the radiant face of his supreme god, White Ulgen. Some things needed to be repeated and remembered always. I did remember them. I knew that I could and would not get lost because I would be healed and summoned by the interior landscape drawn from the experiences of one shaman to another, and I would be guided by the supreme heights of the shamanic cosmos. I realized that I had not told the driver my destination and opening my eyes saw he was heading downtown. I remembered my dream cab driver and gave this one my address.

I was exhausted. I closed my eyes again. Slipping into a trance-like state, I remembered a woman who had called me some time back when Miguel after suffering from a grave illness had left the earth. She said that she was his friend and was in New York, she wished to see me. We met downtown, next to where I lived and the first thing she told me when I gave her the number of the building was that I was protected. She said she was very familiar with numerology and that she had calculated all the numbers which led to mine. She spoke of my Miguel and told me that she was at his bedside when he passed away. She said the last thing he uttered was my name.

All of my chakras were opening and energy flowed through each one. I wanted to touch this luminous body of light and listen to the heart chakra which is the element of air and the leaping light-footed antelope. The car stopped. We were in front of my building and the doorman approached the cab to open the door. I had never come there in a cab and was shy. I asked the driver if he had enough and, smiling, he said that he had more than enough. I thanked him for the ride and saw his eyes in the mirror of the car. They were the eagle's.

I was glad to be back, and after checking the mail headed for the elevator. The studio felt like home and healing. Unlacing my Palladium boots and placing them neatly next to the door, I decided to take a quick shower and clean myself. I lit some incense and turned the messages on. There were many and most were about my upcoming projects. I turned the volume up so I could hear them in the bathroom. I heard Aakash and his sad voice and knew that Ganesha sat at the threshold of all sacred spaces. As the water soothed, cleansed and healed me I closed my eyes and saw the room in my dreams where Ganesha was everywhere gracing and protecting each corner and space. The room was in a house which sat on a lake and overlooked a vast horizon of mountains. It was small and light streamed in from every direction, and in it I saw my beloved mother in a white sari and my divine father taking care of things and telling me that we needed some birds-of-paradise flowers.

Leaving the shower and my flower dream home, I slipped on my Indian cotton night robe and, getting a tall glass of water, lay down with the Mexican script in my hands. The director's son had left another message, asking me to call back as it was very important. Since it was not too late, I dialed his number. He picked up on the first ring and sounded very happy to hear me. He said that something had come up urgently, and they had to leave the day after tomorrow. He asked if it would be possible for me to come the next day. I asked him what time, as I had the rehearsal for the play. There was a pause.

"Come in the morning," he said.

I asked him if I could call him back. Realizing I had the director of the play's number, I dialed him hesitatingly as it was late. He picked up and was both surprised and happy to hear from me. I told him about the situation and he said that I should go ahead and just come right after that. I apologized for calling so late and thanked him. I dialed the little man's number again and told him that I would be there in the morning and would try to memorize as much as I can.

"Don't worry, Just do what you can." he said.

Putting the phone down, I opened the pages of the sacred mountain. There was a silence in and around me. It was the deepest of silences, the silence in which one hears the voice of the holy other. It was a huge script, and it echoed the sound of soul and silence. *This is what I have waited and longed for in my creative career*, I thought. I had no doubts.

Chapter 17: I weep with rain and the drops flood my wounds made by broken souls with fallen wings

The next morning felt new. The dawn light was wet and fresh, and dragonflies danced around the room. I had no idea how they had come in. They were sparkles of light. I decided to wear white. White is the color of child-like naiveté and the ashes of bitter suffering and hard-won wisdom. I took both sides of the long robe and carried the two aspects of its sacred color with me as I stepped out to walk towards the Mexican director's building, carrying the script very carefully in my hands.

I rang the bell and waited for the little one to open the door. He hugged me as I bent down to receive his warm energy. Removing my boots, I walked in quietly. I was anxious. The director was on his throne looking elegant. He was seductive and very aware of it. He asked me to sit down and offered me a glass of water. He told me that they had to leave the next day and he needed to see me today.

"Are you ready?" he asked with his cold and frightening voice.

"I am ready, but I am nervous," I replied.

"You can start then. And use the script if you need to."

I removed the cloak with the two worlds embedded in it – the child and the wise man. I prayed for them to be with me. Taking a deep breath, I began. The lines just flew out of me. I felt every word and carved the inner nuance of each line. My rhythm stemmed from the invisible tapestry, and the shaman sight shaped every move. It was as though the writer, who he had told me was a shaman, was entering me. I wept, I howled, I sat, I rolled on the floor,. I was invaded. And the invasion was divine. I felt every cell in me leaping in flames of light and I was absolutely and completely naked. And in one scene during the initiation that I remembered vividly, the girl had to disrobe herself as a sign of a selfless surrender to the call with no hesitation and no boundaries. I became her, and I felt the change and the transition. I could feel the transformation in me happening as though I was right there in that mountain cave somewhere in South America. Wet with perspiration and trembling, I could not stop weeping. The little boy ran towards me and gave me back my robe so that I could cover myself. I felt like a veined leaf taken and eaten; I had gone through some alchemical process and become someone else.

The room was enveloped in a sacred silence. I gathered myself, my spirit, and my inner tools back inside me. The director took me by surprise. I didn't see him coming. He sat on the floor near me. He was holding me. He had never shown any warmth or intimacy before. He pulled me closer, as though any separation had been broken in him. Captured in his embrace, I felt his arms multiplying like Shiva's. And then he repeated these lines to me as if even in the silence there was a tremor, "I don't see you, but I see you." He touched my hair and the strands were wet from perspiration. The River Ganges itself had flowed through them. I was trembling. He asked his son to bring a clean towel. He wiped my face and his gentleness felt eloquent. His hands were hot like lightening arrows of supernatural energy. I had always known that he had the other also in him. I had felt it in our first encounter but had never experienced it until now. The stone he had asked his son to hand to me at that first meeting fell on the carpet. He picked it up and smiled. I shivered. He asked his son to sit down with us, and taking both our hands, he looked at me. I was sure he could see me and he said that I had the part.

Flowers grew all around and in me. I felt the vines falling from my mouth. The lotus opened its thousandth petal on my head and a red rose grew from my heart as the essence of the flower merged with my blood. I was transformed and the golden sensual pollen covered my body. The visible and the invisible became one and, looking at my right hand now entwined with the little one's tiny hand, I saw little irises sprouting from my fingers as though bridging the unseen worlds. He finally loosened his embrace and slowly got back into his chair as I gathered everything and rose from the white carpeted floor. The son took the towel from his father's hands. He asked me to sit down near him and handed me the glass of water.

"You were magnificent," he whispered. "I knew at the very first moment I saw you that you were her."

Tears filled my eyes. I couldn't stop crying. *Humanity is descended from the very tears of the gods*, I thought. I felt the magical aura surrounding every drop. But suddenly a very strange, haunting feeling of a dark shadow lurking somewhere invaded me, and my eyes started to shed tears of sadness. They were tears for those who are close to what I felt but were deceived and cheated. I felt tiny fingers wiping my tears and smiled at the compassion of a child seer who was born with all the sight.

Clearing his throat, the director began talking about all the logistics and things that had to be done. He told me that he would send me an advance, since he did not want me to take any other parts and needed me to go somewhere quiet to get ready for the journey. I told him that I had two immediate projects I had given my word to that had to be completed. He agreed. He said I should finish them and then concentrate on the part. He asked his son to take down all my details again and make sure that they had my mailing address. Thanking him and his son, I walked to the door and started to lace up my boots, and I felt his non-seeing eyes piercing my every move as though he were devouring me. He asked me to approach him, as he had something he needed to tell me before I left. Leaving my boots, I walked back to him, slightly apprehensive. He pulled me towards him aggressively and whispered in my ear, "Now you are mine and I must possess you completely, body heart and soul."

I stood back as though burnt by flames of fire and I was Scherazade of the Arabian endless nights of unrequited love. I stand in the forest balancing on one leg for one million years, sacrificing all so that I could be one with my creative seed. And I saw all of the distorted portraits of Picasso's women, from when he had lost his fascination with them. I remember the Argentinean poet who sent me a note from across a restaurant, where I was dining with a friend and asked if he could see him. We met later that night and made passionate love and one day in the light of the sun he said to me that he did not believe in anything. I stopped, stunned and told him that I could not be with him and, as I was walking away, he ran and threw me down on the street. Weeping and wounded, I stood up and ran away, trembling and hurt and, though he begged and tried with flowers and gifts, I never saw him again. In a textured village walled room I saw the beatific and fierce visage of the goddess Kali with her red tongue sticking out. On the other side was Krishna who has put his bamboo flute down. And opposite was Ganesha, whose divine swaying trunk is still, and the goddess Sarasvati had put down her sacred instrument. And I knew now why the script had turned to ashes that first day when I held it and why the divine rider had flown through the room. They all came to warn me.

As I was about to turn around to head for the door, I saw a vision where a huge life-sized painted glass fell from its frame and shattered in front of me into a million bits. I walked through all the sharp pieces, carefully avoiding stepping on them, but I felt a pain and bent down to remove a bit from my foot. A cold wind passed through me and I gathered my cloak closer to me. The little one walked out with me, wondering why I had a slight limp. But I said nothing. He was very happy and on the street he held my hands and looked up at me with his blossoming little face, which seemed to truly see.

"I have never seen my father moved like that. Never," he said.

I couldn't tell him what his father had just whispered in my ear, and kneeling down in front of him, I kissed his forehead. "Thank you, my little prince."

He was the little man watering a dying ikebana tree from Japan in Tarkovsky's *The Sacrifice*. And he was the same little kid in the film watching his father being taken away in an ambulance after he had burned down their house as a promise made to god to sacrifice all his worldly possessions for the sanity of the universe. He was little Alexander in *Landscape in the Mist*, crying when he sees the dying horse. He is Anna in *The Spirit of the Beehive* when she looks up to the sky and whispers to the spirits, "*Soy Anna.*" And he was all the little children who can see the angels in *Wings of Desire*. He was my little man.

I embraced him with all the love of my shivering spirit, and kissed his fresh young old face. He held me a long time, and said that he would keep in touch with me and let me know everything. He told me to be confident.I left him and felt Vajra in my hands, the lightening flower, which is the ultimate weapon of the gods to be wakeful and vigilant. Turning back, I saw him rooted at the spot I had left him. He was one with the earth, he was dancing in the space between sky and earth, and I sent him a flying kiss.

As I was walking away, I realized how late it was. Deciding to go home first, I called the studio where the rehearsals were being held. The assistant picked up and I asked if I could speak to the director. She kept me on hold and after a few minutes he picked up. I let him know that I was on my way and apologized for the delay. He asked me to be there as soon as I could.

Hanging up, I rushed into the shower. I needed to wash away everything. I chose a rusty red dress and remembered some words by Theroux that if color is the music of eyes then red would be the sound of trumpets. I felt a radiant energy enter me and strengthen my skin and muscle, as though getting ready for some sort of fierce war. I felt brave like a hungry revolutionary. I thought of Tobias and his fire passion, and I was reminded of the alchemists for whom red was the color for the burning energy of human desire. Placing the script of the sacred mountain on the table next to the altar I felt its body and breath and its ether nuances. I took one of the red roses that my wolf raven had sent me, now a little dry but still elegant in its beauty and I placed it on the script. I knew that he would call me this night and I was excited. My henna hands longed to touch his transparent form and my mouth wanted to feel his lush lips as my snake tongue traveled through his myriad universes. My red, flaming fire feet bent and broke his supple bark body, as his raven wings quivered through my veined mind and left traces of the eagle in flight.

Just as I started to leave, the phone rang and, I picked up quickly. I sat down shocked at the voice I heard. It was Shane. I asked him how he got my number and after a long pause he said that Smila had given it to him. He said that he had tried very hard to get it from Hironobu san who always said that he did not know it. I said nothing as a silent rage arose within me and I cursed Smila for this. But as soon as I did this, I knew that I could not be tainted, and the words fell on the wooden floor like empty kernels and died an instant death. I washed my mouth silently with every flower essence and burning sage smoke to clean these negative shades. He asked if he could see me. "I don't see any reason for us to see each other," I replied. But he insisted and said that he had to explain everything. "It is very important," he cried out like the middle lion he was.

The word closure meant nothing to me, but I felt that this en-

310

counter could lead to a complete cleansing of any residue left by those very bloody wounds. So I agreed, and told him that I could see him the following evening. He said he would call me and let me know where and in the same breath he told me that Hironobu san no longer worked for him. I said nothing, but my heart felt relieved. I placed the phone back into its cradle and my fingers reached out to dial Smila's number but I refrained. My anger at her disrespect was too strong and, gathering my things, I left.

The red felt strengthening and the boots were warm and the Moroccan shawl was a constant reminder of my beautiful, mad gypsy lover. Approaching the door of the building, I didn't see any doorman. Then someone rushed to open the door, and it was my friend. He apologized and said that he was attending to some mail. I told him that it wasn't necessary to always open the door for me. "It's my duty," he replied strongly. Smiling at him, I walked out, dusting off the sand that had engulfed me on those rippling dunes when Shane had attacked me. I headed for the bus stop, which now felt like my very own. Suddenly, I was startled by what I saw. There, right at the stop, was my dream lady from Algeria with her flowing burkha revealing her piercing eyes. She looked as though she had been standing in the same place at the riverbed, giving me a message. I stumbled, and steadying myself, approached her. As I got closer her face unveiled itself. It was Prana. I greeted her warmly and told her that I was very happy to see her. And once again I wondered if she saw what I saw when she nodded slightly telling me that she did know. She apologized for not contacting me earlier and said that she had been travelling all over Africa for antiques and just got back. She was also going uptown and was hoping to see me. I asked her why she didn't ring the bell of the apartment. "I wanted to surprise you," she replied in her usual soft voice. We got in the bus and walked to the back. She was elegant in her suit and high heels. I told her that, and she took my hand and thanked me.

"How have you been?" she asked me.

"I have been thinking of you a lot, especially in the last few days," And told her all that had passed.

I knew that I could trust her implicitly. And I told her everything. I finally came to that afternoon and what had transpired between the Mexican director and me. She looked away from me, away into the distance. She was silent as if taking in every word and sorrow. Coming back, she took both hands and whispered something. I leaned closer to her.

"Be careful," she said.

"How?" I asked.

"You will know," she answered.

I was worried and disturbed. I mentioned to her that I would take a week and go upstate to prepare for the part.

"It is an amazing, powerful role," I told her, "and I feel passionately about it."

Her stop arrived and, getting off, she said that she would call me soon. She stepped out from the back of the bus and as she waved and walked away her tailored suit became a flowing gown, and I gasped in disbelief watching her becoming the divine rider and she and the black, shiny stallion both dissolved into the city scape. I gathered my Moroccan shawl tightly, as though asking it to calm me. My breathing was fast and, placing my right red palm on my antelope heart center, I took deep and long breaths. I needed one of my lovers. I needed their strong and passionate embrace. My stop arrived, and still trembling at what I had just seen, I stepped out. The building where the rehearsal was was a few blocks away and I walked slowly towards it, trying to center and align myself before I got there. In the theater, they were all full steam ahead.

As I stepped in the director nodded and told me to join in. As soon as I began I was back, thrusting forth into my role. It felt good and my words seemed to have broadened and elongated into a larger and clearer shape. The director's eyes were on me. At the break he came to me and remarked that I was better today than I had ever been. I told him that I had been through an amazing experience, which may be reflected in my work.

We continued until late and, finally, he called it a wrap. I decided to walk down to my apartment even though the wind was cool. As I was walking out, I felt the director standing beside me. He asked if he could join me. I eagerly said that I would love that. Out in the streets, we sculpted the evening light with our presence.

"You had a fire in you today," he said.

I explained a little about the film role that I had auditioned for and how it had entered me in an almost unreal way.

"You are a true artist," he said.

I felt a little shy about this compliment, but thanked him all the same. He asked me if I was hungry. "I am famished," I replied. Remembering both the health place and the sushi restaurant, I mentioned them to him. He asked me which one I would prefer.

"I would like some raw fish," I answered.

"Agreed."

The restaurant was quiet and there were only a few people. The waiter who had seated me last time recognized me and asked if I would like to sit at the same table. I nodded and removed my boots. We headed for the lowered table on the floor. He ordered a bottle of red wine.

"It is my poetry," I confessed to him.

"It is mine too," he replied.

The bottle was opened and the waiter poured his glass for him to

taste. He handed it to me, and I smiled. It was perfect. We ordered sushi and sashimi and he began speaking about the play and how happy
he was with all of the actors. I agreed and told him that it was enriching
working for and with him. His hands were sensual and his fingers long
and fine. They evoked many expressions and had eloquence about them.
I felt a sharp tinge in my left foot and remembering the glass piece, bent
down to remove it. He asked me if everything was okay and I told him
that I had stepped on something sharp earlier. Before I could say anything, he was by my side feeling my foot to find the place. His hands were
gentle. He ran his fingers on my foot and my skin felt like a drenched
spring tent covered with the very first blossoms of this new born season,
as every petal sings a melody of birth and freedom and I was the rider on
a horse sitting bareback and feeling every muscle of the shining stallion.

I felt a release and he showed me the glass piece that had been
wedged deep in the flesh. There was a slight bleeding and, taking a paper
napkin, he wet it with some wine and cleaned the wound. I laughed and
felt ecstatic to be healed by this divine liquid. "You have ancient feet,"-
he said, and I knew now that he was part of the tribe of men that would
be in my marriage tent where the courtesan is always worshipped and
honored and where ordinary minds are not welcome. I thanked him. And
the waiter brought us a bowl of water with some napkins. We washed our
hands and continued with the delicious sushi. He asked me how I had
stepped on glass. Looking at him shyly, I said it was part of a sacrifice
that I had to go through. I was sure he would not understand, but he
nodded, "This is why you are an absolute artist."

The sushi was pure sea and the salmon in my mouth dissolved
and acknowledged the journey against the currents, fighting all obstacles and never stopping until the golden liquid was filled in the chalice
of one's absolute creativity. We spoke about the play and my part. I told
him about Miguel and how much he had taught me, and still did. He
asked me what had happened to him and with a trembling voice I told
him that he had passed very early. He was silent and asked me his full
name. When I told him, his eyes widened. He knew of him, and he knew
that he had the reputation of being one of the finest Shakespearean actors.

"Yes, he was," I whispered, "and he was my greatest teacher and
my beautiful rugged singer-lover."

I told him about Formentera in Spain and the time we had spent
there. There was a silence. He poured me some more wine while the sushi and sashimi were sliding through my mouth like the smooth tongues
of the female mind of love and passion, and the bliss of sensuality. Looking up, I saw his palms opened and stretched, and within their lined tapestry every nuance of ecstasy was etched in red. I wondered at the people
that I met or that walked to me and was filled with gratitude.

Krishna is the heart and butter thief, I thought. He is the thief of the heart's butter and this is the element with which he communicates with all creatures, with all women, with his mother, with his beloved Radha and even though "Krishna" means black he is blue or even purple. He is the lover and resembles the bluish stain on Siva's neck where the ocean's poison is concentrated. I thought of the black pelt of a skinned antelope within which the loins of the sacrifice were wrapped. Sacrifice is the continuation in the second act that extracts the essence from the first and then leads to the third act, which is the ordinary life that is then transformed to all the other levels. I felt as though someone had stolen a little candle from my mind.

Johann asked for the check and we left the lush garden of sushi, self, and satisfaction. Lacing up my boots, I began walking and limped a little. He held me and we headed towards the apartment building, which was close by. I thanked him for dinner.

"I'm grateful for a language of symbols and art," he replied. "How is your foot?"

"Raw and open," I told him, smiling.

The night was silent and awake, as though watching us with its secret, haunting, magical eyes. I wanted to touch her and eat her very depth and raised my palms to receive her presence. His gaze was like the antelope. I never explained anything as he walked into the realms with me without any question. Another lover and another birth. And the tree bent from the weight of its blossoms and the lines from Pablo Neruda's poem, 'Every day you play' echoed in my body: "I want to do with you what spring does with the cherry trees." I smiled and leaned on his right shoulder. I was lit. I told him that after the run of the play I would be going away for a week or so to prepare for the part in the film. A sharp, strange pain clutched my heart. He asked me if I was certain that I had the part. I nodded, and my neck felt the swallowed poisons of the cruel, barren, and empty sounds of the dying stallion. He asked me if I had signed a contract. "Not yet," I replied. We walked to the apartment building and he opened the door for me before the doorman could. Smiling, I entered. He paused. He thanked me for the evening and told me to have a good rest, as the rehearsals the next day would be long and arduous. Thanking him for the dinner, I took the elevator to the eleventh floor. As the keys slid into the door, I felt a hand entering mine, and I knew it was Miguel.

The studio was warm and the phone rang as soon as I placed my bag on the couch. Peeling my boots off, I grabbed the receiver, knowing who it was. Yes, it was my wolf raven. I was ecstatic to hear his deep tree voice. He heard my heavy breathing and asked if I was okay. I told him that I had rushed in, hearing the ring of the phone. He said that he would let me relax and call back in a little while. I washed and changed

314

and lit the incense and the candle and lay down on the bed. I took in all that had happened during the day and thought about the part and the approaching performance date. I felt slightly nervous. My eyes closed softly and I was a child climbing up a banyan tree whose branches were so long and ancient that they reached into the ground. I gave each branch a name and they became my trunk friends. The roots of this aged tree spread for miles in and around the surface. It was like a language spreading its stories in the earth and sky. I loved that tree. It was my friend and my solace when I ran away from adults and silly girls who just played with dolls and only spoke about boys. I was never a part of their stories and always walked away whispering silent dreams of faraway horizons.

The phone rang again, I picked up and Ulfhrafn's voice softly invaded me and the whole studio. He wanted to know everything and so I told him all, but left out the Mexican director's last words. It felt like it had to be my own battle and I would have to drink the swords and arrows on my own. A vision quest of sorts when, parched and famished, I would be led to see and not be blinded by selfishness. I told him about the play and how well it was going.

"The opening night is in a few days." I couldn't believe it myself. "I wish you were here," I told him.

He echoed my thoughts. He told me that his mother was still ailing and that he was the only one to look after her. He sounded sad and I threw my snake tongue into his art and soul and plucked his wounding heart out to heal and feel it. He was quiet and listened to all that I said.

"I will go away for a week to prepare for the Mexican film."

"Where?"

"Woodstock. There is a place called Matagiri – Mothers Mountain." I had been there when I first arrived in New York and felt a special strength and peace there.

He asked about the photographer, and I mentioned the trip to the Dominican Republic. I spoke about Shane's call and he was angered to hear that Smila had given him my number. He wanted to know everything. I felt the longing in each of his questions. He asked me if I would see Shane and told me not to. As his voice got soft and cloudy, my inner flight was set free and I was walking somewhere sacred on special stones. Someone handed me a long piece of charcoal and I drew om signs on the flat surface of the stones I walked by, and in another place I was led by some chants and as I closed my eyes a sheep appeared in front of me and kissed my right hand. In another space a man handed me a tray full of seeds that he was ready to plant and asked me to touch these seedlings as he wanted my energy on them, and as I felt them, a fragrant jasmine bloomed in my right hand. "It is for you," he said. And I knew that the gods laughed when men pray to them for wealth.

As his voice caressed me, my poem became my power. A vibration of eons and decades engulfed me as his eyes entered the very tides of my soul. There was a silence in the little studio. "I miss you,"he whispered, and the cry of the howling wolves and the shame of greed became the uncompromised blood-walk. I whispered back with my tongue piercing his ear that I missed him too, and that I longed for his art and his intelligence. He kissed me gently and all the dewdrops of the ether gardens entered and quenched my longing for my raven and my wolf, put together ecstatically.

He told me that he had been in touch with Flora and she sent me all her love and care. "We will see you soon," he told me as he hung up the phone, and every cell in me was haloed and glowing and watched over by the birds of paradise. I moved my body as their feathers tickled me. I made love to myself and to my raven king. I screamed and sliced the Universe. The phone rang again but I waited to hear who it was before I picked up. It was Aakash. He sounded very sad and tired. I felt I wasn't ready to speak to anyone right then.. As my eyes closed and I sank into the other world, he entered my dream with a man beside him. They seemed to be pushing me. His left hand was missing and when I asked him about it, he said that he had already told me about it. I knew then that something was about to happen to him.

I felt cold and pulled the cotton blanket down over me, and watched the last flicker of the candle as Ulfhrafn lay beside me, and his arms held me. I moved into him with my whole self and became a tree toeing the earth, supple and upright in my trunk. Flowing and bending in my branch limbs, my tears mingled with the resin and the rope of endurance. The tree was mine as our souls merged and I felt my birth from a tiny seed coming into existence and weathering every change and vicissitude and reaching up to the sky to absorb all. The bark fitted me and my body was tree-alive, and I guarded my inner life. A goldfish entered my dream and I was reminded of the Swiss artist Paul Klee whose painting, titled, The Gold Fish was of his companion goldfish. A mysterious creature is the center of attention in his water world showing its large, powerful opened eye, warning us not to touch his golden scales, and whose fish-like reveries were revelations. Klee noted in his diary that his paintings were like dreams flowing beneath the waking surface of life. And my dreams are my very axis. They make me whole. They guide me and inspire and inform me and they are my silent warriors always feeding me with the other world, which is the true reality, and where all is born.

As the night slipped in into me I saw my other self. I am wed and the brides are jealous because I belong to no man and yet I am one with the man-bride as he strides through my golden, dripping tent of every color and every perfume and every nuance. I feel Ganga, the goddess of

316

the sacred Ganges, sitting on her fish mount as she prepares to descend from the river's Himalayan source to wet and flow over the vast plains of India. My husband unfurls his rainbow wings and I fly away with him held in his bird embrace.

As dawn entered my small universe, evoking a beginning and a coming into being, I left behind the myth and mystery of the deep, dark night, and I saw a raven feather on my pillow. And I was certain that he was here. I placed it on my altar next to the sun stone from Mexico. I saw the day and felt its pulse. Getting ready for the early call, I started to lace my Palladium boots when the phone rang. It was the photographer telling me that the shoot had been finalized and it would take place in two weeks. *That is perfect*, I thought, as it would be exactly at the end of the run of the play. I mentioned the opening night of the play and he said that Smila had already informed him and that they both would try to be there. I thanked him and hung up.

I continued lacing my boots. I touched them lovingly and caressed the green of the leather and the suede. I loved how the two fabrics balanced each other. I was reminded of Anthony, a young, strong black man who walked in front of me as I was sitting on a park bench in Washington square park and, noticing the boots,he stopped and asked me if I had ever polished them. I had not and he said that he would love to give them a shine, if I didn't mind. I trusted him. He had his shoe polishing tools, and, lacing up his knee pads, began. First he gently wiped the dust off, and then, applying some cream, rubbed and smoothed the surface. He kept speaking about the elegance and quality of the boots and that they needed to be nurtured and taken care off. His fingers travelled on the surface and into my feet and I felt the Indian women's hands painting the henna on them. After carefully finishing, I offered him some change, which he refused, and, as I stood up to walk away, he told me how he loved trees. "I kiss them," he said, "and I tear up dollar bills and place them in the earth of the tree as an offering." I felt my tree self and smiled. "Be strong," he said, "be brave. All is coming to you." Then he asked that I picture his face in my meditations. And each morning since then I have seen his bold, black, clean face.

Arriving at rehearsal, I realized that I was early and was about to walk out when the producer asked me to join him in his office for a few minutes. He told me that there had been some more auditions and parts for plays and maybe an Independent film that had come up that might work for me. He asked his secretary to give me a list with all of the information and I walked out with her, thanking him. As I was about to leave the room he added that the director was extremely happy with my work. I told the secretary that I would be back shortly and decided to walk to the park and visit my trees.

The air was chilly, but I was well dressed and quickened my pace.

317

The trees were barren and etched into the sky cape gracefully. All came back as I walked to the place of the mirror, wondering if by some miracle it would still be there. It was not and grass had grown over that little earth space. I saw the bench where I had sat on that frightening morning when Niyol had approached and saved me. I paused and the memory screamed through me. I knew that nostalgia and I were no strangers. A strange and haunting beauty surrounded and entered me. I felt all the transformation seeping through me with its continuous wail and presence for change. I can never be bitter or closed. This was and must always be my learning.

Manahata, as the Native Americans had originally named this island, a sacred land surrounded by rivers, and even though I could not see the rippling body of the water, I felt the blue orchids singing their soul chants as they carry the consciousness of fish dreams. The forked tree in front of me was the eternal feminine. She carried her form, her shape, and her power, and approaching her, I ran my fingers into her longing curves and beautiful crevices and heard all the women sigh with recognition and admiration and the female song was empowered once again, and the goddess was very much alive as she destroyed all that disturbed the ecology of the universe. She was the slayer of all that upset the balance and the creative core of the body of the earth, and she danced madly, until she was shown a reflection of herself in a mirror, and then she was at peace, and all was restored.

I started walking back to the rehearsal. I had no limp, as my feet walked right through my Paris Palladiums, and I felt the earth and she rejoiced while I respectfully walked all over her. Everyone had arrived and we all got ready for places and positions. Johann stepped in. He had a bounce and a warm smile as he began getting us ready. He caught my eye and we acknowledged each other's presence without any distraction. I liked this. We broke for lunch and he came over to tell me that he had loved our evening together. I felt the still inner center. The sickle moon was now on and in me; all separation dissolved into a completion, and all external aids became distant shadows. My birds were in me. My wolves howled for me. My tiger roared within me. My dragon stuck her fire tongue into me. And my divine elephant held me inside his ivory white tusk.

Johann called for a break and I decided to go to a nearby café. Walking in, I found a quiet corner with a small round table. It had a small glass container with little flowers in it and on the wooden floor was a rainbow formation reflected from the hanging crystals. It had the shape of a cactus pear and, slicing it, I relished the red body of this very special fruit. The seeds crushed between my teeth like little universes of sight and thought.

In India, my husband handed me a plate of this same fruit sliced and skinned. Little Savitri was resting and he fed me with his hands stained blood-red by the fruit.

I ordered a little snack and a green jasmine tea. I removed my journal from my cloth bag, which had not been visited for a while. My thoughts flowed on the welcoming banana skin pages and Kali danced everywhere. But the time had already flown by and, paying, I rushed back to the rehearsal. There was a buzz of excitement in the room as we all felt the approaching premier day. Johann directed and we worked late into the night. When it was a wrap, he gave us all cab fare to go home. Thanking him, I stepped into the cold night as a cab stopped right in front of me. I looked back. Johann was on the pavement waving to me. I felt his ropes on my neck pulling me towards him. It was tight but gentle, and my stallion-self had transparent wings. I leaned back into the seat of the car and, taking a deep breath, closed my eyes.

Little glass mirrors hung from the sky, feng shuing the earth body and Ganesha was sitting inside my right palm. It tickled, and opening my eyes, I realized that I had not told the driver where to go and, just as I was about to, the cab stopped in front of 63 East Nineth Street. Shocked, I glanced at the driver. It was the same beautiful and gentle face that had taken me to Smila's apartment many moons ago. He smiled with a toothless grin, and his mapped life face was that of a desert saint. Stepping out of the yellow cab, I gave him the bills that the director had given us. They were a little moist. I handed the notes to him, remembering the red-stained hundred dollar bill in my palm when I had first entered this city. He refused and his eyes lay exactly where my gold symbol was, underneath my shirt. I nodded and told him that I had the seven turquoise chains with me now.

"I know," he said. "You must always be who you are," he added. His words were like the nectar from the sunflower and the fisherman's sharp, glistening spear as he thrust into the rippling waters searching hungrily for the fish dreams. I bowed to him as he drove off in a ball of light. My eyes wept in gratitude and love for yet another gift given to me and all these messengers that are sent to me to always remind me and show me the way.

I walked into the building in an altered state and the doorman said that there was something for me and then ran into the office to get it. He handed me a large, very flamboyant bouquet of flowers with a card pinned to it. I knew who it was from, and I knew I didn't want it. Shane's name was on the card, and I handed it back to the doorman without even opening it. He stood back but I insisted, and, smiling gratefully, he told me that it was his wife's birthday. "Wish her a happy one from me," I told me, and checking my mail, walked to the elevators.

As I entered the studio I felt a little baby boy on my left shoulder biting into me lovingly, and my mouth felt the fragrant fleshy petals of the **champa** flower in India, the symbol of psychological perfection. The **custi**, the kiss was on me as the sky filled the room, and the feather pen was in my hand as I drew the howl of the wolf woman and carefully placed the ancient child on a soft pillow. The studio was filled with large blooming lilies everywhere and I could hear the hypnotic chants of my karmic song lines, which would always show me my walkabout.

Little Savitri made some cooing sounds and, walking to her crib, I made sure she was covered well. Her fever had not left her completely and there was a tension in the air. The spider web had not been repaired and I was nervous. I lay down behind my sandalwood star man and moved into his sweet-smelling night body. He pulled me in.

Chapter 18: The birds are listening to my call and I will become my talent and my aspiration

The next days were hectic and insane. Rehearsals were intense and we worked every day, almost through the night. We were given off the day before the opening to rest and I took that time to fill in all the other auditions and go-sees. There were quite a few scheduled, which surprised me, but I did as many as I could. In the back of my mind, the Mexican film haunted me. I was so excited and yet very nervous but I knew that I had to do as much as I could before I left for my very own vision quest.

The performance day was finally arriving. I was very nervous. The candle was lit and I went through all the lines and directions Johann had given us. I closed my eyes to rest, taking in all the sounds and the silence of the city night. My little studio was dark and quiet, especially in the evenings and a dream entered me.

Two beautiful women approach me. I cannot make them out but they look familiar. One of them kisses my right foot and, looking up, says that it is a lotus, and my mind wanders to the rippling sand dunes in New Mexico, where I fell ripped and torn on the sand and that one single flower transformed into a lotus. Right in front of me, there is a tall structure, and as my eyes pierce into its very walls it becomes a life size Laxmi temple. I enter and there in its sacred premise is my father. He places **kum kum** on my third eye and the **bindi** place is wet and round. The red powder melts into my skin. I am blessed. The birds are listening to my call and I will become my talent and my aspiration. I want to only know. I want to annihilate all doubt, all fear, and all hesitations. I am Siddhartha, who left his luxurious palace and comforts to be one with the human suffering as he gave himself over to the divine call. And by doing this, I will sculpt my vision and understand why all transformation takes its own absolute time, and in waiting in grace, I will understand why impatience is a sin. I am the motion. I am the change.

The day was here. We had to be at the theater on Second Avenue between Twelfth and Thirteenth Street two hours before the show started. I decided on a long bath before leaving. Ulfhrafn called to wish me good luck and told me that Flora sent her love and best wishes. I held his tongue between my feet and felt it rippling all over my body. I was wet. I told him. He cried. I wore something comfortable and, getting everything together, started to leave. Just then Prana called. I was happy to hear from her. She said that she would try to be there but, if not, she wished me good luck and a great performance. "You will be great," she said. Her voice was healing and inspiring, and my confidence grew stronger and stronger.

Everybody was at the theater and we started getting ready. We all wished each other good luck and Johann came over and whispered something in my ear. He gave me a squeeze and walked away with a twinkle in his eye. It felt good. The time arrived and the curtain went up. It was a full house. We were nervous. I was, at least. I didn't have to go on until halfway into the play. My hands were wet and his tongue slipped in and I kept on taking deep breaths. It seemed to go well. When I walked on I caught the eye of the audience and saw both Shane and Smila sitting side by side. I stumbled a little and then my eyes fell on Prana and everything seemed to align once again. She was the woman in my dreams, and all I saw were her dark and knowing eyes and I was filled with an uncanny strength. The lines came through me like echoes of solitude and pain. That was the essence of the part I played, and I felt one with its depth and spirit. I became her and forgot all else and felt every word and carved the soul and flesh into the character. My voice came from somewhere deep inside of me and I lost all fear or hesitation. There was a moment when I had to scream and cry and I felt every fiber of my being resounding and responding to her agony. I was in flight.

I walked off of the stage in an altered state as Johann hugged me and I heard a huge applause from the audience. I couldn't stop crying. The second act began and, finding a quiet corner, I lay down and inhaled deep breaths. The play was called In the Belly of the Elephant. It was a haunting story of a group of people who had been led into a cave of sacred secrets, which was the only place where they could find their dreams and visions. It was a scary place, filled with huge obstacles and trials that each one had to experience and overcome before finding the final answer. My part was of the one who led them through the whole journey and I was both inside and outside of what they had to experience. I had to become their pain and suffering.

For the first time I realized that the content of the play was not different from the Mexican film, and I wondered why this had never dawned on me before. At this very moment I sat up, startled. The sounds of galloping horses invaded my ears. Not one, but several, and then they shape-shifted into wolves and I saw the green eyes of one of them as they ran by me. Niyol came to give me power. I felt wildly protected, as though the wind herself had woven her arms all around me, surrounding and lifting me. The assistant director came to tell me that I would be on again soon. I got ready. The part in the second act called for the characters transition into a calm and confident one with reassurance, as she led the group to their final realization after the hard journey. It was powerful and called for a tangible stillness and silence. I felt as though I too had gone through a huge catharsis here and in my life. The audience was quiet and the atmosphere was electric. As the play ended, there was a burst of applause and we left the stage.

I felt elated. I changed and, taking all my things, started to walk out. Johann came to me and embraced me very tightly. He told all the others that it had been an excellent play and reminded us to be there early the next day, as he would give us our notes. There was a buzz in the air as we left. I looked for Prana in the audience but I couldn't see her. Many people came to me to congratulate me, and in the corner of my eye I saw Shane and Smila standing and waiting for me. They walked to me and congratulated me. Both were surprised. This was the first time they had seen me work. I thanked Smila for all of her connections. She invited me to join them for dinner and before I could refuse she said that she had already made reservations. I felt like this would be the final ending to this long saga and accepted the invitation.

I watched Johann coming towards us and was relieved. I introduced him to both of them and mentioned to him that it was because of Smila that I got the part or, rather, the audition. He thanked her. They did not invite him to join us. I left with his hungry eyes on my shoulder. I watched him as he looked back, lingering and swaying with his hawk eye. I saw Miguel and whispered his name. Smila sarcastically said something banal and stupid.

They took it for granted that I would join them, paying no mind that I was truly tired. I decided to accept and thought that this would be a good moment to see them both at one time. *This will be my evening of compromise,* I thought. I told them that I would like to stay in the neighborhood, as I really could not have a late night. Smila had made reservations in a place that they both knew which was close by and we walked to it. He looked very dark. His face was chiseled and handsome, and I knew now why I was so easily seduced by this man. My drapes were down. My shaman's tent was dusty even though it hung gracefully and I was shaded by desire and non-fragrant flowers whose flesh bodies, though full and soft, had no perfume. My very own self deceived me, and I learned what sightlessness leads to and the sacrifice was here again in its entire magnificent splendor.

It was a Middle Eastern restaurant and was small and charming with echoes of more. The menu was wonderful and I was famished. Shane looked at the wine list and of course ordered an excellent bottle of red. Smila approved. We all ordered, and then an uncomfortable silence enveloped the table. Shane looked at me and said that he had told Smila all that had happened. He said that he had to see me to express his deep apologies. He added that when I had told him I was pregnant he could not deal with it. "I can imagine how hard it must have been for you," he said. *How can you imagine?* I thought. Smila said that it was wrong that I did not reach out to her.

"I couldn't," I whispered. "I had to face it myself."

They were both very quiet. Smila said that she was very sorry for what I had to go through.

And these words from Hammadi's poem resounded in me: "I am the first and the last/ I am the honored one and the scorned one/ I am the whore and the holy one/ I am the wife and the virgin/ I am the mother and the daughter/ I am the members of my mother/ I am the barren one and many are my sons/ I am she whose wedding is great and I have not taken a husband." Shane poured more red in my glass. Our eyes met for the first time. He was truly a magnificent game player but this time I was covered with wolves and jeweled birds. The wounded walk, which had almost stolen my anima, my dreams, and my wealth of poets and mystics, still sounded in my every cell. I had been saved because I lifted all the fallen roses in filthy subway stations, and brought them to earth, or placed them within the hands of a weeping woman arrow artist whose eyes light up as she sees a dance of youth and friendship.

Suddenly Smila and Shane placed their hands on mine and the henna shrieked through a hollow white canvas. I asked him if he had found the mask that had gone missing while I was there. He was embarrassed and, apologizing, said that.

The cleaning woman had misplaced it but he did find it. We finished the meal in a non-atmosphere. Even sarcasm and cynicism decided not to enter this space that was cold and harsh and sad and lost and hollow. I thanked them both and assured them that without their help, I would not be where I was. We left the restaurant. They wanted to walk me to my studio. I said that I would be fine and left them as I danced into the night.

I was the wolf looking and searching for the light of the moon in fear of losing her love and her passion and her form-changing ways. And there she was peeping through the clouds with her cosmic winking eye. I saw Domenico, the beautiful mad man who, enraged by the carelessness and ignorance of humanity, burns himself and falls from a tall statue in Tarkovsky's Nostalgia. And just at that moment Andrei the poet, who had promised Domenico to walk across the sulfur pool with a half lit candle struggles to reach the other end, but does not give up until he finally places it on the other side and falls down and dies. And the flame burns as a symbol, holding the spiritual insight of the shaman and the true artist.

Just as I was entering the building I heard Smila's voice and, a little shocked, looked back and saw them both standing behind me. "You followed me?" I asked. They both smiled sheepishly and said they just wanted to wish me good night and asked if they could come upstairs. I replied that I really needed an early night. They came closer and hugged me and told me to stay in touch. I said nothing and walked into the building. I did not turn around. This was over. I had expressed my gratitude. I will only bow to the beggar saint and touch his feet.

I took a warm and long shower and lay down, exhausted and

complete. Turning on the answering machine, I listened to all the messages. A long one from my wolf raven said he would call me again this night. I was happy. Flora's voice enveloped me. She said she had no phone number as she and her husband were en route working. She missed me and assured me in her beautiful melodic voice that she was always with me, and knew that I was doing well and that she would see me soon. Prana left a quiet, still line and told me that I was truly magnificent.

On the bed I nestled into the cotton cover and kissed its softness. The phone rang and it was my raven. Before I could speak he started to play the strings of my zither soul. He began to recite a poem. It was The Love "Sonnet XI" by Pablo Neruda from his book The Essential Neruda: Selected Poems:

> "I crave your mouth, your voice, your hair.
> Silent and starving, I prowl through the streets.
> Bread does not nourish me, dawn disrupts me, all day
> I hunt for the liquid measure of your steps.
> I hunger for your sleek laugh, your hands the color of a
> savage harvest, I hunger for the pale stones of your
> fingernails,
> I want to eat your skin like a whole almond.
> I want to eat the sunbeam flaring in your lovely body,
> the sovereign nose of your arrogant face,
> I want to eat the fleeting shade of your lashes,
> and I pace around hungry, sniffing the twilight,
> hunting for you, for your hot heart,
> like a puma in the barrens of Quitratue."

My silence was like a wolf that had forgotten he could speak because of the beauty that had walked into him. I walked, arisen from my spine, taking the ringed structure and threading it into a garland which I flung around the moon so she, too, would wed herself and hum her soft whispers to lonely lovers. "This is the way that I miss you," he said.

Finding my voice again, I told him about the play, and how it went, and that I was forced to dine with both Smila and Shane. He was quiet. We spoke about our long love and the wet ocean shells that howled the bursting wails of the violent sea waves. The seeker knows what he sees and she who sees knows what she has found. I was wounded and healed and the doors were always wide open and, looking back at the last glimmer of the shell song, I knew that I had no doors. I smiled at the entrance to the archway where two women walked in long, white silk robes, one with a sword of ecstasy in her throat, and the other behind her carrying the same sword like a staff of light. They gave and they took and braided everything together as blood turned into the very air they inhaled. The elephant trunk reached out to me and my fingers touch his wrinkled skin of love.

"I want to eat your skin like a whole almond. I want to eat the sunbeam flaring in your lovely body," I whispered in his ears. "I will be back whole and half to unveil you and surround you with thunder and lightning and the hailstones, which fall on the fertile seeded brown earth, will cover all of you. My walk will be crowned by jewels of sunlight and I will place the red ruby on your third eye with my moonbeam finger tips. I will love you."

He wished me good night and hung up. My eyes whispered shaded sounds of night owls as I ate vision and slept in my quest. My feet curled and moved, kissed by one hundred bald eagles and I floated above the little bed in a little studio in Manahata, which a Native American tribe called their own. I was aroused. My skin was on fire and my lovers came from everywhere to lift me.

The phone rang again. I didn't pick up immediately but eventually something made me. It was Johann. He apologized for calling so late. I fell back on the bed and said that I was very awake. He wanted to tell me how good I had been. I teasingly told him that I guessed I had not missed my calling. He said that I had not. He asked me if I ever thought I was meant to do something else. I told him that I had no doubts, but sometimes after so many rejections I felt that I did not have what it took or did not belong here.

"Your exotic visage does not make it easy," he replied, "but that is also your prize and your gift."

"My prize?" I asked him quizzically.

I saw him smiling as he said that it was indeed a gift. I was quiet and listened to his praise as it tickled my heart and worshiped my ego self. But I knew I would not be arrogant and I would not take the wind or the sun or the rain or the seven-lined rainbow for granted. I would serve my heart and soul, and I would scream and hail the entry of the opened, shining peacock feathers, quivering inside my orange dust-driven limbs of desire. He was very silent. I could hear his breath taking a winding journey.

"Your voice has a sultriness that provokes and seduces, a sultriness that is not manipulated," he said.

"I will do even better," I told him.

"You will," he repeated.

And then, as if from nowhere, he said he had something very personal to share with me, and hoped that I would not take it the wrong way. I listened, as my eyelashes gave shade to the lonely warrior.

"I want to make love to you. I want to make love to your howling tears."

I felt surrounded by the sense of the skin soul and green fields of lush growth bending their grass bodies in dewdrop surrender.

"This night is immense," I replied. "I am a woman, and I am all women, and my crown is made only with invisible dust of the gods of love, and Tantra is my bow as the arrows pierce dark dusk bodies of the sublime beings. I remain open like a bud unfolding its petals to the sunlight never fearing anything that may enter to destroy. This is the trust that must and will guide me through the walk of the lioness who has found her own personal song line from the eye of the heart and the song of the soul."

He was silent and open. "Don't stop, please," he said

I couldn't.

"I laugh at the pebbles on the sky, as they bounce back and forth not knowing the difference. They are without boundaries and throb with life and compassion of the very real kind," I finished and we hung up. I felt that I could finally sleep and just then the phone rang again but I refused to pick up and turned off the machine, not wanting to know who would call at such a late hour.

The morning shyly crept in, afraid to wake me. I glanced at the dreamcatcher given to me by a very special Native American elder who had made it himself. It was swaying in the soft breeze, letting all of the special dreams to fly through and catching the negative ones, which were strange and unhealthy, and would be ripped apart by the transparent wings of the butterfly. Johann's assistant called to give me the rehearsal times for the day and I got ready.

It was a misty morning and I thought of all the dewdrops bending the slender leaves of grass. After a warm shower and a moment in front of the altar, I listened to the rest of the messages. Smila and Shane had called. It must have been while I was being loved by wolf raven. Shane commented on how beautiful I looked and that he would love to take me to dinner again. Smila said that she missed me and congratulated me on my work in the play. A strange voice that I did not recognize had left a message saying that Aakash was not doing so well and asked that I call him. I picked up the phone and dialed his number. No one picked up. I left a message. I hoped he was okay.

The play began on time. Everybody was excited by the success of the first night and there was a restless energy in the air. Once again, I walked onstage and felt an uncanny sense of being watched by someone. I felt etched with focus and strength and the words came through me with a life of their own. Miguel's lessons echoed in my mind and I was very aware not to slur my words or eat the beginning or the endings. They felt like pearls freshly found within the oyster, representing the entire universe.

All went perfectly well and, once again, I walked off of the stage sobbing and felt a warm hand sliding through mine. I looked around and knew that it was Miguel. I whispered his name and the waves of the ocean on the Island of Formentera washed over me, as did his voice and his guitar strings. He was the master of the word, and he walked with a limp because once, when he thought I was leaving him, he jumped out of the second story building where we lived in Eaton Place in London and hurt his foot. It was the limping of the sacred beggar. He was my sun horse lover with a face that had travelled every road and path of the inner journey. I had kissed every single part of that mapped face, and his large shaped feet and his bow-shaped lips that he stroked with the burning tobacco in his hand. He was the Native American elder who grounded himself with the brown leaf as he smoked his peace pipe.

I felt all the pound notes that he had thrown all over my naked body one night when he came back after his performance and, standing across the bed, covered me with this green energy and shouted at the top of his voice that it was all for me and that he would always surround me with abundance.. And another sacred moment when some of his friends invited me for my birthday at a beautiful restaurant in London's West End and said that Miguel had asked them to take me out, since he had to work. And then the waiter walked in with a silver tray and on it was an exquisite jeweled box with a pair of earrings. They glistened in the soft candle light and, just as I was about to pick them up, Miguel walked in looking like a Zeus in a white silk suit I had never seen him wear before. He took the earrings and slid them into my pierced ears and held me tight and kissed me on my mouth, my mountain-rugged gypsy man of many men.

"How close you are," I whispered softly as I rested on the couch behind the stage. I was called to go back on and the play ended once again with a big applause. As I got ready to leave, Johann asked us all to gather together and told us that the play had been extended for at least another week or maybe even two. Everyone cheered and I, too, was happy but also worried about the photo shoot and the Mexican film. I expressed my concern to him and he said that he would be willing to speak to the director of the film if I needed him to. Thanking him, I made my way out of the theater. I heard his steps behind me. He stopped me and asked me if I would join him for a quick bite. I sensed Miguel's presence and felt as though he had sent him to me.

We went to the organic place I had been to several times. He told me once again how good my performance had been. I asked him to be very critical, as I wished to learn and expand myself. We ordered and ate in silence. I felt his unspoken desire and his feather caresses. I saw a child fall in a valley and I lifted her and helped her up and just then she drew a yantra with chili peppers through a glass window and the whole entrance was on fire. I touched her head and then realized that she was

328

her, she was the divine Kali and she came to me to eliminate all fear with her sharpened sword and her red fire tongue.

I looked into his eyes and without any hesitations told him that he reminded me of my Miguel. He said nothing and then, taking my hands as though they were fallen, autumn, burnt leaves, placed his mouth on them. His lips fell through me and I felt my red henna feet curling in delight. And here was another lover, another breakthrough, another broken shield, another wedding night of flaming screaming ecstasy when a virgin is born.

"The hero who has come under the protection of the cosmic mother cannot be harmed," said my beloved mother. These were the words for this new dawn-day morning of all mornings. I was free. My beloved parents were with me always and I would carry their legend and flag in every fiber of my being. *Time is the sensible measure in the continuity of mediocrity, and art is a sacred function,* I thought.

The studio was filled with passion and light. "Indeed a golden day," I whispered to myself. Johann and I had not made love but we had. All veils were torn asunder. And the Greek word "*psyche*" resounded in me. It meant butterfly, but it also denotes the soul. Dreams gave my soul wings and images from my dreams became the exquisite patterns on the flight of the monarch orange-black butterfly that brings in the spirit of my beloved father. *I must hold my dreams as I hold the quivering, fragile wings in my quiet palms so that they may always fly,* I thought.

Everything was still as I walked to the bathroom with the wings gently in my palms, and turned on the running water of life and of Ondine, my twin sister of eternal youth and longing and seeing. I sat in front of my altar. I lit one stick of incense. I lit the red candle and watched the flame burn with a purpose. I looked at my spirit beings and inhaled their presence. They were infused with their divine presence. I was empty and full and the unwanted weeds of silly aimless thoughts dropped away and dissolved into the mire of unnecessary noise and confusion. I felt my cells. I saw my cells. I loved each and every one of them. The artist was born.

The morning was alive. The phone rang and the secretary confirmed the extension of the play for another two to three weeks. She asked if I needed any letter for my other commitments. I thanked her and told her I would let her know if I needed any started to get ready. The phone rang again. This time it was Johann, the photographer. He told me that the photo shoot had been postponed for the moment because of several reasons. He was very sorry and truly looking forward to working with me. I was a little startled as the pay would have been substantial. He said that he would be at the play that evening again and commented on how good I was. I thanked him. I realized that the Mexican director needed to be called. I dialed his number but was not certain if they were still in New York or if they had left. Little man's voice spoke first in Spanish and then in English. He said that they were not in and left the number in Mexico. I called that number and he immediately picked up. He was thrilled to hear from me, and I told him that the play had been extended for another two weeks and that I would then leave to prepare for the film. He asked me to hold. I heard some tropical bird sounds and everything in me tingled. Life walked in with its winds of grace.

He was back and said that would be fine but after that, there should be no more delays. He said he was thrilled to hear my voice. We hung up and I thought that I should have asked for the advance that his father had promised me, but decided not to call back. A clay river swam in front of my eyes. My Ganesha was swimming in it and playing with the water. He hit me hard with his trunk and I felt as though the whole world turned around and in me.

The phone rang again and this time it was some agent who I had met some time back. She said that she had several auditions lined up for me in the coming days. I was excited and took all of the details down knowing that I may not be able to commit to them. She also mentioned that some of these people had seen my work in the current play and were impressed. Thanking her, I hung up and, inhaling all the jasmine flowers on every vine in my country of the lotus and of the head, I wondered if this was my time; if I was ready for what was approaching me.

Lost in my thoughts, I remembered the baby kitten of my dreams, sometime, somewhere, who became Sekhmet in front of my eyes and told me that I must always remain grateful and aware of every shining star and each motion of the walking, heaving mountain of delight and in-sight; and she reminded me that when a huge oak tree falls down to die it takes a very long time to decay and integrate back into the body of the soil and, when I will be in that very forest, I will watch only the birth of a million new growths that will be born from the fertility given by the body of the sacred tree.

I decided to wear red and felt all the colors of the painters alive and running in their virgin birth. I called some of the numbers and made appointments for the next two weeks. Lacing up my boots, I was ready to leave when the phone rang again. It was Aakash. He sounded weak and tired and very sad. I picked up. He sounded tired. He spoke and I listened. He asked me to send him energy. I did. I felt hurt by him but I knew that he needed me now and I would be there for him.

In the streets the air was cold but the sun was bright and shin-ing – a beautiful New York day, with its deep blue sky, and its electrifying breeze. The theater felt familiar and had the fragrance of flowers. I looked around and there near the stage was a huge bouquet of lilies sent from some anonymous admirer for I guess the whole cast. Johann was sit-ting making some notes and very quietly I passed him by, not wanting to disturb him. As I walked by he touched my red shirt and once again I felt my luminous body.

"Tonight will be special," he said to me.

"How so?" I asked him.

He looked at me with his strong eyes and whispered some words in Gaelic. I did not need to know what they meant, I knew it already. I went to the dressing room to get ready before the others arrived. His eyes followed me all the way until I reached the room and I felt him removing my boots and touching my feet and caressing the red henna on my skin. Soon all the others began streaming in and I was happy that I had arrived early. I walked to the couch backstage and sat down and stretched myself.

That night the show went more than well, just as Johann was expecting, and the air was filled with a special buzz. After the show he invited the cast for some drinks at a nearby café. He congratulated us and made some comments and corrections, and we wrote everything down. He told other actors that they should take heed as to how I spoke and enunciated my words. I was embarrassed. We all got a little lightheaded and happy. He was an attractive man, and I noticed some of the women in the cast approaching him and flirting with him. A stone Shiva was beside me and as I turned he came alive. I saw all the falseness of society and its mediocrity.

I finished my glass of red and started to leave. Johann followed me; he had felt my unease. I told him that I was fine and just needed to go back and rest. He grabbed my hand and then my shoulder, and kissed me on my mouth. All eyes were on us but, not caring, I sank into this absolute rustic seduction. Miguel had entered Johann's body to touch me. Under the night sky, clear and blue and sharp, he told me that he had wanted this from the first day he had laid eyes on me.

"Your sensuality is like a field of wild harvested grass and broken poppy flowers; it is like the seeds of the pomegranate fruit and the inside of the green fig tree, which knows no difference between its inner and outer self," he said. Shivering in his words, I started to push myself into him. These were the very lines that Miguel had sung to me on that wild night on the sands of Formentera in Spain.

"I was jealous of the women flirting with you. That's why I left," I told him.

He took me in even harder and whispered that there should be no room for that in me, because I was a thousand and one women in one. "That's a lot," I whispered smiling, as my snake tongue wandered into him with an endless curve of desire and ecstasy.

"I will eat you," he said.

"You already have," I said back.

My studio felt special that night, as though some being had entered and left its essence behind. Prana had left a long message, and even though it was late I decided to call her back. She picked up and we spoke for a while. She said that she must see me soon, as she had to leave for a long trip to look for antiques. We decided on the next day. I told her that the play was going extremely well and I felt nervous because I never thought it would be so strong. "You should trust yourself more and be aware of the power you possess and use it well," she told me. I listened with respect as every word settled in me. She wished me good night and, as though in a dream, I heard these words, spoken from her soft and gentle and powerful mouth: "You will break no more."

As she hung up the phone, I lit the red candle and sat on the floor knowing exactly who she was now more than ever. It was as though each time she showed me more, and tonight was the most she had ever revealed to me. I was stunned and saw her once again on that riverbed in Algeria. I was humbled, and changing lay down into the gentle arms of the clouds. My Massai warrior was standing in his ebony skin with a spear in his hand as he held me with his eagle eyes I flew within the self and the metaphysical interiors of the poet's gaze. I had emerged again from the womb of the feminine melody and the song of the Anima. I was here born and was alive.

The next days were hectic and intense. Some problems occurred in the play as some members of the cast fell sick and needed to be replaced. I could see the stress in Johann's eyes and his anxious demeanor. I did all I could to help and became even stronger in my role, which helped hold the play together. He sent me waves of appreciation and I sent him back my cloth of sensuality. During the days I went for as many auditions as I could. One of them came through and required me to start soon after the play finished. I told them that I had to prepare for a large Mexican production and might not be able to. They asked me for dates, which I was not able to give them. I could feel my urgency to prepare for the film. I called some people I knew upstate in a place very close to Woodstock. There was a room available that I could have for a little money. I felt that a week would be enough time to enter this journey.

Prana and I met before she left. We sat in the same restaurant where we had met the first time, when she had told me about the studio. My eyes weaved around her beautiful face and slowly entered hers. She now knew that I knew who she was. We sipped and chose some starters on the menu, and absorbed the silence of the evening, which felt like five hundred nights all merged into one. I told her about my going upstate to prepare for the film. She did not say anything, but had a distant look in her eyes.

"You will learn a lot," was all she said. I told her about the photo shoot being cancelled, and she smiled, saying she knew the client and was not surprised. And then, slowly – as though her voice came from the twin seas of being and not being and from the mountain of bliss untouched by the changing tides -- she said that my walk would be a long and arduous one as I learned to speak from my ether space.

"Enrich your inner tapestry," she said, "and breathe your vision and artistry until it is integrated in every part of your being and until you walk with it wherever you go. Do not be afraid and do not ever compromise, no matter what. Remove all masks and walk open with grace and humility and you will be helped and you will survive and I will always be there for you in your waking and your dream life."

Then, looking at me with eyes so hounding that I almost fell from my chair she spoke again. "Yes I am her, the one you saw in the river bed and in the room in Taman asset, and I see you everywhere."

My eyes filled with tears like the monsoon rains. They fell on the wooden floor of the restaurant. Her voice entered me like the fine point of the swaying crooked bamboo leaf, and she continued: "You will become the storyteller of the invisible magic for those who can hear and see the other. Always remember that it is a continuous task and a constant preparation and process. It is not easy. Yours is a walk on rocky, thorn-filled roads. There are no imitators on this path."

She took a very deep breath and leaned back. I did the same and we looked at each other and started to laugh so loudly that the whole restaurant echoed in this jubilant sound of the goddess of a million faces and a million sacrifices and a million realizations. She was divine, my friend Prana. I touched her hand that sat on the rustic table and I felt the lightning and thunder of the rain gods. She walked me home with her veined hands weaved into mine.

"I love you," I told her.

"I know," she echoed.

> She kissed me on my third eye
> and I knew once again that the
> red ruby had been placed there,
> where true sight belongs. At the
> door she stood in front of me,
> and looked deep into my essence.
> I shivered, feeling the winds of her
> gaze brush all over me. I raised
> my hands and clasped them in
> front of me, and bowed my head,
> whispering "Namaste." She clasped
> my hands and kissed them. Her
> softness was like a golden sky tent
> that clothed and covered me with
> a transparent magic flame.

333

I felt wed. I felt one.

My Satyavan and I were walking into the dusky evening in my India. Savitri was asleep. We were exhausted and anxious as the fever went down and up. He told me not to worry as we hid inside the bamboo groves, and reminded me of that incredible red sari night when I was the one who deflowered him and showed him the madness of love.

The doorman was respectful and waited for us to finish our conversation in silence. I entered, thanking him while Prana stood like a mirrored mountain. I looked back and she shape-shifted, and was the burkha woman with only her kohl-shadowed peacock eyes looking straight at me. I looked at the doorman to see if he was seeing what I was seeing and then she vanished.

I felt different, and removing my boots walked to the bathroom mirror to see what had changed. *Everything and nothing*, I thought, and slipping into my night gown lay down with both candle and incense lit.

I felt the little trembling, warm body of my Savitri lying next to me as her wide child gaze tore inside me. I took her in me and swallowed her fever. I was on fire. Her eyes were all over me. Sleep entered me like a thief who had been waiting all day to make his sweet, soft birth. A baby boy with braided hair came to me and I held and kissed him, and as we sat together on some stairs someone placed a pink rose on my right shoulder. My face bent towards its petals. Both little Savitri and the baby boy formed a circle around me and sang and danced so that I could fall asleep. The one was born and the other yet to be born and my fingers touched my ebony face.

It was the last two days of the play. I had gone to all of the auditions and seemed to have done well. All the cast was back in full swing and the momentum had been regained. I could feel the power of the final performances.

The last night arrived and we were all very nervous, sad, and excited. It was brilliant, without a single mistake or problem. At the end we got a long-standing ovation. People brought flowers and gave us each a bouquet. I saw both Smila and Shane in the audience. They sent me flying kisses. I did not acknowledge them. After finally leaving the stage, I dressed and came out. Much of the audience was still there, waiting to speak to us. Some approached me, a few of whom were directors and producers. They gave me their cards and told me to call them. It all felt comforting and warm. I thanked Smila and Shane again for helping in this journey. I remembered Prana and her words; they were always with me and in me. I asked Shane if he was still practicing Tantra. He cringed; he was uncomfortable.

"You are hurting me," he said.

"I did not mean to," I replied.

He implored me to have dinner with him. I did not reply.

Johann was waiting for the whole crew, as he had reserved a restaurant for us for one final celebration. I said good night to both of them and walked towards the group. Shane followed me and grabbed my hand. He took my face in his hands.

"You are beautiful," he said, "and I am so sorry that I lost you."

I said nothing, even though my tongue almost let herself go to a sarcastic remark, but it rolled off because that emotion had no place in my being.

I walked away in my green almost see-through dress, which I had worn in Taman asset when Tobias stole the pearl from my tongue and swallowed it in his mouth and given it back to me. This was my wedding love dress, the one that I wore whenever I got married to the wind, the rain, and the clouds and to poet men who would always be my lovers. I felt him tearing my clothes off hungrily in that bedroom in Santa Fe on that very lustful, painful night. I shook it off and walked into the eyes of Johann who had been watching us like a hawk.

"Now you are the jealous one," I told him teasingly.

"Very much so," he replied holding me around my waist.

I knew Shane was looking and I knew what he felt. *You hurt me so much Shane.* So much, I thought to myself. And the night began.

There was an excitement in the air. Everyone was jubilant and we praised each other's work. Many told me how strong I had been and how much I had helped them. I thanked them and acknowledged Johann as an amazing and sensitive director. We all stood up and applauded him and sang a toast to him. He said that he was saddened by the ending of the run but was already trying to get the play on the road since it had gotten so many rave reviews. We were all thrilled. He said that he had to return to Europe for a while but would like to stay in touch with the whole cast. We were all famished, and the waiter brought in a whole assortment of delicacies. Some of my beautiful colleagues asked me about my background and training, and they all wished me luck with the film. I was nervous and shared my feelings with them, but they assured me that they felt certain that I would do an excellent job. Everyone got emotional and lightheaded as we shared and exchanged numbers, and wished each other great things.

The night was clear and crisp, enveloping the atmosphere and I felt Johann's hand on my left thigh. It was warm and entered me like the sun slicing into water, and I was in a space of light which had no entry or exit. I travelled into the earth face of my Miguel and I was certain that he had sent this person to me so that I could touch him once again, here in this dry and wet physicality. I looked at him and whispered that I should leave since tomorrow was a huge day and I had to pack and get ready for the retreat, my very own personal one. He asked around if anyone needed anything else and then called for the check.

Suddenly, sadness filled the restaurant. We all felt the end of a very inspiring and unique experience. I knew that I had learnt so much from Johann's direction and from the expertise of some of the cast. Paying the bill, we all rose and spoke our final toast to him, and thanked him for his trust, support, and guidance. There were tears in many eyes as we said goodbye and went our separate ways. I walked out into the night where the goddess conceived of wind had laid a silver egg from which Eros, the golden winged god of love was born while Vishnu slept on the cosmic ocean during the all-encompassing night of nights. I inhaled the words of the Navajo depiction of night as being suspended in ebony space with a pensive moon, under a scattering of mist, while behind her a veiled sun reinforces her sovereignty in the wake of a vanished day. My metaphors are like fireflies roaming around in the sky of my mind. I don't have history in my words, just sliced tongues and sword piercings when the sacred prostitute holds the sacred mountain.

Johann took my hand and we walked together to my studio. "I will miss you," I told him swaying into his body like an ocean wave, which has no inhibitions or fears or doubts and just gushes forth with all its power into the shore. We stopped. He looked up at the sky which was sparkling with stars as the night was dark and the air was clear. He reached up as though to bring one down for me and placed it in my mouth as I lit up with the gold dust of star power, and we kissed and the remnants of all actions seemed to dissolve into us. He told me that he usually never got involved with any member of the cast he worked with and added that this time it was different. You brought me back to my own creativity and my own depths. I have no words to describe it but your femininity has a language of it's own. You truly are 'woman'. He held me very close and asked me what time I planned to leave the city.

"I have a car," he said, "I would be honored to drive you up there."

I was silent, and in my silence he quickly added that he was very aware that I needed my solitude. As my apartment building approached I felt that this would be a perfect start and ending and continuing of an ancient new encounter.

"Okay," I whispered.

Before reaching the entrance he stopped and held my everything. I felt the self-made pearl within me glowing luminously as it got ready to emerge from the wet solitude of its growth, just as I had discovered that pearl in my first oyster on that balmy sultry night in La Cuppole in Paris – my city of mistresses and love howls. We walked to the entrance and kissing my hands he told me that he would be there at 1pm to drive me. I knew this was the secret of our jewel. I felt like a water nymph, possessing his very being, giving him life, and taking it with me.

The doorman opened the archway-less door of my entrance and

as I glanced back Johann spread his eagle eyes around and in me, and I felt my invisible and visible ancestors taking me to my eternal source of life. I was strong and soft and walked into my studio with a very steady and sharp gaze. I was held by more than one desire and by more than one vision of delight and by more than one poet artist man.

There were many messages. Wolf Raven called and I was ecstatic to hear from him. I called him back and told him everything, as excited as a child. I felt the washed colors of the afterlife tracing our language of love. I told him I was off to my vision quest the next day, and that Johann had offered to drive me up there. He was happy. This is what I adored about him. He was so clean and so large, with no place for jealousy or doubt or negativity. He was my very own banyan tree of life. We spoke into the star-filled gold dust night and he told me to take care and that he would call me in a week when I returned. I asked about his mother. He got very quiet and said that she was not doing well and I knew that we were carried by our ancestors. I sent her the mountain of herbs carried by Hanuman and wished him goodnight. His whisper echoed in me and I felt my pearl moving inside of me. I searched for my little Savitri on both sides of me but this night she was not here. I was afraid.

Book Three:
Epiphany

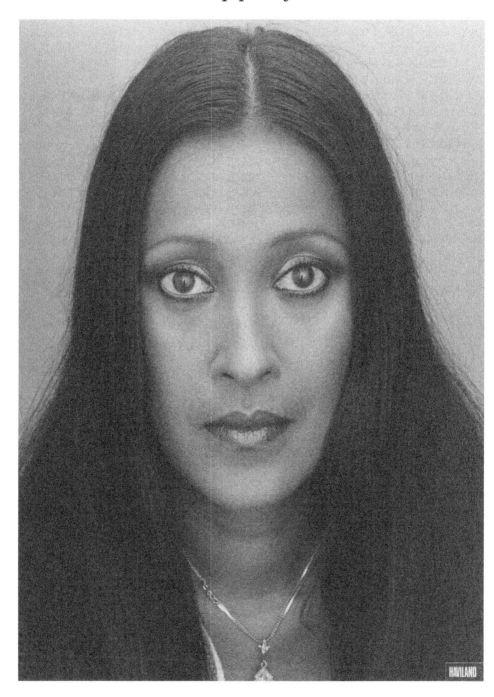

Chapter 19: I will always make love with poet men

The next day came in fast as though to hasten me on my journey into the unknown. The studio was filled with the residue of all things done and undone, and the notes of the bamboo flute streamed through the walls. Hironobu san had left a warm message and I called him before starting the day. He was happy and asked me how I had been. I told him everything, and I was going up to Woodstock. I mentioned that I had seen Shane and Smila and he said that Mr. Shane had called him and told him that. He said he was very happy and working for a wonderful French couple. "They have two little children," he added and I could hear the huge smile on his noble face. I told him that I would call him when I returned. I felt his green tea blessings as all the flower arrangements are based on the formation of nature, and every word that is written on a scroll of paper is perfectly balanced so as not to fly off. *His burning Hanuman tail will always dissolve all that belongs to the lesser nature, I thought.*

Leaving his voice, I took a shower and made some tea while I began packing a few things in a small bag, not forgetting to place the altar on the very top. I felt my mind cracking into my imagination as I picked up the script. I decided not to place it on top of the altar but to carry it separately, as though to maintain a distance from its energy. I made one last call to Aakash. He picked up; his voice was weak. He said that he had been very saddened by my silence. I replied that I had been working a lot and was leaving for a week to prepare for the next project. He asked me why I had distanced myself from him so much. I wished him well. He asked me again what had happened to what we had.

"I felt like what we shared did not grow," I said. "It was as if the roots left the stem and there was stagnation in the water."

"I am not well," he said without responding to my words.

"I know, but why did you not fight for who you stood for, why and why did you not defend what we shared with your family when they accused me of spoiling you?" I asked.

I looked at the time and knew I had to go.

"I will call you when I am back," I said and gently placed the receiver down.

I felt sad but I knew that in order for magic to reign the sword has to be kept sharp, clean and untainted.

The doorman rang the bell and informed me that Johann was waiting for me in the car. I walked out, making sure the windows were closed and everything was in order. All felt good: this move, this motion, this dance with the wolves, this stepping into a new reality. I saw the car and gasped. It was my favorite old sports Mercedes which I had always loved. It was silver, and had such an aesthetic melody to it. Johann stepped out and helped me with my little bag. Sliding in, I told him that I loved his car. He looked at me quietly and wrapping his arms around me whispered that he would miss me so much. We drove off and I un-wrapped my hair and it tumbled around my face like a waterfall in some warm, lush tropical country. He knew the way and we zoomed out of the city into the arms of the valley of the divine, green, winged beings.

My base chakra where the kundalini lies like a coiled serpent tingled as though there were going to be some sort of awakening, and I waited with excitement for the serpent to push through and uncoil my energy. Johann looked at me as though he too felt something. It was about a two and a half hour drive but we made it in two, and as we turned into the entrance of Woodstock, I felt the auras of the trees. They were inviting and I asked him to stop the car. I ran out and caressed the closest ones. They were my absolute and always warriors, my king spir-its, my stallions of stealth and motion and my beings that held the space between sky and earth. They were my masters of silence and nuanced bark. They were my ancient metaphors of agelessness.

We looked at the address where Matagiri was and found it easily. A room had been prepared for me and, greeting the people, we walked in. I let them know that it was only for one, as I saw them looking quizzically at us both. The room was quiet and surrounded by trees. It felt perfect. Johann agreed and after opening my altar and finding the right place for it he said that he would like to have a last breaking of bread with me before he headed back.

"Not last," I said to him passionately. "I will not let you go."

My freedom was as strong as my transparent bond, which was of light and growth and poetry, and I would always make love with poet men. Before he asked about it, I told him that I carry my altar wherever I go. "That is beautiful," he said.

We walked out into the land, and romance and mystery pierced through my skin. My quest had begun. I could feel it. I decided to walk him around before he left and told him all about how this place was born and about the two people who found it and dedicated it to the Mother who blessed it. "'Matagiri' means Mothers Mountain," I told him. He was very quiet as he looked at the books in the library and in the relic room. We entered the meditation room and sat down in front of the images of the Mother and Sri Aurobindo. I started to tell him about them, their yoga and my entry into this country. Glancing at me he said softly that I had come to the perfect place to rejuvenate and prepare myself. I felt Shi-va's presence and remembered something I had written some time back when I had felt his presence invade me. It was an article called 'crushed gold'. It was about the time when I had first come to New York and my feelings and experiences as I began this journey.

I stretched my legs and Johann noticed my feet again. He bent forward and ran his fingers across them, and my ancient being was alive once again.

"They are you," he said.

My toes bent and wriggled with glee. We stood up respectfully and putting on our shoes walked to the car.

"Take care of them, always," he said," they are your soul.

I knew of a special restaurant beside a stream called The Bear Café and we drove there. It was quiet. The food was excellent and the red was blood-like and fierce. The sound of the flowing stream over the body of the wet pebbles was magnificent. We took our time and relished each moment. I was sad and felt the valley of aloneness approaching me. It was scary, but I knew that every curve and imperfection in every tree bark would hold my space and the black raven that had flown by my creative window had picked up my shadows and flung them away into the air. Johann echoed my thoughts as though he saw my mind. "All will be fine," he said. "I will be in New York for about two or three weeks and I will see you when you are back." He made sure that I had his number and, leaving the restaurant, we drove back to the seclusion of my self-exile.

The little house was dark. I was the only one there. He walked in and turned on the tiny lamp near the bed. I lit my candle and incense, and we stood in the center of the room, in this abode in Krishna's forest near the River Ganges as his hands ran down my spine and my soul, and I could feel my invincible weapons, and the whole room drifted like a lotus leaf on the sacred river, and all the divisions were broken into one million and one glass pieces. He caressed my back. My spine walked out.

As Johann left I prepared for my first night in the forest. The mirror in the tiny bathroom was cracked. I liked this. I liked the crack in my face. It gave space for magic to walk in and explore the ancient alphabet of my secret languages and the alchemist's spirit that opened the doors of knowledge and gave birth to my poem. I undressed falteringly as though being watched by some other atmosphere or soul. The bed was cold and I looked for some extra blankets in the little closet next to it. Finding some, I placed them on top and entered quietly into the within and without of my inner world. I left the candle on as I was not familiar with the room and the red glow kept me company. The script was on the little table near the bed and, looking at it, I knew that I would begin rehearsing the following day as my hands shifted and turned the soil, scattering the seeds to allow space for another.

I was exhausted and welcomed my sleep with a longing embrace. The flame of the candle slowly died down and I walked into the realm of my ethereal senses. As I fell asleep I knew that I would have to repeatedly walk and move in the obvious circles until the entry to the inner chore was revealed to me.

The next day my eyes opened quite early. It was misty and mysterious outside. The trees were everywhere as though forming a circle around my little room. Their sturdiness and gentleness was magnificent and looking at them from the bed I felt like I was being transformed into one. I slowly got up and for the first time I could really see the room. It was not very clean, but there was a broom and napkins and I decided to take care of that myself. I hung the few things I had and, entering the bathroom, I took a coldish shower with my sandals on. Looking at the time, I put on something warm and, lacing up the Palladium boots, walked to the main area where there was a small breakfast. A place had been set up. I helped myself to some tea and toast. I was glad I was alone. I did not want to speak. Finishing the little meal and placing the dishes in the nearby sink, I walked out and entered the forest of bliss, script in hand.

I was in the garden here in this lush forest in Woodstock and between the elephant grass feather leaves in India with my dark handsome husband who was a poet man in his own right. As he drank the kohl from around my eyes I knew now why this magical country broke my soul apart. Walking in between these beautiful bark bodies, I remembered reading somewhere that alchemy made the tree a central symbol of its opus, because the tree depicted the nature of an intense inner life and development that follows its own laws, and can reveal the evergreen within an individual. As I found my own path, I thought of Savitri who against her parents' wishes traveled through the worlds on her golden chariot when she saw the prince, Satyavan. Stepping out of her chariot, she approached him and as they both looked at each other they knew that they were meant to be together.

I woke up in my room in India. It was in the middle of the night and hearing little Savitri crying, I ran to her baby crib. I picked her up and her small soft body was hot and wet with perspiration. Removing her clothes, I wiped her down with a cool cloth, as she slowly calmed down and looked up at me happily. I walked around the room with her in my arms. She slowly started to fall asleep. The night was dark and standing near the window I saw the sky on fire with the sparkling stars. I pulled her closer as her baby skin melted into mine, and the child in my dreams walked up to me, telling me I was beautiful. Only then did I know the power of that which is truly beautiful, and how large its hands are. I reluctantly placed her back in her little cot and walked back to my Indian bed. My husband was awake and softly asked me if she was alright. I said I was worried, as she still had a very high fever and was burning up. He held me and I could feel his concern. She had been sick for a long time now and even after taking many tests, the doctors could not find an explanation. The spider web was still broken. He saw me looking up.

I felt as if she had come to tell us something before leaving. A cold wind passed through me and I started crying in his arms. "Don't worry my goddess, my Devi, don't worry. I am with you," he soothed me.

Back in my Krishna wooden forest in upstate New York I spotted an open area where a fallen bark branch invited me to sit down. The energy was sharp and piercing and I knew that I needed to begin the script. I felt little Savitri's burning body in me and started to weep. Looking up at my trees I saw the sun, moon, and stars hanging from the branches and on another one I saw flowers and singing birds, the sign of a spiritual enlightenment. I could see clearly the integration of different forms of life and how the emerging of the imagination is essential in the symbolic process of growth. I was being shown all that I would need to go through to find my own inner wealth My tears fell silently on the leaves of the grass and the harmony of one solitary individual was there, tangible in front of my eagle eyes.

The pages of the script flew in front of me. I cried and read, and read and cried. And green fairies started to fly around me and I rose and followed one like the little girl who believed in their absolute reality in the film, Pan's Labyrinth. As I left the forest entry, I saw the little fairy disappear and, looking at my watch, realized that it was time for supper. I was hungry and remembered that I had forgotten to have lunch.

They were very strict about meal times. I saw dinner laid out for me. I loved this silent absence. I had some kind of soup and a salad. It was wholesome, and eating slowly, I was about to leave when a gentleman came in and asked me if everything was as I had expected. I thanked him and told him it was exactly as I had remembered when I was last there, and he mentioned that there was an extra car in the driveway, and if I needed to get things from the town I could use it. I was surprised and, feeling my excitement, he told me that the keys were always in the car.

I gathered my plates and, taking them to the sink, washed them and set them to dry. He said that was not necessary, but I insisted. Wishing me a good night he walked me to the door and I went to my room, stopping at the meditation room on the way. I felt enveloped by their presence and lit a stick of incense. The pearl rose in me as I wondered about the uncoiling of the serpent. *Maybe they are one and the same*, I thought. My spine stretched up and, on my head, once again, sat my wooden Ganesha, tickling me with his divine feet. My eyes closed into the silence of self and I travelled to the center of my very own mandala where the deity sits. I felt my artistic being becoming full and being painted in great detail with silver and gold. Rising and making sure the incense, was safe I sauntered to my solitary cave.

I washed my whole body, as if to purify myself from all that had to be left behind. I felt like a Zen monk in the beginning of her path. I hid

343

my sensual feline in a soft silk cloth and rested it aside to unfold a little later. I needed my male side now to cross this broken wooden bridge, step after step, yielding to my weight. My female and male, my yin and yang were balanced.

Picking up the script I continued where I had left off. The night walked in and I felt the forest whispers getting quieter as all the little living and breathing beings were also falling asleep. I read some more and then, putting the script down carefully, fell into a deep and heavy sleep.

Dawn walked in with its misty breathing once more, and after a quick shower, I decided to take the car and drive to the Tibetan monastery, which sat on top of a hill and hosted a magnificent golden life-size sitting Buddha. I wanted to sit in front of him and touch him and feel his huge almond eyes slice into me. I found the way easily and drove up the hill. It was just off Tinker Street, the main street in Woodstock. I loved this place, where the true bohemians still lived in and around the town and where many artists and musicians made their home. The car was a stick shift and I felt aligned to the moan of the engine as I changed gears.

The monastery was at the very top and in the center was the main house where the shrine was. Parking in the lot I walked to the entrance, hoping it wasn't closed. Artists perform rituals in the same way worshipers do and this was my ritual on that day. Removing my boots, I walked to the main hallway where there were a few devotees in meditation. Finding a quiet corner and a cushion, I sat on the very shiny, very clean wooden floor. The candles were all lit in front of the Buddha and the glows from the flames lit his golden body. He looked with compassion on humanity in its effort to achieve something more than just the ordinary. Looking at him with my whole eyes I saw birds fly out of his chest. It was the scene from Nostalgia, by Tarkovsky when the main actress of the film watched as one of the women worshippers in the cathedral opened the Madonna's chest and birds flew out, and it was right there, in front of my eyes. Suddenly I felt pulled, as though elongated into a bigger space. I could almost see his eyes and my inner mandala sparkled with this experience; and, right at that moment, I was certain that making art was about unique experiences, it was about feeling something greater than life, it was about invoking the unspeakable. Like the ritual dancers who danced themselves into the status of gods, artists too sought the opportunity to transform into another; and it was a dance that could never be taught, because it was a dance about unique and personal experiences.

As my mind was filled with thoughts of incredible and unspeakable realities, I suddenly felt formless. The eyes of the golden Buddha were shadowing mine, and looking down I knew I was in flight. I was reminded of the first scene in Fellini's film 8½ when a man breaks open the car window in the midst of traffic and flies above and into the sky. His foot has a rope tied to it, and so I wondered who was holding me down. Right then a pack of wolves appeared with a silver weaved rope held in their fierce jaws and they looked up at me and in the language of the howl let me know that they would not let me go yet. In a strange way I felt relieved. Then with a bump I landed back on the green Zen cushion. I looked around shyly to see if anyone had noticed my flight and my landing. But they were all in deep meditation, eyes closed. I thanked the golden Buddha and got up and walked towards the exit, stopping to get some grains of rice. Lacing up my boots and placing five grains carefully in my green bulging wallet, held by a green rubber band, I walked up and looked at the sky, knowing that I had touched the clouds and was one with Ganesha and his all-seeing eye. He is the mighty one, the one who treads the earth with such elegance and grace and who never misses anything or anyone and I felt his wet trunk, like in a dream I had once had where he placed some coins within my palm. I felt the wet interiors of a magnificent vision and I knew those coins would be my birthright and my future abundance. It was a sign of what was to come, and his beautiful wrinkled cloud body was always in a state of absolute bliss.

As I walked towards the car, one of the grains fell back onto my hand again. And in it the whole universe was given to me.

I was in India. In the kitchen lunch was about to be prepared. The same grain of rice fell onto my feet. I gave it to my Savitri, who was now always with me. She was my bigger self in a baby body. We decided to go to the temple. It had been a long time since our last visit. I wanted to see her, my toothless warrior beggar.

As we approached the sacred building, there she was, with her torn white sari, her golden cloak. I bowed in front of her and touched her all-knowing hands. Holding the little one in my arms, we sat to receive her blessings; and she smiled, and, opening her toothless mouth, showed me once again all that there was to see in the white light that flowed out of her.

I walked to the little car outside the temple and noticed something sparkling in the field across from the monastery. Reminded of that similar scene back in Central Park, I decided to walk over to the spot. I needed to step across a kind of a barrier. But I didn't see any foreboding signs. I crossed the threshold and, walking through the trees, saw the open area and looked for the little sparkle. But it wasn't there anymore. It had just been a sign for me to enter, and butterflies rested on my eyelids as little sparrows nestled on my lips. The sun was streaming through the trees warming the cool day, and finding a sun-drenched spot, I sat down.

A rustle awoke me. I looked around and the same pack of wolves that had held me to earth were running through the trees with their eyes glistening in the sun and eating the light. I knew Niyol was among them. I had not seen him for so long, and the Navajo and the Sioux in me ached with his memory. I remembered walking here some time back with a husband. We were lost and were looking for an area, which we were told was a very sacred Native American spot. This was it. I was sure of it and that was why I had been guided there. Held in that awake space that I called "the child's gaze," where all is realized and manifested, I saw my Native American sage lady walking towards me, carrying her abalone shell with burning sage in it. I began to rise. But I felt heavy. I just couldn't move. I sat back down and closed my eyes.

I was back in the body of a tree, and I felt it swaying with me. The script was in front of me and I touched its pages, recalling my divine rider burning it into ashes. My hands were still. I felt all my lovers kissing them from near and from far and I knew that I would never wait for the ordinary, silly small ones, and that I would always and ever be open to the magician's haunting whistle, to the one who would always see the cracks on and in my face, and the one who would always touch the wild gaze of the artist mendicant who pulled the threads of his self, made brilliant by a pearl and a coiled snake tapestry of creativity.

I was being chiseled. I was being carved. I was being shaped. I was being molded. And the river body pushed her way into me, and all the carp with blue light glistening on their scales that swim against the stream brush passed me. I was still lying on the grass, unable to move. I was in my other world, my real world. The feathered mountain divided itself to reveal what was hidden within its dream body and all the birds flew over us in fluid formation defining some kind of wind victory and the sharks were alive and they would swallow all the guns and weapons so that the human race could finally understand the power of peace in its waking state. And **Durga** was on her tiger destroying all the demonic manifestations and when they began to overwhelm her, Kali was born from Durga's third eye and she with her blood-red sword slaughtered all ignorance and mediocrity and I sat here in this sacred grass spot and became the sword in her hand and felt the edge of my blade. I would be sliced into pieces of vermillion sand dunes where the feminine mystique would emerge with rust colored feet and walk the earth and henna the soil.

My feet tingled and my eyes opened. I had just had a vision quest. I stood up, holding on to my tree that was now erect. I was walking towards the parking lot when a group of people who belonged to the monastery shouted that I was on forbidden land and that I was trespassing. "Too late," I whispered, as I placed my foot across the boundary with a very wide stride so my legs opened to move away from the so-called no man's land where I had seen the invisible. They followed me with disapproving looks as I approached the little car and they reprimanded me for being disrespectful to their property. Very loudly, I told them that land cannot and does not belong to anyone and since that was clearly a sacred area, it could not be forbidden. "This is the very reason it is out of bounds," they replied with their angry and blind tones. Getting into the car, I heard them say that I was an intruder and an outsider. But they were the pure ones because they lived in a monastery, I thought.

I drove out of the parking lot furiously, knowing that I would not be welcome there anymore. I didn't care, because I knew that the golden one's eyes saw right through and he was laughing at their pathetic small-ness.

In the car my throat was parched and the sun settled inside my voice chakra. I drove down the winding road carefully. I had returned from a journey and I needed to fit into this tangible visibility. I thought of the World Trade Center in Manhattan which was built on a Native Amer-ican sacred burial ground. They had protested against the buildings but were ignored. *There will be many more burial grounds until the predators of the sacred realize the horrible result of defying the sacred law.*

I shivered and needed to stop the car for a bit. I took a huge breath. All this had been given to me and I couldn't stop crying. I didn't understand why this was happening. I felt the burning body of my little Savitri who was always telling me something and I knew that I had to be conscious and awake and aware to every sign and message given to me. I must listen to my intuitions or all would be lost. I was the oyster and the little car was my shell.

Starting the engine, I rolled down the hill slowly. It was a beau-tiful windy road surrounded by trees. I made a left at the junction at Tinker Street, remembering a store called Dharmaware behind which was a tiny little café with some snacks. Finding parking, I walked into the courtyard of the store and found the café open. It was small and cozy with organic homemade food. Ordering some mint tea and something sa-vory, I sat at a little table and got the script from my bag. Opening to the page where I had left off I was startled. It was the scene when the young girl begins her initiation by the master shaman, who shaves her hair. She surrenders completely to this journey of sacrifice and a lit interior. Her walkabout had begun. The same sensation of being lifted enveloped me and unconsciously my hands clung to the small, used wood table for an anchor. The girl behind the counter gave me a quizzical look and I shy-ly released my hands and continued reading. I felt absolutely aligned to the story and to her and could not believe how fortunate I was to get this role. And just at that moment, I heard the sound of galloping. I glanced out to see if there were some horses grazing but there were none and I knew that once again I had been given a sign. I walked through the pag-es. I had to finish the script in the next few days which were flying by.

The café was closing and, gathering my things, I walked to the car. The evening was getting cooler and I wrapped the shawl around my-self, Parking the car where I had originally found it I looked at the time and saw I had a few hours. I decided to walk through my forest and find my path in the sky. I found the spot where I had sat the previous day and, touching all the trunks and leaves, sat and breathed in the silence and the shadows.

Little Savitri was awake and smiling. I was happy and, lifting her from her little cot, carried her to our bed. Placing her on my knees, I rocked and tickled her, as she giggled and kicked her sweet, carved feet. Satyavan played with her and the three of us rejoiced and celebrated her smiling, dimpled divine face. The maid brought in the tray with tea and some special food for her. She was also happy to see her smiling. We bathed and oiled her and after my bath we sat in the balcony with the streaming sun. My mother-in-law seemed to be in a better mood and, though she was still not smiling, seemed relieved too that her little granddaughter was feeling better. My husband said goodbye to us, as he had to leave for work, and Savitri and I settled in comfortably on the large divan enjoying the sun and the birds and the dragonflies.

It was getting dark and I started to walk back to the center. I went to the meditation chamber and lit some incense, and placing the script in front of me, melted into the stillness of the room and knew that psychologists approached the soul from without and the poet from within and the path I had chosen was a solitary expedition into unknown lands, where logic and reason had very little place. I had a baby tiger and a flying dragon in the inner chambers of my mind. They flew to me when I ask them to. Temple bells were ringing somewhere. I looked around, very aware that I was not in India. But then again maybe I was.

In the dining area I sat at my place and had what had been laid on the table for me. I had placed my red soma blood in a golden urn for a while.

After the small meal I washed my dishes and headed back to my room. The lamp had been lit near my bed and I wondered who had been there. I noticed that both the bedroom and bathroom had been cleaned, even though I had never complained or mentioned anything. It felt better and I knew I would sleep well. Night became me and I loved her starry drapes and her floating visions and her sightful dreams that she has always brought to me. My eyes closed and a white Ganesha entered with a red rose and a true warrior must recover all that is beauty. I woke up to a loud thud and fumbling for the switch on the little lamp, I turned it on. The script had fallen on the wooden floor. It felt as though someone had pushed it. Turning off the lamp, I tried to go back when I was awakened again by a presence.

My India husband and I were asleep when my eyes shouted open. I saw two eyes at the windowsill against the very dark night. The owl that I had seen there before was there again. Near the little one's cot was a figure bending over her. I jumped off the bed and ran to her. It was my mother-in-law holding my baby and scolding me because Savitri had been crying and I did not hear her and instead had been carelessly just sleeping. I tried to take her from my mother-in-law but she resisted. My husband was now beside us and asked what was going on. His mother said that she was awoken by Savitri's crying and rushed into the room. The little one was very hot and he took her from his mother's reluctant arms. She left angrily, looking at our bed in disgust as she walked out. The air was sick with her bitterness and her hopeless hatred towards me. The soul had flown away, afraid to reside in such a hollow shell. We took the little one to the bed with us and she fell asleep happily in between us. He got up again and locked the bedroom door, angered by his mother's intrusion. He looked at me sadly and I felt his pain. Taking me in his arms with the little one in the middle, he kissed my face and said how sorry he was that his mother didn't understand me.

The dawn dream entered the room and, lifting it up, I decided to arise even though it was very early. This day was going to be strange. I thought I saw an owl on the tiny windowsill. I looked again and it was gone. Something was going to happen. I showered and glanced at my reflection in the cracked glass and remembered the openings for the river body to flow in and I saw a beautiful black bird fly across the window outside. *May the invisible always be beside me and may the visible be fleshed with the full moons of every life and may the rain and fire and morning dewdrops breathe a constant presence for the red rose petals that swim on my snake tongue and may my lovers feel all of me. My skin is the flavor of my soul and sits perched on the shiny silky neem oil's surface of cells and birds and blue horizons where the muse of the harvests dwells.*

I was famished and hoped that breakfast was ready. I walked in very quietly and sat down. The toast was slightly burnt just as I loved it, and the tea was dark and perfect. I ate a lot and enjoyed each bit. The person in charge came in and wished me a good morning, asking me how I was. I replied it had been a very important few days. He asked me how much longer I would be there and realized that I only had few more days left. I asked him if I could leave it open and he said that would be fine. He wished me a good day and. noticed how hungry I was. "It is the air," he said as he walked out.

In one corner of the room there was a little alcove with a statue of a Buddha. It had a lotus on top of his head. The sun was falling right on his face and I felt as though I might rise up but the toast and the tea were my anchors this morning. I took care of the dishes and decided to go to the library to continue with the script. I was close to the end and I had read every page very slowly, absorbing all. Her head had been shaved and my hands went to my energy strands and I felt a pang inside me and knew it was going to be a huge sacrifice I mused at the shape of my head, which could be a vessel of transformation and wholeness and where seeds of new and eternal life would be planted.

I remembered reading somewhere that ancient peoples believed that reason and mind resided in the heart and chest while the head contained psyche and the fertile essence of an incorruptible life. Dusk was entering night, and I realized how long I had been sitting there. I had a few pages left and decided to go for a long walk. I saw a *yoni* tree, slit and long and elegant and strong. The leaving sun touched the curves and hollows of the tree, and I knew that my words would come from other realms and that I would marry one more time when the sky and earth met and my youth would sing forever and I would love and make love and I would be touched and tongue-spoilt because I was learning to be alone and here was another victory.

The dusk was wet and soft and wrapped herself all around this little wild orchid forest of my solitude. I felt the strings of my body being tightened and tuned and I was certain that when I would play their notes they would be in a perfect key. Something or someone touched me with a sophisticated sensual sound and I wondered who was sending me these remembrances. My mind felt feathered and wild and the sacred owl's eyes floated into my inner chamber and I knew that she was here to tell me something wise and true.

It was getting dark as Shiva danced all into being and with his feet thundering inside my heart and mind I felt their echo. I suddenly realized that I had left the script on the ground and rushed back to get it. The slight wind had opened the pages. It was exactly the place where the shaman removes her hair. I couldn't stop crying. It was a wolf howl and it screamed through the forest, and it was a string of pearls around my neck. They were my precious jewels and my silent warriors of release, and cleansing and filled me with the nectar of human compassion. I was relieved. My amber raindrops had stained the page. I felt the urgency to find the clear path. A full and heavy force pushed me out of the forest and I stepped into the clearing.

Back in the center I spent some time in the meditation room and placed the script near the altar. I lit the candle and an incense stick and watched the spiraling smoke merging the material and nonmaterial realms of being. I sat up straight, as though being pulled by some invisible strings and felt my back opening as though the coiled snake was beginning to move and uncoil. Everything was shaking inside. The earthquake had entered me. Even the bones in me felt warm and lit and flower-filled. The eyes of the snake pierced through the centers and I knew that my galloping stallion would return with the narrative of life because it was his.

I picked up the script from the serpent's uncoiled head and completed the last few pages. The main character took them through the cave of knowing and walked them through the realms of the unknown, as they followed obediently. They had entered the threshold and then each one would return alone with the gifts given to them. But their guide never returned. Sadness filled me and rivers rained down my eyes. She was the selfless guide taking people to find their way and she sacrificed herself while doing this. My back opened even wider as I moved towards the wall to protect any false entry. I put the script down, hands trembling, and hoped nothing would go wrong with this project.

I walked on the pebbles outside, feeling each round body stone as I carried my boots in my hands. They were cold but my feet needed to touch the earth. Back in the dining room, there was a candle on the table near my plate and a little note instructing me to help myself. It was a simple Indian meal and the time was so right for this. I had ached for the smell and taste of my land and loved each bite. The lentils were soft and pungent and the rice grains were my wedding song.

In the ornate Indian house dinner was being served. It was just the three of us, with little Savitri in my lap as I fed her some of the soft rice. She loved it. We were served and the food was delicious. My mother-in-law did not look at me and I humbly finished what was placed on my plate. After the meal my husband suggested a little walk in the gardens and the three of us entered the gentle India night. He walked towards the jasmine bushes and picking some flowers weaved them into my hair. The little one giggled as she too inhaled the scent of this eternal flower of grace and fragrance. I could feel my mother-in-law's eyes piercing my back and I walked in front of him to avoid any shadow-sounds from entering.

The candlelight was falling on the Buddha statue in the quaint musty Woodstock room and I melted into his silence and his love. I sat at the table after finishing the meal and stayed there until the flame went out. Then, slowly clearing the table, I walked to my room. The bed was turned down and the lamp was lit. I lit another stick of incense on the altar and, as I turned, I noticed a red rose placed in a tiny glass tumbler on the table. Removing it, I took it to the altar near my bed. It was late and I felt exhausted and complete. I loved the script and was mad for the part. Changing and washing I lay down and Zen hands large and small entered me. I turned the lamp off and entered the axis of my horse dream language of an ancient vocabulary. All was silent and still, except for the night sounds as white sail boats floated by in the river of the jeweled muse and the tribal warrior was slicing the reflection of the sickle moon with his spear.

I fell into a deep and silent restful sleep and wandered into the twilight of fearlessness. My armor had been left behind sitting silently on the rugged wooden half-carpeted floor awaiting my return from the other space where the feathers of the winged beings trace the shades of my dreamscapes. Suddenly an antelope poked me with his horns and I felt a body beside me violently trying to rape me. I tried to wake up but didn't' seem to be able to. I heard myself screaming for help to anyone and was struggling with this flesh body that was attempting forcefully and crudely to violate me. Still in a semi-dream state I vaguely saw who this being was and, with a shock, realized that it was the Mexican director, except now he could see and his eyes were burning through me wildly and violently. I jumped up and turned the little lamp on. I looked around to see any signs or remnants of this visitation and only noticed the wrinkled sheets from my struggle and the fallen pillows. I was completely wet and, slightly unbalanced, decided to get out of the bed to get a glass of water. Looking at the filled tumbler I noticed with a start that it was slightly murky, like that very first time in South Hampton. I shivered and, lying down left the lamp on. Going to the bathroom, I emptied the glass and filled it again with the running water. This time it was clear and I drank it all in one whole gulp. Filling it up once again, I lit the candle and incense and lay down. I took deep breaths and felt the galloping horse hoofs all over me. Their feet were leaving marks on my skin and I knew that the sacrifice had begun.

All would be burnt and I would be homeless and in exile in the forest, away from the laughter of outsiders, away from earth sounds and the cries of waste-land plastics, where there would be broken and unbroken formations which would lead me to the body of the work that would be given to me to manifest.

I lay very still in this tree house. It felt as if it was perched on top of the trees, and the trunks grew inside this little room. I could not move and decided to stay motionless for a while, until the butterfly was ready to emerge. I fell into a light sleep for the rest of the night.

Waking up the following morning, I had a long warm shower. The water was healing.. I put on something warm and strong and laced up my Palladium boots that Anthony had polished and nurtured and I walked to the dining area. The manager was having some tea. Greeting him warmly, happy to see another presence, I sat at my regular place. He served me some of the hot tea and prepared the toast. I wondered why he was here this morning since he had never been there before.

After we finished I told him that I needed to leave today. He looked up a little surprised and asked me how I planned to get back to the city. Remembering Johann's sincere offer to call him if I needed anything I decided against that and asked if I could take a bus back. He looked for the timetable and gave me all the times. I chose the early afternoon one, as I would have liked to take one more walk around before I left. We decided on the time and he offered to give me a ride to the stop. Thanking him, I asked him to give me the bill so that I could take care of it. He said he had enjoyed me being there. "Me too," I whispered, adding that I would come back again. He smiled and gave me a receipt and a little blessing package from the hands of the divine Mother. It walked right into my green, ever-bulging, struggling to burst open wallet of many, many years. I stood next to the Buddha statue and gently passed my fingertips over him. I walked to the meditation room and lighting an incense stick sat down to absorb all the power and energy of their presence. The night had exhausted me and fear tried to push into me. I fought it with the curling smoke of the incense and pulled the armor tighter to me.

After a long silence, I walked to the woods and touched every single bark body as my own. The mist had left the trees but the grass was still moist and fresh. There was a gentle aroma in the air and the birds sang in tune with this fragrance. Finding my bark place I sat down, feeling the damp moisture seeping through me as though to cleanse everything.

I thought of the scene from the Greek director Theo Angelopoulos's brilliant film *Landscape in the Mist* where Voula, the 12-year-old protagonist of the film, after being violated and raped by a truck driver, sat alone near the ocean waves as it washed over and in her. Her blood-stained hands had marked a tree inside the truck wall and I felt its formation as my red hands stroked the rough bark that I was sitting on. Absorbing all that I could and, running my fingers over the swaying grass leaves, I ringed the fear cloth that had floated in and squeezed every bloody drop from this false presence that invaded to lessen and weaken and rob us of all belief and trust. I wished that She, my divine horse rider, would slaughter it without any hesitation, like a demon in need of annihilation. This all-time monster of greed and lust that never stops trying to steal our beauty and our truths. I knew my strength was shy and had been attacked and the last words of the Mexican director, 'you belong to me now', stood right in front of my eyes as the pine needles pricked my skin and blood drops trickled on the body of the green grass. Prana had told me to be careful but I did not know how I could be.

Wrapping myself with the forest wishes, I stood up and slowly left my soft and gentle sanctuary where the exile was coming to an end. The clearing was sunny, and walking to the room I gathered my bag and looked around to make sure that I had everything. I made the bed as my hands trembled and decided to leave the still very awake rose on the little table near the bed. I walked to the bathroom and glanced once more at my cracked reflection as my fingers slid through the crevices in the glass and my skin. I closed the door and walked to the driveway where the manager was already in the car.

He got out and, placing the bag in the back, opened the door for me. We drove through another windy, woody Woodstock road and he told me a little about the area. I replied by telling him a little about the script and the reason why I needed to prepare for this project. He wished me well as we approached the bus stop. He walked me to the enclave where there was a wooden bench and, thanking him, I told him that he did not need to wait. He left wishing me goodbye and my eyes wandered to the stream across the road. The murmur was musical and melodious and, leaving my bag in a corner of the shelter, I ran across to get a glimpse of the flowing water. It was healing and transforming, and I wanted to touch its liquid body but right at that moment I heard the bus approaching and ran back.

In the bus there were a few gentle people. I walked where there was a row of empty seats and took my place near the window. Settling down I closed my eyes. The bus started with a slight jerk and looking out I noticed that we were not on the highway. It was a local bus and it would take longer, but the route was lush and green. We made many stops and people walked in and out, but I was always left alone in the back. I was thankful as I once more shut my eyes and breathed in the feeling of the last days.

I am in a hut in some unidentified place covered in mud. A man and a woman are there and when I enter they start to smear the mud all over and around me. I sink into this wet, cool earth and just then everything turns into gold and I sit in this brilliant, warm glow. And then right at this point my brilliant, jeweled bird muse flies in and picks me up and places me on her feather back, as my hands reach out to make sure the red ruby is safe on her third eye. It is, and it is round and whole and transparent. Perched on her back I see Krishna destroying all the demons around him as he rises triumphant on the head of the ocean serpent. We fly, my bird and I, as I feel her feathers becoming one on my back as though she is giving me her wings to fly with; and just then the warrior with his sickle moon slaying spear appears and flies with us and we are the warriors of the air and they want me to eat back the strength that was stolen from me. I feel the sharp poke. It is Garuda with the soma held in his magnificent beak.

I looked out of the window and there galloping alongside me was my divine rider on her shining, smooth black stallion. His limbs were like flames of fire and his muscles rippled like the River Ganges rolling down Shiva's locks of hair. His eyes pierced the horizon as his rider draped his back with her dark, black, flowing robe. He seemed to be keeping up with the speed of the rolling bus and rode alongside it. I saw her hand touch his mane. It was that magnificent hand that showed me the way when I had fallen on that desert dune on the edge of New Mexico and Colorado. Her fingers were silver clad and they caught the sunbeams that reflected the hidden and shaded silhouette of the new moon. And then as though from nowhere in her hand was the very same lotus flower that was in front of my eyes on that barren, rippling, nuanced body of sand. The stallion and she came closer to the side of the bus as though on purpose.

I looked around to see if any of the other passengers were witnessing what I was. But they were either sleeping or reading and were unaware of all of this. And I could almost touch this enlightened flesh. My hands tried to open the window but they were of course sealed and my red henna palm stayed on the glass panel wanting to touch them so badly. They had never been so close. And then I saw her head turning and my breath left me. I sat back absolutely still as her hooded visage kept turning and then, as though sunflowers had eyes of diamonds, she revealed to me her face. The script which had been perched on my lap fell on the floor of the bus with a thud and an artist was painting my interior with an indigo blue color and the thunder of the spirit hunter was here, right in front of my eyes, and here looking straight into my cracked rivers was no other than the divine Goddess Kali. I fell from the seat of the bus on my knees hands clasped. Some passengers looked back but I paid them no mind. She had shown me her face, today of all days, and the silk basements of veiled tarnished days would be slaughtered and broken and destroyed. There would be no time for niceness or trivialities. This would be a war of blood, swords, and wounding arrows. This was the beginning and she had come to tell me so.

In India, I was walking to the temple, her temple. My beggar saint was sitting there smiling as I approached. The priest nodded as he chanted to the Kali image during the evening puja. She was lit and, as I walked into her eyes, she moved and I heard the galloping stallion on the earth. The lady smiled and told me that I had been given a sign and that I must be strong and ready for what was to come. The priest gave me the blessings of fruit and flowers and bowing to both of them I walked away like a child who had just seen its own birth and transformation.

On the bus, my hands shaking, I ate the blessed fruit, only to realize that my hands were empty. "But they are not," I whispered to myself and placed the invisible blessing in my mouth and a ball of light floated by me and I knew it had been sent from my beggar, brilliant, temple-body, lady saint.

We arrived in Manhattan. The Port Authority was teeming with people rushing, pushing, and shouting impatiently. I stepped down as though in slow motion, in a daze. Nothing and no one affected me. I had seen Her. Taking my little red leather bag and carrying the script in my left hand, I decided to walk down to the studio. It was not that cold and I wanted to feel the concrete pavement and remember the touch of it when I had walked on the wet surface, bare feet with a barren belly many moons ago. I noticed the steaming manholes and smiling stepped on one, not burning my feet this time but feeling the heat. The cries of those who had been slaughtered at wounded knee echoed in my mind as I walked with all of the warrior tribes to regain what belonged to them and to remind mankind that money could not be eaten and that land could not be owned and all is in harmony with the law of nature.

I decided to walk down on the West Side next to the Hudson River and hear its ripples speak to me. I wanted to continue my nature marriage and stay within her balance and feel beauty in front, behind, above, and all over me. It worked and my stride shifted to a very slow and aware pace. It was a beautiful sun-drenched day, and the sun settled on the water and some of the rays reflected off the moving liquid expanse. The week up in Woodstock was still alive in me and it was hard to come back. I felt alone and this solitude was not the same. I desperately called to the hunter spirit of this island. I wanted to see her and feel her protecting wings around me right now. I had entered an altered state and everything felt different. All I could hear were the galloping horse hoofs and all I could see was that beatific face.

And there, once again, in the distance she emerged from the river sword-first, like the sword in *Excalibur*, except this one is the sword of all swords and I know that she was everywhere as my fingertips touched the flowing water and the nails fell on the belly of the wet whale. All songs seemed sung before and stale human dust would be bladed away as the goddess Kali's red tongue drips with fresh, conquered blood and the river was now a stunning red. Bending down I unlaced my Palladium boots and with my red feet echoing the color of the river I ran down the rest of the way.

My footsteps left red marks on the concrete and I was certain that all the sati brides would arise from the burning ashes of the flames that they had jumped into to follow their husbands and claim once again what it was to be the birth of the feminine revolution and grace would be alive and well again. I became the horse and the sacred tail was behind me and my neck was elongated into the black stallion head spliced by red arrow drawings of longing women by my artist friend. And a very brown, beautiful woman walked towards me as I galloped with my horse hooves down this hardened surface and gave me what looked like cowry shells to put in my lemon morning water as she pulled my cheeks and shouted that I would get all that I wished for and that patience was the gift of the gods and the hardest to hold in the body.

My pace slowed down and my feet were cold but I wanted to stay in my bare feet. And in a dream a young girl takes Kali postures and stands very tall above me. When she holds the second pose she falls into a valley and is hurt. I help her and lift her dark feet and she becomes a child as she draws a goddess yantra with chili peppers through a glass window.

I noticed I was very close to my studio and, sitting on a bench, put my boots back on and walked across town towards the building. There would be many messages for me and one would be from Mexico. I knew that. I shivered and pulled the shawl tightly around me. Before approaching the door, I carefully removed the wings given to me by my ruby

356

red muse bird and hid them under the wedding shawl, and even though they were visible only to me, I made sure that no strange, prying eyes could see them.

My friend Reynaldo was at the door. He was happy to see me and told me that there were some things for me. He brought in a beautiful bouquet of flowers I knew were from my wolf and some packages and large envelopes that did not fit in the mailbox. I collected everything and thanked him. He said that I looked different. "I feel different," I said, anxious to step into my studio. The elevator door opened and out stepped that same mysterious little girl with braces. She looked like someone from one of my dreams. She, too, smiled and wanted to hug me but restrained herself because the lady accompanying her didn't seem very encouraging or warm.

It always felt like a long walk to the studio from the elevator and today it really was. The key happily slid in and I opened the door gently. My invisible friends were happy to see me and I them. Unlacing my Palladium boots, and placing them very carefully against the wall, I unpacked my bag, and placed the altar on its table. Some of the clothes needed to be washed and I piled everything aside in the laundry basket. My hands ran to dial the phone but I stopped. Something told me to take a bath before. I unfurled the wings and placed them in a corner, which glowed and became my very own hot spot. I smiled and ran the water. I missed the cracked mirror in the Woodstock bathroom. It reflected the imperfections of reality and reminded us that Only when the mask of falseness and superficiality is removed will man remember his true visage because if he forgets, it will dissolve into him and he will become his façade andall will be lost.

My hand traveled to my face to make sure there was no artificial skin laced to my skin soul. Undressing luxuriously and feeling every caress from my clothes, I watched them fall on the tile floor. I fell gently into the full liquid as it enveloped each corner and curve of a voluptuous abundance given and gifted to me by my beloved ancestors of noble birth and beginnings. I thought of Ondine and her water birth and felt her presence sinking into mine. It felt good to be back in my own space. Leaving the water, I decided to stay in this evening and feel all that had transpired. Putting on something light and fresh and lighting the candle I placed the flowers in a large bold chiseled vase. They were twelve red magnificent roses, and they had a heady fragrance. I gently unpeeled one petal and placed it on my tongue. It melted into me with all its superior and high vibrations.

Lying down, I listened to the messages. I was nervous. The first two were from little man. He asked me to call back as soon as possible. Wolf Raven had left many lush and warm messages and Johann had said that he was leaving very soon and hoped I was back from Woodstock and

357

that he had to see me before his departure. I wanted to see him, as well. Prana called from London on her way to Rome and then Africa. She said that she would be back in a few days. She sounded different, as though she was closer to me in a physical way. I now knew that there was a reason for her slight distance: I had to learn. She was a strong and powerful teacher. Aakash had left a sad message and I decided to call him that very evening. It was time. I must restore and find this friendship, which maybe could be saved. It was beautiful and people could change. I will try to give him my own growth or atleast help him see his. Lying on a rocky surface, hands in a pool of water I looked up to see the sky and my hand held one single cloud. Some producers and agents had left messages, as well, but I might have missed the auditions. I would contact them all in the morning anyway.

I dialed Mexico first, and a little voice answered in Spanish. He was thrilled to hear my voice and said that they should be in the city in a couple of days, and that his father wanted to speak to me. I asked him if something was wrong. There was a hesitation in his voice and then he just said that his father had to see me again. Very boldly, I asked him if his father had changed his mind about the part. There was another silence, at which point another voice came on the phone. It was the father who gruffly said that it was very important for him to see me as soon as they were back. I began to tell him that I had been away for almost a week preparing for the part, but he just handed the phone back to his son without even letting me complete the sentence. I could tell that his son was not free to speak openly, and just said that he would call me as soon as they arrived in New York, which would be in two days or so. Everything shook inside me and the mountain erupted and the hot lava began to roll down and burn me. My hands were trembling.

The phone rang and I was thrilled to hear Raven's voice. I started to weep and told him about the call. He was quiet and asked how my retreat was. "It was amazing." I described everything in detail. His voice embraced me and I fell into his liquid and sensuous gaze.

"I want you," I said with a trembling voice. He spoke lovingly, with an intelligence that pierced my skin and I knew that it was time to unfold my soft, throbbing, eternal, sensual that I had kept aside in a very silk cloth. It felt richer and stronger and softer and alive. It had grown. I had grown, and the red soma had also entered me full-bodied and dry like an aged forest bark with all its transformations soaked into its blood liquid. I would sip this warm glow and it would make me mad and I longed for its wild entry. "I am with you," he said softly. I told him that something was wrong and then revealed the night's visitation.

"I like his films but I never liked him," he said. "In his arrogance he is a master game player and a manipulator."

"The part is amazing," I said, "and it is almost written for me."

Ulfhrafn was helpless and, after a silence, said that because he could not work due to his mother's illness he might have to travel to make up in the next months. My heart ached. The flowers had left my bones. He added that his mother was not doing well but that he had to leave. We were both sad and felt the weight of the dead horse as the women throw drops of water on his every orifice to purify his life breath so that all of him could be magnified – his breath, his sight, his hearing and his voice. My voice felt feeble, as though the power had left it. I told Ulfhrafn that the roses were spectacular and that one petal was melting on my tongue.

"Give it to me," he said. And I sliced his delicious body with the sharpened edge of the red petal on my snake-coiled and uncoiled tongue.

Even the pearl floating inside me throbbed and vibrated as I dissolved into his deep, dark, wet absolute sensuality.

"Don't worry," he said as he kissed me and swallowed the petal from my tongue. "You are Sekhmet, the lioness-like cat goddess. You will cleanse and burn all decadence with your fire sparks." All was moist and youthful and alive as I hung up the phone.

I asked my husband if I could visit Kali's temple in Calcutta. He hesitated because he knew what had happened to me the last time I had gone there. I told him that I had to go and that it was very important for all of us. He said that he would agree only if the maid would go with me. I nodded and he made arrangements for the car to pick me up. "Don't tell your mother," I whispered in his ears. I would have liked to take my baby girl with me, but she was not well enough. He said that he would take care of her while I was away.

I left quietly, making sure the ogre did not notice my departure. Gauri was already in the car and looked back to make sure that no one had noticed us. We left the driveway and headed for the city. It was crowded and mad with noise and traffic. I recalled the time when we were returning with the little one from the doctor's office and the image of the goddess that was being carried to be immersed in the Ganges fell on the car and her head almost entered the car. We ambled through the streets and I hoped my mother-in-law would not notice our absence. The car stopped, pushed by a huge crowd of people singing a song that I was very familiar with – the song sung when somebody passes. And there in front of us once again a huge procession appeared, carrying a garlanded pyre with someone who had just left this mortal world. My heart missed a beat and my hand traveled to Gauri's as she gave it a strong squeeze. The driver once again told us that it was good luck. I asked him to hurry up but he could not, so I leaned back and waited.

We finally arrived at the entrance of the temple. As usual, it was filled with people and sacrifices and blood, and everything came back to me. I was afraid to get out of the car and I looked at Gauri. She nodded and we both got out together. I asked the driver to stay close to the temple. Gauri was very close to me as though anticipating the same thing to happen again, but we both knew why we were here. At the entrance a lady in white came to us and looking at me very intensely told me that I would help the women of the world one day and it would be huge. I looked at her puzzled and didn't know what she meant. We walked inside the grounds of the temple, careful not to step on all the remnants of sacrifices which were on the floor. And there was the image. I began to shake and tremble and fell down but this time I was still conscious. The priest was singing his prayers when he turned and noticed me. It seemed like he was the same one who I had seen when I had come before. He beckoned me to get closer. I did, as Gauri held me and he gave me some of the offerings and whispered something in my ear. I got up with her help and, trembling, we walked to the car. No one said anything and this time the driver decided to take a route through the outskirts of the city that made it quicker to get back.

He parked away from the house and, getting out of the car, we pretended we had just gone for a walk in the gardens. I saw my mother-in-law in the distance looking for us and as we got closer she demanded to know where we had been. I told her that we had gone for a long walk, as I needed some air. "Your child needs you," she said angrily. Noticing us, Satyavan ran out of the house and after my mother in law walked away we told him what had happened. Gauri assured him that I had not passed out, and I told him what the priest had said. He had asked me if I breastfed my child and if not I should begin immediately. I was baffled and didn't understand how he even knew that I had a child. "They know," my husband said, "especially the ones who truly see."

He seemed happy because he had always wanted me to, but my mother-in-law had forbidden it, giving some stupid superstitious reason. She thought the child would be contaminated by my brown skin. I told him that the priest had also told me that if I had fed her from the beginning she would not be sick now. *How did he know?* I thought again.

Wounded and damaged in this precious protected and secure cage by superstition, prejudice, and empty rituals, everything I did was wrong because I was not of the desired hue and because my skin was sunburnt and because I loved the breath of art and dreams and because I had given birth to a little goddess. I was not surprised that she was sick. Why would she not be? It had hurt me so deeply but I had followed the rules like a lost lamb in a strange herd of sheep where I knew I did not belong. But there was nothing I could do except fly away in my dreams.

We walked to the bedroom and he locked the door behind us. I washed and changed, and taking her very warm body unbuttoned my blouse as the sari fell off my shoulder and hoping I still had milk fed her. It was ecstatic and rejuvenating, and she giggled and kicked and didn't stop drinking. My husband shyly looked away and I took his hand and placed it on my other breast. The three of us were united and born again. I looked up and was sad that the web was still broken. I wondered where the spider was and why he or she was neglecting the web. Savitri fell asleep with her little mouth still on my breast and I slowly placed her back in her little cot. My husband took me in his arms and we lay down together as he pulled the sari from me and kissed me all over. His sandalwood jasmine mouth was now brave and bold, and I loved this new courage in my beloved man. I asked him if she would be okay. He said that he did not know, but that he would be by my side always and passion sang her sweet sultry melody and even Shiva and Parvathi paused in appreciation. And the eyes of the sacred cow walked in with their almond entry and the evening temple bells were louder than usual. We were suddenly interrupted by my mother-in-law's voice announcing that dinner was served. She was relentless in her ability to destroy our oneness.

My nipples felt tender. I decided to call Johann. He picked up and my silky basement was alive with windows again. "I just got back a few hours ago," I told him. He asked if we could have dinner the next day, as he was going to leave shortly.

"Tell me all when I see you," he said.

"I will," I replied.

I hung up the phone and dialed Aakash's number. He picked up immediately and hearing my voice did not stop crying. He said that he was very sick and I felt he was leaving. I didn't want to ask him what he had, but I thought I knew. We spoke for hours and he apologized for everything that had happened. I just listened and felt his gentle soul and realized that I too had missed what we shared. I told him of the script and how amazing it was. "But I am not certain if I will get the part," I added. In turn he told me that even though he didn't feel much better he wanted to be in the city to do some shots of me, but he was leaving for India for some special Ayurvedic treatment.

"When I am back I will come straight to New York," he said.

I asked him what the shoot was about and he mentioned some Indian bridal theme.

"Why me?" I asked.

"Because you would be perfect and unique."

"I left all that Aakash. I'm not that 'India' anymore," I said

"I know, that is exactly why you are perfect. I want that other look, or rather both looks in one; and you have them. I know I have changed but what we had and have can never die. I will email you from India and call you as soon as I know my plans. Please never forget me, Mrina."

I hadn't heard anyone call me that for a long time, and even though things were changed I was glad that we had picked up the threads and I was happy I had called him back. The sword of true compassion is never mediocre or sentimental. Hanging up the phone, I recalled Hironobu san's words, and I knew I had to be careful. My sleep was welcome and deep and peaceful that night.

Waking up in the morning light, I missed the misty trees and so watched the sun fall on the shiny surface of the concrete buildings instead. My altar breathed a new life and I smiled, knowing exactly why. Making a strong and hot cup of tea I started calling various agents and producers. Two of them mentioned that the auditions had been a few days ago. Others said that their projects had been cancelled. The photographer with the Domincan Republic project had left a message and I dialed his number. He said that it was still on hold and would let me know as soon as he heard more.

Since I had some time, I decided to do my laundry and went down to the basement. The elevator door opened and I missed not seeing my dream girl. Leaving the clothes in the washer, I checked my mail and then went back up to the studio. I was not centered today. I missed the forest and the silence, and felt alone and strange. I thought of the black Madonna and how she inspired Goethe to write the closing lines of *Faust*. It is not the divine element in woman but the divine as woman, and I wanted to wrap myself in the sky and feel all the forest shadows etching into my skin, carving their ancient wisdom on my nuanced surface. When the inner meets the outer the work is finally made.

The script was on the table and I started to pick it up but stopped. I would not look at it again until I knew what was to be. Just at that moment the phone rang. It was little man and he told me that they would be arriving late tonight and that his father wanted to see me the next day, with the script. He asked me to hold on as he spoke in Spanish, and then coming back, told me that I should be there early evening as his father wanted to invite me for dinner. It all felt strange and odd. There had been no mention of the check that was promised to me.

I went down to put the clothes in the dryer and just then, who should enter the laundry room but my little dream girl? She had a little basket in her hands and said "Hi." I asked her if she needed any help but soon realized that she knew exactly what and how to do it all. I was surprised to see her alone and asked her where her mother was. She said that she was upstairs, not feeling too well. We didn't say much but we both felt comfortable in the other's presence.

"Are you an artist?" she asked. "Did you see the fairies in the forest?"

Startled, I looked at her wondering how she had known that I was in the forest. She simply smiled and I knew that she knew.

362

"Yes," I replied.

We were playing in the circle made by the blue-bodied people as they dance around the white sparkling tree of life and as she and I left the circle and touched the tree. She had no braces there.

She smiled and, finishing everything, left the room. My eyes followed her as she turned and waved at me. I sat in the lobby waiting for the dryer cycle to end. My journal was with me and I started to write about everything that had happened in the last days. Folding the dry clothes and placing them in the basket, I went back upstairs. I thought of the girl. She was like a solitary star with her two shining, bright eyes. Little children and their gaze of magnificence is like a breath of fresh air.. Opening the door to the studio, I saw the red flashing light on the machine and listened to the messages. Johann called to ask what time and where we should meet. We decided on seven and I felt armed with invisible baby bodies of love. It would be a special night and I needed to see him and a little child crawled towards me and kissed me on my mouth and giggled with joy.

I dressed carefully and decided to wear the magic green one. The kohl flew around my eyes and the gold dusted my lips and I knew that the wrapped silk sensual was around and in me once again. The wings were in the hot corner of the studio. The doorman rang and announced a visitor. I took a last glance at my reflection, remembering the cracked mirror and all the doors that needed to be re-opened and aired. Johann was sitting in the lobby downstairs and at first glance I stopped, shocked. It was Miguel with his rugged, rough, exciting face. Walking towards me, he asked if everything was alright. "Everything is fine," I told him. "I just thought it was Miguel sitting there."

He was quiet. Then he said that he had discovered a very quaint Moroccan restaurant on the West Side where he would love to take me. I loved the idea. He said that I looked exquisite. He took a pack of cigarettes from his trousers and lit one, and I noticed they were the exact same French ones that Miguel used to smoke, with a gypsy on the blue cover. "I didn't know you smoke," I said. And he laughingly said that he did on special occasions.

"This is one?" I asked.

"This is one," he replied. He wanted to know everything and I told him about the week, leaving out the flying in front of the Buddha statue.

The restaurant was small and inviting. We were led to a table and he ordered a bottle of red. I was excited to feel the liquid magic soma in my mouth again after so long. The first sip was like an entry into a field of one million and one secrets.

My body was warm and the golden urn was transparent as spirit and sense blended together in ecstasy and pleasure. I told him that I had not had any wine while I was on my retreat and my rivers were parched.

"Wine suits you," he said as he filled my glass again. He spoke about the play and the rave reviews it got and all that he was doing to organize a tour with it both in the states and in Europe. "That would be wonderful," I said. He asked about the film and I told him that I had prepared very hard, but that I had a strange feeling about it.

"He has been very vague about everything," I said.

Johann asked again if I had signed a contract.

"I have not yet, but I will be seeing him tomorrow and I guess will know all the details."

I told him that I did not get the advance the director had promised. He was silent and just said he was sorry he had to leave the following day.

"This is not professional," he added. "It worries me."

"The script is amazing," I replied, "and the part is challenging and powerful."

We spoke and laughed, and I remembered the glass piece he had removed from my foot not too long ago after I had left the Mexican director's apartment. "I love Paul Gauguin," I suddenly said, especially *The Moon and the Earth.*"

He looked at me and the sharpened dagger held by master painters and poets slid through my pores and the setting sun reflected a translucent luminous body on the gliding river. The mountain waves lashed their wings on the pebbled shore, leaving a thousand stories lost in ancient translations. The sharpened sword held by the virgin queen reflected the burning shades of a new language yet to be born, a language crushed with the wings of mythology. And the truth would be as fierce as war but it would gallop across the sands of time, merging into every single grain. My eyes walked into his and my passion was as red as the burning sun. I was ready.

The next day was throbbing with every woman's fulfilled passion written in Sanskrit on the leaves of my burning, widened anima. The evening approached and I dressed to kill. I was red and, though it was chilly, I wore my very sexy string sandals, which I laced up beyond my calves. The Mexican director's apartment was close and since I didn't have to walk far I wanted the vision of my feet and their ancient howls, because today they would have invisible hooves as I would become the stallion once again. I wore my special oil made from the bark of the trees, my very own calling card. People always followed me to ask what it was, and I replied it was the fragrance of my soul. My hair was unraveled and flowing and my eyes had extra kohl around them because the trees must enter them and I should be her in Satyajit Ray's film, *Devi* and my sanity would be my burning spear. My sword was in its sheath. I was nervous and yet ready for this on coming battle, and my chariot was not driven by Arjuna, but by the night winds. They gave me their divine back to walk

364

on so my naked henna feet did not get cold. What more could I ask for?

I rang the bell and little man opened the door. He looked warm and sun-drenched and he hugged me very strongly. He started to say something to me but was interrupted by his father, asking who it was. He looked at my feet and smiled. He announced me and I walked into the very white and much manicured battleground. The director was sitting in his throne as usual, dressed in synthetic white, and I shivered as I remembered his invasion into my bed that night in my little grass cave in the mountains of Peru.

There were also some people whom I had not expected there and pretty girls crowded around him like hungry slaves, with their tongues dripping like stupid tame dogs ready to do anything for their monster owner. I accepted the anger that entered me, because tonight it was absolutely okay. More than okay, I thought. He was swollen with pride and arrogance and introduced me as being part of the film, but he did not mention me doing the main role and I knew something was wrong. They glanced at me but paid no attention and continued to grovel around him as he spoke of Zen and philosophy like a fallen priest. I took a seat quite far from his disciples and watched him. Little man came with a glass of red wine and sat next to me. He was embarrassed by his father's behavior but said nothing and glanced at me helplessly. I suddenly realized I had forgotten to bring the script with me and told Little man so. "That's all right," he said. The caterers walked around the room with many delicacies and the little man explained each thing to me, making sure there was no meat in the ones I chose. I was famished and enjoyed his attention.

The girls started to get tipsy and giggled and talked a lot, echoing conversations that had stepped aside and not inside. And I watched the dragonfly falling from vast horizons where the finality of smallness languishes in smallness, like unripened beings falling into blankets of stale dreams.

Some of them began to leave and the room felt like it was getting smaller. He said something to his son who in turn asked me to get closer to him. I was trembling. The earthquake was inside of me. I sat exactly where I had that first time when I read from the script. He asked me to come even closer and as I did he peered into my eyes and looked me up and down.

"You look good," he said. "You have been preparing. I can feel it."

I began to relax just a little and remembered that it was this kind of breeze that had excited me when I had first laid eyes on him on that stone-wrapped mystical day when I had seen my burkha-clad, Algerian, dream lady standing within a circle of light. He asked me what I had done and I told him everything, deciding to leave out my Buddha flight.

"Where is the script?" he asked.

"I forgot to bring it," I replied, saying that I was sorry.

He seemed annoyed but did not say anything. Then he invited me to the table where there was a sumptuous meal laid out for three. I guessed the little giggling geese were not included. Sighing with relief, I was happy I would not have to listen to loud vocals of pretty faces with walls, decked with dead art and non-grace. I would not have to see the stealth of dust on vagrant souls and tired faces and stolen looks and the typical weddings and aged faces and a mouthful of laughter from warped mouths and crooked forests. I was not them. They were not me.

The meal was amazing and the wine suited the winged feline inside me. His eyes very near me, straining to see and seemed to be watching me very closely as though even my eating was important. He asked about the part. I spoke passionately and forgot all else. I winded my way through all of her nuances and moods and reflections and searchings and growth and how all that would be made into a tangible reality. He listened carefully and little man touched my left hand. The director asked me why I sat so far from the group of girls, adding that they were all very talented aspiring actresses, some of whom he was considering using for the film.

"I felt uncomfortable," I answered, "I am not a groupie," I added.

"So you were not running after the Beatles when you were in London?" He asked sarcastically. "They were running after me,"I said, boldly.

I liked their music but that was all. In the same tone he continued saying that in this business there were a lot of must-does in order to get ahead. The words of the photographer fell in front of me, plodding off with no impact. I thought of Smila repeatedly telling me that I had to meet important people with money in order to be successful on that night in the back of the taxi cab driving through Central Park with my tree warriors standing erect in my city as I felt chilled to the bone. My now-healed barren belly felt a pang as tough stabbed by a blunt knife. We were served more dishes and wine.

The director was getting heady and a little tipsy and asked me to join him on the very large ornate sofa. The waiter brought over the rest of the wine and poured into our glasses. He told his son to go to bed and little man reluctantly left the room, taking my hands in his before he left. The servers left after tidying the room and we were alone with the candles and the red flow. He spoke about the part and what had been happening, and now for the first time began to tell me why he had to see me so urgently. My skin tightened and all the grok people that I knew from the world sent me their invisible understanding of my mystery and magic. He said he had been fighting with investors, some of whom were very big, because they wanted a big name for the part and did not approve of an unknown like me. He said that he had convinced them that I would be perfect, but they insisted that they could not finance him unless there was a name involved. Silence crashed in like a greedy thief. The snakes in the dream in Southampton in the cave that I walked into who became the shenai played at weddings, were right here writhing in front of me but this time they did not turn into gold. This time they had fire in their eyes and slid inside the two-thousand-year-old Shiva temple in Kerala to find the inner sanctum. Words fell out of my mouth as though through me and not of me. "I thought you never compromised," I screamed. He said that he did not, but the film had to be made.

"So you will just take anyone they suggest," I told him with my sweeping voice.

"I am helpless," he replied, adding that he had not given up the fight and would prove to them that I was the right one.

Suddenly he pushed himself closer to me and then said that he had to see and feel my body, because in the initiation scene the girl would be ripped off all her clothes. I knew this and standing up slowly and proudly undressed like a naked bamboo erect and strong. I looked around to make sure that my little man was not there. He quietly re-assured me that we were alone. My body is the instrument of the wind held by forest whispers and birdcalls and baby beings. It feels clean and sharp. I am proud, in an ether-filled way. I sat down in my skin and watched him watching me.

He got very close and started touching me. My nakedness lost its magic and a dark veil fell on it. The river got polluted and green. He be-gan kissing my mouth and grabbing my breast and clawing at my thighs. His breath was heavy and disjointed like an animal without its head and heart, crawling through the forest paths, lost in its lust. All that had happened that night in my solitary cabin was right here and I howled with anguish. He covered my mouth and continued and insisted that he had to possess me to know me. And I remembered the words of an actress and a singer who once told me that I had to go to bed with every producer if I wished to make it in this business and I told her that then I would rather not make it. And she laughingly said that that was why she was so popular. And now she is no one, lost in oblivion of nothingness. I would never succumb to that temptation for my work. He had ripped his clothes and climbed on top of me like a deer without his horns, like the wolf without its growl, like a camel without his hump and like the lion without his grace.

I slid away from beneath him and started to weep. The horse enters and throws lotus buds in the air one of which floats in front of my eyes. It is the same one that I had seen in the sand, sweating and na-ked and raped by greed. He tried to grab me again, I remembered those men in the spa and I pulled away. It was as though he was all of them merged into one. And the memories of my afternoon of blood in London were there in front of me. I was with Miguel who was filming a series and

I had sauntered out in some country town for a walk. I heard approaching footsteps and looking back saw a man hurrying towards me. At first I took no heed but when the steps got even faster I began to quicken mine. He began to run and before I knew it he was at my side dragging me to a field. I remembered distinctly that there were farmers all over when I began my walk but now there was not a soul in sight. Throwing me on the ground he mounted me like a dog in heat and when I started to scream he clasped my throat, almost choking me. Miguel cried when I told him later and after kissing my wounded self with his lips of love went out to kill the rapist.

The Mexican director tried to pull me back again but I pushed him with full force and he stumbled. I started to dress, trembling and crying, and all I heard him say was that he would never forgive me for this. "Never!" With these words echoing in my ears, I ran out to the door sandals in hand, like a frightened child lost in its fresh dewy youth.

The night was large and it was raining. Horse heads floated on the river, lotuses had been strewn on the now dry riverbed, the flying dragon fell in his mate flight and died and was now sitting in art and gold leaf, the fragrant spring violet flower was dry and pierced the blue beaded earth where sits a goddess head. The rooted leaf had entered a bowl of earth and the sacred elephant's wet trunk was reaching out to a man to be fed and a red heart held within a black-lined lip sat within the jungle of flowers. And the scratched concrete had a coiled snake etched into its body with imprints of the guru feet. I was wet and raw and scarred with pain. My feet bled from some glass pieces left on the pavement. They were not like the broken glass art piece of the last encounter and no man mate was there to softly remove them. My heart ached. My soul ached. My voice ached. My eyes ached. My hands ached. My sight ached. And my vision was masked with a white plastic hue I could not peel off. I was lost and I had lost. I was warned many times but I had to find out myself.

What would have been my flight in passion and expression and art was taken away from me. I stumbled and fell on the concrete, and in front of me through the stinging rain, I saw huge lights coming towards me. It was the very same bus which had carried me so many times uptown to my rehearsals and auditions. It looked like the wheels were going to ride over me and with much difficulty I moved onto the edge of the pavement, fallen and wounded and the huge chariot drove by just missing me, empty with lights inside but not a soul in sight. I struggled up and, taking my bag and sandals, somehow walked toward my apartment building. In the distance I saw the doorman. It was my friend and as he saw me he ran towards me with an open umbrella as we walked towards the building. Opening the door, he helped me in and, seeing my feet bleeding, ran to get the first aid box from the office. I said that I was okay but he insisted and very gently cleaned the wound, making sure there were no glass pieces left inside. He put several Band-Aids on and helped me to the elevator. I thanked him. He was from Portofino, in Italy, a very gentle and sweet man. He was embarrassed and looked away as I was drenched with my dress clinging to me in this wild, windy rainstorm, faltering, weeping, howling, laughing, stumbling, frightening, and enlightening process of what was to be.

The studio felt barren and strange and I didn't understand this. I ran a bath and sank into its warm embrace. My tears didn't stop and fell into the water like red pearl drops. After what seemed to be hours I dried myself and lay down and lit the candle and watched the smoke curling up to the sky as I swallowed each crystal blue moon. Kali's face was drenched with red and black from the fallen child kite's hands. I wished to speak with my wolf but knew he had left and silence seeped into every cell and my tongue felt trapped in its own chains, as the grasshopper elephant ambled along with chains on his feet. I wanted to rip them off but they were too heavy and, looking up at his sad eyes, I cried with him and gave him my blue world ball to play with. He smiled at me and threw it back to me with the wet tip of his trunk and I knew that I would rise again from my own ashes And on the edge of the water he made me an *Om.*

I lied on my bed of nails and fell into a dusty, empty, barren, concrete dreamless sleep as shadows surrounded the entry arches and the birds were silent. I was aware that the steel points might have sliced through me but I cared not. I was helpless and wounded and lost. I was the dead flower, trampled by unconscious man. I was the raped one, left slaughtered and in agony on barren earth. And I was the little girl, violently deflowered by an old bent drunk truck driver.

Crows woke me the following morning. I recalled the crows in the Hamptons when I opened my eyes that first morning and the murky glass of water that stood next to me. I wondered who had passed away because in India it is believed that crows carry the spirit of a loved one. My desire and longing to do this part had been killed and the death was as big as the herd of divine elephants who had been murdered and slaughtered and whose tusks had been cut off by greedy poachers for money.

My mind was vague and cloudy and covered with emptiness and nothingness. The shamiana marriage tent was stooping and falling all around me and I did not have the strength to hold it up. Most of the petals from the red roses that raven had sent me dropped sadly on the wooden surface like the earth of my creative imagination which had been robbed from grace, and my human body became part of a rock painting of animal and man by a bushman tribe in South Africa. The hero is able to shift between the worlds to avoid being caught in the dream catcher's wheel. He or she remains fluid and is able to hide this process which is his magic and allows him to become invisible. We are shape-shifting, always, because life eludes stasis and the more genes we discover the more alteration and myriad forms of life are revealed to us. Those who retain these otherworld initiations – mystics, shamans and healers – inspire both awe and fear as their never-ending metamorphosis expresses and threatens the very nature of our being.

I felt bent in this world of light and dark and in this battle with evil. I remembered the broken, half table lamp somewhere in my journey, inside of which were the words of the artist Bruce Neumann: "The true artist helps the world by revealing mystic truths." And maybe this huge bleeding obstacle had been given to me to jump into the unknown and to eat and become the very essence of what is transformation. The phone rang and it was little man. All he said was that his father wished to see me that afternoon with the script. He asked how the rest of the evening was and I realized that his father had not mentioned anything. Reluctantly, I told him I would be there

I was going through my own metamorphosis and transformation by magic and this would be the reward of the gods. Maybe this would be a reward an entry into my own initiation in a found mountain where a secret, sacred shaman dwells and waits for my arrival by choice and sacrifice so that I would then be able to inspire and hold the trembling hearts and souls of the seekers. This time it would not be in a film. And there would be an alchemical process leading to a transformation from darkness to renewed life and the lead in me would be transformed into gold after all the vulnerability, rage, anxiety, and loss had been burnt and baked into a valuable blood red pigment with a vermillion hue. And my work would come to life because I would and should give everything for this and would sacrifice all I needed to, like Alexander, in Tarkovsky's, The Sacrifice who kept his promise to God that he would give up all that was his if the balance was restored. He did and burnt his house and left his wife and beloved son,

The time had come and, checking my foot, which was healing, I wore some warrior clothes appropriate for the occasion. I was not in my full form but then the warrior too falls and sinks and breaks and is attacked and slashed and torn apart; the difference is he understands that the psyche also initiates its own transformation. Picking up the script, and lacing up my Palladium boots, I left this heart space.

My friend was at the door of the apartment building and inquired about my foot. Assuring him that it was healing, I walked to the director's apartment.

Before I rang the bell, the door opened and little man was standing there. He took my right hand and kissed it gently with sadness in his eyes. I was certain that he now knew what was to be. The director was sitting in the same throne and around him were some of the same semi-actresses that had been there the day before. I was certain that he had them there for his protection and to wound me even more and all this because I refused to succumb to his dangerous and arrogant deception. He asked me to walk toward him and told the girls to make space so that I could sit nearby. At first I did not and, still standing, I looked down at this strange and damaged soul. He was irritated and rudely demanded that I take a seat. As though nothing had happened, he told me in a very casual manner that he had really tried to get me in the film but had not succeeded and that the producers had decided on a big name. The girls giggled and sighed in disbelief when he said who would play the part, and he added looking at me, though not seeing that he had only agreed because she had a resemblance to me. Shaking, I stood up and started to give the script to him when an invisible force, grabbing it from my hands and threw it at him. My hands did not move. He noticed this and sat back in shock.

I stood back and there she was, the furious beatific goddess, sword in hand and Shiva was right behind. He was startled and looked behind him, maybe feeling her presence. He made some kind of strange motion as though shielding himself. I saw his head falling off bloody and raw. This was the second time I had witnessed this. The first time was when I saw Shane again at the party given by Smila's friend.

Trembling, he picked up a check and handed it to little man to give to me. My eyes were beginning to fill but I would not cry, not in front of this man again, and I spoke with hot pebbles falling out of my mouth with a power that I knew did not belong to me. It was as if she had sliced me open with her sword and was speaking through me. I opened my mouth and words just flew out,

"I knew it. I felt it and was warned but did not take heed because I had to walk through this deception and now I thank you for giving me the opportunity to prepare myself for something bigger than you, bigger than your pathetic lies and pride and false pretense of someone who you are not. You want someone who worships you, who moves at your beck and call, who would be your slave. You think you are some kind of Zen master. You are not. You are like all the rest, a caricature of your own egoistic play. You are not a true artist, not the artist you pose to be. You are pathetic, and weak, and bow down to fools who have no integrity or vision and you will create one more typical, formulaic and diluted piece of shit film that you will try to call art. You have compromised and you and your work will never be the same. You will regret this. You are a very ordinary man."

The girls around him were all shocked, and gathered closer to him. But I had not finished. "Lust after your little disciples and be the king in a circle of fools. You are a fake king with a crown of death on your

371

head and you will never be forgiven and your arrogance and stupid pride are the thieves who stole your eyes. You are fallen.

You are nothing and no one. You will be burnt by greed and the godhead will never forgive you. Death stands in front of you. You are a rapist."

Little man came to me and with wet eyes gave the check to me. I walked to his father, this time made bold by the same force that had entered me and taking the check tore it up in front of him, and threw the pieces on his lifeless body. I turned around to leave and he shouted that I would regret this. I looked back and there she was merciless and mad, with his head in her hands.

Little Savitri was crying and I jumped out of bed. The night was still and heavy and humid and foreboding. I picked her up. She was burning. My husband was beside me and rushed to get a wet cloth and wiped her down. She finally calmed down and opened her eyes wide and looked at me with an ancientness that stunned me. The eyes of the wooden stallion and the brass head of another and the eyes of the two-hundred-year-old Krishna and the burning eyes of the goddess Kali all swam into me through her and I was certain that she pointed her little tiny beautiful brown fingers towards the cobweb in the corner of the ceiling. I didn't dare to look and as she fell asleep I placed her back in her little cot. We stood near her for a long time until her breathing was even, and then we lay down.

"We will see who regrets this," I said standing in this false, white, stupid, pathetic room in my beloved warrior city as I watched him quiver a little because I was certain he could feel Kali's presence.

Boots in hand, I stormed out bowing to her silently and on the street I put them on. I had to sit down in order to pull them on and lace them up. My eyes were filled and I could hardly see what I was doing. A soft voice and a gentle tap made me look up and there he was crying with me, my little man who was his son but not a part of his deceit and pride. I told him not to say anything. "It is done and I am so happy I met you," I told him. Taking the sunstone, which I didn't even know was in my hand, I placed it in his little palm and closed it. He held me tight and asked me to please keep it. He explained that although his father had asked him to place it on my foot that night, he had found it himself, and I saw the young Algerian boy on that magic day who had placed the three stones on the table in the café. They were almost the same and they were the divine language that soothes my soul and my heart and my creative field of perception, imagination and vision. I took his face and kissed both cheeks. Just then a helper ran to us and in Spanish told him that his father was very angry and wanted him to get back in immediately. He nodded and I stood up slowly.

"I hate my father," he said through his tears.

372

"No," I told him, "you cannot and must not do that."

"But he has hurt you so much," he added. "He is a fool. You are the part and nobody else will be able to do it. The film will be a failure and I don't even care."

I kissed him again and told him to stay in touch with me. He would not let go of my hand and then squeezing his little hand I walked towards my building. I looked back and he was still standing there and then once again he ran to me. He was my little man and he was carrying two buckets of water to feed my Ikebana tree after his father had been taken away to his freedom in The Sacrifice.. I am the Ikebana tree. My roots are wet and the soil is fertile. His child's gaze had saved my soul.

For some reason, I decided to just walk and walk I felt like I wanted to see the immense Zen-like grandeur of the Brooklyn Bridge, where so many lost their lives during construction. What a perfect bridge it is, maybe one of the most beautiful bridges in the world. In the very middle grew a plant in a concrete column and I always touched and admired it. I wondered how it found its nourishment and was amazed at its ability to survive and thrive where there was no earth.

I walked slowly and sat down in the center on a bench and felt the eternal language of the East River speak to me, as I perched above its magnificent languid body. Dusk was dancing in and I watched the blue become a burnt vermillion and the ball of the sun merged into this solid, soft rippling melody of one million and one evening ragas. I heard the sitar, the veena, the double headed violin, the mandolin and the flute as the cowherds ran from their homes, leaving all their household chores behind to be with the blue-black god of love, Krishna. He who carries me back and forth between the two worlds. Between the self who stayed and the one who left. The gypsies dance to the flamenco as the **hota** screams through the fire waves and the women with symbolic tattoos move their bodies with magnificent grace. And I knew that I too was a gypsy and had no possessions and walked the earth held and caressed by the bronze electric magic of the burnt prairie. And the gypsy women in Rajasthan wanted to tattoo my face with henna. When I asked them why, they promptly replied that I was a gypsy and had to be initiated.

The evening cowbells broke my ether space and, leaving the bench, I walked back towards my studio. At the edge of the bridge was written: "You have beautiful dreams," and I knew this message was for me. I was hungry and checked my wallet to see if I had any money. I had a little and I desired flesh and blood. My footsteps led me to that Japanese restaurant where Johann had first taken me and where he carefully pulled out a piece of glass art from my red, red feet. It was quiet and the maître d', recognizing me, sat me at the same low table. My feet felt clean and falseness was dripping out of the inner pours. He brought me a balloon of red without even asking. He enquired if I was alone, and I nodded and he left with a smile on his face as the raw lean sushi slid on my tongue.

The tall, elegant bamboo tree near the table touched me as I reached out for its graceful trunk, strong and unbreakable. He brought me another glass and said that this one was on the house. I looked up to thank him and noticed his eyes and hands quietly flirting on my skin. I enjoyed it and wore it like a loose garment, which flowed all over me. My aloneness had to be met and adorned and married before all else. My mouth formed a thank you and I knew he wanted to kiss my lips so I left them carved and full, floating in the air. I paid the bill and noticed that he had not charged me for any of the wine. Lacing up my boots, I waved back to him and swayed into the dark and transparent night.

My art was robbed and lied to by a sinner. He had taken my gifts and tried to sell them to the highest bidder. Those filthy hands had touched me and undressed me. I would not hate, I would not be blind. I would grow sharper and with my shining samurai sword I would slaughter him and his entire unholy tribe of pretending minstrels and masked fools. His mask would stick on his slimy skin. It would have to be cracked open and when it fell off, his face would be distorted and he would become the demon. I would walk away and fly above him with my eagle wings aflame and my art regained and re-captured.

The building was welcoming and after checking my mail I entered the studio. Something had shifted, as though man and animal were one and the great sacred Ganesha had entered and cleaned all obstacles away. I heard him breathe and heard his gentle footfall, and this time it was unchained. Washing and changing and lighting I lay down and listened to the messages. Prana was back and wanted me to call her. Johann called from London, wanting to know what happened with the director and giving me the good news that the play almost certainly would be on tour. This made me happy. My raven said that he missed me madly and was in love with every tree that he touched because he knew they were me.

Getting out of the bed, I gathered the red petals, which I had discarded, near to me on the table. *This is what happens when you fall into the dangerous folds of mediocrity*, I thought. Little man's sunstone sat amidst the other pebbles. And then I heard the voice of my Flora after so very long. She said that she and her husband had been travelling in remote villages doing unique projects. She wished so much that I was there with her and she missed all of me and always every single morning saw and felt my altar. She had no number to leave but would try to call back that night as she had felt she needed to speak with me. Machu Picchu and its sacred secrets gathered in this special and powerful sunflower warrior. I was certain she felt what had happened. Hironobu san left a wonderful Zen message too, and then there were two from Smila and

Shane.

    In my dream that night I was in India being initiated by a howling tribe of gypsy women where all the preparations were being made for a special ceremony. It was a unique ritual done after a loss, It was a celebration of life so birth could be evoked again. They painted my hands and feet with sacred sandalwood paste and turmeric clove imprints, which arched my eyes like the symbolic tattoos on the face of the gypsy woman who rides the camel, her dark hair flowing and her laced boots up to her thighs. Her spear at her waist is fierce because she is hunting the man who stole her spit and soul and her secret word, and abused it because of which she lost her shape-shifting power. I was she and my art soul and my sacred spit were stolen by an outsider. But I should regain all my powers and my creativity and would shape-shift into the white wolf.

    I called Hironobu san. He picked up immediately. Hearing his voice was like eating the holy herb mountain that he in his Hanuman form always carried. I clung on to his burning tail as he burned the vicious kingdom of **Ravana** and set everything on fire after he had found Sita, Rama's beloved wife. His wise voice made me weep and he was very silent as I howled into the phone. And then slowly he told me that he had felt something very strong, and reminded me what he had spoken to me earlier that all this would be rewarded in tens of thousands of ways. Peace entered me like a ripe fruit and bounced in and around me as I crushed the flesh joyfully in my not burnt tongue. "It has been hard," I said.

    Before we hung up he told me he would make sushi and green tea for me "very soon". I loved his broken English and his soft water liquid voice and his accent, which was ancientness itself. I placed a petal in my mouth and wet it to life and Flora called. I was beyond ecstatic to hear her mountain voice. Her first question was if I was okay. I told her that I was, after hearing her voice. She of course asked about the director. I fell silent and said nothing. I knew she could hear my breath as she asked me to feel the winds from Machu Picchu surrounding me. "You will be fine," she added and the line was cut off.

    Then I dialed Prana's number. After a few rings she picked up and said my name. She said that she needed to meet me tomorrow and that it was very important. I was quiet and she said that she knew all that had happened and she would help me.

    I watched the misty moon sliding through the window and as I closed my eyes I thought of the way of the samurai and the Maori people of New Zealand. The concept of **mana** was at the center point of their philosophy and depends on the spark of life one is born with and is determined in each being by relationships with the living and their ancestors. I saw all my ancestors floating around me as my grandmothers poetry became me.

Two glowing eyes pierced through my sleep in my mosqui-to-net-draped bed in India, as I woke up. The owl was at the window-sill, exactly in the same place as before, staring at the little one's cot. I fell back because right next to the cot was the divine rider without her stallion, her robes covering the entire cot. As I sat up she slowly turned her head slightly. She placed her hands in, and lifted my child and then she was gone. I screamed and my husband jumped up, as I told him in Bengali that she had taken our child. I saw her.

"Who?" he asked.

"Kali came," I answered.

We ran to her and he took her hand and lifted her. She had left us. And now I knew why she had pointed her little fingers to the cobweb. She knew. All was dark, and I fell.

When I came back to my senses the room was filled with com-motion. I was lying in bed and the doctors were around me. The entire household was in upheaval. I felt nothing and didn't even remember what had happened. The lights were glaring and I heard wailing and cry-ing. "She has left us," my mother-in-law screamed and beat her head on the wall. Though my heart hurt so much I could feel my skin stretching inside, I felt comforted that Kali had come and showed me her face to as-sure me that my child would be protected. I could not tell that to anyone, as I was the only one who was blessed and could see her. My eyes walked to the web in the ceiling; it was completely destroyed and broken. I woke up and I saw death. I woke up and I saw gold. I woke up and I saw the face of creation and the destruction of ignorance. I woke up and I saw Ganesha. I could not weep. Tears did not come to my eyes and I remem-bered Tagore's play **Chitrangada**. It is the story of a princess who was brought up like a prince, but once, when she saw **Arjuna** the lord of love, she fell madly in love with him and asked the lord of beauty to grant her one-day of perfect beauty. He gave her a whole year but after they were together, she realized that everything was a lie. So she ran and ran and ran in the forest path filled with **shephali** flowers. At a lonely brook she fell down and tried to weep and to cry but no tears came to her eyes. I was she today and I could not cry.

I watched everyone hurrying around, and several doctors checked her. I knew she had gone but said nothing until finally the last doctor said it was useless. Everyone was shocked and I was certain my moth-er-in-law would blame me for this occurrence. The only person I wished to see was my beggar, saint.. I started to get up, but I felt very weak and then I saw my husband bringing her to me. Her little body was still warm and filled with life. Her face was calm and smiling. I was maybe dreaming but I was certain her little hand grabbed mine and just for one moment her eyes opened and she smiled at me as though to wish me goodbye and assure me that she was in divine hands. My eyes didn't leave her for a single moment as I held her to my breasts and kissed her and kissed her and kissed her.

All around they were making all kinds of preparations as I held my blue, bold blossom girl-child who had come to tell us so much and I knew I could not be sad because that would hold her down. And death was the final glorious transformation.

The priest was informed and began elaborate preparations as her little body was bathed and dressed so that she could be carried to the temple. I bathed and, trembling from the shock, wore a very white sari, because from its milky waters emerged saps and elixirs and the white cow of all desires, and **Airavata** was the moon-white elephant emblem of the **Visudha**, the throat chakra. And I saw my favorite white buffalo cow woman dressed in white buckskin that gives to the Sioux tribe the sacred pipe and all the holy rituals honoring mother earth came in front of me.

I carried her to the temple with the whole household following me. My feet were not touching the earth. I felt as though I was being carried by her little spirit. I wanted her to kick me and suddenly her tiny feet pushed into my chest. I wept with joy and knew that I should and would rejoice. The white sari-clad lady was right there and I could not even distinguish between her and the temple. She was the temple.

From afar I saw the shine and knew that she had her mouth open and was showing me the Universe. I glanced sideways at the others but no one could see her. Approaching the temple, I handed the little body to the priest who took her and placed her gently in the lap of the goddess. I bowed down in front of the image and as I rose it was as though her stone eyes opened and looked straight at me. I fell on my knees again at this vision, and held it within myself. I placed myself into her lap not caring what my mother-in-law would say. But she said nothing and also bowed down to her hesitatingly. The Universe One held my head and assured me that her leaving was very important and that I should not grieve. Now the tears flowed and they were not red pearls but wild, found ones and they were very white and translucent. I knew the little one would have clutched them in her baby hands and giggled. I howled and couldn't stop as she rubbed her rough life hands on my face and whispered various healing mantras in my ears. The priest was also in tears and did a very long **puja** as we all sat around and waited, stunned and numb and heavy with her little, big loss. Finally, it was done and he instructed us what to do. I was not part of this and did not wish to be either. Certain rituals had to be performed and then she would be cremated. My husband and mother-in-law helped me rise as I stumbled to the house. I looked back to get another look at her and now I only saw in her place a circle of light. There was no physical form but I heard her voice and in Bengali she said that she would be back in many different forms. And I knew this. This is what she told me with that last sweet ancient gaze, my absolute shaman shape-shifting child. To my surprise my mother-in-law was also looking at her, and in her eyes I saw she had heard it too. She took me by my shoulder, almost hugging me. I was not used to this, and glanced at my husband who had tears in his eyes. He smiled at me. "Finally," he said, "finally."

Prana and I met the next day. She took me to the restaurant we had dined in when we first met. She ordered wine and handed me the menu. I chose fish of course. I am a Bengali, hailed from an ancestry of poets, artists, philosophers, and powerful, uncorrupt politicians. I love fish. They are my very own stream-of-consciousness and my personal narrative. They live in the flowing waters of dream and of liquid realms and the salmon and the carp always swim against the current but never forget their roots. I hail from dignity, respect, and humility.

She was stunning. Her eyes were beacons of light and wealth. We raised our glasses and as she ran straight into my gaze she said that she knew all that happened and had seen it and knew that I needed to face it by myself. What can you say when a woman who represents and embodies every branched tree structure of her female tree trunk also manifests the divine feminine? She was a mythical beast and I had no words.

"Your growth has cracked you open and the retreat or your little vision quest was given to you as a gift. Nothing is forgotten, Mrinalini. Nothing is not seen and nothing stays unrecognized, absolutely nothing. There are no separations or boundaries. There is no sin or guilt or those pathetic, moralistic values of what is good or bad. You are being trained to become a true shaman and a true artist and this is exactly why you had to and needed to go through this and you will be given more trials and tribulations and obstacles and each inhumane obstacle will enlarge you and widen you beyond belief. How did you feel when you were on the same height and could see into the eyes of the Buddha?"

I looked at her stunned, even though by now I was used to her presence and wisdom. I had no words. It was as though the wind and the sky caressed and held me and her eyes lit me with a fierce and calm fire. I still didn't know what I knew but the facades of worship or just physical postures meant nothing to me. My entire being is a posture offered to the gods and the universe. She smiled and said very quietly that the artists, the real ones, are the shamans of the world. A lightning sliced the sky and I felt alive. The sky was listening and the rain poured down and thunder roared within my veins and the white wolf unchained me and I would be free.

"I love you," I told her as my almond eyes carved gratitude onto the skin of her being, my Prana, my breath. I thanked her. She lifted her glass and I mine, and **Garuda** poured his soma into our open mouths, drenching our lips and staining his entry. My head and face bent back-

378

wards as he flew off with Vishnu on his bird back, because he is his carrier.

"I know what you went through after Shane stole your womb and ate your virgin self. I know what you had to do at that spa because I was there. But you are Kamala, the courtesan, and will always be and you will save and nurture all who come to you, like Siddhartha, who after all his ascetic ways was taught everything by Kamala. You are she and you are also Siddhartha. You left your palace of wealth and comfort to serve your art. You saw and will see all. You will bleed and sacrifice and burn down all your possessions because you are the true nomad. You live to give." I thought of Abrihet. I felt Flora and I looked at the eagle eyes of my shape-shifter Goddess-woman sitting right in front of me. They were all my tribe of the ecstatic feminine and I will do anything for them.

I listened with eyes wide open and recalled the woman in a gallery in Taos, New Mexico telling me that I was the female Siddhartha. How strange it all was.

"I will always love you," I told her with my lips arching their very own sensual curve, "because I trust you." My blood merged with Garuda's soma and all was in harmony and in balance.

We left the restaurant and she walked with me on this strange mystery-whispered night towards the apartment building. There was not much traffic and our breathing was carved. Just before we reached the entrance, she stopped in front of me and kissed me on my lips as her mouth poured all the knowledge of the courtesan warrior in me, like a freshly cut fig and the blossoming tree began to rise within me. She took my hand and weaved her veined fingers into mine. The doorman opened the door. It was my friend, Reynaldo, and he smiled at Prana, recognizing her. She waited until I was inside and I carried her gaze as I walked to the elevator. Her hands were still wrapped in my fingers and my dream-spirit woman saint filled me with an uncanny new strength as I slid the key in my lock.

As soon as I opened the door the phone rang. It was Prana. "It will not be easy, but your biggest learning and journey has begun. You have just started. That is why you went to your exile, not to prepare for the part in that stupid film but to prepare for what and who you will be. For your chosen part in this life time. Your scars and your deep red, bloody wounds will carve and sculpt you and the beauty that you have now will sit deeply within you and you wll finally accept it and claim it and the lines will etch your eternal face of youth. Take what you have learned and felt and become all of that and rise to the journey. Remember the levitating up in the temple when you met the eyes of the illustrious one. Remember the fairies guiding your way. Remember the turquoise one who walked towards you in that sacred spot in the hill to sage you and now live your very own vision quest."

379

Her words walked into my every pore as she said: "You will break no more."

My sandalwood Indian husband was lying next to me and the night was young. I had not returned yet from my sense of loss, even though I knew my Savitri was in divine hands. He wrapped his dusky arms around my shoulder, as my body slid closer to him. The door was locked, as was our ritual now. Nobody valued any privacy here. But I wanted to make certain and I whispered in his ears if he had remembered to lock it. He nodded and for the first time I unwound my cotton gaze and my blouse and all that trapped me down and revealed my whole skin soul naked body to him. He was overwhelmed and with tears in his eyes, which fell like fragrant garlands on my nipples and belly and **kundalini** place, kissed me with a wild and tantric passion which shed light in every cell in me as I howled with pleasure and divine erotica and received his entry with a thousand throbbing lotus flowers. My body was silk and soft and I slid in, around, underneath and on top of him. My pleasure was beyond sighs of the rippling river, as all the rose petals entered me and I was fulfilled. We lay side by side on the dampened and wrinkled sheets and his hands rested on my wild breasts and he took my mouth and ate my lips like a pomegranate, not missing a single crunchy seed. He had become the man. He had left behind all of his fears, insecurities, sexual inhibitions caused by hypocrisy and social constrictions, and superstition distorting the physical being, making Kama, the god of love, mad and angry and on fire.

"You taught me everything," he whispered gently in my ears. "How did you know so much? Who trained you?"

"I am the **Khajurao** temples," I replied, "where the voluptuous woman is celebrated with her many moods and facets and desires and her supple body is entwined in ecstasy with her male consort."

Kama was happy with our union and shot arrows of flowers from his bowstring made of bees and with his sugarcane bow of love. The juice from the sugarcane dripped on my skin and I asked my husband to kiss each drop. And right then I turned my head, because something pulled me, and I saw Kali standing by the little one's cot, but this time she was placing something into the cot. I started, and he asked me what was wrong. I quietly told him that she was in the room next to the cot putting something in it. He listened, not questioning me, because he had so much faith in me and we both were very silent.

We lay like this for a long time as dawn came in with its dewy presence and my eyes wandered up to the ceiling and I cried in joy because there, where the ripped cobweb was and which my darling child had pointed her dimpled fingers to, was a whole complete web intact and beautiful. He looked up, too, and we both smiled in joy. Holding me, he asked if I still felt that call, that voice from far that distracted me and

380

made me sad. I was quiet for a long time and said that I finally felt that I was one with myself, and that I was free from that maddening desire and now I would be able to do what I always wanted, which was my paintings, and that maybe now his mother would accept me for who I truly was. "I don't feel ugly anymore, my art has entered me.," I said.

"My mother has no choice," he said as he jumped out of bed and prepared a bath for me. "I will bathe my Devi now with all the sandalwood soaps from Arabia and everywhere else and rub you with jasmine oil and dress you in red."

"Why red?" I asked him, smiling with joy.

"Because today you are my bride again, and today we are married again, and today something has begun, and today new seeds have been planted, and today I love you once again, and today and forever I will let no person, man, woman, or child ever hurt you and your absolute divine beauty."

We walked to the bathroom stopping at the little cot where Kali had stood and I bowed in respect and knew that she had placed life back there and right in front of my eyes I saw it rising up to the ceiling, floating all over and above us. He saw me looking up and asked me what I saw. I smiled and said that our love made me fly. After bathing and dressing me he opened the door and there outside the room was a tray with a steaming pot of tea. "Let's have this outside," he said as we walked into the tropical sun filled garden of delight. His mother smiled at us and said gently that breakfast would be served soon.

> "My dreams are my warriors
> and my reflections and my myth-
> makers, and my journal is filling
> up and I now write with red ink
> flowing from a fountain pen.
> They call me primitive. I call
> them ignorant."

I stepped out of the little, hot, shifting studio in my city of knives and knew I had to drink the sky and eat the world. I ran down Third Avenue and watched my feet becoming horse hooves. They were red, as the henna had merged into them. I touched my gold circle and remembering the ancient cab driver who had seen it in his dreams looked back wondering if he would find me this evening of a burdened body of love. *I will eat somewhere new tonight*, I thought and decided to walk around for a bit.

Hearing some faint refrains of a Spanish song, I went towards it and saw a very romantic little Spanish restaurant. It was perfect. There was a little corner where a musician was singing "Malaguenia," a song that I adored and which Miguel used to serenade me with on the sands of Formentera in Spain. His voice was like the entry into the fire dragon's mouth. I heard his tongue. I listened to his lips and walked in as though pulled by a magnate of sorts.

He looked at me and sang these words in Spanish: "Rose leaves of Malaga"/" to kiss your wanted lips, to kiss your wanted lips"/" and telling you beautiful girl"/" that you are pretty and magical"/" that you are pretty and magical, as the innocence of a rose...and telling you beautiful girl..." The maître d' welcomed me and, leaving my bag at the table, I asked where the restroom was. It was clean, with wild, fresh flowers in a handmade blue vase. I inhaled their language into me. I washed my hands in a very round ceramic bowl with some natural liquid soap. I hesitatingly glanced in the mirror. The bride was asleep in her beloved husband's arms. I was just a little envious. Her husband had transformed into a man and a shining silky bronzed stallion. Walking to my table, I asked the waiter what he would suggest, since I was not familiar with Spanish wines. He brought me a glass and said that it was compliments from the singer. "Kiss my wanting lips," I whispered to my wolf raven, to Miguel and to Tobias. It was time for magic. I bowed my head to him. I ordered some paella filled with seafood. I ordered another glass and asked the waiter to send one to the singer. His voice was like the rippling dunes of red deserts where gypsy women undulate to the sounds of the flamenco. He sang some other tunes and then my song again.

I asked for the bill and when I opened the folder found a poem written on it. " The world is you and you are the world." I looked up and the waiter said that the singer paid for it. I didn't know what to say and, leaving a tip, I got up and looked for him but didn't see him. I asked the waiter to please thank him for me. Gathering my things, I walked to the door and there standing next to it was the musician with a large stainless steel bowl in his hands filled with water and a white napkin on his left arm. My feet were now of dust and yellow rose petals and fading ferns and owl eyes.

"This is to clean your hands, your heart and your wounded self forever," he said. "The water is from the rivers of my alma." His eyes were deep pools of endless light and mystery and mythos. I saw all my animals and all my trees and all my poet men sitting in the midst.

My fingers touched the folds of his vibrant voice and slid through *Ondine's* feather water of all waters. They fell to the bottom of this endless bowl and, looking into his wild eyes, I was cleansed and renewed, and the snakeskin had fallen on the wayside, as his heart became my new skin. "Come back beautiful girl, you are magical," he said giving me the very white cloth to wipe my hands with. And I loved the red henna from my hands, which left the stains of the fallen women and the weeping widows and the ones who are abused and thrown aside after they have been raped and used like wasted fruit on this pure white surface. They will and are rising again and I will shield and protect them in my very own shamiana tent until they are healed and made whole again and their femininity will save the world.

I started to walk towards my studio, still filled with his melodious voice, as all my women ran with me and I took the symbols the gypsy women had painted on my face and played with the fire of who I was becoming as I walked through this forest in search of silence and grace and I felt the rain of my soul. I was born a thousand years ago, and pollen from the everlasting lotus flower glided down and life and death and love and fear all united in me. With a mind like the silk inside of the ancient seashell, I came again and again to the earth, and dancing with the divine in this life, I flowed with word and presence, and I felt her, and became her sister, her mother, her daughter, her lover, her sacred prostitute. And my whole body was now fearless and one. We had united. I was she. She was me. The bride who stayed. The warrior who left.

Chapter 20: The child's gaze has saved my soul
I will awake alive within the womb of my own creativity

Aakash was back from India and called me. He told me that he wanted to finally shoot the bride sequence in the studio. He was different. He was frail and had lost some of his buoyancy and energy. He said that he had missed me violently. I said nothing to him about the massage parlor where my soul almost slid out of me.

The trees in the forest surrounded and closed the entrance to that place to tell me that I needed enter there no more. The sacrifice was made, the wounds were felt, and the blood was spilt, and all the rivers were now celebrating the red glow within their very own rippling flowing bodies. That was why the divine one on her shining stallion had entered the room to tell me I had given my blood and Prana's magic piercing eyes had said the same, and my courtesan limbs which were trained and sharpened for the dance of death were left behind on the bed of the glittering artificial red pleasure room, and my Godot had found his soul and I needed to wait for him no more.

We spoke about the shoot. It would be a visual montage of a Bengali bride, with all the makeup and appropriate attire. He had someone to do the makeup. I missed my Flora. It had been so long.

We decided on a day and began. He was a master with the camera. I felt Ulrafhn's eyes enter me through the lens and I worked for him moving and shaping and becoming flawlessly supple. Aakash was pleased. "I have been trained by the best," I said.

"I can see that," he said.

We took a break, and I closed my eyes. My creative core was alone and had wept and longed for my return. And now I could listen like a child and I gazed from crystal eyes, and every day, every hour, every minute, every second, I would awake alive within the womb of my own creativity. It was fed by pain and tears and power and vision. I would speak from cracked veils where both arrogance and ignorance were crushed into dust. The wind swallowed my scars as I licked her whirling dervish dance. I was the Sufi whirling dervish dancing the **Sema** and my skirt reached the sky. My thighs were scarred and my cloud lovers would kiss every single story of the skin line. These were my gypsy tattoos, and I would find the soul-snatchers and spit thieves and slice their heads off. And I would fly in and out of the white wolf tribes and shift and shape and play with man. I laid on my little bed and dreams flowed once again. It had been so barren and so long. A Hasselblad camera was lying on the floor. Through the slit of my eyes I watched the open lens as a haloed being entered the box. As I watched, the image became Krishna and then Kali and then Durga and Laxmi and then right there within the scope of this amazing camera sat my very own Ganesha. His trunk was weaving with joy and celebration. I was reborn, finally reborn.

Aakash knocked and walked in with a whole box of things. We began again and continued until very late. We took a break and went for a bite. I left my make up on and people stopped and looked. I was married to my own transformation. Aakash smiled and shyly took my left hand and kissed the outer palm. I remembered everything we had shared. "You are beautiful Mrinalini, and this is exactly what I wanted," he said.

He took me to the Tibetan restaurant we had gone to some ten thousand years ago when I was a stolen bride child after watching Satyajit Ray's film *Devi*, when he had fed me and I him. My hands were fresh with henna then. My hands are raw and open with blood now. His were trembling. He tried to hide this but I missed nothing. "Are you okay?" I asked him. He looked at me sadly; he did not have to say a word. I knew that this was the last time I would see him, and it was.

We returned and continued until we finished, since he had to be back in San Francisco to develop and print all the shots in a couple of weeks. The pace was fast and nostalgic and I saw the serpents dance and become the wedding instruments like in my dream once again, and I become my dream. I am the alchemist of all alchemists. As the camera got closer and breathed into me I saw the reflection of my bride self in the same lens, and I watched her walking out of the lens and dissolving into me. I felt her limbs melting into mine. I felt her skin stretching into mine. I felt her eyes swallowing mine. I felt her voluptuous lips licking mine. I felt her tongue slicing mine and I touched her soul as it merged into mine.

We stopped, and I could not stop crying. And I saw it all: the wedding day, my hennaed feet and hands, the clove sounds on my face, anklets on my feet and a blood-red sari wrapped around my lived waist as I walked through the dusty paths in a village in India and flowers sailed by me and this was the day of Kali puja and also my wedding day. I had met myself and wed the other half. We were now one as the throbbing sound of choral Om chants filled the valleys and hills of this absolutely divine, brilliant, ecstatic Universe where the two-thousand-year old sage tree weeps in joy of what she has witnessed. This was the birth of the new consciousness, when the invisible becomes visible and all falseness is slain and slaughtered. And now the world was ready for true art and the whispers of brilliance and the poet filmmakers would finally change the language of cinema.

My sandalwood husband and I walked through the garden and the sweet gentle gardener handed me twelve red roses and another bunch for the priest. We headed to the temple and offered the flowers to the priest, who was in the midst of the morning worship. We sat in front of him to receive his blessings. He was happy that I was in red and he commented on this. I looked for my beggar saint and just then, as though from nowhere, she appeared smiling and transparent. I touched her feet in respect and so did my husband and she blessed us both. After receiving the **Prasad**, we got up to leave and I bowed in front of her as she took my head and rubbed it hard. I felt a light sword piercing through, all the way down and as I looked up at her she, once again, opened her mouth and in that glowing toothless space I saw my little Savitri held in the light of the universe, smiling and giggling at me.

We walked back to the house, the twelve red roses captive in my trembling hands. We had breakfast quietly. My mother-in-law served me and encouraged me to eat well. I thanked her and after we had finished I went to her and touched her feet. This was the very first time I had done that. All was at peace and in harmony and in balance.

In the evening my beautiful husband asked the maid to dress me up and put jasmine garlands in my hair and the special gold earrings in my ears and the ornamented gold toe rings on my feet and the brocade red sari on my body. She took her time and finally walking to the mirror I looked at my reflection through the twelve red roses with their superior vibrations. And there beside my bride self was the other stallion warrior whose call I always listened to and longed for and now this moment at this time she and I became one and she was I and I was she. And the sable antelope entered and with his dark mysterious incredible eyes looked at both of us, as his carved sickle horns were in perfect balance and had become one with themselves. We were one.

My husband came to me and kissing my red *sindoor* space where the almond shaped eye dances between my two eyes said, "**Devi.**"

"Yours," I replied, whispering to him that his seed had met mine. He ate my lips and crushed my breasts and flowered my soul and all the chains were broken and fallen in the dust. I was free and the baby boy who was always in my dreams had entered me and would be born. I knew that my divine golden Savitri had sent him down to me. My mother-in-law would be happy and maybe wear red herself again. I would weep in her heart and bring joy back to her because true compassion has no end. I love love. And the temple lady walked right in front of me with her mouth wide open and there once again was my baby goddess, Savitri, smiling and sublime. And I saw a baby animal man in my dream.

386

I kissed his throbbing heart and he said that he was my child. My wings unfurled. His eyes walked through my trembling soul. I sailed through jasmine blossoms and stood erect and drenched with illuminated Zen monks and walked on dusk-hewed rippling rivers.

This morning my altar had shifted and the gods had fallen from the sky. My feather hot spot corner was glowing and the sickle moon slicing spear warrior was now on his way to catch the rays of the full moon, to bring me back her radiance and her round gentle and powerful beauty. I was the moonchild and she was the moon goddess.

I stepped out of the building. My friend, Reynaldo the door man, said that I looked like the sun. I laughed and stepped out with a bounce in my stride. I was with my pack today, my Niyol wolf pack. I had become the wolf. My power was back.

I walked two blocks when a very soft voice stopped me.

"Excuse me?"

I turned around. A chiseled face in a green skull cap with eyes belonging to a king and a voluptuous mouth in a renaissance face asked me in broken English if I was from South America.

"I am from India," I said proudly, and he laughed. He handed me some post cards from the Metropolitan Museum. They were of the Egyptian prince, Tutankhamen. He looked like him. I was breathless. He was a blue Austrian stallion. He took out a little blue book, which was his German-English dictionary and looked for a word. He showed it to me. The word was "marry." His blue-green eyes were like an eagle in flight over rugged stone rocks and red burnt mountains as he said, "Will you?" I smiled.

This was the past. It was healed. It was ripped open and burnt with sage. Even the blood had not left any stains. It was honored and remembered with respect and then sent free. The husk of the coconut was filled again and this was offered to the gods. It was transformed and my metaphors had entered my body.

My antelope princes. They will all sail to me. Not one husband but one million godheads walking on one beam of light floating in the blue, brown, blood-wet sky and I am Urvasi, the Apsara, the female spirit of the clouds, sent down to please man I will catch them in my feather wings and feel their eyes with the skin of my heart and the sense of my soul. I will take their mind lines and find stories of flight. I will rapture their limbs and flame their fires. They will wed me because I am all women and death will bow his head and weep at this absolute power and even he will walk away. I will steal a little candle from their minds and light the flame. And the feline feminine will drink deep from the mystic cup of ecstasy and wounds are your ink and all true poetry will be written in blood.

I will belong to no man.

My steps got lighter and faster. I looked back and saw the laughing hearts of man and groom in the dancing wind and all my lovers were standing there at the threshold of love and longing and desire and I became the blue stallion and the howling wolf and wed every shooting star that fell in each grain of sand and broke into a thousand whispers of magic and twilight. All my poet men rode around me and fell into the windmills of my turquoise eyes and a relentless yearning was given to me as I waved to them and they became my wolf walk. I made love to each and every one of them and this time I did not destroy them. I gave them my trembling orgasm. Leaving my Palladium boots behind on the rough and cold concrete, I stepped on a translucent lit earth surface and then on the heart center of the sand dunes where one single lotus flower saved my life. I have arrived, and alchemy has become me, and I can see through this transparency and all the fish are swimming against the current with blue light glistening on their wet bodies to keep in pace with me, because they now know that I am one with them. I swim against all manmade rules and restrictions and traps and prisons and mediocrity. My red feet sink into the sublime consciousness and leave their fire scales and step on sand and sink into its nuanced shades. The little ankle bells tinkle to the sound of the waves as my silver flower toe rings marry each grain of sand, and I walk around the image of the goddess, which is now bleeding red and black. And in the distance I see a girl running towards me, and as she approaches she becomes the doe-eyed bride child I had left behind. Her vermillion red circle on her forehead merges with mine and I feel my third eye piercing through bone and flesh, and her red brocade silk sari winds around me and cuts open my flesh. We are one as we enter the history of the found inner child and the quivering rhapsody of a whole being. I look back and see red petals strewn on the sand leaving a trail of new blood. They fell out from her waist pouch. They fell out of my heart mouth when I had swallowed them as I howled in pain. They have left me and with them my aching heart, which is now in union with absolute bliss. Gold light shines everywhere and the Universe is transparent as we run into the light and carve out our visions. And etched on the skin of my heart with a quill pen in red ink is written:

"I will express myself.
I must express myself.
The Sacred is Art.
Art is Sacred."

There is only one question:
EVOLVE OR DISSOLVE?
EVOLVE OR DISSOLVE?

This is the fiery message, seen in the eye of the elephant and in the glowing face of the woman warrior. This is the light she wraps around the world with her words of blood.

Index

Savitri...10
Satyavan...10
Shlokas...17
Ardhanari...19
Sutra...26
Darshan...27
Numinosity...45
Apsara...57
Devi...82
Meera...85
Bhajans...85
Kungalini...90
Shiva Lingams...96
Mantras...99
Shamiana...103
Tantra...109
Muladhara...109
Kali's...110
Hanuman...111
Ondine...118
Hozho...122
Mrtyu...123
Dhenuka...123
Atman...124
Seele...124
Ba...124
Alma...124
Lakshmana...126
Soma...131

Mudra...133
Yoni...135
Samana...141
Gazals...163
Athma...165
Vajra...193
Grok...193
Rishi...201
Bauls...201
Mirabai...201
Siddhartha...201
Curandero...217
Yantra...222
Khepri...237
Ra...237
Vrindavan...243
Purusha...243
Prakriti...243
Dakini...262
Ardha...263
Nari...263
Triahule...264
Sat-Chit-Ananda...276
Gandharvas...280
Ayurvedic...291
Yasoda...301
Gokula...301
Kum Kum...319
Bindi...319

Index

(Continued)

Dugra...344
Hota...371
Ravana...373
Mana...373
Chitrangada...374
Arjuna...374
Shephali...374
Airavata...375
Visudha...375
Khajura...378
Kama...378
Prasad...384

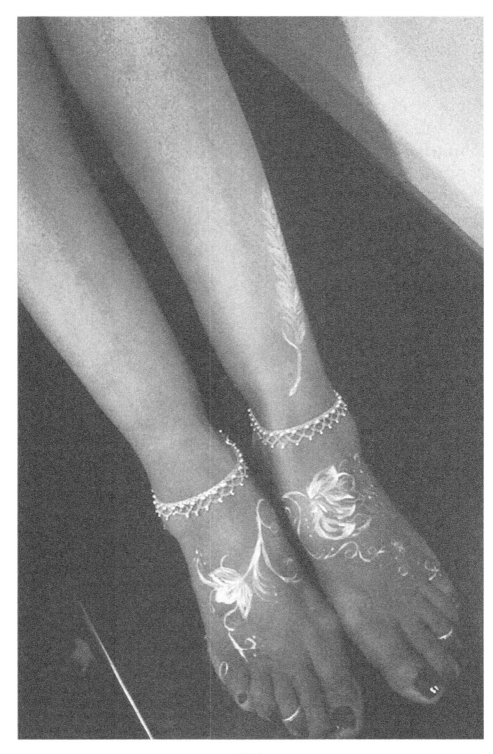

392

THANK YOU

And with deep gratitude to
Francois Wilson, who recognized the alchemy
of Blood Words and who had the passion and courage
and belief to publish it.

To Albert Fernandez for
introducing me to Francois Wilson
To Sheril Antonio who took the time to delve deep
into the book and write a visionary foreword

To Katya who reflected the
Moon and Sun to me and filled
my cracks with Gold dust

To M, my torchbearer, who kept
my wings dry so I could fly

....

To Robert who always said
I played above the ring and never
stopped believing in me

To Scott for being an exceptional
artist and who made sure I had a lemon
for my morning water and who always inspired
me with his eclectic taste in music,
literature and art

To B who never stopped believing in
Blood Words and me

To Elly who saw the birth
and success of the book from
the very first day

To Ame for our conversations
on art and cinema

To Jake for his sense of perfection
when designing the website

To all those young warriors
who read *Blood Words* and

found their own personal truths

And

To all the trees that I have touched
who bless and protect me,
to every pebble, every star, the sickle,
half and full moon,
the arrows of the sacred sun
and all the fallen flowers
and leaves on concrete
that have been
crushed by careless feet

And

To all those mad artists
who encouraged me
to never stop
and never compromise

CPSIA information can be obtained
at www.ICGtesting.com
Printed in the USA
BVOW08*1826251016

465981BV00002B/3/P